Miss Eliza Takes The Reins

A Sweet Regency Romance with Wounded Warriors, Willing Hearts, and a Home Worth Fighting For

Catherine Bilson

Shenanigans Press

Copyright

Contents

Trigger Warnings

This book contains scenes that may depict, mention, or discuss: Abandonment, Animal death, Animal illness & injury, Death of a pet, Injury (physical), Loss of vision, Military service & deployment, and Racism.

Miss Eliza Takes The Reins takes place during a busy foaling season at a Regency estate breeding horses to supply to the military. Nobody at Belle Haven is under any illusions as to what will happen to most of those horses.

Foaling is a hazardous business even today with all the advantages of modern veterinary medicine. In the Regency era, it would have been even more risky, and I do not pretend otherwise. There is loss in this book, and if animal death is not something you can bear to read, this book may not be for you.

Chapter One

MARCH, 1815

ELIZA BELL STOOD MOTIONLESS in the chaos of Belle Haven's main stable yard, watching grooms and stable boys dart between stalls like startled sparrows, leading out horses, gathering tack, securing provisions for journeys no one could predict the length of. Hooves clattered on cobblestones. Men shouted. Horses nickered in confusion. Yet Eliza kept her expression composed, her chin lifted in imitation of her father's demeanour. At eighteen, she had not expected to find herself responsible for one of England's premier horse breeding establishments. But then, no one had expected Napoleon to escape from Elba either.

Yesterday's afternoon routine had been shattered by the arrival of a dispatch rider, his horse lathered and heaving, its sides streaked with dust. Eliza had been in the small paddock with a young filly, settling a saddle on the youngster's back for the first time, when she heard the commotion. By the time she reached the main house, her father was already reading the message, his face grimmer with each line.

"He's escaped," Sir Richard said, his voice tight. "Bonaparte has left Elba and returned to France; he is even now gathering an army and marching on Paris. The Prince Regent has ordered every available horse requisitioned for the cavalry. I am to report to London immediately with as many as we can spare."

Those words still sat cold in her chest. War had been a distant thing these past months, a shadow lifting after years of darkness. Now it loomed again.

Her father's voice pulled her back. "Eliza! Where is that list?"

She hurried to his side, pulling the carefully prepared inventory from her pocket. "Here, Father. I've marked the twelve best trained horses, suitable for officers, in red, as you asked."

Sir Richard scanned the list, nodding. "Good girl." His eyes softened as he looked at her. "I know this is a terrible burden to place on you, with your mother at Molly's side for the birth, and Clara and Anna still in Vienna. But there's no one else."

"I can manage," Eliza replied, willing her voice steady. "You've taught me well."

And he had. Since she could toddle, Eliza had followed her father through the stables of Belle Haven, learning the bloodlines of every horse, the proper feed for each season, how to spot the first signs of illness before they took hold. She might be young, but horses spoke a language she understood.

"Mr. Pearson will help with the accounts," her father continued, "and old James knows the breeding schedule better than anyone. Mrs Fallon will be moving in from the vicarage today, to manage the house until your mother can return. But the decisions on the horses..."

"Will be mine," she finished. "I understand."

He clasped her shoulder, and she saw the conflict in his eyes. She forced a smile, one that looked more confident than she felt. "We'll manage splendidly, Father. Don't worry about a thing."

She watched him mount one of their finest stallions, a horse who should have been turned out with an unbred mare that very afternoon but was now bound for London. Behind him, forty horses waited in a string, ridden or led by men who had returned home just months earlier and were now heading back to war.

She swallowed against the ache in her throat. "Godspeed, Father."

Sir Richard's gaze swept over the estate one last time before he signalled to the waiting line. "Move out!"

The procession filed through the gates, her father tall and straight-backed at their head. Eliza stood watching until the last horse disappeared from view. Her smile dropped only when she was certain no one could see.

"Miss Eliza."

She turned to find Mr. Thornton, the head groom, at her elbow. His weathered face was creased with worry, his cap twisted in gnarled hands. At sixty-four, he had been at Belle Haven since her grandfather's time, but had never seen a slip of a girl left in sole charge.

"Yes, Mr. Thornton?"

"Begging your pardon, miss, but there's matters need attending to. With so many men gone..." He hesitated, clearly uncomfortable bringing troubles to someone so young.

"Speak plainly," Eliza said, squaring her shoulders. "I need to know everything."

Thornton nodded, reassured by her directness. "Well, miss, the breeding schedule; your father had planned thirty-six coverings this month, but we've just lost more than half our stallions and all the young colts. You'll need to look at suitable crosses for the mares from what we have left."

"What else?" Eliza prompted when he paused.

"Sixty foals due in the next three months, miss. We usually have four men just for the foaling barn, and a dozen more to muck the stables and train the youngsters to saddle." He gestured to the remaining workers in the yard, mostly boys of twelve or thirteen, with a few men too old to return to service. "We've got eight in total, and only three with any real experience."

Panic flickered through her. Sixty foals, each requiring skilled hands for safe delivery. The breeding schedule, planned over years to produce the right crosses. Almost two hundred horses still at Belle Haven: mares in foal, mares waiting to be bred, yearlings and two-year-olds who needed to be broken to saddle before their delivery to the cavalry at three. All of it, hers now.

She looked at the ledger in Thornton's hand, then to the anxious faces of the staff who had gathered around them. They were looking at her. Not at Thornton or old James, but at her. Waiting.

Her father's words from years ago surfaced: *Horses sense fear, Eliza. If you're frightened, they'll be frightened. Show them calm authority, and they'll follow you anywhere.*

People, she decided, weren't so different.

She straightened and spoke in a clear voice that carried across the courtyard. "Mr. Thornton, I want a complete inventory of our feed supplies by noon, so we can order replacements for what my father had to take with him. James, start revising the breeding schedule around the stallions we still have; prioritise the mares already in season. My sister Charlotte has an excellent grasp of our bloodlines and what crosses will suit. I'll ask her to come and help you."

"Phillip, Adam," she said, turning to the stable boys. "You two will begin training for the foaling team immediately. You've shown good hands with the yearlings; it's time you learned more."

Her voice firmed as she saw respect dawning on the faces around her. "The old rotation won't work with our numbers. We'll create new teams; every man and boy will learn tasks outside their usual duties. We'll recruit. Anyone you know who wants work, boys or girls, I don't care, send them to me. Belle Haven horses will be cared for as well as they always have been."

Thornton's face split into a grudging smile. "Very good, Miss Eliza. Where shall we begin?"

"With breakfast," she replied, returning his smile with a flash of her usual impish grin. "A good decision is rarely made on an empty stomach. Then we'll get to work."

As the staff dispersed, Eliza permitted herself one glance toward the road where her father had disappeared. Belle Haven would endure. She would see to that.

Eliza chewed on the end of her pencil, a habit her mother constantly scolded her for, and recalculated the spring breeding programme for the third time. The breeding ledger lay open before her on the study desk. With three of their finest stallions now en route to London, dozens of carefully planned crosses needed revision. She traced her finger down the column of broodmares, mentally matching each with the remaining stallions before passing them to Charlotte, who would check the crosses were not too close to work.

"Lady Daphne," she murmured, tapping the page where the grey mare's name was written in her father's careful hand. "Originally planned for Poseidon, but he's gone now." She considered the alternatives. "Hephaestus has the speed but not the bone... Beech... no, he's her uncle..."

The door burst open so hard that Eliza's pencil skidded across the page, leaving an ugly mark through three entries. She looked up, ready to scold, only to find young Tommy, one of the stable boys, cap in hand and flushed with excitement.

"Miss Eliza! Miss Eliza!" he gasped, plainly having run the entire way. "There's a soldier at the gate! An officer, miss, leading a horse!"

"Calm yourself, Tommy," she said, rising from the desk. "What sort of officer? What regiment?"

"Cavalry, miss, looks just like Major Blair-Fortescue's uniform. All proper with brass buttons and such. But he looks tired, miss, awful tired. And the horse..." The boy's eyes widened. "It's a fine big stallion, but there's something wrong with his eyes."

Eliza was already moving, straightening her plain grey dress as she hurried from the study. "Find Mr. Thornton and tell him to meet me at the front gate immediately," she instructed, lengthening her stride across the entrance hall.

"No!" She caught the collar of Caesar, one of her father's mastiffs, as he made to bolt out ahead of her. The dogs were trained to defend Belle Haven and might bark and spook the officer's horses. "You stay inside!" She edged through the front door and closed it on Caesar's disappointed whine.

She shielded her eyes against the afternoon glare. As her vision adjusted, she saw the tableau at the gate: a tall figure in a dust-covered uniform stood between two horses. One was a nondescript bay, clearly spent from long travel. The other...

Even at a distance, the second horse commanded attention. A powerful light dapple-grey stallion with the lines of superior breeding. The arch of his neck, the depth of his chest, the balance of his proportions; all spoke of quality. A Belle Haven horse, without doubt, though she didn't recognise him. But as she drew closer, she noticed what Tommy had tried to describe: the stallion's eyes were clouded, milky with blindness. Jagged scars covered his face, black lines scored against the lighter grey coat.

The officer straightened as she approached and removed his hat. Despite the travel stains on his uniform and the weariness that hung from him, he held himself well, shoulders squared.

"Miss Bell?" he inquired.

"I am Eliza Bell," she confirmed, stopping a few paces from him and reading his rank from his uniform. "How may I help you, Lieutenant...?"

"Llewellyn, miss. Lieutenant David Llewellyn, 16th Light Dragoons." His voice carried an unexpected lilt. Not the clipped tones of London or the drawl of the aristocratic officer class, but something softer. Musical. Welsh, she realised. He bowed slightly. "I've brought him home."

Her gaze shifted to the stallion, who stood perfectly still, his blind eyes turned to nothing, ears swivelling at the sound of their voices. Something in the way Llewellyn said *home* made her certain this was no ordinary military horse.

"May I?" she asked, gesturing toward the stallion.

Llewellyn nodded. "He's gentle enough, miss, though cautious now he can't see."

Eliza approached slowly, not from fear but respect. She spoke softly as she extended her hand. "Hello, beautiful boy. You've had quite a journey, haven't you?"

The stallion's nostrils flared, sampling her scent. His head turned toward her voice, ears pricked forward. When her hand touched his neck, he stood still, accepting her.

"He's one of ours, isn't he?" she asked. "But I don't recall him."

"He's ten, by his teeth," Llewellyn explained.

Which perhaps explained it. The stallion would have been an unfinished three-year-old when he left Belle Haven, and Eliza only eleven.

"We met rather... unexpectedly." The lieutenant's gaze turned distant, as if seeing beyond the peaceful Hampshire countryside to somewhere far grimmer. "My mount, Osiris, was shot from under me in my first engagement. Skirmishers had cut off our retreat. I was surrounded, certain I'd be killed or captured."

His hand rose to stroke the stallion's scarred face. "Then I remembered something Miss Molly showed us at Sandhurst. She said all Belle Haven horses are trained to respond to a distinctive whistle."

Llewellyn put his fingers to his lips and produced a three-note call that rose sharply at the end. The stallion's ears pricked forward, his blind head turning toward the sound.

Eliza nodded. It was part of the training they gave every horse, but only a Belle Haven horse would respond to it.

"Just like that," Llewellyn continued, smiling at the horse's response. "I was desperate enough to try anything. This stallion came to me through smoke and gunfire, his rider already fallen. I don't know his original name, but I called him Hermes, for his speed." His voice softened. "He carried me to safety that day, and through countless battles after."

Eliza watched the lieutenant's hands as he spoke. She noted the calluses of a horseman, the steady sureness of his touch on the stallion's neck. Not the soft hands of an officer who sat astride his mount for parades. These hands knew the work.

"We fought together for two years," Llewellyn continued. "He seemed… invincible." His voice caught. "Until a cannon blast caught us, too close. We both went down. My arm broken, his face…" He gestured to the scarring. "The horse doctors couldn't save his sight."

"Yet here he is," Eliza said, watching how the stallion leaned into the lieutenant's hand.

"They wanted to put him down at once," Llewellyn said, and a flash of defiance crossed his face. "Standard procedure for a blinded mount. But I refused. Belle Haven stallions aren't Army property to be disposed of; they're to be returned when their service ends." His chin lifted. "That's the agreement."

Eliza nodded, impressed. Most officers wouldn't have remembered the terms her father negotiated with the cavalry regiments, let alone honoured them in the chaos of war. Few Belle Haven stallions ever came home. She could think of only one other: Apollo, whom her sister Molly had brought back from Sandhurst. She could wish for Apollo now, but he was at Molly's home in Oxfordshire, their father having given him to Molly and her husband Tim as a wedding gift to start their own breeding programme.

"I thought…" Llewellyn hesitated, his confidence faltering for the first time. "He may be blind, but you could still use him for breeding?" The statement turned upward into a question, his tone almost pleading. "His courage, his intelligence; surely those qualities are worth preserving?"

Eliza studied the stallion, assessing his conformation, his movement as he shifted position. Despite the blindness, Hermes still carried himself with balance and grace. Powerful hindquarters, clean legs, depth of girth. Her father had always said that breeding was about more than appearance; it was about heart, the intangible quality that separated a good horse from a great one. There were excellent reasons this horse had not been gelded as a youngster. Reasons that might serve her very well now.

"Yes," she said, her mind already running through potential crosses, mares that might complement this stallion's strengths, once she had looked up the year he was sent to the cavalry and traced his bloodlines. "Hermes has more than earned his place at Belle Haven. Thank you for bringing him home."

The relief that washed over Llewellyn's face told her how heavily the stallion's fate had weighed on him. This was more than duty. This was a debt of honour, a bond forged under fire.

"Thank you, Miss Bell," he said simply, the Welsh lilt thickening. "Thank you."

Hermes nickered softly, as if adding his own thanks, his blind head tilting toward Eliza.

"Follow me to the stallion barn," she said, turning on her heel. "We'll need to prepare a special stall for Hermes." She led the way across the courtyard, calling to a passing stable boy without breaking stride. "Phillip! Tell Mr. Thornton I'm putting this stallion in the north barn. And have cook prepare a warm bran mash with molasses; he's too thin." She glanced back at Llewellyn, who followed with Hermes' lead rope held carefully, the bay trailing behind. "Stallions get the north barn; it's quieter there, away from the mares."

The stallion barn stood apart from the main complex, a long building of weathered stone with high windows. As they approached, two more young grooms appeared, clearly alerted by Phillip. Eliza addressed them without slowing.

"Robert, fetch the soft halter from the tack room, the padded leather one we use for the sensitive yearlings. Adam, check there are no obstacles in the stall or the corridor, and then take the lieutenant's gelding to the main barn and see to him." The boys hurried off, and Eliza caught a flash of surprise on Llewellyn's face. His brows lifted, his gaze reassessing her.

"I confess, Miss Bell," he said as they entered the barn, "I expected to deal with Sir Richard or his steward. Your father's reputation in cavalry circles is considerable."

"My father was summoned to London yesterday," she replied, leading them down the central aisle. "Napoleon's escape has disrupted many households, Lieutenant."

They reached a stall vacated just hours earlier. Spacious and deeply bedded with fresh straw; the boys had done a good job, no doubt on Thornton's instruction.

"And is there no man left in charge?" Llewellyn asked. His voice was carefully neutral, though Eliza caught the concern beneath it. "A steward, perhaps?"

"My mother is with my sister Molly, who is expecting her first child any day," Eliza said, running her hand along the stall door and checking for rough edges that might injure a blind horse rather than looking at him. "My other sisters, Clara and Anna, are in Vienna; Anna was recently married there and Clara is also expecting. So it's just me." She turned to face him. "Managing all of it."

Llewellyn glanced around the stable, then through the open door to the yard beyond, where the stable boys hurried about with buckets and tack. His gaze returned to her.

"Just you," he repeated slowly. "In charge of all this? During wartime?"

There it was. The doubt she'd been expecting since dawn. She'd already seen it in the grooms' eyes that morning, though it had vanished quickly enough once she'd asserted herself.

Whatever she might privately feel about her own readiness, Eliza Bell was not going to let anyone see it.

"I am perfectly capable, Lieutenant," she replied, cooler than she'd intended. "Belle Haven has been my home since

I was a baby. I've assisted my father in every aspect of its management."

Llewellyn held up a hand. "I meant no offence, Miss Bell. It's only that these are uncertain times, and Belle Haven horses are valuable beyond measure to the cavalry. The best mounts in Europe, many say, myself included."

The compliment softened her slightly, though she kept her posture. "Indeed. Which is why they will receive the best care, regardless of who oversees it."

Robert returned with the padded halter, and they turned their attention to settling Hermes. Eliza watched as Llewellyn guided the stallion into the stall, speaking to him all the while, showing him the space by touch so he wouldn't startle.

"Three steps forward, that's it," Llewellyn murmured. "Straw under your feet now, good depth of it. Wall to your left, water bucket straight ahead."

He moved carefully, Eliza noticed, positioning his body to favour some injury. He moved his weight off his left leg when standing still, and though his right arm seemed to work, he relied more on his left. The shadows beneath his eyes spoke of long roads and longer battles.

As Hermes settled, turning once before finding a comfortable position, Eliza was struck by the likeness between horse and rider. Both bore the marks of war. The stallion's blindness and scars were plain to see; the lieutenant's wounds less visible but no less real.

"He'll need time to map his space," Llewellyn said, stepping back and closing the stall door. "Blind horses build a picture of their surroundings. Once he's learned the dimensions, the position of his feed and water, he'll move confidently enough."

"You've studied this," Eliza observed.

A faint smile crossed his tired face. "I've had to. The regiment thought me mad for insisting on bringing him home." Something hardened in his expression. "But I owed him that much. I owe him my life, many times over."

Eliza nodded. Belle Haven horses were not tools or weapons. They were partners, deserving of honour in return for their service. Her father had taught her that from her earliest days.

Llewellyn cleared his throat. "Miss Bell, I wonder if I might make an offer." He paused, seeming to weigh his words. "I'm on extended leave while my injuries heal. The regiment doesn't expect me back for at least two months, even with Napoleon's escape; I can't fire a rifle or ride with my troop until I'm whole again."

He glanced around the stable, then out to the yard where the reduced staff hurried through evening chores. "With your father away and your staff depleted, perhaps I might stay and help? I have experience with cavalry mounts, and..." His gaze went to Hermes. "I owe a debt to Belle Haven."

The practical part of Eliza's mind saw the value at once. An experienced cavalry officer who understood military horses would be invaluable while her father was away. But her pride stiffened at the idea that she needed rescuing.

"I assure you, Lieutenant, we have matters well in hand," she said, more stiffly than she'd intended.

"I don't doubt it," he said quickly. "But Bonaparte's escape will cause ripples we can't yet foresee. Additional protection for the horses might prove prudent."

Protection. The word sat between them, pointing to a worry Eliza had been pushing aside. Belle Haven horses were valuable not just in pounds and shillings but as potential targets for anyone wishing to disrupt Britain's preparations. With only boys and old men remaining to her, the estate was more exposed than it had been in years.

Still, to accept help felt like admitting she couldn't cope. She was about to refuse again when Hermes turned his blind face toward her and whickered softly. The sound was gentle, almost questioning.

And she saw past her pride to the truth. Sixty foals coming soon. Breeding decisions that couldn't wait. Security she hadn't fully thought through. Here was a man who'd risked his superiors' anger to save one of their horses, who understood the value of Belle Haven bloodlines, who offered help not because he doubted her, but because he respected what she protected.

"Very well," she said. She extended her hand as she had seen her father do when concluding business. "But understand this is temporary, Lieutenant Llewellyn, and I remain in charge. Belle Haven is under my authority until my father returns."

Llewellyn took her hand. His grip was firm, his palm rough from reins and weapons. "Of course, Miss Bell. I wouldn't have it any other way."

Hermes nickered again, softer this time.

"Now then," Eliza said, practical once more, "you must be famished after your journey. We'll see Hermes settled with his evening feed, and then you'll join my sisters and me for dinner. We have much to discuss about Belle Haven's operations if you're to be of any use."

The ghost of a smile crossed Llewellyn's lips. "Yes, Miss Bell. Whatever you think best."

Eliza nodded. Perhaps accepting help wasn't weakness. Her father would understand; he might even approve. For now, it was enough that Belle Haven had an unexpected ally.

Chapter Two

Eliza had been awake since before dawn, pulling on boots and a shawl to check on Hermes in the stallion barn, then walking the foaling paddocks with old James, who reported two mares showing signs of imminent labour. By the time she returned to the house, her fingers were stiff with cold and her mind was already compiling lists of tasks, calculating what resources she could assign to them. Her stomach growled. She took off her boots in the mudroom, washed her hands, and went to find something to eat.

The breakfast table looked wrong. That was the only word for it. The long oak table could seat fourteen, and when her parents were home it was more often than not full: family, visitors, horse buyers, cavalry officers passing through. This morning it held only her twin sisters Charlotte and Laura, and Lieutenant Llewellyn, who sat at one end with the stiff courtesy of a man accustomed to eating among strangers. He had changed into a clean shirt, though his uniform jacket was the same one from yesterday, brushed but unmistakably travel-worn. He ate methodically, breaking bread with his left hand, his right resting beside his plate but doing very little.

Charlotte was talking about bloodlines, as Charlotte generally was. At fourteen, she possessed an encyclopaedic knowledge of equine pedigrees that bordered on the supernatural, and she had taken the news of Hermes's arrival with undisguised excitement. "If he's a grey, and you believe he's ten now and was sent out as a three-year-old, that puts his birth in 1805," she was saying, her porridge growing cold as she scribbled on a scrap of paper. "Which means he could be out of Lady Arachne by Dorado, or possibly by Dorado's half-brother Donatello..."

Laura, Charlotte's twin in face but not in temperament, was eating steadily and saying nothing, her expression suggesting she had heard quite enough about Dorado and his relations.

The front door opened, and a gust of chilly March air swept through the entrance hall, carrying brisk footsteps and a voice that rang with the clarity of someone who had been organising things since before she could walk.

"The kitchen garden is in a dreadful state, Mother, someone has let the cabbages bolt entirely, and I counted three broken panes in the glass house on the way past. Poor Lady Bell has clearly been too busy to attend to things..."

Miss Louise Fallon appeared in the doorway, her dark hair escaping its pins, her cheeks flushed from the walk, her eyes bright with the kind of purpose Eliza found both welcome and slightly alarming. Behind her came her mother, Mrs Helen Fallon, carrying a basket that undoubtedly contained provisions from the vicarage kitchen, because Helen never arrived anywhere empty-handed.

Charlotte and Laura were both smiling to see Louise, who was just their age and their closest friend. Louise plopped down in the chair on Laura's other side and at once included them in her opinions about the kitchen garden.

Helen paused in the doorway. Her gaze took in the room in a single sweep and landed on Lieutenant Llewellyn. Her eyebrows rose. Her smile, warm and ready, did not falter, but something behind it shifted. She looked at Eliza.

"Aunt Helen," Eliza said. "How nice to see you."

"Good morning, my dear," Helen said, setting down her basket and kissing Eliza's cheek. Her eyes returned to the officer at the far end of the table. She was still smiling. It was, Eliza thought, the smile of a woman reserving judgement.

"Mrs Fallon, may I introduce Lieutenant Llewellyn of the 16th Light Dragoons," Eliza said. "He arrived yesterday afternoon with a Belle Haven stallion he saved from the war. The horse is blind but sound, and perhaps valuable for the breeding programme. Lieutenant Llewellyn has offered to assist us while his injuries heal, and I have accepted. We are very short-handed." She heard the note of apology in her own voice and did not like it. Her father had left her in charge; she had every right to hire anyone she saw fit. Not that she had discussed compensation with the lieutenant, she thought with a flicker of guilt. She must do so, when she got an opportunity.

Llewellyn was already on his feet, his chair pushed back. He bowed. "Mrs Fallon. I've taken one of the vacant grooms' rooms above the stallion barn. Miss Eliza was kind enough to invite me to breakfast."

He said it simply, and Eliza appreciated the economy of it. The information was complete: he was not staying in the house, the arrangement was proper, and the invitation had been hers to extend.

Helen studied him for a moment perhaps two seconds longer than politeness required. Whatever she found seemed to satisfy her, because her smile warmed from assessment to something approaching approval.

"How very good of you, Lieutenant," she said. "And how fortunate for us. Louise, take this basket to the kitchen and ask Cook what stores she has. I shall need a full accounting before noon." She turned to Eliza. "Your father sent me a note before he left, requesting that I come to stay until he or your mother are able to return home. I have instructions." The last word carried a gentle weight. Helen had been given authority and intended to use it, but she understood that someone else held authority here too, and the lines between them would need drawing with care.

"The horses are mine," Eliza said quietly. Not a challenge. A boundary, laid down with the same certainty she might mark a fence line.

"The horses are entirely yours," Helen agreed. "I shall manage the house, the kitchen, the laundry, and these two." She gestured at Charlotte and Laura. "And I shall attempt to manage Louise, though history suggests that is an ambition rather than a certainty. She will stay with us, rather than annoy her father at home. He will be quite fine; I arranged with Mrs Myers from next door that he shall step over to their house for his dinners, and the maid will take care of everything else."

From the hallway came Louise's voice, already issuing instructions to someone about the state of the linen cupboard.

Something loosened in Eliza's chest. Helen's presence transformed the house from an echoing, half-empty shell into something more functional. The horses, she was confident she could manage. The household had been quite another matter.

Helen gave her a smile that said she understood everything Eliza was not saying, then sat down and poured herself tea, producing a jar of blackberry jam from her basket that she set beside Laura's plate with a murmur that she had brought Laura's favourite.

Llewellyn resumed his seat and his breakfast, and for a few minutes the dining room held the sounds of ordinary morning life: the clink of cups, Charlotte's muttering about sire lines, Laura spreading jam, Louise's voice somewhere in the hallway saying something about beeswax candles.

Then the mastiffs began to bark.

The sound came from the front gate, deep and savage, the full-throated alarm of dogs bred to guard. Caesar and his brother Pompey had voices that could rattle windowpanes, and they used them now with a ferocity that startled Laura into dropping her knife. She bent to fumble for it, Charlotte reaching down at the same time, and they cracked heads, both yelping. Helen jumped up to comfort them.

Llewellyn set down his teacup. His hand was steady, but the cup rattled on the saucer. His eyes went to the window, then to Eliza, and in that glance she read something that had nothing to do with breakfast and everything to do with the instincts of a man who had heard too many alarms to ignore one.

Eliza was already rising, her napkin dropped beside her plate. Through the window she could see dust on the lane, and the shapes of horses, many horses, approaching Belle Haven at a purposeful walk.

The column filled the lane like a slow grey tide. Eliza counted twelve mounted soldiers and behind them a string of led horses, coats dull with road dust. At the head rode a man whose bearing spoke of decades of command, his uniform immaculate despite the early hour and the state of the roads, silver at his temples and along his jaw. She read the golden bars on his shoulders with the ease of a woman who had spent years amongst officers. A colonel. Not a man she could dismiss, nor one even her father could have.

Eliza shut the mastiffs in the boot room, where they howled their displeasure against the heavy door, and went out to meet him.

The colonel dismounted, removed his hat, tucked it beneath his arm, and produced a folded document from his breast pocket.

"Is Sir Richard Bell available?" he asked.

"I'm afraid not," Eliza said. "He departed for London yesterday, with a string of mounts for the army."

The colonel nodded, as though not at all surprised. "And you are...?"

He had a good voice, level and unhurried.

"Miss Bell." It still felt odd to say that, when she had been Miss Eliza her whole life, but her three older sisters were all married now, even if she hadn't yet met Anna's husband. "I am in charge here, in my father's absence."

The colonel did not look surprised about that either. He held out the paper. "Colonel Ashworth, 4th Dragoon Guards. I carry requisition orders from the War Office, authorised by the Minister, for the procurement of horses suitable for cavalry service."

Eliza took the document and read it standing in the yard, conscious of Helen watching from the front step and Llewellyn somewhere behind her, a presence she felt rather than saw. The orders were explicit. Every horse at Belle Haven was to be assessed and, if suitable for military service, taken immediately. Compensation would follow at the standard government rate, roughly half what Belle

Haven horses normally fetched when sold to Sandhurst as officers' mounts.

Her father had taken forty horses yesterday. The remaining saddle-broken stock numbered perhaps that many again, and included mares she had planned to breed this season, stallions critical to the programme, and a handful of youngsters still too green for her father to have taken.

"Colonel Ashworth," she said, folding the paper with steady hands, "my father departed yesterday with forty of our best cavalry mounts, at the direct request of the War Office. Surely that contribution has been noted."

"It will surely be appreciated." His tone carried genuine respect. "Belle Haven's horses are the finest in England. Which is precisely why we need more of them."

"Then you will understand that what remains is not surplus. These are breeding stock, Colonel. Broodmares carrying next year's cavalry mounts. Stallions whose bloodlines represent decades of careful selection. To take them now is to cripple not this season's campaign but the next, and the one after that."

Ashworth inclined his head. "I understand the argument, Miss Bell. I have heard it at five estates in the last two days. But Bonaparte is marching, and a theoretical foal is no use to a dragoon who needs a horse beneath him today. If we cannot stop the French, there may not be a British Army to purchase your horses next season."

The words were cold and flat, and she read the truth of them in his eyes. There was no cruelty in it, which was what made it so hard to fight. He was not a bully or a fool. He was a man with clear orders, and there was nothing she could say that would change what was about to happen.

All she could do was try to save what she could.

They began in the main stable yard. Eliza had sent Robert running for the breeding ledger, and she met the colonel at the first stall with the book open in her hands.

"This is Artemis," she said, as they looked at the handsome chestnut mare. "Seven years old, in foal to Hephaestus. Due in May. She carries bloodlines from both the Dorado and the Mercury lines, the foundation of our programme. Taking her risks both the foal and the mare."

Ashworth looked at the chestnut's swollen belly and nodded. He made a note in his own book. "Agreed. She stays. Any mare due to foal this spring or summer is exempt, Miss Bell; you have my word on that, and I will leave you a paper confirming it should any further requisitioners come through."

The next horse was not so fortunate. A five-year-old bay mare, she had been bred to Hephaestus just days earlier, and they hoped she would foal next spring. Eliza argued her temperament was unsuitable for battle, that she shied at loud noises. It was not quite a lie; the mare had once startled at a dropped bucket. But Ashworth was not easily deceived. He had a sergeant fire a pistol at fifty yards, and the mare merely flicked an ear.

"She goes," the colonel said quietly. "If she survives, she will come back to you to have her foal." He nodded to one of his men, who brought a halter and took the mare from the stall.

Eliza gritted her teeth and looked away.

Horse by horse, stall by stall, she fought. She argued age; what use a twenty-year-old broodmare?

"Likely more use to us than she is to you," Ashworth countered. "She could pull a cart, even if she couldn't carry a rider. She goes."

Some arguments held. Most did not. Ashworth had an eye as sharp as her own, and the patience to examine every animal before making his decision.

Throughout, Eliza was aware of Llewellyn. He stood near the door to the stallion barn, arms folded, weight shifted onto his good leg. He did not approach. He did not speak. He simply stood, watching the systematic stripping of Belle Haven's stock, and she understood his silence was deliberate. To speak would undermine her. To intervene, even with his commission, would mark her as someone who needed a man's voice to be heard. She was grateful for his restraint the way one is grateful for a wall that holds without being asked.

The hours ground on. The sun climbed. Eliza's voice grew hoarse. She saved the demonstrably pregnant mares, every one. She saved three young colts by insisting they hadn't been broken to saddle and, being ungelded, would take longer to prepare than Ashworth had. She saved the two-year-olds, who hadn't yet carried a saddle and were far too unformed. But every finished horse, every gelding and mare broken to saddle and sound of limb, was led out and added to the string in the lane.

Llewellyn's bay gelding went without protest. The plain, road-weary horse that had carried the lieutenant to Belle Haven was exactly what the cavalry wanted: sturdy, sensible, and ready to ride. Eliza did not attempt to argue. He was not a Belle Haven horse, he had no breeding value, and the requisition orders covered any horse on the premises suitable for service.

She watched the bay join the string and felt something close in her throat that had nothing to do with the gelding himself.

The stallion barn was the worst, and from the sympathy in Ashworth's face as he watched her push open the door, he knew it.

Hephaestus, the black Thoroughbred and one of the fastest horses Eliza had ever seen, put his elegant head over his stall door and whickered, hopeful for a carrot or a slice of apple. Eliza blinked against the sting at the back of her eyes and reached up to stroke his soft nose.

"He's nine," she said, unsure how she was keeping her voice level. "He is very fast. Won quite a number of races before Father purchased him. I don't know that he has ever been ridden in anything other than a racing saddle."

"And he is sound?" Ashworth asked, writing in his notes.

"Perfectly." She wanted to lie, but Ashworth would only ask to see the stallion trotted up. She gave Hephaestus one last pat and moved to the next stall. "This is Beech. He is from a long line of horses bred right here at Belle Haven."

The big bay, more solid than Hephaestus, extended his neck to sniff at her hand, eyeing the strangers warily.

"A fine animal," Ashworth said.

"He has already been to war, and was returned to us because he went lame. Father nursed him back to health and he has been sound for years, but he is almost twenty, Colonel. Surely..."

"A battle-experienced mount is priceless, Miss Bell," Ashworth said, almost gently. "Despite his age, if he is sound, he meets the criteria." He looked past her at the last occupied stall. "And who is this fine fellow?"

"The one horse here you cannot have." She was sure of her ground in this if nothing else. "Hermes is blind, Colonel," she said, when Ashworth looked at her questioningly. "See for yourself."

One look at Hermes's scarred face, and Ashworth nodded. "Then I am glad not to have to take all your stallions, Miss Bell," he said, making a note as Beech and Hephaestus were led out.

In all, thirty-seven horses were assessed, documented, and led away. The compensation vouchers, written in Ashworth's careful hand, sat in a stack on the mounting block like dead leaves, worth nothing until the government chose to honour them.

"Miss Bell." The colonel paused at the gate, hat in hand. "For what it is worth, I am sorry. Your father's contribution to the cavalry is unmatched, and I will ensure the War Office knows the full extent of what Belle Haven has given." He hesitated, then added more softly, "You argued well. Better than many a steward or estate manager I have dealt with. You saved at least three horses my orders would otherwise have required me to take."

Three . She had saved *three*.

The column moved off, and the sound of hooves on packed earth faded down the lane, carrying the work of years with it. Eliza stood in the yard, the ledger pressed against her chest, and looked at what remained. Stables that had held nearly two hundred horses two days ago now housed foaling mares, unbroken youngsters, and a blind stallion. The silence gathered around her.

Llewellyn had watched it all with his arms folded and his jaw set and his rank sitting useless on his shoulders.

A lieutenant did not countermand a colonel. A lieutenant on medical leave, technically detached from his regiment, did not even have the right to address a colonel unless spoken to first. He had known this from the moment Ashworth dismounted, and the knowing had sat in his chest like a stone swallowed whole.

He had watched his bay gelding led away without a word. The horse had no name; he had never named it, which perhaps said something about the state of his heart these past months. The animal had been borrowed from a remount depot, sturdy and willing and entirely unremarkable. It joined the string without protest, head low, ears slack, and Llewellyn felt the loss as one more small subtraction in a year made entirely of subtractions.

Ashworth had not been unkind. That was the worst of it. A cruel man could be hated, resisted, reported. But

Ashworth had been thorough and fair and genuinely sorry, and his orders bore the seal of the War Office, and there was nothing in any of that to push against. Llewellyn had learned, across three years of campaigning, that the most damaging blows were often the ones delivered with courtesy.

The gate swung shut. The last horse vanished around the bend, and hooves thinned until it was indistinguishable from wind in the hedgerows. The yard fell quiet. Not the comfortable silence of a stable at rest, but the hollow quiet of a place that had been emptied.

Stall doors stood open along the main barn, their occupants gone. A water bucket sat beneath a tap, catching drips. Two of the youngest stable boys stood near the mounting block, uncertain what to do, their faces carrying the bewildered look of children who had witnessed something they did not fully understand.

Llewellyn watched Eliza.

She had not moved. She stood where Ashworth had left her, the ledger held against her chest, fingers pressed into the leather binding. Her back was to most of the yard, angled toward the lane as though some part of her still expected the horses to come back. Her shoulders were rigid beneath the grey wool of her dress, set in a line so straight it looked as though it might snap.

He knew what that posture cost. He recognised it as a man recognises his own handwriting, because he had stood exactly that way himself. After his first engagement, with Osiris dead and blood on his hands. After the surgeon said "permanent" about his arm. The body held itself together through sheer effort, every muscle recruited for the single task of not falling apart, and from the outside it looked like composure, but from the inside it felt like drowning on dry land.

He saw the moment she cracked.

It was small. Her shoulders dropped, not in relaxation but in collapse, a fraction of an inch as if something inside had given way. The ledger pressed harder against her sternum. Her head bowed. Just slightly. Just enough.

And in that unguarded instant he saw her face in profile, and what was written there was not grief or anger but something worse. The look of someone who believed they had failed. Who had been trusted with something precious and watched it carried away despite everything they could do. Who was eighteen and had just had her first real test end with thirty-seven horses walking through the gate.

He understood that look. He had worn it himself, staring at the ruin of Hermes's eyes while the horse doctors argued over the pistol.

Then her chin came up.

It was deliberate, visible, a conscious act of will. Her shoulders squared. Her grip on the ledger moved, became purposeful rather than desperate. She turned, and her face was composed, and her voice carried across the yard with the same clear authority she had held all morning.

"Phillip, close up the empty stalls and clean them out. Robert, redistribute the hay to the occupied stalls; I want nothing wasted. Mr. Thornton, I'll need the revised numbers by this evening. Every horse we still have, their status, their condition, their schedule. This eases our manpower crisis, at least. One small silver lining."

The boys moved. Thornton appeared from somewhere, nodding, his face grim but steady. Belle Haven stirred back into motion, diminished and bruised but functioning, because the woman at its centre had decided it would function.

Llewellyn did not cross the yard. He did not offer comfort or reassurance. He had seen what lay underneath, and he knew that to acknowledge it now would strip away the armour she had just rebuilt. She did not want sympathy. She wanted to work.

So he turned to the stallion barn, where Hermes stood with his blind face toward the sounds of the diminished yard, ears forward, nostrils working. Llewellyn let himself into the stall and ran his hand along the stallion's neck, feeling the steady pulse beneath the warm hide, the patience of an animal who had already lost the worst thing he could lose and found a way to keep standing.

"Just us now, then," he said quietly.

The horse leaned into his hand, that great scarred head pressing against his shoulder. Outside, Eliza's voice continued, steady and controlled, marshalling her reduced forces.

He would stay. Not because she was fragile or incapable. Because this place, these horses, this woman who rebuilt herself between one breath and the next, deserved every hand that could be spared. And because he recognised, with a soldier's instinct for solid ground, that Belle Haven was the first place in a long time that felt like it might hold his weight.

Hermes sighed, a long exhalation that stirred the straw at their feet, and Llewellyn stood with him in the quiet of the barn and listened to the sound of someone refusing to break.

Chapter Three

Eliza sat down in her father's chair without ceremony, without hesitation, because there was no one else to sit in it and the breeding programme would not reorganise itself while she stood on propriety. The leather was worn smooth where her father's elbows had rested for years, and the desk still smelled faintly of his pipe tobacco, though he had given up smoking two winters ago at her mother's insistence. She pushed the scent aside the way she pushed aside every soft thing that threatened to slow her down, and opened the first of the stud books.

Charlotte had already colonised the left half of the desk and was advancing on the right. Three volumes lay open before her, their pages marked with scraps of torn paper, and she had produced from somewhere a sheet of foolscap on which she was constructing a pedigree chart like a general planning a campaign. A cup of tea sat beside her, cold and abandoned, a skin forming on its surface that Charlotte had not noticed and would not notice if the house burned down around her.

Laura sat in the window seat with one of the mastiffs, Caesar, his great head in her lap. She was listening, her face turned toward the room, her fingers moving through the dog's coarse fur. Laura's silences had a quality Eliza had never been able to name, a kind of alert stillness, as though she were hearing frequencies the rest of them missed. She probably was. Laura's blindness had sharpened her other senses until they more than filled the space her sight had left.

"Right," Charlotte said, not looking up. "A grey colt. Ten years old now, by his teeth, so foaled in 1805. Sent to the cavalry as a three-year-old, which means he left Belle Haven in 1808." Her pencil tapped the page. "Father sent four ungelded colts to Sandhurst that year. Two bays, a chestnut, and a grey. The grey was out of a mare called Celestine, by Mercury's son Donatello."

"Celestine," Eliza repeated. "I don't remember her."

"I don't remember her either, which means she must have passed, or perhaps been sold." Charlotte turned pages in the broodmare ledger, cross-referencing at the speed of someone who carried half these charts in her head and used the books merely to confirm what she already suspected. "Celestine, Celestine... here she is."

Charlotte stopped.

Her pencil hovered above the foolscap. Her hand, which had been moving with brisk confidence, went still. Not the stillness of confusion. The stillness of someone who has found something and needs a moment to believe it.

Eliza watched her sister's face. She knew that expression. She had seen it once before, two years ago, when Charlotte had worked out that a certain mare's foal would carry the combination of speed and stamina their father had been trying to breed for a decade. Charlotte had been twelve then, and their father had checked her work three times before admitting she was right.

"Charlotte," Eliza said quietly.

"Wait." Charlotte held up one finger without looking at her. She pulled the third book toward her, a heavy volume bound in green leather that contained the purchase records from every horse Sir Richard Bell had ever bought for Belle Haven.

Charlotte found the page she wanted. She pressed both hands flat on the open book and stared at the entry.

"Celestine's dam," she said, her voice different now, stripped of its usual breezy authority, "was a mare called Dorado's Gem." Charlotte looked up. Her eyes were very bright. "Dorado's Gem was a daughter of Eclipse."

The name dropped into the study and the room went still.

Eclipse. The greatest Thoroughbred racehorse of the eighteenth century, perhaps the greatest ever born, and as a sire unparalleled. Undefeated in every race he ran, his descendants had reshaped the breed. Every horseman in England knew the name. Every breeder alive would give a great deal for a great-grandson of Eclipse.

Eliza felt the understanding arrive before the words, something shifting beneath her ribs. She looked at the pedigree chart Charlotte was building and saw the line drawn clear: Hermes, through his dam Celestine, through Dorado's Gem. To Eclipse.

"His dam was a granddaughter of Eclipse," Eliza said, half disbelieving.

"Father paid a fortune for her." Charlotte tapped the purchase ledger. "Eight hundred pounds."

Eliza whistled between her teeth. She had never heard of such a sum paid for a horse; certainly her father had never hinted that he might consider such a price reasonable for any animal.

"What happened to her?" Laura asked quietly from the window seat.

Eliza looked at the broodmare book, still open before her. The tragically short entry for Celestine. "She died. Hermes was her only live foal, a son of Mercury. Father put her back to Mercury but both Celestine and the foal died the following year." She wondered what her father had felt. Eight hundred pounds on a mare who had given them one foal.

"What a waste," Charlotte said, but then pulled the foolscap toward her and began writing rapidly. "Father has been trying to strengthen the dam-side quality in our stock for years. He's said so a hundred times. Sire lines get all the attention, but it's the mares who carry the endurance, the heart, the..." She gestured impatiently, as though the vocabulary of the English language was insufficient for her purposes. "He can't be wasted, Eliza. Do you understand? He cannot be wasted."

"I understand," Eliza said, and she did.

With Hephaestus taken by Ashworth that morning, and Beech gone the same way, and Poseidon and the other stallions gone with their father, Hermes was not merely a useful addition to the breeding programme. He was the programme. The sole remaining adult stallion at Belle Haven, and more than that, the carrier of a dam line no other horse in their stable, perhaps no other horse in England, could replicate. A line they had not even known Belle Haven possessed until a blind horse walked through their gate with a Welsh lieutenant at his side.

Charlotte was already working through the implications. "His sire is Mercury. So he cannot be put to any mare carrying Mercury blood in the last three generations or we'll have overcrossing problems. But that's less than a third of the mares in the yard, by my count. If we choose carefully..."

Laura spoke from the window seat. "Lieutenant Llewellyn should know."

Both sisters turned. Laura's face was calm, her hand still resting on Caesar's broad skull. She did not elaborate. She rarely did.

"Yes," Eliza said. "He should."

She looked at the pedigree chart taking shape on Charlotte's foolscap and thought of Llewellyn standing in Hermes's stall, stroking the stallion's scarred neck, saying *just us now, then*. He had brought this horse home because he owed it a debt. He had no notion of the treasure he had carried through the gates of Belle Haven.

She pressed her palm flat against the desk and felt the solidity of the oak beneath her hand, the generations of careful work that had built this place. Thirty-seven horses had walked out of the gate that morning. One had walked in the night before. And that one, broken and blind and scarred by cannon fire, might be worth more than all the rest combined.

"Get me the mare list," she said to Charlotte. "Every mare we still have who could carry to him, once they've foaled. I want options by this evening."

Charlotte's answering smile was fierce. "I've already started."

Llewellyn had been summoned to the study by one of the stable boys, who delivered the message with the breathless gravity of a child entrusted with important business. He followed the boy across the yard and through the front door, past the mastiffs who regarded him with the tolerant suspicion of animals who had not yet decided whether he belonged, and into a room that was clearly the working heart of Belle Haven.

Stud books covered every surface. The desk, the side table, the chair by the window where a volume lay open face-down across the armrest. Charlotte sat at one side of the desk with a pile of open registers before her, her fair hair escaping its ribbon, a pencil behind one ear and another in her hand, surrounded by scraps of paper covered in pedigree charts that looked, to his untrained eye, like the plans for a siege. She did not look up when he entered.

Eliza occupied her father's chair with a naturalness that struck him. She did not sit in it as if borrowing it. She sat in it as though it had been waiting for her, and the papers before her and the ink on her fingers and the slight crease between her brows all spoke of someone deep in necessary work. She looked up when he appeared and gestured to the chair opposite.

"Lieutenant. Sit down, please. Charlotte has found something."

He sat. Charlotte launched into an explanation covering Eclipse, dam lines, and the relative merits of female-side inheritance at a pace that assumed her audience could keep up. Llewellyn followed perhaps two thirds of it. He understood horses well enough to ride them into battle and care for them after, but breeding theory was another country, and Charlotte spoke its language as a native.

What he did understand was the weight of the words. Hermes's dam was Eclipse's granddaughter. The sole remaining carrier. A line that could not be replicated.

He looked at Eliza. She was watching him, gauging his reaction, and in her expression he read the thing she wanted him to understand: the blind horse he had led through the gate, the animal the army had deemed worthless, was more valuable than every horse Ashworth had taken that morning.

"I had no idea," he said. It sounded inadequate, and was.

"Nobody did," Charlotte said, without looking up. "That's rather the point. He left as an unfinished three-year-old."

"Why did your father let him go?"

"An interesting question," Eliza agreed, tapping a line in a book before her. "Father actually thought him unpromising as a three-year-old. Perhaps because of his pure Thoroughbred lines, he was slow to mature. Gangly and awkward, Father wrote in his training notes; not particularly brave or fast."

Hermes was the opposite of those things. Solidly built, sure-footed, the fastest horse Llewellyn had ever sat on and courageous beyond belief. He said all of that, and Eliza nodded without questioning him.

"They mature," she said.

"And now he's come home," Charlotte said, sounding happily satisfied.

The room settled into quiet as they absorbed the implications. Llewellyn turned it over in his mind. He had brought Hermes home because it was right, because the horse had saved his life countless times and deserved better than a bullet. He had not imagined that this act of conscience might matter to anyone beyond himself and one blind stallion.

Charlotte excused herself to fetch another volume from the library, gathering her skirts and papers and disappearing through the door like a terrier on a scent. Laura followed her out, murmuring something about tea. The study fell quiet. Through the window came the distant sounds of the yard, reduced and thin; boys calling to one another, a bucket clanking.

Eliza was looking at the ledger before her, but her eyes were not moving across the page. She was looking through it, at something farther away.

"If I had argued better this morning," she said, her voice low and even, as though reporting a fact rather than confessing a failure, "I might have saved Beech. He was our best covering stallion. Thirteen seasons of proven get. I should have found a way."

She did not look at him, and Llewellyn understood she was not asking for sympathy. She was stating the debt as she saw it, entering it in her private ledger the way she entered everything: plainly, honestly, without ornament.

He knew this reckoning. He had done it himself, in field hospitals and on long marches, tallying the men lost against the decisions made, calculating whether some different choice at some earlier moment might have changed the sum. It was the burden of command, and it was always wrong, because it assumed you could have known what you did not know.

"You couldn't have anticipated what happened," Llewellyn said. He kept his voice plain. No softness, no sympathy, because she would reject both. "Ashworth arrived with sealed orders and a full column. Your father departed yesterday with forty horses he believed were sufficient. Nobody could have known the War Office would send a second requisition separately. Nobody. You saved the pregnant mares. You saved the colts. You argued three horses out of his hands that his orders entitled him to take." He paused. "That isn't failure, Miss Bell. That's the line between what you could control and what you couldn't."

Her eyes met his. Dark brown, very steady. She was weighing his words the way she weighed everything, testing them for soundness before she would accept their load.

Whatever she found must have held, because she nodded once and turned back to the breeding ledger.

"Then we work with what we have," she said, and began turning pages.

They worked side by side in the quiet study, Eliza turning through the broodmare register while Llewellyn examined the records of Hermes's year, trying to piece together the horse's early history from entries made in Sir Richard's careful copperplate. Clouds moved across the March sky outside, shifting the light on the desk.

Eliza reached for a volume at the same moment he did.

Their fingers met on the spine of the stud book. Her hand was bare and warm from the fire, rough in places where he might have expected softness; calloused at the base of her fingers from years of handling reins and halter ropes. His own hand, reaching from his left side because his right was slower these days, covered hers for an instant before he registered the contact.

Something jolted through him, sharp and physical, that had nothing to do with the book and everything to do with the warmth of her skin against his.

She looked at him. He looked at her. The moment held for one breath, two.

He withdrew his hand.

He did it deliberately, pulling back to rest his fingers on the edge of the desk, because in that instant of contact the distance between them had become abruptly, painfully measurable. She was Miss Bell. Daughter of Sir Richard Bell, master of Belle Haven, breeder of the finest horses in England. She sat in that chair by right of blood and competence and a lifetime of belonging to this place. And he was David Llewellyn, second son of a farmer in Carmarthenshire, a lieutenant on half pay with a damaged arm and a lame leg, who owned nothing in the world but the uniform on his back and a name that meant nothing east of the Brecon Beacons.

She had not pulled away. He had. The distinction mattered, though he could not have said to whom.

"Excuse me," he said, and reached for a different book, one safely distant from her hands.

Eliza took the stud book he had relinquished and opened it without comment, though he thought, perhaps imagined, that her fingers paused on the spine where his had been.

They returned to work. Charlotte's footsteps sounded in the corridor, returning with her prize. And Llewellyn kept his hands carefully to his own side of the desk and did not look at Eliza Bell's fingers and told himself that the warmth still lodged behind his breastbone was nothing more than gratitude for being useful.

He was not at all convinced.

The March air hit Eliza's face when she stepped from the study into the yard, sharp with the smell of damp earth and hay and the absence of horses. She had spent her whole life walking through a stable yard alive with the sound and warmth of two hundred animals, and the quiet that met her now had weight. Empty stalls gaped along the main barn, doors unlatched, bedding still carrying the impressions of bodies that had stood there that morning. A water bucket dripped beneath a standpipe. Somewhere a loose latch knocked in the wind.

Charlotte walked beside her, the pedigree chart clutched in one hand, her bonnet abandoned somewhere in the study. Laura had remained inside with Caesar, and Llewellyn had excused himself to check on Hermes, which left the two sisters alone as they turned toward the broodmare barn along Belle Haven's southern boundary.

"Artemis first," Charlotte said, consulting her chart without breaking stride. "She's the obvious choice. In foal to Hephaestus now, due in May, but she can be covered again after she foals. Her dam line is pure Dorado on the female side, no Mercury blood at all. She's clean."

Eliza pushed open the barn door and the warm breath of horses met them, thick with the sweetness of hay and the earthier notes of straw and manure. Twenty-three mares occupied the stalls, most of them heavy with foal, their sides round and low-slung. Several turned their heads at the sound of the door. A chestnut near the entrance nickered and pressed her nose against the stall gate.

"There she is," Eliza said, stopping at Artemis's stall. The chestnut regarded them with calm intelligence, her dark eye liquid and watchful. "She foaled easily last year. Good milk, good temperament. And she's deep through the girth, which would complement Hermes's length of leg."

Charlotte studied the mare with an appraising eye. "Agreed. An excellent choice." She marked her chart and moved on.

They worked their way down the aisle, pausing at each stall. Charlotte carried the pedigrees in her head as readily as other girls carried the steps of a country dance, producing dam lines and sire connections with the fluency of recitation. Eliza supplied the physical knowledge: which mares foaled easily, which were difficult breeders, which had thrown foals with conformational faults that suggested the cross should not be repeated. Between them, the two kinds of expertise fitted together seamlessly.

"Lady Daphne," Charlotte said, pausing at a grey mare with kind eyes who stood dozing in a patch of watery sunlight. "She was meant for Poseidon again, who went with Father. Her dam is by Mystery Star out of a Mercury mare. Mercury blood on the dam's side." She frowned. "Hermes's sire is Mercury. So we'd have Mercury on both sides. Too close."

"Ruled out, then."

"For Hermes, yes. We'll need to find her another match." Charlotte's pencil moved, striking through a name.

They crossed the yard to the separate paddock where the three young colts stood together, the ones Eliza had saved that morning by insisting to Ashworth they were unbroken. Two-year-olds, leggy and unfinished, with the gangly proportions of adolescence and the nervous energy of young horses who had seen too many strangers in a single day. They clustered at the far fence as the sisters approached, then curiosity won out and one, a tall bay, extended his neck to investigate Charlotte's outstretched hand.

"This one," Charlotte said, running her palm along the colt's neck, "is out of Thistle, who is by Red Cloud. His sire is Beech. Excellent lines, both sides, and look at the bone on him." She lifted the colt's foreleg and examined the cannon bone, running her thumb along its flat surface. "Clean as a whistle. Dense and flat, not round. He'll make a stallion, given time. Possibly a great one."

Behind them, old Thornton had appeared near the gate, and with him Robert and Phillip. They leaned on the fence, faces carefully blank, and Eliza recognised the look at once. The particular scepticism men reserved for expertise delivered by someone they considered too young, too female, or both. She had seen it directed at herself often enough.

Charlotte, absorbed in the second colt, did not notice the looks. Or, Eliza thought, did not care. Charlotte's confidence was not the brittle sort that needed outside approval. It was the confidence of someone who knew what she knew and had the evidence to prove it, and if the evidence was not enough for her audience, that was rather their problem than hers.

"This chestnut is the weakest of the three," Charlotte announced, straightening. "He hasn't the bone of the other two, and his dam threw a roarer two seasons ago. I don't know why Father didn't geld him already. I would have."

She moved to the third colt, a leggy black who stood apart from the others with his head high and his nostrils flared. "But this one. Oh, Eliza, look at him."

Eliza looked. The black colt had presence; the quality that could not be quantified in stud books or pedigree charts, the indefinable thing their father called heart. He stood as though the paddock belonged to him, watching the humans at his fence not with fear but appraisal.

"He's out of Silver Star, by Hephaestus," Charlotte said, her voice softer now. "And Silver Star is out of Mystic Moon, who Father bought from an auction of Spanish stock in London eight years ago. No Mercury blood anywhere. He could stand with Hermes's daughters in three years' time and give us a whole new line. But in the meantime, he can cover every mare meant for Hephaestus. He's the one, Eliza. Him, and Hermes; between them we have options for every mare still at Belle Haven."

Something shifted in Eliza's chest, warm and unfamiliar, and she recognised it after a moment as hope. Not the brittle, desperate kind she had clung to that morning while Ashworth's men led her horses away. Something steadier. Built on Charlotte's charts and her own knowledge and the young colts still standing in this paddock because she had found the words to keep them there.

She looked at Charlotte, who was scribbling notes with the pencil from behind her ear, hair in her face, cheeks pink from the cold, utterly absorbed. Fourteen years old and carrying the future of Belle Haven's breeding programme in her head.

Eliza did not hide her pride. There was no one to perform for, no audience to manage. She simply watched her sister work and let herself feel the thing she rarely allowed: gratitude for the people who had not left. Who were here, and capable, and hers.

"Charlotte," she said.

Charlotte looked up, pencil poised.

"That's excellent work."

The smile Charlotte gave her was quick and bright and pleased, the smile of a girl who was still, beneath the expertise and the bloodline charts, young enough to glow at her elder sister's praise. Then she turned back to her notes, because there was work to be done and Charlotte Bell was not the sort of person who let a compliment slow her down.

Thornton had uncrossed his arms. He was watching Charlotte with an expression that had shifted, almost imperceptibly, from scepticism to attention. Eliza filed this away and said nothing. Charlotte's gift would prove itself. It always did.

She looked across the yard at the stallion barn where Hermes stood in his quiet stall, mapping his world by sound and scent and the geometry of walls. A blind stallion with a pedigree worth more than gold. Three colts saved by stubbornness. A sister who could read a bloodline the way other people read faces. It was not much. It was not nearly enough.

But it was a beginning.

Chapter Four

Llewellyn woke in the dark with his right arm aching and the taste of gunpowder in his mouth, though neither had any business being there. The dream dissolved before he could catch it, leaving only residue: a tightness across his chest, a ringing silence where cannon fire had been. He lay still and let the world reassemble itself. Rough wool blanket. Straw mattress, thin but clean. The smell of hay and horse and old timber, nothing like the mud-and-iron stink of a bivouac. The groom's room above the stallion barn at Belle Haven, where he had slept two nights now. The first birds were singing; dawn must be close.

He dressed in the dark by feel, pulling on his shirt and breeches and the boots he had placed beside the bed with the tops turned down, the way he had done every night for three years so he could find them without a light if the alarm sounded. Old habits. The war followed him into small rituals he could not seem to put down.

He descended the narrow stairs to the barn aisle, one hand on the wall, his bad leg taking each step with care. The air grew warmer at the ground floor, where the heat of four horses collected beneath the roof: Hermes and the three colts who would be asked to do the part of grown stallions within just a few weeks. Grey light was beginning to reach the high windows. The barn existed between night and morning, and the shadows had a softness to them, as if the building itself were still half asleep.

He heard her voice before he saw her. It came from Hermes's stall at the far end of the aisle. Quiet, unhurried. The voice of someone who believed herself alone.

Llewellyn stopped in the doorway of the feed room and did not announce himself.

Eliza stood inside the stall with one hand on Hermes's neck. Her back was turned, her dark braids coiled tight against her head, her shawl slipping from one shoulder. She was telling him about Celestine, about Eclipse, about the blood that ran through him now. Her voice was so low Llewellyn had to hold his breath to hear it, and what he heard was not the brisk authority of the woman who ran Belle Haven. This was tender, almost reverent, the voice of someone speaking truths too fragile for daylight.

"You were her only living foal," Eliza was saying, her hand moving along the stallion's crest. "Everything she was, everything Eclipse gave her, it runs through you now. Just you."

Her voice caught on the last two words, and Llewellyn felt it land in his chest. She was speaking about more than a horse. She was speaking about what it meant to be the last carrier of something, the sole repository of a line that would end if you did. And he thought that she was speaking about herself. Because Eliza Bell was a Bell, a daughter of Belle Haven, but Llewellyn had known Molly Bell at

Sandhurst before she became Mrs Blair-Fortescue, and he knew that none of the Bell daughters were Sir Richard and Lady Bell's by blood. One look at the sisters here would tell anyone that; while Charlotte and Laura were twins, not identical but alike in their blonde prettiness, Eliza could not have been more different. Her hair was black as midnight and her skin only a few shades lighter. Her parents must have been from Africa, or the West Indies, and how she had come to be adopted by the Bells was surely a story in itself.

He watched her hand come up to rest against the stallion's scarred face, slender dark fingers tracing the ridges of healed tissue with a gentleness he had not seen her show to anything in daylight. Hermes leaned into her touch, and the two of them stood together in the dim stall like figures in a painting.

He recognised what he was seeing because he had done the same thing. Saying things to an animal that he could not say to any human being. The private language of people who had learned that vulnerability was safest when its only witness could not repeat what it heard.

Hermes's ears turned. The stallion's head lifted, nostrils flaring, and Llewellyn knew he had been discovered; not by Eliza but by the horse. Hermes nickered softly, and Eliza went still.

She turned. The grey light had strengthened just enough for him to see her face, and what he saw was the moment the door closed. The softness pulled inward, folding itself away, and in its place came the composure she wore like armour. Not false. But not the whole of her, and now he had seen what lay behind it.

"Lieutenant," she said, her voice reset to its daytime register. "You're up early."

"Old habit." He did not step closer. "I came to check on him."

"He's well. His appetite is good and he's moving more confidently in the stall." She ran her hand along Hermes's shoulder, a practical gesture now. "I was just assessing his condition before the yard wakes."

She had not been assessing his condition. They both knew it.

"I'll leave you to it, then," Llewellyn said, and turned toward the feed room. Behind him he heard the soft rasp of the brush as Eliza began to groom the stallion, the silence between them filled with bristles moving over a horse's coat.

He did not look back.

Charlotte began her interrogation over breakfast.

"When you say he came through smoke and gunfire," she said, buttering her toast with one hand and holding a pencil in the other, her tea cooling untouched, "do you mean willingly? Or did you have to call him more than once?"

Llewellyn set down his teacup. Laura ate quietly across the table, her knife gliding butter over bread by sound and touch. Louise sat beside her, already on her second slice of toast, eyes bright with the acquisitive interest of a magpie spotting something shiny.

"Once," Llewellyn said. "I whistled once, and he came."

"Straight to you. Through musket fire."

"Through musket fire and a line of French skirmishers. His rider had fallen and he was loose, but he wasn't panicking. It seemed as though he was waiting for someone to tell him what to do."

Charlotte nodded. "And in subsequent engagements? Under cannon fire?"

"Steady. He never balked at a charge. Never refused to advance. He went where I pointed him, every time, at whatever speed I asked for."

"And the speed?"

"The fastest horse I've ever ridden. On a retreat in the Low Countries, I carried a message across open ground under fire. He covered the distance so fast the French marksmen couldn't track us. My troop called him the grey ghost after that."

Charlotte smiled, fierce and satisfied. "Courage, speed, willingness, and intelligence. All heritable, all desirable, and consistent with what we'd expect from an Eclipse dam line crossed with Mercury." She tapped her pencil against her book. "Thank you, Lieutenant. Extremely useful."

She returned to her charts as though the conversation were a tap she had turned on, obtained what she needed, and turned off. Louise caught Llewellyn's eye and grinned. He found himself grinning back.

Later that morning he walked to the broodmare barn to check on the heavy mares. The barn was warm and close, thick with the smell of clean straw and the deeper scent of horses working hard to build new life. Most stood quietly, heads low, hips cocked. But in the fourth stall, one mare had been restless for days, a dark bay with a white blaze, enormous with foal and fractious with discomfort. She had kicked her water bucket over twice that morning.

She was not pacing now.

Laura sat on an upturned bucket inside the stall, her back against the wall, hands folded in her lap. Caesar lay at her feet. The mare stood over them both, head low, muzzle touching Laura's shoulder, eyes half-closed, breathing slow. She looked like a different animal.

Laura's face was turned toward the mare, though her sightless eyes saw nothing. Her expression was patient, unhurried. Her hands rested on her knees, not touching the horse. Simply present.

Llewellyn stood in the aisle and watched, reluctant to break the scene. He had seen skilled horsemen calm difficult animals through technique. This was something older and stranger, like perfect pitch. The mare had not been trained to be calm. She had found calm, because Laura was there.

He backed away without speaking and left them to it.

He was crossing the yard when a sack of carrots nearly collided with his chest.

"Oh! Lieutenant!" Louise moved the sack to her opposite shoulder, a streak of dirt across her cheek. "I've been at the kitchen garden all morning. The carrots have gone entirely to seed, but the horses won't mind, will they? Horses aren't particular about the aesthetics of a carrot."

"I shouldn't think so," Llewellyn agreed.

"Good. Because there are rather a lot of them." She hoisted the sack and set off toward the broodmare barn before he could offer to carry it, calling back over her shoulder about reorganised herb beds and a forgotten row of turnips she had sent up to Cook.

Llewellyn shook his head, smiling. That girl was a force of nature.

He became aware of a weight against his left leg. Pompey, the second mastiff, had planted himself against Llewellyn's thigh with the immovable solidity of a dog who has made a decision and sees no reason to discuss it.

"Right," Llewellyn said. "You've decided, have you?"

Pompey leaned harder. Llewellyn scratched behind the mastiff's ear, and the dog's eyes closed with such contentment that something loosened in Llewellyn's chest, a tension he had been carrying so long he had forgotten it was there.

The dog followed him for the rest of the day. Into the stallion barn, where Hermes tolerated the mastiff with weary patience. Across the yard, where Pompey sat beside the water trough while Llewellyn helped Robert repair a fence rail. Into the tack room, where the dog curled on a folded blanket and watched him clean bridles with the grave attention of a supervisor who takes his responsibilities seriously.

By evening, Pompey preceded Llewellyn into the dining room and took up position beside his chair as if the arrangement had been ordained since the house was built.

Dinner was lamb with roasted potatoes and the first spring greens. Helen presided with quiet authority. Charlotte talked pedigrees. Louise talked turnips. Laura said nothing, though she smiled when Louise described the gooseberry bushes in terms that suggested a personal affront.

Llewellyn cut a sliver of fat from his chop and, under cover of reaching for his napkin, lowered his left hand beneath the table. Pompey's nose was already waiting. The dog took the meat with jaws that closed around the morsel with the delicacy of a duchess accepting a bonbon.

Llewellyn straightened and reached for his glass. As he did, his gaze met Eliza's across the table.

She was watching his hand, the one that had just returned from beneath the tablecloth, a little grease on his fingertips evidence of what he had just done. Her dark eyes tracked from his fingers to his face. Her expression did not change. She simply held his gaze for a beat longer than necessary, and returned to her meal.

It was the closest thing to approval he had received from Eliza Bell that did not involve horses. He ate the rest of his dinner with a warmth in his chest that had nothing to do with the lamb, and a warmth on his leg from Pompey's great head resting upon it.

Eliza returned from the broodmare barn the next morning to find Helen and Llewellyn at the kitchen table with a pot of tea between them, talking as though they had known each other for years.

Helen sat leaning forward in her listening position, the one that drew words from people much as a farrier drew nails. Llewellyn sat across from her, his long frame folded into a too-small chair, and he was speaking with an ease Eliza had not heard from him before. His Welsh accent was markedly stronger as he talked of his home; his father's sheep farm below the Black Mountain, the Welsh cobs his father bred, the winters harder than anything he had met in the Peninsula though the French were considerably less pleasant than Welsh rain.

Helen laughed, warm and sudden, and Llewellyn smiled at the sound of it in a way that took years off him. He looked like a young man of twenty-four rather than a soldier carrying the weight of twenty more.

Eliza felt something prickle beneath her skin. A small, pointed sensation, like a splinter she couldn't locate.

"Good morning," she said, more briskly than she intended.

Helen's expression was serene. Llewellyn's smile settled back into its usual restraint. He rose from his chair, an automatic courtesy, and reported that Thornton credited Laura with settling the dark bay mare overnight.

Eliza poured herself tea and sat at the end of the table, setting a distance between herself and their conversation. She asked Helen about the laundry account; Helen had already ordered the soap. Helen turned back to Llewellyn as though the interruption were a brief gust of wind, mildly refreshing but not worth remarking upon.

Eliza drank her tea and observed. The irritation sat in her chest like a cinder that would neither catch fire nor go out. She could not name it, which irritated her further. There was nothing improper about two adults sharing tea in a kitchen on a cold morning.

And yet.

She finished her tea and went to the study. The prickle followed her.

An hour later, she was deep in calculations when Louise appeared in the study doorway with the brightness of expression that meant she had identified a problem nobody else had noticed and was preparing to solve it whether or not anyone had asked.

"Eliza!" Louise advanced into the room, stepping neatly over Caesar, who had stationed himself across the threshold like a furry barricade. "Charlotte says the feed delivery is coming tomorrow, and you'll want Lieutenant Llewellyn to know, because he'll need to have Hermes out of the stallion barn while the men are carrying in the sacks and barrels, so they don't upset him. Shall I run down and tell him? I don't mind at all. I was going that way anyway."

She had not been going that way. The stallion barn lay in the opposite direction from everywhere Louise had been that morning, which included the kitchen garden, the laundry, and the linen cupboard, all of which she had reorganised with cheerful thoroughness and absolutely no mandate from anyone.

"That's kind of you, Louise," Eliza said, looking up from her papers, "but I'll tell him myself when I see him later. There's no hurry."

Louise's face fell. A flicker, there and gone, the brief collapse of a plan that had seemed so promising thirty seconds earlier. Her smile recovered quickly, but Eliza had seen the disappointment, and it was disproportionate. No one looked that crestfallen about failing to deliver a message about a delivery of feed that wasn't even happening until the following day.

"Of course!" Louise said brightly. "I just thought I'd save you the trouble. You're so busy."

She retreated, navigating Caesar with the agility of long practice, and her footsteps faded down the corridor. Eliza heard her begin a conversation with Laura on the landing, something about whether the gooseberry bushes could be saved, and then the two of them moved out of earshot.

Eliza sat back in her chair and considered.

Louise was fourteen. Cheerful and warm and constitutionally incapable of passing a problem without attempting to solve it, but also at the age when a cavalry officer with a Welsh accent and a war wound might seem the most romantic thing imaginable. He was tall and well-built, broad-shouldered without being heavy. Quiet in a way that suggested depths rather than shallows. He had saved a blinded horse from cannon fire and refused to let anyone put it down. He had a way of listening that made you feel heard rather than merely waited upon. And he was, Eliza admitted to herself, quite handsome.

She had not examined this fact before. She examined it now, briefly and with deliberate calm, as if it were an entry in a ledger she had overlooked. Good bones. A strong jaw, though not heavy. Eyes that were a particular shade of grey-blue, like river stones. The way he held himself, straight-backed despite the injuries, carrying the damage without complaint. The slight crook of his nose where it must have been broken at some point, which ought to have marred his face but instead gave it character, like a flaw in good wood that proved it was real.

She caught herself. Her pencil had stopped moving and she was staring at the wall above the desk with the breeding schedule forgotten beneath her hand.

Louise had a crush. That was all. Perfectly natural and entirely harmless, and Eliza would keep an eye on it, because Louise's heart was large and generous and easily bruised, and cavalry officers on temporary assignment were not a suitable object for the affections of a fourteen-year-old girl. Llewellyn was a sensible man who would not dream of encouraging her, but that didn't mean Louise could not break her heart over him anyway.

She picked up her pencil and returned to the breeding schedule. The prickle in her chest had not gone away, but she chose not to investigate it further.

Some problems, Eliza told herself firmly, did not require solving today.

The routine took shape by repetition, the same feet crossing the same ground until the grass lay flat and a direction emerged. By the third morning the rhythm was recognisable, if still ragged at the edges, the way a young horse's canter finds its beat after the first unsteady strides.

Dawn brought the feed round. Then mucking out, which took twice as long with half the hands. By mid-morning Charlotte was at the desk with her charts, Laura in the broodmare barn, Louise somewhere being useful in ways no one had requested, and Eliza in the yard directing the work.

It was during the second water round that she noticed the look.

She had told Thornton to move some yearlings from the east paddock to the larger field behind the stallion barn. A straightforward instruction. Thornton hesitated. A beat, perhaps two, his gnarled hands on the gate latch, his face turned not toward her but past her, toward Llewellyn, who stood thirty paces away mending a fence rail. The look was instinctive, the reflex of a man who had spent sixty-four years taking orders from other men and whose body sought confirmation from the nearest one available, regardless of whether that man held any authority at all.

Llewellyn did not look up. He drove another nail, shifted the rail, tested its hold.

"Right you are, Miss Eliza," Thornton said, and went to move the yearlings.

She watched him go. He was not hostile. He did what she asked, and did it well. His loyalty was to Belle Haven itself, which extended to her by inheritance whether his instincts were comfortable with it or not. But the look cost her. A small deduction from a reserve she could not replenish, because what Thornton's eyes sought when they drifted past her was not skill but category, and she could not argue herself into a category she had not been born to.

She crossed the yard to the standpipe. Llewellyn was already there, filling buckets, sleeves rolled, forearms bare despite the March cold. Eliza noticed the rope of scar tissue along his right wrist before it disappeared beneath the cuff.

The rhythm established itself: pump, fill, set aside. Take, carry, pour. Return. They moved around each other without speaking, bodies that had learned the dimensions of a shared space. The silence between them was comfortable enough that neither felt the need to fill it.

On the fourth pass, she reached for a bucket at the same moment he did.

Her hand closed around the rope handle. His hand closed over hers.

His palm came to rest against the back of her hand, warm even through the chill of splashed water, fingers curling around hers. His calluses pressed against her knuckles. The heel of his hand rested against her wrist, and she felt his pulse there, or perhaps her own.

Neither of them moved.

Phillip led a skittering yearling across the cobbles. A wren sang from the tack room roof, three bright notes in the cool air.

She did not pull away. He did not pull away.

One breath. Two. Then he let go.

Llewellyn returned to the pump. Eliza walked to the next stall, and her mind went without permission to the study two days earlier. The spine of the stud book. His fingers covering hers for an instant, then withdrawn as though he had touched something hot. She had not withdrawn. He had. The distinction had lived in her since, unexamined, like a coin in her pocket she kept reaching for without knowing why.

He had not looked at her differently since. She had watched, without admitting she was watching, and found nothing. No lingering glances. No manufactured closeness. He maintained between them a distance that was scrupulous and, she was beginning to suspect, effortful. He never once looked at her the way he had looked at Helen in the kitchen, with that unguarded warmth, that easy smile.

She flexed her hand. The warmth was still there, sitting on her skin like a print left in soft wax.

She thought of Louise's disappointment, and her own tidy explanation. She thought of the prickle when she had found Helen laughing with him over tea. She thought of the way he had looked driving nails into a fence rail with his sleeves rolled and the scar on his wrist catching the light, and how she had catalogued it all as though assessing a stallion's conformation, and how that comparison seemed considerably less reasonable now.

Eliza curled her fingers closed, trapping the warmth against her palm, and turned back to the yard, where Llewellyn was pumping water and not looking at her, and she was not looking at him, and the careful distance between them was exactly the width of everything neither of them was prepared to say.

Chapter Five

A LITTLE MORE THAN a week at Belle Haven, and he had settled into a rhythm. Not comfort, but the working approximation of order that emerged when the same tasks were done in the same sequence enough times that the body learned the pattern before the mind had to think it through. Llewellyn rose before dawn. Checked on Hermes. Fed the three colts. Walked the broodmare barn, counting breathing rates and watching for the subtle shift in posture that meant a mare was close. By midmorning he was in the yard, mending what needed mending, carrying what needed carrying, fitting himself into the gaps left by absent men the way water fills the spaces between stones.

He was replacing a damaged plank on the stallion barn door when the sound reached him. Hooves on the lane, measured and unhurried, the cadence of horses being ridden rather than driven. A column or riders. He straightened, hammer still in hand, and watched the bend in the road.

A dozen riders came around the curve of the lane and stopped at the gate. An officer in front, troopers behind, and no led horses. A requisition party travelling light, which meant they intended to leave heavier. The officer rode well, sat deep, his uniform newer than Llewellyn's and better kept. A captain. The crowns on his shoulders caught the sun like a rebuke.

Pompey, dozing by the barn wall, rose and produced a single resonant bark that echoed off the stonework. Llewellyn set down the hammer, quieted the dog with a hand on his broad skull, and walked to meet the riders.

The captain dismounted and removed his hat. He was perhaps thirty, fair-haired, with the neatness of a man who had spent his career at staff desks rather than in the field. His boots were clean. His gloves were whole. He looked at Llewellyn's worn uniform jacket.

"Lieutenant," he said. "Captain Harding, remount service, attached to the War Office procurement division. I carry orders for the requisition of horses from this estate." He held out a folded document, offering it to Llewellyn with the easy assumption of an officer addressing a junior.

Llewellyn did not take the paper.

"Miss Bell has the authority here, sir," he said. "She manages the estate in her father's absence. You'll want to present your orders to her."

Harding's hand stayed extended for half a beat. His gaze moved past Llewellyn to the yard. "Miss Bell," he repeated.

"Sir Richard Bell's daughter. She has full authority over the horses and the breeding programme."

Harding tucked the document back into his pocket and resettled his hat. "Very well. Would you be good enough to inform her I'm here?"

Llewellyn turned to send one of the boys, but Eliza was already crossing the yard. She must have heard the hooves; he did not know where she had been, only that she was here now, moving toward them at the same unhurried pace she used for everything. Her grey dress was plain, her braids pulled tight, her expression composed. She carried no ledger this time. Her hands were empty, which struck him as deliberate, as if she had decided the arguments would have to stand on their own.

"Captain," she said, stopping three paces from Harding. "I am Eliza Bell. You have orders?"

Harding produced the document again. If her youth or her sex or the colour of her skin gave him pause, he concealed it behind the brisk courtesy of a man with a job to do, though Llewellyn saw the incredulous looks the troopers behind him traded with each other. "Captain Harding, Miss Bell. War Office procurement. I'm tasked with assessing and taking possession of any horses on these premises suitable for cavalry service, with particular emphasis on young stock of three years and above."

Llewellyn watched her read the orders. Her eyes moved down the page carefully. He saw her reach the relevant clause. Her fingers tightened at the margin, so slightly it might have been invisible to anyone not watching for it.

"Three-year-olds. Broken or not," she read aloud.

It took everything he had not to wince. He knew what that meant; two dozen fillies they'd planned to put in foal, some twenty geldings that were in the early stages of saddle training, and those three colts in the stallion barn. The bay with the dense, flat bone Charlotte had praised, the chestnut whose dam had thrown a roarer but was still a viable option for some of the bigger draft-cross mares, and the black, the one Charlotte had called the future. She had built the entire revised breeding programme around those colts and Hermes, and the future was standing in the barn fifty yards away, ears pricked, unaware of what was coming.

Eliza folded the paper along its original creases and lifted her chin. "Captain Harding. You should know that Colonel Ashworth was here ten days ago and took thirty-seven horses, including two stallions critical to our programme. My father departed the day before that with forty more. Belle Haven has given the army nearly eighty horses in a fortnight, every ridable horse we had."

"The War Office is aware of Sir Richard's contribution, and grateful for it," Harding said. He was not unkind. He was a man doing arithmetic, and the numbers would not bend for gratitude. "However, the situation on the Continent has deteriorated faster than anticipated. Wellington needs every mount we can provide."

"The three-year-olds left to us are unbroken," Eliza said. "They have never carried a rider; some have never carried a saddle. Colonel Ashworth agreed they were unsuitable for immediate service."

"Colonel Ashworth's orders did not extend to unbroken stock. Mine do." Harding's expression was patiently implacable. "The remount service will complete their training at the depot."

Llewellyn stood behind Eliza and to her left. Close enough to be present. Far enough not to crowd her. He held his silence for the same reasons he had held it with Ashworth: to speak would be to step in front of her, and he would not do that.

She squared her shoulders. Her chin came up.

She began to argue.

She made every argument he would have made and several he would not have thought of. She cited the breeding records. She pointed out that a horse taken now, before his growth was finished and his bone hardened, would make an inferior cavalry mount compared to the same horse taken at four or five. She argued yield: give us one more year, give us six months even, and these youngsters will be worth three of any horse you could take today. She argued the economics, the long war, the need for horses not just this season but every season after it.

Harding listened. He did not dismiss her or interrupt. He nodded at the right moments and made notes in a small leather book, and when she had finished he closed the book and said, "I understand what we are demanding will do damage to your breeding programme and potentially to the horses themselves, Miss Bell, and I will ensure your objections are recorded in full and passed on to my superiors. But the orders are explicit. Three-year-olds, broken or unbroken, are to be taken for the remount depot. I do not have the authority to make exceptions."

The worst of it was that Llewellyn understood Harding. He had been a cavalry officer who needed a horse beneath him. The system stripping Belle Haven was the same system that had given him Osiris, and then Hermes. He could not hate it without hating the thing that had saved his life.

But he could hate the particular flavour of uselessness. *I might stay and help*, he had said to Eliza, as though help were a thing he could provide. He had offered himself as protection, and protection meant absolutely nothing against sealed orders and the weight of the War Office.

Eliza led Harding to the stallion barn last, after all the young fillies and geldings had been brought in from the fields and tied together in a string the troopers would have quite some task to handle. They were too young. They needed a handler each, not one to manage four of them. And the colts probably needed two men apiece; Llewellyn hoped Harding was not taking them too far before handing them over, or there might be a disaster on the road somewhere.

That argument too would fail. Harding would just come back tomorrow, or the next day, with however many men he needed, and he would be more annoyed. So Llewellyn held his peace and carried halters and calmed the youngsters as best he could as he passed them over to the troopers.

The colts knew something was wrong. Heads high, nostrils wide, the nervous energy of young horses who had not yet learned to hide their fear. The bay stood at the back of his stall with his ears pinned. The chestnut paced. The black stood at his door with his neck arched and his dark eyes fixed on the strangers, not frightened but affronted, and the look reminded Llewellyn of the woman who had fought to keep him.

Eliza held the halters. She insisted on that. She would not let Harding's troopers handle the colts; she slipped the leather over each head herself, murmuring to them, her hands steady. She checked each buckle, adjusted each noseband, ran her hand down each neck.

She handed the first lead rope to the waiting trooper. The bay went quietly. The chestnut pulled once, then settled. The black colt planted his feet in the barn doorway and refused to move, his whole body braced. One of the troopers reached for a crop. Eliza stopped him with a look.

"Give him a moment," she said, and stood beside the colt with her hand on his shoulder until the tension left his body and he walked forward of his own accord.

Llewellyn did not watch the long string of horses go through the gate. He turned away because he knew what would be on her face, and he knew she would not want him to see it. He stared at the plank he had been mending, the hammer lying where he had set it down. The nail was half driven. The job half done.

The hooves faded. The gate swung shut. The yard fell into the same hollow quiet it had held ten days ago, though worse this time because they had built something in the interval and watched it carried away.

Charlotte was standing by the mounting block. She must have come from the study when she heard the commotion, because she still held a pencil and her foolscap was crumpled in her other hand, the pedigree chart with the crosses mapped out. Her face was white.

"We were depending on them," she said, her voice thin and young, stripped of its usual authority. "I'd worked out all the crosses. Every mare, every combination. The whole programme."

"I know," Eliza said, quietly.

Charlotte pressed her lips together, nodded once, and turned back toward the house with the chart still clutched in her hand, walking quickly, shoulders hunched.

Llewellyn picked up the hammer, crossed to the barn door, and drove the nail the rest of the way home. The plank sat flush. He tested it, swinging the door back and forth. A small thing done well in a day of large things done badly.

He did not speak to Eliza. He had learned in the field that there were moments when words were not a bridge but an intrusion, when the only respectful thing was to stand on your own side of the silence and let the other person have theirs.

He moved to the next task. A water bucket with a cracked stave, kicked over for the umpteenth time by the bay mare who was restless and angry waiting for her foal.

He fetched it, brought it to the tack room, and began working the damaged wood free. The anger sat in his chest like something swallowed sideways, too large to go down. Not anger at Harding. Anger at himself, for being here with his damaged arm and his lame leg and his lieutenant's insignia that meant nothing, offering help he could not deliver.

He had thought Belle Haven felt like solid ground. He was beginning to understand that solid ground could be taken from under you piece by piece, requisition by requisition, until you were standing on air.

He worked until the bucket was mended. Then he filled it with water, put it back in the bay mare's stall, and looked for the next thing he could mend. It was all he had.

She recognised her mother's handwriting on the letter before Phillip had even left the study. Theresa Bell wrote in a neat, slightly cramped hand that always slanted to the right, as though the words were leaning toward the reader, eager to be kind. The seal was plain wax, pressed with the edge of a button rather than a proper stamp, which was so entirely Theresa that Eliza felt her throat constrict before she had opened it.

Molly was well, enormous, and impatient. Tim had been called up, of course; despite his hearing loss there were plenty of tasks a man with his skill at horses could do for the army. He had been sent to manage a remount depot, Eliza say with a twist to her lips; she wondered if the Belle Haven horses would come under his eye, if he could recognise them. The baby was expected any day, and Theresa wrote with the practical optimism of a woman who had attended enough births to know that most went right, and the quiet faith of a woman who prayed for the ones that didn't. The doctor had confined Molly to bed, which was going about as well as could be expected. A dry, weary chuckle escaped Eliza as she imagined Molly's temper about that, and even Theresa's near-saintly patience strained to the breaking point managing her.

The second page turned to Belle Haven. Theresa had received Sir Richard's letter about Napoleon's escape and the departure of the horses. She offered advice for the breeding programme, carefully framed as suggestions rather than instructions, because Theresa never imposed. She wrote about the importance of the young stock. *Charlotte will know the bloodlines, but trust your eye for conformation. Those colts are the bridge between what we have now and what we will build next. Don't let anyone take them from you if you can help it.*

Eliza set the letter down and pressed her fingertips against its edge. The advice was excellent; Theresa knew Belle Haven's stock as well as any of them, though she rarely involved herself in the daily business of the horses, preferring to keep the house as her domain. It was precisely the strategy Eliza and Charlotte had devised. It was also, as of four hours ago, entirely useless.

She folded the letter carefully and placed it in the top drawer, where her father kept his important correspondence, and sat for a while without moving.

Dinner that evening was quiet, especially so since Helen was absent, having gone to the village to attend a young mother having her first child. Cook had made a pie from the last of the mutton, and Louise contributed a dish of roasted carrots that she presented with solemn pride. Charlotte ate without speaking, which was so unusual that Laura reached across the table and found her twin's hand and held it for a moment. Louise filled the silence with an account of the seeds she had planted in the herb garden that nobody had asked for and everybody was grateful for.

After dinner, Eliza returned to the study and took out paper and ink.

She wrote to her mother, choosing her words carefully. She reported that the household was well. That Helen and Louise had arrived and the house was in good hands. That the broodmares were progressing and the first foals would come any day now. She described Llewellyn's arrival with Hermes, the blind stallion, the Eclipse dam line Charlotte had discovered. She mentioned that Llewellyn had known Molly at Sandhurst, that it was Molly's demonstration of the whistle that had brought Hermes to him on the battlefield. She thought her mother would like that detail, and that Molly would like to hear that one of her trainees had made choices that brought him back to Belle Haven. The thread connecting Molly's teaching of Llewellyn to Hermes' survival to the future of the breeding programme had the quality of a story that would matter to Belle Haven for decades to come.

She did not describe the requisitions in detail. She wrote that they had given horses to the army and that the numbers were reduced, which was true without being the whole truth. She did not mention that Belle Haven's remaining breeding stock consisted of a blind stallion and sixty broodmares heavy with foals that would not be ready for anything for years.

There was nothing Theresa could do about any of it even if she was here, and Eliza did not want her mother to worry, or to feel torn. Molly needed Theresa right now far more than Eliza did. She wrote a loving wish for Molly's child to arrive safely and soon at the bottom of the letter, signed her name, and set down the pen. Reading back over the letter again, she sighed. There was nothing more to say.

Charlotte had come back to the study with her after dinner. Of course she had. She had spent the evening with the stud books open and a growing pile of fresh sheets of foolscap covered in her small, fierce handwriting. She was rebuilding. Not the same programme; that was gone with the colts. Something new. Crosses that could be made with Hermes alone. A narrower path, but Charlotte had found it, or was finding it, because Charlotte Bell could no more stop working a problem than water could stop running downhill.

But her head was down on a stud book now, her pencil still in her hand, her breathing slow and even. She had fallen asleep mid-calculation. A strand of fair hair lay across the open page, and in the lamplight she looked younger than fourteen, younger than the weight the last eleven days had put on her.

Eliza touched her sister's arm. "Charlie. Come on. Bed."

Charlotte stirred, blinked, and sat up with the disoriented frown of someone waking from a dream. "I wasn't finished."

"You are for tonight," Eliza said gently, closing the stud book and collecting the pencil from Charlotte's loosening grip. "The mares will still be there in the morning."

Charlotte allowed herself to be guided to the door, still murmuring about dam lines. Eliza listened to her footsteps on the stairs, uneven with sleep, and then Laura's voice from their shared room, soft and welcoming, and then quiet.

She returned to the desk. The study was very still. The candle threw guttering shadows against the bookshelves, where decades of Belle Haven records sat in ordered rows, broken occasionally where Charlotte had pulled one out.

She ran her finger along the spine of the nearest volume and felt the leather, cracked with age, supple from use.

One stallion. Sixty broodmares, once their foals were born. Whatever she and Charlotte could build from that.

She heard his step before she saw him. The slight unevenness, the way his left foot fell fractionally heavier than his right, had become familiar enough that she could pick it out from every other footfall. He appeared in the doorway, one hand on the frame, lamplight catching the planes of his face.

"Just done the rounds," Llewellyn said, his voice pitched for the hour. "Nobody looks like they'll foal tonight. The dark bay is restless but not close. Phillip's on watch; he'll come for us if anything changes."

Eliza nodded. She ought to have said thank you and let him go. It was almost midnight. The day had been long and hard and they both needed sleep.

He hesitated in the doorway. His eyes moved across her face, reading what was written there, and she did not have the energy to close herself up the way she usually did. Let him see.

"There's nothing you could have done," he said quietly. Plain, not pitying. The voice of a man stating a fact, the same voice he might use to report that a fence was mended or a horse had cast a shoe. "The orders were sealed before he left London. Nothing you said would have changed them."

She knew that. She had known it while she was arguing, known it as you know the ground is hard before you hit it. But hearing it from him, from a man who understood sealed orders and the weight of authority because he had served beneath both, loosened a shift in her chest. Not the grief or the anger, but the knot of believing she ought to have found a way.

"Get some rest," he said, shifting his weight from his bad leg. "There'll be plenty to do tomorrow. Sleepless nights coming soon enough, when foaling starts."

He did not wait for a reply. His uneven footsteps retreated down the corridor, through the kitchen where the mastiffs stirred and came to rest, and out the back door toward the stallion barn where Hermes stood alone in his dark stall, mapping his world by sound.

Eliza sat in her father's chair a while longer. The lamp guttered. Charlotte's fresh charts lay on the desk beside the sealed letter to Theresa, beside the stud books, beside the stack of compensation vouchers she wasn't even sure what to do with. The quiet of the house pressed in.

She blew out the lamp and climbed the stairs to her room. She slept, and if she dreamed, she did not remember it in the morning, which was perhaps the kindest thing the night could have given her.

Chapter Six

THE BEDROOM SMELLED OF lavender water and hummed with boredom. No sickroom, in Theresa Bell's experience, was complete without both. Molly Blair-Fortescue lay propped against a fortress of pillows, her dark hair loose around her shoulders, her belly a considerable landscape beneath the counterpane. She had a woman's expression, one who had been told to stay still and was obeying under protest, her jaw set, her fingers picking at the embroidery on the pillowcase with the restlessness of someone who would far rather be picking out hooves.

"Letter from Belle Haven," Theresa said, settling into the chair beside the bed. The paper was warm from her pocket, the seal already broken. She had opened it downstairs, standing in the hallway with her heart in her throat, because letters from home during wartime carried a particular weight and she had wanted a moment alone with whatever the news might be.

"Read it," Molly said, pushing herself higher against the pillows. "All of it. Don't leave out the horses."

Theresa smiled, because Molly's priorities had been the same since she was eleven years old and had walked from London to Hampshire on blistered feet to find Theresa and Belle Haven. Horses first, then people, then everything else, though the people she loved she loved with a fierceness that could stop your breath.

She smoothed the pages on her knee and began to read aloud. Eliza's voice came through the careful handwriting, steady and measured, reporting that the household was well, that Helen and Louise had arrived, that the broodmares were progressing and the first foals would come any day.

"She sounds like Richard," Molly murmured, and Theresa heard the affection in it. Richard's letters had always carried that same calm reassurance, and Eliza had learned it from him as surely as she had learned to assess a horse's conformation.

The second paragraph brought news that tightened Theresa's hands on the paper. A lieutenant of the 16th Light Dragoons had arrived with a blind stallion, a Belle Haven horse he called Hermes. Charlotte had traced his dam line. Celestine's foal. The granddaughter of Eclipse. Theresa remembered that mare, remembered Richard's agonising over the purchase price. She had encouraged him to buy her, thinking of the future; had grieved with him when all that investment yielded just one unpromising, gangly colt.

"Eclipse," Molly breathed, her restless fingers going still.

Theresa read on. Llewellyn had known Molly at Sandhurst. It was Molly's demonstration of the whistle that had brought Hermes to him on the battlefield.

Molly's face changed. The boredom fell away, and beneath it was something raw and bright. Her hand went to her belly, an unconscious gesture, as if the child inside could hear the story too.

"Llewellyn," she said quietly. "David Llewellyn. Yes, I remember. I gave him Osiris."

Theresa continued with the letter, but she was no longer reading only what was written. She was reading what was absent. How many horses remained was not enumerated, only *the breeding programme has been adjusted*, which was no answer at all. *The routine is new but functioning* told her the old routine had been destroyed. And the single sentence about reduced numbers carried beneath it a silence so deliberate it might as well have been written in its own ink: things are worse than I am telling you.

She knew her daughter. Eliza would not ask for help. She would sooner set her own arm than admit it was broken.

Theresa folded the letter and pressed her fingers against the creases. Through the window, the Oxfordshire countryside stretched green and quiet beneath a pale sky. Tim and Molly's house was comfortable, but it was not Belle Haven.

"I should go home," she said.

Molly's hand found hers. Quick, strong, calloused from years of reins. "No."

"Eliza is only eighteen, Molly! She's running everything alone."

"She is running everything brilliantly, from the sound of it." Molly's grip tightened. "She has Helen. She has Charlotte and Laura and Louise, and Thornton and old Jenkins. She has Lieutenant Llewellyn." She paused, and her voice was quieter when she spoke again. "There is nothing you can do there that Eliza and Helen cannot manage between them. And I don't think I can do this without you."

There it was. Beneath the stubbornness that was at the very core of Molly's personality, the admission that she was frightened. Tim had been called up the very day Richard's note arrived, two blows landing within an hour of each other; his hearing was damaged, but there was nothing wrong with his body or his mind, and the army knew it. The baby was coming. And Molly, who could calm a rearing stallion with her voice and her hands, was afraid of the one thing she could not control by being braver than it.

She was also right.

Theresa turned her hand beneath Molly's and held it properly, palm to palm.

"You are going to be perfectly fine," she said. "And so is the baby. And so is Eliza."

She was not certain of any of these things. But certainty, Theresa had learned, was less important than steadiness, and steadiness she could provide.

Molly released her hand and reached for the writing box on the bedside table. "Give me paper. I want to write to Eliza."

"The doctor said you were to rest."

"Writing is restful. Writing is practically sleeping. I shall be horizontal the entire time." Molly was already uncapping the ink. "I remember Llewellyn well. That summer at Sandhurst, there were forty young cadets and most of them sat a horse like a sack of oats with ambitions. Llewellyn was different. Good hands. Better instincts. He listened." She dipped the pen and began to write. "I liked his face. Honest. A little bit sad, even then. Tim said he was the finest natural horseman of the intake." She paused, pen hovering. "That grey gelding, Osiris. Beautiful animal, very willing. I matched him with Llewellyn myself, and it was a great decision. They were the best pair of the class, by a country mile." She wrote a few more lines, then added, almost to herself, "I'm glad he's alive. So many of them aren't."

The pen stopped. Molly stared at the page, her dark eyes distant, and Theresa saw the weight of it settle across her shoulders. The young men she had taught that summer, laughing and clumsy and so young.

Theresa took the note when Molly handed it to her and promised to include it in her own letter. But as she rose to go to her writing desk, her mind turned in a different direction. Eliza had written only what she wanted her mother to believe. A kindness, and Theresa recognised it as such. But kindness was sometimes a very effective wall, and she needed to know what was on the other side of it.

She would write to Helen as well. Helen Fallon, who saw everything and said only what mattered, would tell her the truth.

She looked at Molly, who had already dozed off with the ink bottle still uncapped on the writing box, one hand on her belly, her face softened by sleep. Theresa capped the ink, moved the writing box to the table, and drew the curtain against the afternoon light.

Then she went downstairs to write her letters.

The letter arrived with the morning post, tucked between an invoice for hay and a note from the farrier. Eliza opened her mother's reply at the breakfast table.

Charlotte was eating toast and reading a stud book propped against the teapot. Laura sat beside her with Caesar at her feet, slipping the crusts to the dog, knowing they would all be watching but equally aware they would all pretend they saw as little as she did. Louise occupied the chair nearest the door, from which she could monitor the hallway, the kitchen, and any passing crisis that might benefit from her attention. Llewellyn sat at his end of the table with Pompey's great head resting on his boot.

Three days since she had posted her careful letter. The roads were busy with military traffic; she was surprised it had come so quickly.

Her mother's reply was warm and steady. Molly was well, enormous, and the doctor had instructed her to stay in bed, which meant the doctor did not know Molly. The baby would come when it chose. Theresa did not ask the questions Eliza had been dreading. She did not press for numbers or details. She simply wrote that she trusted Eliza would know what to do, and the trust sat in Eliza's chest like a gift she was not sure she deserved.

A second sheet was folded inside the first, written in a bolder hand. Molly's script was looser than Theresa's, the letters tall and confident, ink blotted where the pen had been dipped too eagerly. Eliza could almost hear her sister's voice in the writing.

Molly remembered Lieutenant Llewellyn. The summer of 1812, forty young men in the riding school, most of them hopeless, a few with promise. Llewellyn had been the best. *Good hands*, Molly wrote, *better instincts. He listened, which is rarer than you'd think. I liked his face. Honest, and a little sad. Tim said he was the finest natural horseman of the lot, and Tim does not say that about anyone he doesn't mean it about.* Eliza glanced up at Llewellyn without meaning to. He was breaking bread with his left hand and was not looking at her.

Molly wrote about choosing horses for the recruits, matching temperament to rider. *I chose Osiris for him myself. A dapple grey gelding, very willing, with a lovely mouth and not a mean bone in his body. I hope he is well; give him a pat from me.*

The words sat on the page, cheerful and certain, written by a woman who did not know.

"Molly is asking after Osiris?" Eliza said, looking up from the note. The question came out naturally, directed at Llewellyn across the table, carried on the easy current of breakfast conversation.

And then she remembered.

Eliza's fingers tightened on Molly's note. He had told her on the first afternoon, standing in the yard with dust on his uniform. *My mount, Osiris, was shot from under me in my first engagement.* She had heard the words and filed them the way she filed facts about bloodlines, and she had not, until this moment, felt the full weight of what they meant. Molly had chosen that horse for him. Matched him personally, the way Molly matched all her pairs, with an instinct that was almost uncanny. And the horse had died in the first hour.

A shadow crossed Llewellyn's face, quick and controlled. His jaw tightened, then released. His left hand set down the bread he had been holding.

"Osiris was killed," he said, his voice level. "In my first engagement. The French had sharpshooters in the trees. He went down in the first volley."

Charlotte had gone very still, her toast forgotten, her quick mind visibly assembling the chain: Molly chose Osiris, Osiris died, Llewellyn whistled, Hermes came. Laura's head had turned toward his voice with that particular attention she possessed, and her expression held a gentleness that was not pity but recognition. Laura, who had lost her own sight to illness as a young child, understood something about the world being taken from you without warning. Louise, for once, did not speak.

It was Charlotte who asked. "Will you tell us? About Osiris. About how Hermes came to you."

Llewellyn looked at his tea. His thumb traced the rim of the cup, one slow circuit, and Eliza recognised the gesture as the private negotiation of a man deciding what he owed and to whom.

"Miss Molly arrived at Sandhurst in the summer of 1812," he said, and the Welsh lilt softened his voice in a way Eliza had not heard before. "She was the only woman most of us had seen in the riding school. Small. Dark. Wearing a bonnet that had seen better days. She walked into that yard as though she owned it, and within an hour, she did. Major Blair-Fortescue didn't know what to do with her. I laughed when I read in the newspaper that he'd married her."

He smiled. It was slight and genuine and looked as though it cost him something.

"She could read a horse in ten seconds. She walked the line of us and matched the horses she'd brought. By temperament, she called it. She said the horse had to want the same things the rider wanted, or neither of them would survive." He paused. "She chose Osiris for me. A grey gelding, sixteen hands, with a soft mouth and an honest eye. He was willing. That was the word she used."

He spoke about the major teaching him to ride, about Molly teaching him the whistle. She said every Belle Haven horse would answer it, and he should practise until he could produce it in his sleep, because he might need it when he wasn't awake enough to think.

Eliza's throat tightened. Molly had been twenty that summer. Teaching a whistle to a young cavalry recruit as if it were a trifle.

"We shipped out in the autumn," Llewellyn said. The music was leaving his voice now. "Osiris loaded without fuss, was quiet on the crossing, walked off the transport at Lisbon as though he'd done it a dozen times. I thought we were invincible." He stopped. His hand closed around the edge of the table, knuckles whitening, then deliberately relaxed. "You believe that, at twenty-one. You have to. Otherwise you wouldn't go."

He told them about the first engagement. A village he could not remember the name of. Screening an infantry advance. French sharpshooters concealed behind a ridge line. Osiris going down in the first volley, a ball through his neck, so fast Llewellyn barely cleared the stirrups. Alone on the ground with a dead horse beside him and the French advancing through the smoke.

He raised his left hand and mimed the gesture. Two fingers to his lips.

"I didn't believe it would work. We were a mile from our own lines, the field was full of smoke and noise, and I was calling for a horse that almost certainly didn't exist. But I had nothing else."

The room was very still.

"I heard hooves," Llewellyn said quietly. "Through the gunfire and the shouting, I heard hooves, galloping straight at me. And then he was there. Coming through the smoke, a dapple-grey stallion, bigger than Osiris, with blood on his shoulder from a sabre cut and his rider lost somewhere behind him. He came straight to the whistle. He stopped and stood while I mounted, with musket balls cutting the air around us, and then he ran."

His voice caught and held.

"We went through the French line, back to our own troop. My sergeant said, 'Thought we'd lost you, sir,' and I said, 'Not today,' and we went on." He looked at his hands. "Nobody noticed it was a different horse. One dapple grey looks much like another in dust and smoke, and nobody cared that I went out on a gelding and came back on a stallion. I never corrected them." what might have been a smile touched his mouth, rueful and private. "I should have reported the switch, declared Hermes as captured stock, done the proper paperwork. But I was twenty-one and I had just survived my first battle on a horse that came to me out of nothing, and the bureaucratic implications were not foremost in my mind. He was a stallion, too.

Probably meant for someone of much higher rank than me, and I didn't want to lose him."

Nobody moved to break the silence.

Laura spoke. "I'm glad he came," she said.

Her voice was quiet and clear, and she did not specify whom she meant.

Charlotte reached for the teapot, poured Llewellyn more tea, and the morning began to move again. Eliza remained where she was a moment longer, looking at Llewellyn, who was looking at Laura. His expression held something she had not seen on his face before: the relief of one who had set down something heavy and found that the ground held.

She folded Molly's note, slipped it into her pocket, and carried it with her for the rest of the day.

The study door was ajar, which was unusual. Llewellyn paused outside, one hand raised to knock, and through the gap he saw them.

Eliza sat in her father's chair with her head in her hands, elbows resting on the open stud book, her braids falling forward. Charlotte occupied the chair beside her in an identical posture, fair head bowed, her foolscap covered in crossings-out, the fierce handwriting obscured by line after line of cancellation. The charts from that morning were still there, but they had the look of maps to a country that no longer existed.

He knew the feeling. He had sat that way himself, in field hospitals and empty barracks, staring at the space where a plan had been. The temptation was to stay sitting, to let the weight hold you down, because standing up meant admitting you had to start again.

He knocked on the doorframe. Both heads came up. Eliza's face rearranged itself with the speed of long practice. Charlotte was slower; her eyes were red-rimmed and her chin had a set to it that dared anyone to mention it.

"May I?" Llewellyn said.

Eliza gestured him in. He took the chair opposite and looked at the wreckage of charts between them.

"The two-year-old colts," he said. The thought he had been turning over all afternoon, walking the fields, watching the young horses. "The ones still in the south pasture. There are four ungelded, by my count. They're too young for Harding's orders, too young to carry a rider. But their instincts will tell them what to do with a mare. They're old enough for that."

Charlotte looked up, her eyes brightening. "Father would have gelded them already if he didn't think they were the right type."

The words landed with quiet force. Sir Richard Bell did not keep entire colts by accident. Every ungelded two-year-old in that pasture had been evaluated by a man who had spent thirty years breeding horses, and each one still carried his potential because Sir Richard had seen something worth preserving. That judgement, made months or years before this crisis, had left them the raw material they needed.

"How many?" Charlotte asked, reaching for a clean sheet of foolscap.

"I counted four. A bay, two chestnuts, and a grey."

"The grey will be out of Moonstone," Charlotte said, already writing. "She was one of Father's favourites. A granddaughter of Mercury, so unfortunately ruled out for the same mares as Hermes." Her pencil moved faster. "The bay, I don't know, I'll need to look him up, but he could be one of Beech's, and the chestnuts are probably Hercules sons or grandsons…"

Eliza had been silent. She watched Charlotte work, then looked at Llewellyn, and in that look he read something he had not seen from her before. Something close to recognition, as though he had spoken a language she understood but had not expected to hear from him.

"We'd need to assess them properly," Eliza said, and her voice had shifted, the flatness of defeat replaced by something with an edge to it. "Conformation, temperament, movement. Charlotte can check the bloodlines. I'll evaluate the horses." She pulled a fresh sheet toward her. "We should do it tomorrow. First light, before the yard is busy. We'll get them into the stallion barn and start handling them."

"I can help with the temperament assessment," Llewellyn offered. "In the cavalry, we test horses for courage by exposing them to unfamiliar sounds and situations. The ones that recover quickly and approach rather than retreat are the ones you want."

Charlotte looked at him over her foolscap with grudging approval. "That would be quite useful."

From Charlotte Bell, Llewellyn understood, this was high praise.

The afternoon turned, and the three of them worked. Charlotte rebuilt her breeding charts around the two-year-olds, mapping possibilities with the concentration of an architect redesigning a building whose foundations had been knocked away but whose ground was still sound. Eliza produced lists: foaling dates, the logistics of introducing young stallions to the programme when the stallions themselves were still adolescents. Llewellyn contributed what he knew of assessing young horses, the practical knowledge of a man who had watched hundreds of remounts arrive at the depot.

It was a narrower programme than the one they had lost. But it was a programme. A path forward, built from what remained.

At some point, Eliza moved her chair closer to his to share the broodmare register. He did not remember the exact moment it happened. One minute the full width of the desk lay between them; the next, her elbow rested six inches from his, and the pages they were studying overlapped, and the faint scent of her reached him: hay, and horse, and something that was just herself, warm, like sun on dark wood. He turned a page with his left hand. She pointed at an entry with her right. Their arms lay parallel, almost touching, and neither of them moved apart.

Charlotte excused herself to fetch another volume. She was gone before Llewellyn registered the quiet, and then it was just the two of them, side by side, the stud book open between them, the study warm and close from hours of work.

Eliza's finger rested on a mare's name. Her hand was steady, her breathing even. She was reading, or appeared to be reading, but the page had not turned for some time.

Footsteps in the corridor. A pause.

He looked up.

Helen Fallon stood in the doorway. Her gaze moved across the scene: the two chairs drawn together, the shared book, the parallel arms, the six inches of charged air between his sleeve and Eliza's. Her eyes met his. They held for one beat. Two. The corner of her mouth did not quite smile, but something turned in her expression that was worse than a smile because it suggested understanding.

"Dinner in ten minutes," Helen said, mild as milk. She turned and left.

Eliza straightened, pulling the stud book toward her side of the desk, the movement so natural it might have been coincidence. She began gathering the scattered papers, aligning edges.

Llewellyn stood and busied himself straightening volumes on his side of the desk. He told himself that what Helen had seen was two people working. That the hours had passed quickly because the work was absorbing. That the proximity was practical. That the warmth in his chest was the simple pleasure of useful work, the relief of a plan taking shape after a day of loss.

He told himself all of this as he followed Eliza down the corridor toward the dining room, Pompey falling into step at his heel, and the telling was thorough and reasonable and he did not believe a single word of it.

Chapter Seven

The broodmare barn held its own weather at night in foaling season. The air was thick and close, warmed by the bodies of twenty-three mares and sweetened with the scent of clean straw and molasses feed, and when Eliza pushed open the door the warmth pressed against her face like a hand laid flat. Outside, a March wind cut through the yard, but in here the lanterns cast pools of amber light along the aisle and the straw rustled softly beneath shifting hooves, and the whole place felt set apart from the world beyond its walls.

She began her rounds the way she always did: stall by stall, hands and eyes doing the work her mind compiled into lists. The first mare, a chestnut with a star, stood quietly, hips level, udder unchanged. The second had waxed since morning, small beads of colostrum like drops of candle grease at the tips of her teats. Eliza noted it in the ledger she carried and moved on. The third was dozing, weight shifted to one hip, and did not stir when Eliza ran a hand along her flank to feel the foal's position beneath the taut drum of skin. Head down. Good.

From the fourth stall came a sound so soft it might have been imagined. Singing. Not a melody, more a thread of sound, a voice moving through notes the way water moves over stones, finding its own path. Laura sat in the clean straw with her back against the wall and her skirts tucked around her knees, her sightless eyes closed, her lips barely parted. Caesar was not with her tonight; the mastiff had been left in the kitchen, because the broodmare barn belonged to quieter creatures. The dark bay mare who had kicked her water bucket over twice a day for a fortnight and bitten young Robert's sleeve clean off his arm stood directly above Laura, head low, muzzle nearly touching the girl's shoulder. Her eyes were half-closed. Her breathing was slow and deep, the breathing of an animal at perfect rest.

Eliza paused in the aisle and watched.

The mares did not settle this way for the boys. Phillip was gentle enough, and Robert willing, but neither of them could walk into a stall and have a fractious eight-hundred-pound animal simply decide that the world was safe. Laura approached with nothing but her presence, and the mares surrendered.

It was not a trick or a technique. Laura was simply calm the way other people were tall or fair-haired, as a native condition rather than an achievement, and the horses read it in her the way they read the weather.

A movement at the edge of her vision. Llewellyn stood three stalls down, watching Laura and the mare, and his expression was one Eliza recognised, because she wore it herself when she encountered something in a horse that exceeded explanation. He was seeing it proved.

His gaze shifted and found hers. The lantern light caught the grey-blue of his eyes and turned them amber at the edges. He did not speak. He inclined his head, a gesture so slight it might have been nothing, and returned to the hay he'd been forking into a barrow.

Eliza moved on. Three more mares checked, three more entries in the ledger, the scratch of her pencil a small industrious sound in the warm quiet. She reached the stall at the far end of the aisle and stopped.

Ballerina stood with her head over the door, watching Eliza's approach with the alert patience of a horse who had seen twenty-two years of the world and found most of it tolerable. She was a beautiful bay, coat still lustrous despite her age and condition. Her mane was long and fine, threaded with grey at the roots, and her dark eyes held a depth that younger horses lacked, the look of an animal who understood the rhythms of this place because she had lived through more of them than anyone currently standing in it.

Eliza opened the stall door and went in. Ballerina turned her head and pressed her nose against Eliza's chest, breathing her in. Eliza scratched behind the mare's ear.

Llewellyn appeared at the stall door. He leaned against the frame, arms folded loosely. The hay was done. He had found his way here without being asked, which was becoming a pattern she did not know what to do with.

"This is Ballerina," Eliza said, her hand moving along the mare's crest. "She belongs to my mother. Father gave her to Mother before they were even married. She's twenty-two."

Llewellyn looked at the mare properly, as a horseman looked, reading the body beneath the coat. "She carries her age well."

"She does. She always has." Eliza smoothed the grey-threaded mane. "Mother loves this horse more than she loves most people, though she'd never say so. When she left for Oxfordshire, the last thing she did was come to this stall. She stood here for ten minutes. I don't know what she said."

Ballerina moved her weight, her belly low and heavy, and sighed the long, patient sigh of a mare who had done this many times before.

"This was meant to be her last foal," Eliza said. "Mother and Father decided together, last autumn. One more, and then she retires to the pasture and lives out her days getting fat on grass." She paused. "But that was before we lost so many of the mares who were to carry for next year. Before Hermes came. Charlotte says Ballerina is an excellent match for him on paper; she shares no ancestors with him in at least seven generations. Their foal could be the foundation of a whole new line."

She heard herself laying out the argument as if reading from Charlotte's charts. Beneath it sat the thing she could not put into the language of facts: that Ballerina was old, and breeding was hard on old mares.

"I don't know whether to breed her again," Eliza said. It came out plainly, but it cost her something. She did not enjoy uncertainty. She preferred problems with solutions, ledgers that balanced. This one sat on the border between what the programme needed and what the mare deserved, and she could not find the line.

Llewellyn was quiet for a moment. He looked at Ballerina, who had returned to dozing, her lower lip drooping, one ear cocked toward Laura's distant singing.

"You don't have to decide yet," he said, his voice pitched to the hour and the barn and the drowsing mare. "Let her foal first. See how she comes through it. The answer might be clearer then."

It was permission. Permission to wait, to not know, to let the question sit without forcing an answer. And Eliza, who had spent the last fortnight making decisions because no one else could make them, felt something in her chest ease. Like a girth loosened one hole after a long ride.

"Yes," she said. "That's sensible."

They stood together in the stall while Ballerina dozed and Laura's singing drifted through the warm air, and the broodmare barn held them all in its close, patient dark, waiting for what would soon begin.

She knew when Laura shook her awake, face white.

The lantern in the aisle still burned. Two o'clock, perhaps a quarter past. Llewellyn was there already. He stood inside Ballerina's stall with his shirtsleeves rolled and his hands wet to the elbows, and his face told her everything he did not say.

The foal lay on the straw. A bay filly, dark as her dam, with four white socks and a narrow blaze and legs that looked too long for her body, in the way that a newborn foal's legs always do. She was utterly, perfectly still.

"The cord," Llewellyn said, his voice level, but his accent strong in the way she was coming to recognise meant he was feeling something very strongly. "It was knotted. Wrapped twice and knotted. She never had a chance."

Eliza dropped to her knees beside the foal. Her hands found the small ribcage and pressed, feeling for the flutter that was not there. She cleared the filly's nostrils, wiped the membrane from the muzzle, tilted the delicate head to open the airway. Nothing. She rubbed the ribs with a twist of straw, hard, the way her father had taught her, trying to provoke the gasp that would start everything.

"Eliza." Llewellyn's hand was on her shoulder. "I've tried. She hasn't breathed."

She rubbed harder. The straw rasped against the wet hide. Beneath her hands the filly's body felt cool and slack, wrong in a way that went beyond temperature or muscle tone, wrong in the fundamental sense that the thing which should have been inside it had never arrived.

She stopped. Her hands rested on the foal's ribs, fingers splayed, and she felt the stillness travel up through her palms and settle in her chest like water filling a glass. She sat back on her heels.

The cord lay in the straw, a twisted rope of blood and tissue, knotted on itself. It happened sometimes. The foal turned in the womb and the cord looped and tightened, and by the time the birth began the damage was done. There was nothing anyone could have done. No mistake to learn from, no adjustment to make. The cord knotted. The foal died, possibly a day or two ago, and there was never any chance of her taking a breath. That was the whole of it.

Ballerina stood over her daughter.

She had delivered cleanly; the afterbirth lay in the corner, the straw was dark with fluid but not excessively so, and the mare herself appeared hale and hearty. She stood with her head low, muzzle nearly touching the filly's haunches, and she was doing the thing that mares do: nudging, and whickering. Gentle, insistent pushes of her nose against the foal's hip, the instinct that said *get up, get up, you must get up, I am here and you must stand and drink*. Each nudge rocked the small body in the straw. The filly's head lolled. Her legs did not unfold.

Ballerina nudged again. And again. Patient, unhurried, with a faith that was absolute and terrible.

Eliza could not look away. She had seen dead foals before; she had grown up at Belle Haven, where birth and death shared the same barn. But this patience was worse than any cry or thrashing. This was a mother doing exactly what she was meant to do, following the ancient instruction written into her blood, and the instruction was wrong. It would not work. And the mare did not know that.

Laura's hand found Eliza's shoulder, and she sat down in the straw beside her. Eliza leaned into her sister. Laura leaned back. Shoulder to shoulder, Laura's slim hand finding Eliza's and holding it. Laura's fingers were cold. Eliza's were wet and sticky from her futile effort to revive the foal.

She did not cry. The grief sat behind her eyes, heavy and hot, but it did not fall. Eliza Bell did not cry in barns, or in yards, or anywhere that someone might see and mistake the tears for weakness. She held the grief inside her the way she held everything, with her jaw set and her shoulders straight, and felt it press against the walls of her chest like water against a dam.

Laura's thumb moved across her knuckles. Small, steady strokes. Not comfort, exactly. Presence. The declaration that she was not alone in this stall with a dead foal and a mare who did not understand.

Ballerina nudged the filly one more time. A long, slow push, her muzzle travelling the length of the small body from hip to shoulder. The filly did not move. Something shifted in the mare then, something behind the dark eyes. She raised her head. She looked at Eliza and Laura, and the sound she made was not a whinny or a nicker but something between, low and questioning, the noise of an animal asking for help from those she trusted to give it.

Eliza rose. Her knees ached and her hands were stiff with cold and drying fluid. She went to the mare and put her arms around Ballerina's neck, pressing her face against the warm bay hide that smelled of sweat and twenty-two years of being loved. Laura followed, her hand finding the mare's shoulder, her fingers moving in slow circles.

They stood together, the three of them, in the lantern-lit stall with the still foal on the straw, and Eliza held the old mare and felt the great body trembling beneath her arms, and she did not have anything to give except her hands and her weight and herself, and she gave it, knowing it could not be enough.

He stood outside the stall because the grief inside it was not his to share.

From the aisle he could see Eliza's face in the lantern light. The composure she wore like chainmail had loosened at the seams, and through the gaps he read what was written there. Grief, yes. But beneath it, threaded through it, guilt. The quiet belief that she ought to have done something. That if she had been in the stall instead of asleep, if she had somehow reached inside and unknotted the cord before it tightened, the filly would be standing now.

He knew the shape of that belief. He had carried his own version after every engagement, tallying losses against decisions. It was always wrong, because it assumed the person doing the reckoning could see around corners and through time and into the coiled interior of a womb where a cord lay looped and lethal.

He did not say *you couldn't have known* or *it wasn't your fault*. Certain griefs had to be carried whole. You could not halve them by sharing. You could only stand nearby and wait for the person carrying them to set the weight down on their own terms.

The hours turned. The lantern burned low and was refilled. Eliza and Laura remained with Ballerina while the mare stood over her foal and the foal did not move. At some point Eliza rose and covered the small body with a clean cloth, tucking the edges as though it mattered, as though the filly could feel the cold. Laura stayed beside the mare, humming something so quiet it was barely distinguishable from breathing.

Llewellyn took away the soiled straw in a barrow. He brought fresh bedding and spread it without being asked. He filled Ballerina's water bucket and placed a measure of bran mash at the front of the stall, knowing the mare would not eat yet but knowing too that the smell of food was its own kind of comfort, a signal that the world continued.

They did not speak. They moved around each other in the wordless coordination that had become their way, and once, her shoulder brushed his arm, and neither of them pulled away, and the contact lasted no longer than a heartbeat and said everything that words would have ruined.

Dawn came slowly. The high windows turned from black to grey to the thin, washed blue of early morning, and the birds began their noise outside, indifferent to what had happened beneath the roof. The other mares stirred and called for breakfast. The world, as it always did, went on.

Llewellyn left the barn and crossed the yard.

He found Thornton in the feed room, measuring oats. The old groom looked up, and his weathered face read the news before a word was spoken. His hands stilled on the scoop. His jaw clenched.

"Ballerina's foal," Llewellyn said.

"Stillborn?"

"Knotted cord. Never breathed."

Thornton set down the scoop. He wiped his hands on his leather apron, slow and deliberate, as though the wiping were a kind of ritual. He reached behind the door and took down a spade that hung on a nail, its blade worn bright from use. He passed it to Llewellyn and took another one down for himself.

They walked together past the stallion barn, past the south paddock where the two-year-olds grazed in the early mist, past the old orchard where the last of the winter apples rotted in the grass. Beyond the orchard, at the edge of the property where a stone wall marked the boundary, a line of graves ran along the fence. Some were large, sunken with age. Others were small. Foal-sized.

Thornton walked to the end of the line and stopped. He drove the spade into the soft earth, and Llewellyn measured with his eyes where the other end of the grave should be and set to work.

They dug in silence. The earth was dark and loamy, softened by spring rain. Thornton worked with the steady rhythm of a man who had done this many times. Llewellyn dug from the opposite end, and they met in the middle, and the grave took shape between them without a word exchanged.

When it was done, Llewellyn went back to the barn alone. He lifted the foal himself, folding the cloth about her gently and letting Ballerina sniff her one last time. She weighed almost nothing. Her body had stiffened, the legs locked at awkward angles, but he settled her against his chest and walked back through the orchard with the dew soaking his boots and the early light catching the white of her socks.

He laid her in the grave with care, settling the small head on the earth. He did not cover her face. Thornton would do that. It seemed like the old groom's right.

The mastiffs arrived as Thornton began to fill the grave. Caesar and Pompey came through the orchard side by side, moving with the silent purpose of dogs who know where they are going and why. They sat at the graveside, one at each end, and did not move.

The soil went back in. Spade after spade, the dark earth closing over the bay hide, the white socks, the blaze that had been so like her dam's. Thornton worked until the grave was level and then stood with both hands on the spade handle, chin lowered to his chest.

They did not speak. There was nothing to say that the work had not already said. The line of graves stretched along the wall, the accumulated losses of a place that had bred horses for generations and understood that birth and death were not opposites but neighbours.

Thornton shouldered his spade and walked back toward the yard. Llewellyn watched him go, back straight despite his years, boots leaving dark prints in the wet grass. Then he looked down at the fresh earth, already darkening as the dew settled, and at the two mastiffs who had not moved.

He stood with them a while longer. The sun cleared the treeline and reached the orchard wall, warming the stone, and somewhere in the broodmare barn a mare whinnied, sharp and demanding, the sound of life continuing whether you were ready for it or not. He wiped his hands on his trousers, leaving dark smears that would not come out in the wash, and turned back toward the yard to begin the morning's work.

Chapter Eight

Two days had passed since they had buried Ballerina's filly beneath the orchard wall, and the barn still carried the memory of it in its timbers, in the quiet way the stable boys moved through the aisle. Eliza sat on the overturned bucket outside the bay mare's stall with her back against the wood and a ledger open on her knees and her eyes burning from a tiredness that went deeper than sleep. The lantern flame bent and steadied, bent and steadied, marking time much as a pulse does.

The bay mare had been restless since midnight. Not the irritable restlessness of the past fortnight, the bucket-kicking, sleeve-biting temper that had made her the terror of the barn and Laura's particular project. This was different. Purposeful. She paced the stall in a tight circle, pausing to paw the straw, swinging her head to look at her own flank with the wide-eyed attention of an animal listening to something inside herself that she could not see. Sweat darkened her neck and the hollows behind her ears. Her breathing came in short, hard pushes, each one punctuated by a grunt that sounded as if it were being forced from her against her will.

Eliza set the ledger aside and rose. She had watched enough mares to know the difference between discomfort and progress, and the bay had crossed that line. The muscles along her barrel were contracting visibly, great slow waves that rippled beneath the hide and drew the mare's hindquarters down into the straining posture that meant the foal was coming.

She sent Phillip for Llewellyn. The boy went at a run, boots clattering on the cobblestones, and Eliza let herself into the stall and spoke to the mare in the low, steady voice her father always used. The same words. The same tone. As though Sir Richard's calm could be borrowed like a coat.

The mare went down. She dropped to her knees with a groan and rolled onto her side, and the first white membrane appeared, pale and glistening in the lantern light, and inside it the dark shapes of two small hooves and the line of a muzzle pressed between them. Textbook. A perfect presentation. Eliza breathed out.

Llewellyn arrived as the shoulders cleared. He said nothing, just knelt beside Eliza at the mare's hindquarters and caught the foal as it slid free in a rush of fluid, a dark bay filly, wet and impossibly small, already shaking her head against the membrane that clung to her face. Eliza cleared her nostrils. The filly sneezed, a sound so tiny and outraged it might have been comic in any other hour.

The mare groaned again.

Eliza looked. Her hands, still wet from the first foal, went cold.

A second set of hooves. Pale, smaller than the first, already emerging inside a fresh caul of membrane. Two white crescents pressing into the world where no second foal should be.

"Twins," she said, and the word tasted like iron.

Llewellyn's head came up. Their eyes met across the mare's body, and she saw her own understanding reflected back. Twins in horses were not a miracle. They were a catastrophe: two foals sharing a space meant for one, each taking from the other, both arriving undersized and weak. Even if both survived the birth, even if the dam survived, the odds were vicious. She had read her father's records. She knew the numbers. She wished she didn't.

The second filly came faster, as though in a hurry to prove the night wrong. Smaller than her sister, lighter in colour, a chestnut with a crooked blaze and legs that looked as though they had been assembled from spare parts. She lay in the straw and blinked, and her first breath was a thin, reedy gasp that barely moved the air.

Two foals. Both alive. Both fillies.

Eliza rubbed both dry with a warm cloth and waited for the afterbirth. Five minutes. Ten. The mare strained but nothing came. The contractions continued, purposeless now, the body labouring against something that would not release. Eliza pressed her hand against the mare's flank and felt the muscles clench and hold, clench and hold, the rhythm growing ragged.

"It's retained," she said. She could hear the flatness in her own voice, the professional register that held everything at arm's length. The placenta had not separated from the uterine wall. It happened sometimes with twins. The womb, overtaxed, simply failed to complete its work.

"I can try..." Llewellyn said. She shook her head.

"I'll do it. My hands are smaller." It was inarguably true, and though he looked like he wanted to argue, perhaps say something about it not being a suitable activity for a young lady, he had the sense to hold his tongue.

She tried gentle traction. Llewellyn held the mare's head while Eliza worked, her hands inside the warmth, feeling for the edge of membrane, trying to coax without tearing. The mare groaned and kicked weakly. The straw beneath her hindquarters darkened.

Blood. Not the expected fluids of a normal birth but something heavier, thicker, the deep arterial red that meant a vessel had torn somewhere inside. It soaked the straw in a widening stain that crept toward Eliza's knees. She pressed harder, trying to find the source, knowing even as she searched that her hands were not enough.

"Too much," she said. "She's haemorrhaging."

The mare's head dropped to the straw. Her breathing changed, the hard labour-grunts giving way to something shallower, quicker, the sound of a body losing its argument with itself. Her dark eye rolled toward Eliza, and in it was not pain but confusion, the bewilderment of an animal who had done what was asked of her and could not understand why the world had not held up its end.

Eliza stayed with her. She pressed her hands against the bleeding she could not stop and watched the light go out of the mare's eye by degrees, the way a candle dies when the wax is spent, not all at once but in a long, flickering surrender.

The bay mare died at four in the morning, with her head in the straw and her two daughters wet and shaking beside her.

The barn went quiet. Not the comfortable quiet of sleeping horses or the hollow quiet after a requisition. The quiet that comes when something has been subtracted from the air itself, leaving a space that sound has not yet learned to fill.

The foals lay in the straw. The larger one had found her legs, or was trying to; she pushed herself up on her front knees and then collapsed, and pushed again, and collapsed again. Her sister lay flatter, breathing in quick, shallow pulls, but her head was up and her ears were forward, watching the world she had entered with an expression that might have been curiosity if it were not so plainly bewilderment.

They were the only sounds in the barn. The wet scrabble of hooves on straw. The small grunts of effort. Every other noise had withdrawn to give them room, and in the quiet their struggle seemed enormous, the most important work being done anywhere in the world.

Eliza sat back on her heels. Her hands were red to the wrists and her dress was ruined, the grey skirts black with the mare's blood, and the grief sat in her chest beside the grief that was already there, the two losses stacking like stones on a cairn. She looked at the twin foals and ran the calculation she did not want to run.

Twins without a dam. No milk, no warmth, no mother to nudge them to their feet and teach them the shape of the world. Hand-rearing was possible in theory, with a bottle and warmed cow's milk, every two hours through the night, for weeks. They had done it before with single orphan foals, the entire Bell family working as a team around the clock, and some had survived. But two. Both undersized, both weakened by sharing what should not have been shared, both needing more than she had to give with half her sisters and both her parents gone.

The larger filly finally got her front legs under her and wobbled there, swaying, her wet coat steaming faintly in the lantern light. She turned her head and found her sister and pushed her nose against the smaller foal's neck, and the smaller one lifted her chin in response.

The idea did not arrive like inspiration. It arrived the way most useful things arrived in Llewellyn's experience: slowly, through the back door, while the front of his mind was occupied with something else. He was watching Eliza kneel in the bloody straw with her ruined dress and her steady hands, watching the twin foals struggle against the simple impossibility of standing, and the thought assembled itself from pieces he had not known he was collecting. A mare three stalls down with a full udder and no foal to drink from it. A mare who had nudged her dead daughter for an hour, asking her to stand.

"The old broodmare," he said. His voice sounded rough in the quiet barn. "The one who lost her foal two days ago. Ballerina."

Eliza looked up. Her face was drawn, her eyes shadowed, and the lantern threw the hollows of her cheekbones into sharp relief. She looked older than eighteen. She looked as old as the work demanded.

He saw the thought land. The recognition, the assessment, the swift calculation of odds and costs. She had done this before. He could see it in the way her eyes moved to the foals and back to him, measuring.

"I've seen it done," she said. "Good broodmares with lots of experience will sometimes take a newborn orphan. Sometimes." She paused. "But never twins. Surely she won't take them both."

"No," he agreed. "Probably not."

They looked at each other across the dead mare's body and the wet, trembling shapes of her daughters.

Eliza's shoulders rose and fell. A shrug so weighted with exhaustion it barely qualified as a gesture. "I suppose we might as well try. Even if she accepts one, that's something."

One foal saved out of two. A fraction of a victory extracted from a morning made entirely of loss. Llewellyn nodded and went to fetch what they would need.

Ballerina stood in her stall at the far end of the aisle, head low, weight on three legs. She had eaten little in the two days since her stillborn daughter was carried away. The bran mash Thornton brought each morning was picked at rather than consumed. Her udder was tight and full, the teats swollen with milk that had nowhere to go, and she shifted with the discomfort of it. She looked up when Llewellyn unlatched the door, ears coming forward, and the sound she made was the same low questioning sound she had made over her dead foal, as if she were still waiting for an answer.

He spoke to her. Quiet, unhurried. Welsh words no creature on this estate would understand, but it was the rhythm that mattered, the cadence of animals tended in the dark hours by men who understood that tone counted for more than language. He ran his hand along her neck and felt the heat of her, the faint tremor in the muscle. Then he knelt beside her and placed the wooden pail beneath her udder.

The milk came easily. Ballerina stood patient while he worked, her head turning to watch him. The milk was rich and yellow with colostrum, warm against his hands. He was gentle, not taking too much. He wanted the foals to drink most of it.

He carried the pail back to where Eliza waited. She had covered the dead mare's body with a blanket, to await the many hands it would take to move and bury her in the morning, and the twin foals now lay together on fresh straw, the larger one's chin resting on her sister's back.

They had stopped trying to stand, their energy spent, and lay blinking in the lamplight with the stunned look of creatures who had arrived in the world and found it nothing like what they expected.

Eliza took the clean cloth he held out. She dipped it in Ballerina's milk and wrung it until the fabric was wet but not dripping. Then she knelt beside the foals and began to wipe the milk across their coats.

Llewellyn watched her work. The cloth passed over the larger filly's neck, her back, along her ribs, beneath her jaw. The foal flinched but did not pull away. Then the smaller one, more gently still, the cloth tracing the line of her spine, circling the base of her ears, covering every surface a mare's nose would investigate.

"The scent has to be consistent," Eliza said, not looking up. Her voice had changed into the register he associated with her expertise. "She'll smell them before she sees them. If the first thing she recognises is her own milk, it might be enough to override the instinct that tells her these aren't hers."

Or it might not. Neither of them said so.

They carried the foals together, one each. Llewellyn took the larger filly against his chest, her body hot and damp through his shirt, her legs dangling. Eliza carried the smaller one with both arms beneath the foal's belly, and the filly's head rested against her shoulder as though it had found the only safe place in the world.

Ballerina's head came up as they approached. Her nostrils flared. She drew in air in long, searching pulls, reading the information carried on it, and Llewellyn saw the moment the milk scent reached her because her whole body changed. Her ears shot forward. Her neck extended. She pressed against the stall door with a force that rattled the latch.

Eliza went in first with the smaller foal. A deliberate choice; the weaker one needed a mother more urgently, and if Ballerina rejected her, they would know quickly. She set the filly on the straw near the back wall, giving the mare room, and stepped aside.

Ballerina turned. Her head swung low, muzzle almost touching the floor, and she advanced on the foal with the cautious intensity of a mare investigating something she badly wanted to believe. Her nostrils worked, tasting the air above the foal's body. The filly lay still, too weak to move.

The mare snorted. Her head jerked up and she backed a step, ears flat, and Llewellyn felt the moment teeter. Wrong smell beneath the milk. Not mine. The ancient calculus of recognition, which asked for more than scent, which asked for the memory of carrying, of contracting, of the specific weight and warmth of your own.

Eliza pressed her hand against Ballerina's neck, squeezed lightly at her wither. "It's all right," she murmured. "You're all right, sweet girl. You don't have to. Just try, please... for me."

Ballerina lowered her head again. Slower this time. She nosed the tiny filly's hindquarters, her flanks, her neck. The milk-wet coat. The smell of colostrum that was, undeniably, her own. Her ears came forward, went back, came forward again. Her muzzle rested against the foal's ribs, and she breathed there, long and deep.

Llewellyn set the larger filly down inside the door. Ballerina's head swung toward the movement, nostrils flaring, and she snorted a warning. He backed away. The larger foal struggled upright on her front knees and swayed there, blinking, and Ballerina looked from one small body to the other with an expression that was not acceptance but the suspension of disbelief.

They waited. The lantern burned. The barn held its breath.

It was the smaller one who moved first. She could barely stand, but stand she did on shaking, spindle-thin legs, staggering across the straw toward Ballerina with the dogged, graceless determination of a creature operating on nothing but instinct and need. She did not know where she was going. She did not need to know. The smell of milk was in the air and her body was following it as a compass needle follows north, without thought, without choice.

Ballerina watched her come. Her ears moved between forward and sideways, the indecision written in every line of her body. She shifted her weight. Her tail swished once, hard. When the foal reached her front legs and nosed blindly along the curve of her belly, Ballerina turned her head away, staring at the far wall as though she could deny what was happening by refusing to look at it.

The foal found the udder.

It was not elegant. The filly's muzzle bumped along the mare's flank, slid past the stifle, caught on the fold of skin where the udder began, and then, with a sideways lurch that nearly sent her sprawling, found a teat and closed her mouth around it.

Ballerina's hind leg came up.

Llewellyn stopped breathing. The mare's hoof hovered above the straw, the muscles of her haunch bunched, and for one suspended instant the arithmetic was simple and terrible; one kick, and this would be over.

The hoof did not fall. It hung there, trembling, and then lowered slowly back to the straw. Ballerina's head whipped around, and she stared at the foal latched to her udder, nostrils flaring, breathing in the scent of her own milk rising from the small dark body.

The filly swallowed. A single gulp, audible in the quiet stall, the noise of something going where it was meant to go.

Ballerina's body changed. The tension ran out of her like water from a cracked jug. Her head lowered. Her breathing slowed. She nosed the foal's hindquarters, not with suspicion but with something older, something from the same deep place as the nudging she had given her stillborn daughter. The same instruction. *Get up. Stand. Drink. Live.* Except this time there was a body capable of obeying it.

The milk let down. Llewellyn could see it in the way the udder softened, the teats plumping, the filly's throat working in rhythmic swallows. Ballerina stood absolutely still, and her dark eye held an expression he could only call peace.

The larger filly had been watching, or sensing, or simply responding to the smell of milk now flowing freely. She got her front legs under her. She wobbled. She fell. She got them under her again, and this time she stayed, swaying like a sapling in wind, her long legs braced at improbable angles. She took one step. Two. Her hooves slid on the straw and she caught herself with a lurch that brought her crashing against Ballerina's shoulder.

The mare's ear flicked. She turned her head and regarded this second arrival with what Llewellyn could only describe as weary assessment. She sniffed the filly's face, her neck, the milk-wet coat that carried her own scent. Her nostril twitched.

Then she nudged the filly toward the udder, on the opposite side to her sister.

The filly found it, latched on, and drank. Two small heads pressed against the swollen udder, two sets of jaws working, and above them Ballerina stood with her head low and her eyes half-closed.

A sound at the stall door. Llewellyn turned.

Thornton stood in the aisle with his cap in his hands, his weathered face arranged in an expression Llewellyn had never seen on it before. His mouth was slightly open. His eyes were bright. Behind him, Phillip and Robert crowded on tiptoe, craning to see past his shoulders, and their faces held the uncomplicated wonder of children witnessing something they would remember for the rest of their lives.

Nobody spoke. The scene said everything that words would only diminish: the old mare with her adopted daughters, the milk flowing, the small sounds of swallowing, the straw warm and golden in the early light now reaching the high windows.

A month. Llewellyn leaned against the wall outside the stall and counted. A month since he had led a blind stallion through the gate and asked for a place to rest. In that time he had watched dozens of horses walk away. He had stood in empty stalls and mended fences and pumped water and done every small thing his damaged body could manage, and none of it had been enough to stop the losses from coming. He had dug a grave for a dead foal, and today he would help dig a larger one.

The foals were undersized. Twins carried risks that would not resolve for weeks. Ballerina was twenty-two and grieving and her body had already been through labour. She might reject them tomorrow, when the novelty of their need wore thin and the ancient instinct reasserted itself.

And yet.

The foals were nursing. Their small tails flicked with the involuntary happiness of newborns receiving exactly what their bodies demanded. Ballerina's head swung gently side to side as she checked one, then the other, and each time her nose confirmed what her udder already knew, and each time she eased a fraction deeper into her stance.

Thornton opened the door. He held a bucket of bran mash, warm and freshly made, and he set it inside the stall with the quiet care of a man placing an offering at an altar. Ballerina lifted her head. She looked at the mash. She looked at Thornton, who had known her since she was a foal herself, who had groomed her and shod her and held her through twelve previous foalings and who was watching her now with his cap in his hands and his eyes full.

She dropped her muzzle into the bucket and ate.

The sound of a horse eating bran mash was not, by any standard, remarkable. The wet grinding of molars, the soft splashing of nose in warm water, the occasional pause to chew. But in that stall, on that morning, it was the sound of a mare choosing to go on. Choosing nourishment, choosing to stand over these two small creatures who were not hers and feed them from a body that had carried its own grief for two days and found, somewhere beneath it, a reason to continue.

Llewellyn looked at Eliza.

Her braids had loosened; a spiralling coil of dark hair had come free at her temple and lay against her cheek, and she had not pushed it back. Her dress was stiff with dried blood. Her hands, resting at her sides, were still stained from the night's work.

She was trying to hide it. He could see the effort in the set of her jaw and the careful stillness of her mouth. But her eyes betrayed her. They were bright, not with tears but with the thing that comes before tears or instead of them, the pressure of an emotion too large for the space allotted to it. Hope. Fragile and unwanted and present despite everything she had done to keep it out.

She caught him looking. Their eyes held for a moment across the stall, across the nursing foals and the eating mare and the old groom with his cap in his hands, and what passed between them did not need to be spoken. They had lost and lost and lost, and this morning, in a barn that smelled of milk and clean straw and the first real warmth of spring, perhaps they had won.

Eliza looked away first. She pushed the loose curl behind her ear with fingers that were not quite steady, and when she spoke her voice was brisk and practical and only someone who knew her well would have heard the fracture running through it.

"Phillip, more fresh straw. Robert, warm water for the mare. Mr. Thornton, I'll want someone watching them all day. Never leave her alone, not for a minute." She straightened, squaring her shoulders against the morning. "And someone tell Charlotte there are two new fillies for her charts."

Thornton nodded. "Right you are, Miss Eliza," he said, and this time his eyes did not drift past her to find a man's confirmation.

Llewellyn pushed himself off the wall and went to help Phillip with the straw. Behind him, in the golden stall, Ballerina finished her mash and lowered her head to the smaller foal, and began to lick the tiny body, and the foal's tail flicked.

Chapter Nine

A WEEK OF FOALING had worn the edges off everything. Eliza's hands were chapped from washing in cold water between stalls, her back ached from sleeping upright on buckets and hay bales, and the hours between midnight and dawn had lost their individual character, blurring into a single long watch lit by lanterns and punctuated by the sounds of mares labouring in the dark. Four foals born alive and well. One more lost, a colt with a twisted leg who had never been viable; Thornton had quietly put it out of its suffering. And the twin fillies, who grew stronger each day beneath Ballerina's patient guardianship, their legs steadying, their appetites fierce.

Eliza had asked Llewellyn to name them, which had surprised him into silence for several seconds before he offered, quietly, Seren and Eira. Star and snow, he had translated. Charlotte had approved on the grounds that neither name appeared anywhere in the stud books, which made them easy to track.

Tonight it was the dun mare in the sixth stall, a proven broodmare with three clean deliveries behind her and the calm temperament of a horse who understood what was happening and was not especially impressed by it. Eliza had come down to check on her after dinner, and never left. The waxing had been textbook, the restlessness predictable, and when the mare went down at half past ten, she did so with the unhurried competence of a professional settling to a familiar task.

The foal came easily and quickly. The white caul appeared, and inside it the pale crescents of two hooves and the dark line of a muzzle, and the mare bore down twice and the shoulders cleared and then the whole foal slid free in a single warm rush. A colt. Big. Bay, like his sire Beech, with a broad forehead and a long white sock on one hind leg. Eliza cleared the membrane from his face, wiped his nostrils, and sat back to let the mare do her work.

The dun scrambled to her feet with the urgency all good mothers showed, the instinct that said *the world is dangerous and you must be standing between it and your foal.* She turned and found him with her nose, nickering, the low vibrating sound that foals were meant to answer. She licked his face, his ears, his neck, long sweeping strokes that cleaned and warmed and said *I am here, and you are mine.*

The colt lay on the straw and did not move.

Eliza waited. She counted his breaths. They were there, but shallow, the faintest rise and fall of ribs that should have been heaving. His nostrils did not flare. His legs, folded beneath him at the angles of arrival, stayed where the birth had placed them. He did not lift his head or twitch or flinch or do any of the things a healthy newborn should do in the first minutes of life, the frantic inventory of limbs and air and light that meant the body had received its instructions and was carrying them out.

She gave him five minutes. The mare nudged harder, pushing her muzzle against his ribs, his hip, the soft hollow behind his ear. Nothing.

Eliza knelt beside him, one eye on the mare, who did not seem to mind her, perhaps sensing she was there to help. She took a twist of straw and rubbed it briskly along the colt's ribs. She tickled inside his ear with a piece of clean hay, a trick her father had taught her, one that made most foals jerk their heads up in outraged surprise. The colt's ear flicked once, weakly, and was still.

She cleared his nostrils again, though they were already clear. She pressed her palm against his chest and felt the heartbeat, steady but slow, slower than it should be. His body was warm. His colour was good. There was nothing wrong with him that she could see or feel, but he lay in the straw like a parcel delivered to the correct address but never opened, and the life inside him was fading for want of someone to tell it that it had begun.

She knew this kind of foal. She had known three of them in recent years at Belle Haven, and they had lost all three.

The first had been a filly, six years ago, when Eliza was twelve and still learning at her father's shoulder. Sir Richard had tried everything: rubbing, tickling, lifting, propping, speaking to the foal in the voice he used for the most difficult horses, the voice that assumed you were going to do the right thing and simply needed reminding what it was. The filly had breathed for forty minutes and then stopped, as gently as a candle going out.

Eliza rubbed the colt harder. She was pressing with the heels of her hands now, pushing along the barrel of his body, trying to produce the gasp, the jolt that would tell his lungs to fill and his legs to unfold and his head to come up. The mare stood over them, nickering, nudging, and each unanswered nudge was a small wound, because the dun

was doing everything right and her foal was not responding, and Eliza could feel the minutes running through her
hands like water.

"Come on," she said, and her voice was too loud for the
barn, too urgent, stripped of the low steadiness she used
with horses. "Come on, breathe. You need to breathe."

The colt's ribs rose. Fell. Rose. The intervals between
breaths were growing longer. She could count three heartbeats between each one, where there should have been one.
She knew what came next. The breathing would slow further, the body would cool, and the heart beneath her palm
would lose its rhythm, and in the morning there would be
another small grave beside the orchard wall.

She pressed her forehead against the colt's warm neck
and shut her eyes. The straw was rough beneath her knees.
The mare's breath was hot on the back of her head. Somewhere beyond the barn the first birds were beginning, the
same indifferent chorus that greeted every dawn, and the
sound felt like mockery, because the world was waking up
and this colt was not.

She had run out of her father's tricks. She had nothing
left but her hands and her voice and the desperate, useless
pressure of wanting something to live.

He heard her voice before he reached the door. Not the
words but the tone, pitched wrong, too high, too fast, the
voice of someone who had run out of calm and was spending what came after it. Llewellyn had been saying good
night to Hermes, about to go upstairs to his bed, when the
sound of the dun mare's labour drew him out. He had not
hurried, hearing Eliza's voice in the broodmare barn. Eliza

was capable and the dun experienced. But something in the quality of the silence that followed the birth changed his pace. He crossed the yard in the darkness and pushed open the barn door.

The lantern showed him everything he needed and several things he wished it hadn't.

The dun mare stood over her foal with her head low and her neck rigid. The colt lay on the straw, big and well-formed and utterly still. Eliza knelt beside him with her hands pressed flat against his ribs, her braids falling forward, and when she looked up at his boots her face was stripped bare. Fear, plain and unguarded, the face of someone who had watched too many things die in this barn and could feel another one slipping.

"He won't try," she said, and her voice was shaking.

He had not seen her frightened before. Angry, yes. Grieving, yes. But fear was new, and the sight of it landed somewhere behind his breastbone and stayed.

"May I?" he said.

She looked at him. Her hands were still pressed against the foal's ribs, and he could see the effort it took her to lift them. To move aside. To let someone else try. Eliza Bell did not easily yield ground she was standing on, and the ground beneath this colt was hers by right and by every hour she had spent in this barn since her father left.

She nodded. A single sharp movement, as if more would cost her something she could not spare.

Llewellyn knelt in the straw beside the colt. He placed his left hand beneath the foal's belly and his right arm over the top, wrapping both arms around the barrel just behind the withers. The colt's body was warm, damp, heavy with the density of a newborn that has not yet learned to carry its own weight. He could feel the ribs beneath his forearms, the slow rise and fall of breathing that was more suggestion than commitment.

He squeezed.

Not gently. Hard, a compression that drove the ribs inward and held them there, both arms locked, his chest pressed against the foal's spine. He counted to three. Then he released. The ribs expanded, barely, and he squeezed again. Held. Released. Squeezed. Held. Released. A rhythm like breathing itself, like the contractions of a birth canal around a body passing through it, the pressure that said *you are being born now, you are arriving, the world is pushing you into itself and you must push back.*

His right arm burned. The scar tissue along his wrist pulled against the effort, a bright wire of pain that ran from forearm to elbow. He ignored it by acknowledging its presence and giving it nothing. His father had taught him this in a lambing shed in the shadow of the Black Mountain when he was twelve years old, a lamb limp and blue on the straw, and his father's thick hands wrapped around the tiny barrel, squeezing with the deliberate force of a man who understood that gentleness was not always kindness. It worked for foals as well as lambs, but it took a strong man to squeeze a foal into life.

Squeeze. Hold. Release.

The foal did not move. The wet coat was warm under his arms, the ribs compliant, offering no resistance and no response. He was aware of the mare above him, her breath on his neck, her muzzle investigating his hands. He was aware of Eliza, watching silently.

She had not retreated. She knelt three feet away, close enough to touch the foal if she reached out. Her hands were balled in her lap, fingers white-knuckled, and the stillness of her was the stillness of active restraint.

Squeeze. Hold. Release.

His arms were trembling. The effort of compressing a foal this size was not trivial, and his right arm had been weak for months. He shifted his grip, settling his weight lower, using his chest and the cradle of his arms rather than brute strength. He pressed his cheek against the colt's shoulder and felt the heartbeat through the hide, slow, too slow, but still present.

He thought of his father's hands on the lamb. The lamb had lived. It had stood on legs like bent wire and found its mother and drunk, and three months later it was indistinguishable from any other lamb in the flock, and his father had said nothing about it because a Welsh sheep farmer did not make a fuss about the things that worked. He made a fuss about the things that didn't, because those were the ones you learned from.

Squeeze. Hold. Release.

The colt lay beneath his arms, warm and heavy and still, and Llewellyn squeezed again, and again, and did not stop, because stopping meant deciding it was over, and he was not prepared to make that decision in a barn where Eliza was watching with fear on her face and her hands clenched in her lap, trusting him to do the thing she could not.

Squeeze. Hold.

Something turned beneath his arms. A tension, faint as a fish moving beneath the surface of still water. A gathering in the muscles of the foal's barrel, the first suggestion that something inside was waking up and beginning to object.

Release.

She saw it before she understood it. A tremor ran through the colt's body, visible beneath Llewellyn's arms, a ripple of muscle that started at the hindquarters and travelled forward. The foal's ear flicked. Not the weak movement of ten minutes ago. A proper flick, sharp and startled, the ear of an animal that had just noticed something and was not sure it approved.

Llewellyn squeezed again. Held. Released.

The colt's head came up.

It was not graceful. It was a lurch, sudden and uncoordinated, the head lifting from the straw at an angle that suggested the neck had not been consulted. But the eyes were open, and they were wide, and in them was something that had not been there before: the outrage of a creature that has been disturbed.

He squeezed once more. The colt flinched. A full-body flinch, legs jerking, spine arching against the pressure of Llewellyn's arms, and then the breath came. Not one of the shallow, reluctant whispers Eliza had been counting. A gasp. A great heaving inhalation that expanded the ribs against Llewellyn's grip and filled the stall with the sound of lungs that had suddenly, belatedly, understood their purpose. The colt sneezed. He shook his head. He breathed again, deeper, the air whistling through nostrils that flared wide, and his legs began to move, not with purpose yet but with the involuntary thrashing of a body that had woken up and wanted very much to be somewhere else.

Llewellyn released his grip and rocked back on his heels, and the colt lay in the straw breathing in great hungry gulps, his sides heaving, his ears forward, his dark eyes fixed on the world he had only just agreed to join.

The dun mare was there in an instant. She lowered her head and nosed her son with an urgency that was almost frantic, the nudging that had gone unanswered for so long now met by a foal who twisted his neck toward her and answered with a thin, wavering whinny that was the most beautiful sound Eliza had ever heard.

The colt got his front legs under him. One attempt, two. On the third he stayed, his haunches still flat in the straw, forelegs braced wide. His mother licked his face. He shook her off and tried the hind legs. Down. Up. Down. The fourth attempt held. He stood, trembling, all four feet planted at improbable angles, and the mare nickered and the foal nickered back, and the sound of them together was the sound of the world working the way it was supposed to.

Eliza turned to Llewellyn.

He sat in the straw with his sleeves dark to the elbows and his right arm cradled against his side. His hair was disordered, his face flushed, and he was watching the foal with a broad smile she had never seen on him before.

"What was that?" she said. Her voice came out raw, scraped thin by the past twenty minutes, and she did not care. "What did you do?"

He flexed his right hand, slowly, testing whether it still worked. "My Da called it the birth squeeze. Did it on lambs, but it works on foals too. Just takes more strength."

"The birth squeeze."

"Sometimes, if the labour is too fast or too easy, the foal doesn't know it's been born." The Welsh lilt was more pronounced than usual. "The pressure of the birth canal is what tells the body to start. To breathe, to move. If the foal comes too quickly, it misses the signal. Squeezing the ribs mimics the pressure. Tells the body what it needs to hear."

He said it simply, much as a man describes something he learned young and carried without knowing it was remarkable. The knowledge had travelled from a Welsh hill farm to a broodmare barn in Hampshire and saved a life, and Llewellyn spoke of it as though it were nothing more interesting than the correct way to drive a nail.

Eliza sat back on her heels. Her hands were still shaking. She looked at them, the tremor visible in the lantern light, and folded them together in her lap.

"I've seen foals like this," she said. "They die."

It came out flat, but beneath it lay the weight of every foal she had knelt beside in this barn and failed to save.

Llewellyn met her eyes. "Sometimes it works," he said. Not always. Sometimes.

She looked at the colt. He had found his mother's flank and was nosing along it with the blind determination of a creature following the oldest instruction in the world. His muzzle bumped past her hip, slid along the curve of her belly, and found the udder. He latched on with a sideways lunge that nearly toppled him, and his throat began to work, and the dun mare dropped her head and sighed the long contented sigh of a mother whose world had righted itself.

"Your Da," Eliza said, "is a miracle worker."

Llewellyn laughed. It was a tired laugh, rough-edged, the sound ofthe noise of someone who had been holding himself taut for a long time and could finally let something go. He shook his head, and the smile that remained was genuine and unguarded, one that took years off him.

"He'd be embarrassed to hear that," Llewellyn said. "He'd say any hill farmer worth his salt knows it, and that the real miracle is the ewe who does it all on her own at two in the morning in a snowdrift, without any fool squeezing anything."

Eliza heard herself laugh. A small sound, almost startled, as though her body had produced it without consulting her. She could not remember the last time she had laughed. The sound surprised her and then warmed her.

The colt drank. His small tail flicked with each swallow, keeping time. The mare stood steady and patient over him, and the lantern light caught the sheen of his wet coat and turned it to rich bronze.

Llewellyn rose, favouring his left leg, and brushed straw from his trousers. He stood and looked at the foal drinking and the mare content and the stall warm and golden in the early light, and his face held the expression she was learning to read: the careful look of a man who did not trust good things to last but was grateful for them while they did.

She looked at him, and the catalogue she kept without meaning to added another entry. The way his arms had wrapped around the foal without hesitation. The pain in his right arm that he would not mention. The tired laugh. The smile. The knowledge passed from father to son in a lambing shed, carried through a war, arriving in her barn at the moment she needed it.

"Thank you," she said.

He inclined his head, the slight gesture she was coming to know, and turned toward the mare's water bucket.

"He needs a name," Eliza said.

Llewellyn paused. He looked back at the colt, who was still drinking, his small body braced against his mother's flank as if the udder might try to escape.

"Arthur," he said.

"Arthur?"

"A great Welsh king." The corner of his mouth lifted, sly and warm. "Though the English have tried to claim him."

Eliza felt her own mouth curve in answer. "King Arthur, then. For the stud book."

"King Arthur," he agreed, and held out his hand to help her up. She took it, and they stood together for a few moments watching the colt drink, holding hands as though it were the most natural thing in the world, until he let go and picked up the water bucket to go and fill it.

Chapter Ten

MAY HAD COME IN softly, the hedgerows thickening with hawthorn blossom, the paddocks greening in earnest, and the broodmare barn emptying stall by stall as each mare delivered and was turned out with her foal to the spring grass. Thirty-five live foals thus far. The arithmetic was good. Eliza knew it was good because she had run it against her father's records from previous years, and the numbers held, and Charlotte had confirmed it twice with the quiet satisfaction of a girl who trusted figures more than feelings. Two foals lost, the stillborn filly and the twisted colt, and one mare, the mother of the twins Ballerina had accepted as her own. More than Eliza wanted, but far fewer than she had feared, in those first black nights when the barn had felt like a place where things came to die rather than to be born.

The kitchen table at half past seven on a Tuesday morning looked like the aftermath of a minor siege. Charlotte had her cheek pressed against the wood grain beside an untouched cup of tea, her fair hair escaping its pins in all directions. Laura sat upright but had fallen asleep with her hand resting on Caesar's head, the mastiff wedged beneath her chair like a furry ottoman. Louise, who had been running between stalls all night carrying hot water and clean cloths, was still talking, though her sentences had begun to lose coherency. Llewellyn sat at his end of the table with Pompey's chin on his knee. He held his teacup in his left hand, his right arm resting on the table, and his eyes were half-closed in the way Eliza had learned to recognise as not sleeping but very close to it.

Three mares. Three foals in a single night, between ten in the evening and five in the morning, as though the animals had conspired to test every person and every lantern Belle Haven possessed. The first had been straightforward, a chestnut mare with a history of easy births who produced a leggy bay filly and stood up looking mildly inconvenienced. The second had taken longer, a breech presentation that required Llewellyn's hands and Eliza's steady voice and two hours of patient, exhausting work to turn the foal before it suffocated. A colt, alive and breathing, though the mare had needed stitching afterwards and Eliza's arms still ached from the effort.

The third had foaled while they were fully occupied with the second, and Phillip, Charlotte and Laura had handled it between them, the three youngsters white-faced and shaking when Eliza found them in the stall with the foal already standing. She had told them they had done well, and meant it absolutely.

She poured herself tea and sat down. The chair creaked beneath her. Her hands were raw, her back a column of dull protest, and behind her eyes a headache pulsed with the slow insistence of a horse pawing at a stable door. She drank the tea and tasted nothing.

Helen's footsteps in the corridor. She appeared in the doorway with the post, two letters and the folded newspaper, and set them on the table beside Eliza's elbow. She looked at the exhausted faces around the table and said nothing, but poured more tea and placed her hand on Laura's shoulder, shaking gently to waken her without startling her.

Eliza recognised her mother's handwriting before she had fully registered that the letter was there. The familiar rightward slant, the cramped neatness, the plain wax seal pressed with the edge of a button. She broke the seal with clumsy fingers.

The first line. She read it, and read it again, and the headache behind her eyes receded as if someone had opened a window.

"Molly's had the baby," she said.

Charlotte's head came up from the table. Laura's eyes opened. Louise stopped mid-sentence, whatever word she had been searching for abandoned in favour of a gasp.

"A boy," Eliza said, scanning the page. Her mother's words blurred and steadied as her tired eyes found their focus. "Born on the ninth of May. Mother and child both well. Molly is already trying to get out of bed, and the doctor has threatened to tie her ankles together if she attempts the stairs before the week is out."

Louise clapped her hands. Charlotte sat up properly, blinking, a smile breaking across her face that was the first uncomplicated expression of joy Eliza had seen from her in weeks. Laura reached across the table, found Charlotte's arm, and squeezed it. Caesar, sensing the shift in the room's weather, thumped his tail against the floor.

"What has she named him?" Laura asked.

Eliza kept reading. Her mother's hand continued, steady and warm, describing the baby's dark hair and considerable lungs.

"Alexander," Eliza said.

From the end of the table, a sound she had not expected. Llewellyn laughed. Not the tired, rough-edged laugh she had heard on the night Arthur was born, but something lighter, genuinely amused.

"Of course she did," he said.

Eliza looked at him. Her brain, operating on the dregs of whatever fuel it had left after seven hours of foaling, turned the name over without finding anything to hold on to. "What?"

"Alexander the Great," Llewellyn said. His eyes were warm, the grey-blue of them catching the morning light, and the smile on his face was the unguarded one, the one she had first seen directed at Helen weeks ago and had since learned to covet without admitting it. "The most famous horseman in history. He tamed Bucephalus when he was a boy. No one else could ride the horse, but Alexander saw that it was afraid of its own shadow, so he turned it to face the sun." He lifted his teacup. "Of course Miss Molly would name her son after a man who understood horses better than people."

Charlotte's laugh joined his, bright and startled. Laura smiled, her sightless eyes crinkling. Louise said, "Oh, that's lovely," in a voice that suggested she might cry, which at this hour and this level of exhaustion was not an unreasonable response to anything.

Eliza looked down at the letter and felt the warmth of the news settle into her chest. Molly was safe. The baby was well. Tim had a son; she hoped he would be able to get home soon to meet him. And Molly, being Molly, had stamped the child with horses before he was a day old.

The room was bright with morning light and warm with the smell of bread and the sound of people she loved being happy, and for a moment the war and the empty stalls and the tiredness that sat in her bones all receded to the edges of the room and left the centre clear.

She looked at Llewellyn across the table, and he was already looking at her, and neither of them looked away.

The others were still talking about the baby when Eliza turned the page.

Theresa's letter continued on the reverse, a few more lines about Alexander's arrival, a note about Tim being able to come from his depot for a brief visit to meet his son. Ordinary news, warmly delivered. And then, at the bottom of the page, set apart by a line of space that seemed deliberate, a postscript in smaller, tighter script, as though her mother had added it after the letter was finished and was trying not to take up too much room.

Have you heard from your father of late?

Eight words. Eliza read them twice. The first time they passed through her mind unremarkably, a mother's idle enquiry. The second time they caught. They snagged on something, the way a thread catches on a rough nail, and the pull of it drew tight a line she had not known was slack.

When had she last heard from her father?

She set the letter down on her knee, beneath the table where no one could see it, and searched her memory. The weeks since March had blurred, each one consumed by the rhythms of the barn: the foaling schedule, the feed rounds, the nightly watches, the slow accumulation of small victories and smaller losses that made up a breeding season. She had written to her father twice. She had received only one reply; a brief note, written in haste, the handwriting less steady than usual. Sir Richard reported that he had delivered the first string of horses safely and been asked to take a consignment across the Channel to Belgium. The army's need of skilled horse handlers was urgent. He expected to be gone a few weeks at most. He would write again when he could.

That letter had arrived in the first week of April. Six weeks ago. She had read it at the desk in the study, noted the salient facts, filed it with his other correspondence, and returned to the evening feed round, because there were pregnant mares to manage and the work did not pause for worry.

Six weeks. No second letter. No word at all.

She had not noticed. The realisation sat in her stomach like a stone, the ripples spreading outward through everything she had done and failed to do. She had been so consumed by the foaling, by the daily business of keeping Belle Haven alive, that her father's silence had registered as nothing more than an absence of post, another small gap in the routine that would resolve itself in time.

But her mother had noticed. Theresa, two hundred miles away in Oxfordshire with a new grandchild and a household not her own to manage, had noticed, and the fact that she was asking Eliza rather than writing to Richard directly meant she had already tried and received no answer.

Around her the breakfast table continued. Louise was speculating about what Alexander might look like. Charlotte was considering how old he might be before Molly would put him on a horse and from where she would source his first pony. Laura had asked Helen whether they might send a gift, and Helen was already making a list. The joy in the room was genuine, and Eliza could not bear to puncture it.

The newspapers. They arrived each morning with the post, folded and ink-fresh, delivered to the study as they had been for as long as Eliza could remember. Sir Richard usually read them over breakfast. In his absence, they had accumulated on the study desk in an untouched stack that grew by the day, because Eliza had neither the time nor the inclination to sit and read about a war she could not influence when there were horses to attend to.

But Llewellyn read them. She had noticed weeks ago. Each evening, after the last round of the barns, he would collect the day's paper from the study and carry it to his room above the stallion barn, and bring it back the following morning. She had seen the light in his window late at night, the candle burning while the rest of the household slept, and she had understood without asking that a soldier did not stop following a war simply because he was no longer fighting it. He would know what was happening on the Continent. He would know what Belgium meant.

She waited until the conversation turned to whether Molly would attempt to ride before the doctor permitted it, a question whose answer everyone already knew, and spoke beneath it.

"Lieutenant." She pitched her voice for him alone. "Would you have a moment to meet me in the study after breakfast? There's a matter I'd like to discuss."

Whatever he read in her face, he did not ask. He simply nodded, and returned to his tea.

Louise glanced between them. Her gaze lingered a beat too long, and the brightness in her expression shifted to something speculative, but Helen caught her eye from across the table, a look so mild it might have meant nothing and so pointed it clearly meant everything, and Louise returned to her toast.

Eliza drank her tea. It had gone cold, and the taste was flat and bitter, but she drank it anyway, because the routine of lifting the cup and setting it down gave her hands something to do that was not pressing against the letter in her pocket, feeling for the shape of the question her mother had asked and the silence where her father's answer should have been.

The study door was open. Llewellyn paused at the threshold the way he always did, a habit from the army, assessing a room before entering it. The desk, the stacked ledgers, Charlotte's charts pinned to the wall, the accumulated paperwork of a breeding programme rebuilt from almost nothing over the past two months. And Eliza, standing at the window with her back to the door and her arms folded, looking out at the yard where the morning's work was already underway. Her shoulders held the tension he associated with a decision already made but not yet spoken.

She turned when she heard his step. The uneven rhythm of it was, he suspected, as legible to her as her expression was to him. They had spent enough hours in shared spaces to learn each other's sounds: the weight of a footfall, the creak of a chair, the scratch of a pencil on paper at two in the morning when neither could sleep and neither would admit it.

"Close the door, please," she said.

He closed it. Caesar, who had been following at his heels, was shut out and registered his objection with a single thump of his tail against the floorboards before settling on the corridor side with a sigh.

Eliza produced the letter from her pocket. She unfolded it, turned to the second page, and held it out so he could read the postscript. Her finger marked the line. *Have you heard from your father of late?*

"When did you last hear from him?" Llewellyn asked.

"The first week of April. A brief note." Her voice was level, controlled. "He wrote that he had delivered horses and been asked to take a consignment across the Channel. To Belgium."

The word landed in the room with weight. Belgium. Llewellyn had been reading that word every night for weeks, turning it over in the candlelight of his room while Hermes shifted and breathed below. He had read it in editorials that alternated between confidence and dread, in the careful language of correspondents who were not permitted to say what they plainly meant.

"You didn't know he'd gone across," Eliza said. He knew his face had changed when she said the word.

"No." He had assumed Sir Richard was somewhere in England still. The Channel crossing changed everything. "You said he expected to be gone a few weeks?"

"That was six weeks ago. And letters can still cross the Channel, can they not? There are ships going back and forth?"

He looked at her across the desk, and what he saw was not panic but a woman's particular stillness, the stillness of one who had identified a threat and was waiting for information before she responded. She had brought him here because he had information she did not, and she trusted him to give it straight.

He would not insult her by doing otherwise.

"The news from the Continent is not good," he said. He leaned against the edge of the desk, taking the weight off his left leg, and chose his words with care. "Napoleon crossed into France in March and marched north. Every garrison he passed, the men went over to him. The Bourbon king fled Paris without a fight. By the end of March, Bonaparte had the French army again, or enough of it. He has been gathering men and materiel at a rate the papers describe as alarming, which means the actual rate is worse."

Eliza's arms tightened across her chest. She did not interrupt.

"Wellington is in Brussels. He has been assembling a coalition force: British, Dutch, Prussian, Hanoverian. The papers suggest he is preparing for a major confrontation, though the when and where are not reported, assuming anyone knows." He paused. He would not soften what came next. "Belgium is not large. If Wellington is massing his forces there, it is because he expects to fight there. The entire country is becoming a theatre of war."

"And my father is in it," Eliza said. "With horses."

"Your father is not a soldier. He should not be near the front lines, and the army would have no reason to place him there. His role would be delivery and handling, not combat." He met her eyes and held them. "But if battle comes, the lines become unclear very quickly. Supply routes cross battlefields. Depots are targeted. And horse lines are always close to the action, because the cavalry needs its remounts within reach."

The silence that followed was the kind that came when two people had arrived at the same conclusion and neither wished to say it aloud. Sir Richard Bell was a civilian in a country that was about to become a battlefield, and the last anyone had heard from him was six weeks ago.

Eliza's jaw tightened, and her eyes moved to the stack of unread newspapers on the desk, the accumulated record of a war she had been too busy and too tired to follow. He saw her register the stack, calculate its size, and understand what it represented: weeks of information she had not had, sitting three feet from where she worked every day.

"I'll read them," she said. "Tonight."

"I can mark the relevant articles," he said. "Save you some time."

She nodded. A concession, small but real. They had come a long way from the morning he had withdrawn his hand from the stud book.

They stood looking at each other across the study, and the distance between them was not the careful, measured space of two people avoiding something. It was the distance of two people standing on the same ground, facing the same direction, watching the same horizon for a shape they hoped would not appear.

A sound in the corridor. Quick footsteps, lighter than Helen's, less purposeful than Charlotte's. A pause outside the door, the quality of which suggested someone pressing an ear to the wood. Then the door opened and Louise's face appeared around the edge, her dark eyes bright, her expression cycling through several states before settling on a grin she attempted, unsuccessfully, to suppress.

She giggled.

It was the giggle of a fourteen-year-old girl who had found two people alone in a room with the door closed, and whose imagination had supplied a narrative considerably more interesting than the one actually taking place. Her cheeks flushed pink, and her gaze moved between them with delighted speculation.

"I'm sorry to interrupt," Louise said, in a tone that suggested she was not sorry at all and was thrilled to have something to interrupt. "Only Mr Thornton is asking for you, Eliza. He says it's urgent, but he said it in the way that means it's not actually urgent, he just wants it done before lunch."

Eliza's expression changed. The taut stillness was gone, replaced by something that was not quite exasperation and not quite amusement, the look of a woman confronted with evidence that the world contained problems less grave than the one she had been contemplating and yet equally demanding of her attention.

"Thank you, Louise," she said. "Tell him I'll be there directly."

Louise beamed, glanced once more at Llewellyn with an expression that promised she would be reporting this encounter to someone at the earliest opportunity, and withdrew. Her footsteps retreated down the corridor at a pace that suggested news was being carried.

Llewellyn exhaled. The breath was not quite a laugh, but it sat in the same territory, the involuntary response of a man whose chest had been tight with grave matters and had been abruptly loosened by a girl's giggle. He straightened from the desk and looked at Eliza, who was pressing her fingers against the bridge of her nose in the manner of someone counting to a specific number before trusting herself to speak.

"I'll mark those articles," he said.

Eliza dropped her hand. Her eyes met his, and beneath the weariness and the worry he saw something else, something Louise's interruption had not displaced but merely covered, as a cloth thrown over a lamp does not extinguish it but only changes the quality of the light.

"Thank you," she said, and went to find Thornton.

Chapter Eleven

She went out to find Thornton, because it was something she could do right now when she did not want to think about what the absence of letters from her father might mean. The old groom was in the tack room, mending a headcollar that had been chewed through by one of the yearlings, a colt with a taste for leather and a total absence of anything resembling restraint. He looked up and nodded, his weathered face arranged in the expression Eliza had come to read as deference offered grudgingly but offered nonetheless.

"Miss Eliza. Ballerina's in season."

Those words changed the shape of the morning. In season. The mare's body declaring itself ready, six weeks after the stillborn filly, six weeks after she accepted the twins, six weeks of patient recovery during which Ballerina had eaten her feed and nursed her adopted daughters and stood in the spring grass growing sleek and round, her bay coat darkening to a rich mahogany as the season turned.

"How long?" Eliza asked.

"Since yesterday evening, I reckon, but proper this morning. She's flagging and winking and rubbing up against the fence posts." Thornton's mouth twitched, the closest he came to humour, and he set aside the headcollar. "She's not subtle about it."

Eliza followed him out of the tack room and across the yard. The morning was warm, the days beginning to feel like proper summer, the kind of warmth that sat on the skin and made the stone of the stable buildings radiate heat. The hawthorn hedges had thickened into full bloom, white and heavy-scented, and somewhere a lark was singing.

Ballerina stood at the fence of the near paddock with her head high and her tail lifted. Her coat gleamed. The grey at the roots of her mane, which had seemed so stark in the lantern-lit stall on the night of the stillbirth, was less visible in the sunlight, threaded through the darker hair like silver wire. She looked, Eliza thought, like a mare ten years younger. Like a horse who had found something to live for and was living for it with considerable determination.

The twin fillies proved the point. Seren and Eira frolicked in the grass behind Ballerina, full of youthful energy. They had grown astonishingly in six weeks, their legs losing the splayed-footed wobble of newborns and acquiring the angular grace of young horses who had discovered that the world contained grass and sunshine and the reliable presence of a mother who came when they called. Seren, the larger, the bay who had been first to nurse, was already showing the broad forehead and clean legs of her sire's line. Eira, the chestnut with the crooked blaze, was smaller but quicker, her movements sharp and certain, a filly who had arrived undersized and had been making up the deficit ever since with a will that bordered on the vengeful.

They were not Ballerina's blood. They carried nothing of her in their veins. But they carried everything of her in their bodies, every ounce of milk and warmth and patience she had given them, and watching them now, glossy and fat and alive in the May sunshine, Eliza felt the weight of the decision she was about to make settle across her shoulders.

She leaned on the fence rail and gave Belle Haven's three-note whistle, softly, so she did not call every horse within earshot. Ballerina turned and walked toward her, ears pricked, and pressed her muzzle against Eliza's chest. The mare's breath was warm and sweet with grass. Her dark eyes held the calm of her twenty-two years, and Eliza scratched behind her ear and thought about what Llewellyn had said in the barn, weeks ago, in the quiet of a different night. *Let her foal first. See how she comes through it.*

The foal had not survived, but it was no fault of the dam's; the knotted cord was just one of those things that could happen to any mare. Ballerina had come through it. Not just survived but thrived, taking on two fragile orphans and raising them with a devotion that bordered on the ferocious. She had regained her health, her appetite, her spirit. And now her body was telling them what it wanted.

Charlotte's voice in Eliza's memory: *Ballerina shares no ancestors with Hermes in at least seven generations. Their foal could be the foundation of a whole new line.*

Against this, the other calculation, the one that sat in her chest rather than her head. Ballerina was twenty-two. Carrying a foal at twenty-two was not the same as carrying one at twelve or fifteen. The risks were higher: complications in pregnancy, difficulty in labour, the simple fact that an older body had less to spare. *Mother loves this horse more than she loves most people*, she had told Llewellyn, and it was true, and if anything happened to Ballerina because of a decision Eliza made, the weight of it would sit between them for years.

The sound of hooves on cobblestones drew her attention. Llewellyn was leading Hermes out of the stallion barn for his daily walk, the blind stallion stepping with the care of a horse who mapped the world by memory and sound. Hermes had grown more confident over the weeks, his mental geometry expanding daily. He knew the yard, the path to the paddock, the distance between the barn and the water trough. He walked with his head slightly raised, his ears working constantly, reading the air the way other horses read the ground.

They were fifty yards from Ballerina's fence when Hermes stopped.

His head came up. Not the gradual lift of a horse noticing something at a distance, but the sudden, electric attention of a stallion who had caught a scent that spoke directly to the oldest part of his brain. His nostrils flared wide, pulling air in deep, searching draughts. The thick muscles along his crest tightened. His tail lifted.

He called. A full stallion's call, resonant and carrying, the sound rolling across the yard and the paddocks and probably halfway to the village. It was the first time Eliza had heard Hermes produce that note since his arrival, and the power of it surprised her. This was not the careful, contained horse who navigated his stall by memory. This was a mature stallion doing what stallions did when they scented a mare in season, and the sound was as old as the species and as unmistakable as thunder.

Ballerina answered. She swung away from Eliza and trotted three strides into the paddock, her tail flagged high, her neck arched, the picture of a mare who knew exactly what she was about. She whickered. A low, inviting sound, coquettish, the equine equivalent of a glance over one shoulder.

The twin fillies watched this performance from a safe distance, their ears pricked, their expressions suggesting they had absolutely no idea what was happening but found it thoroughly interesting.

Hermes pulled toward the fence. Llewellyn let the lead rope run through his hands, giving the stallion his head, and Hermes walked forward with a ground-covering stride. He reached the fence rail and stretched his neck over it, nostrils working, and Ballerina came to meet him, and they stood nose to nose, breathing each other in, and the sound they made together was the oldest conversation in the world.

Eliza watched them. The blind stallion and the old mare. Eclipse blood and twenty-two years of faithful service.

She turned to Thornton, who stood three paces behind her with his cap in his hands and his face carefully neutral, waiting.

"We'll try," Eliza said.

Thornton nodded once. He put his cap back on his head, the gesture of a man who had received his orders and found them satisfactory.

"I'll set up the breeding paddock," he said, and went to do it.

The stallion's whole body had changed since he caught Ballerina's scent. He walked with his head high and his nostrils wide, each breath pulling information from the air, and beneath Llewellyn's hand the lead rope hummed with contained energy. Hermes did not pull. He was too well-mannered for that, or too experienced. But every muscle in his body said *forward*, and the sound he made, a low rumble deep in his chest, was not a sound that required eyes.

The breeding paddock was a small square of level ground behind the stallion barn, bounded on three sides by post-and-rail fencing and on the fourth by the barn wall. Phillip stood at the gate, pale with the solemnity of a boy witnessing something he understood to be important without entirely knowing why.

Llewellyn led Hermes in and unclipped the lead rope. The stallion stood for a moment, reading the space, ears turning. He pawed the ground once, a sharp strike that sent a divot of turf spinning, and called again. The sound bounced off the barn wall and came back to him, and Llewellyn saw the horse adjust, tilting his head, using the echo to confirm the dimensions of his enclosure.

Eliza came around the corner of the barn carrying a thick bundle. "Leg wraps, for his front hooves," she said, and held Hermes's head while Llewellyn put them on. They had been cleverly made; soft leather padded with felt, buckles so they could be adjusted to fit different stallions. Hermes flattened his ears as he tested his hooves to the ground, but he had been a cavalry horse, accustomed to far more onerous tack than this, and then Thornton brought Ballerina in from the far gate and Hermes scented the air again and forgot all about his hooves.

Ballerina walked calmly beside the old groom, her ears forward, her tail already lifted. She had done this a dozen times or more in her long career, and her body carried the memory of it in the easy way she moved, unhurried, patient, her dark eyes taking in the stallion with an expression that could only be called assessment. She was, Llewellyn thought, a mare who knew her own worth, and one who had already judged the stallion before her worthy.

They released her. She walked into the centre of the paddock and stopped.

Hermes approached. His steps were measured, but there was nothing tentative about his direction. He went straight to her. His muzzle found her shoulder first, travelling along the curve of her barrel, and Ballerina held steady, allowing the investigation. He nosed her hip, her tail, her hocks. She turned her head and nipped his shoulder, not hard, a mare's correction that said *I am ready but you will do this properly.* Hermes accepted the reprimand with the good grace of a stallion who understood that cooperation was required.

What followed was unremarkable in the way that fundamental things always are. The mechanics of equine breeding were neither elegant nor romantic, and the people watching were not looking for either. They were looking for safety, for timing, for the signs that told an experienced horseperson whether the covering had been successful. Llewellyn stood ready to intervene if Hermes stumbled or Ballerina objected, but neither horse gave him cause. Hermes was sure and steady, his blindness irrelevant in the face of his instincts. Ballerina bore his weight without flinching, her legs braced, her neck level, a broodmare who had earned every grey hair in her mane.

It was over in minutes. Hermes dismounted and stood, sides heaving, his scarred head turned toward the morning sun. Ballerina shook herself, walked to the water bucket, and drank, and the prosaic ordinariness of the gesture made Llewellyn smile. The world's great dramas, he had learned, were followed not by speeches or fanfares but by a horse drinking water and a groom reaching for a lead rope.

Thornton clipped the lead to Hermes and led him back to the stallion barn. Phillip took Ballerina back to the pasture where Seren and Eira were calling for her, two small voices pitched high with the indignation of children who had been briefly abandoned.

Llewellyn remained at the fence. He rested his forearms on the top rail, taking the weight off his left leg, and turned his face into the warmth. The sun sat above the treeline now, full and generous, the sort of late-spring sun that heated the wood beneath his arms and drew the scent of hawthorn from the hedgerow and made the yard feel, for a few minutes, like a place where nothing was wrong.

Eliza came to stand beside him. She leaned on the rail in the same posture, forearms flat, and the distance between his elbow and hers was the width of a hand.

She was looking at Ballerina. The old mare had reached the twins and was submitting to their urgent inspection as Phillip removed her headcollar, both fillies pressing against her flanks, nosing for milk.

Llewellyn was aware of Eliza the way he was aware of the sun: as warmth, as presence, as something his body oriented toward without instruction. The light fell across her face and shimmered against the dark brown of her skin, the tight braids pulled back from her temples, the line of her jaw, the place where her collar met her neck. She was not beautiful in the way that paintings were beautiful, arranged and distant. She was beautiful the way a well-made thing was beautiful, in the fitness of every part to its purpose.

He looked at the paddock where the breeding had taken place, and at the pasture where Ballerina minded her adopted daughters, and at the stallion barn where Hermes stood in his stall, and the thread that connected them all ran through the woman standing beside him.

"The next generation will come," he said quietly.

Eliza did not answer immediately. She watched the twins jostling for position at Ballerina's flank, and the corner of her mouth lifted, and the expression was not her brisk professional acknowledgement. It was softer. Unguarded. The face of a woman who had carried the weight of this place for months and could feel, just for a moment, that the weight was shifting.

"Yes," she said. "It will."

She smiled, and turned her face up to the sun, and closed her eyes, and Llewellyn stood beside her and said nothing more, because the sunshine was doing the talking for them both, and it was saying everything he could not.

The rosemary needed cutting back. Helen had said so at breakfast, in the mild tone that meant it was not a suggestion, and Louise had taken the shears and gone to the kitchen garden with every intention of being thorough and returning with a basket of herbs that would demonstrate her value to the household beyond question. She had, in fact, cut approximately three sprigs of rosemary before the noise of a stallion calling from the breeding paddock reached her over the garden wall, and her hands went still, and the shears hung forgotten at her side.

The kitchen garden occupied a square of south-facing ground behind the house, bounded on three sides by a stone wall that was taller than Louise even when she stood on her tiptoes. It was a productive, well-ordered space, the beds ruled into neat rows of sage and thyme and parsley, the soil dark and freshly turned where she had planted seeds weeks ago that were now showing the first brave shoots of green.

But the wall. The wall was the thing. Because if one stood on the upturned crate that someone had left beside the compost heap, and stretched one's neck just so, one could see over it to the breeding paddock behind the stallion barn, and the whole morning's drama could be seen like a play performed for an audience of one.

She had not meant to watch. Or rather, she had meant to watch the breeding, because she was fourteen and the mechanics of horse reproduction were interesting in a purely scientific way that she was certain Charlotte would approve of. She had not, after all, grown up at Belle Haven itself, as her friends had. This was new to her. But by the time she had fetched the crate to the wall and clambered up on it, the breeding was over, and what she saw instead was actually even more interesting.

Two people stood at the fence, angled side-on, right where she could clearly see both their faces. Side by side, leaning on the rail. Close enough that a handspan would bridge the gap between them. Eliza's face was tilted toward the sun, her eyes closed, and the expression she wore was one Louise had never seen on her. It was not the capable, guarded composure Eliza carried through her days like armour. It was simpler than that. Eliza was smiling. Not the brisk, functional smile she offered when a foal stood for the first time or a mare ate her mash. A real smile, unguarded, the kind that started somewhere behind the ribs and arrived at the mouth without being inspected along the way.

And Llewellyn was watching her.

Louise knew that look. She had seen it on her stepfather's face a thousand times, directed at her mother across the supper table, across the churchyard, across any room that happened to contain Helen Fallon. It was the look of a man who had found the place where his attention wanted to rest and saw no reason to move it. Llewellyn stood with his weight on his right leg, his damaged left one bearing less, and his face held the face of someone gazing at something infinitely precious.

He did not touch her. They did not speak. They simply stood together in the May sunshine, and the distance between them hummed with something Louise could feel from forty yards away, the charge that gathered in the air between two people who were not saying the thing they both knew.

She had been right.

She had known it for weeks, with the conviction of a girl who paid attention to people the way Charlotte paid attention to pedigrees. She had known it when her mother caught her eye across the breakfast table and redirected her gaze with a look that said *not now* and also *yes, I see it too.*

The shears fell from her hand and landed point-first in the rosemary bed. Louise did not retrieve them. She climbed down from the crate, wiped her earthy hands on her skirts, an act that would earn a reproach from Helen and was entirely worth it, and ran.

She found Charlotte in the study, naturally, surrounded by charts and open stud books. Charlotte sat cross-legged in Sir Richard's chair with a pencil behind each ear and a third in her hand, frowning at a chart with the concentrated displeasure of a girl who had found an error in God's arithmetic and intended to correct it.

"Charlotte," Louise said, and she was out of breath despite the distance being approximately fifty yards, because urgency had its own respiratory demands. "Charlotte, listen. I was in the garden. I *saw* them."

Charlotte looked up. The pencil stilled. Her blue eyes sharpened with the focus she brought to new information, the look of a mind that sorted it the way other people sorted a hand of cards: rapidly, by suit, into the correct order.

"Saw whom?"

"Eliza and Lieutenant Llewellyn." Louise pressed her palms flat on the desk and leaned forward, and the grin she had been suppressing since the garden wall broke free. "I was right. They're in *love.*"

Charlotte's eyebrows rose. Then her mouth curved, slowly, a girl's smile, one who dealt in pedigrees and recognised a good cross when she saw one.

"Are you sure?" Charlotte said, but she was already smiling, and the question was not scepticism but an invitation, because Charlotte Bell did not accept conclusions without evidence.

"Completely sure. She was *smiling*. Actually smiling, Charlotte, with her eyes closed and her face in the sun, and he was watching her as though she were the only horse in the paddock." Louise paused, aware that the metaphor had got away from her. "That is to say, the only person. You know what I mean."

Charlotte laughed. It was the bright, startled laugh that came out of her rarely, the sound of one who spent so much time being serious that laughter, when it came, arrived with the force of something uncorked. She set down her pencil. Louise sat on the edge of the desk, because the chairs were all occupied by books.

"I noticed at dinner the other night," Charlotte said. "Their hands touched when he passed her the salt, and she didn't react at all, as if it were something she was quite used to."

"And the way he looks at her when she's not looking," Louise said. "Every single time."

"And the way *she* looks at *him* when *he's* not looking."

"Do you think they know?"

"I think," Charlotte said, with the decisive authority she brought to all matters of matching, "that they are the last two people on this estate to work it out. Which is saying something, because Hermes is a horse and blind and even he can probably tell."

They dissolved into giggles. Louise laughed until her ribs ached, and Charlotte pressed her hand over her mouth, and the study filled with the joyous music of two teenage girls sharing a secret they found unbearable and delicious.

"What are you going to do about it?" Laura asked.

Her voice came from the window seat, where she sat with her knees drawn up and Caesar's head in her lap. Louise had not noticed her when she came in, which was not unusual; Laura had a gift for stillness that made her as easy to overlook as furniture. Her sightless eyes were directed toward the sound of their laughter, and her expression held the gentle amusement of someone who had been listening to the entire conversation and had waited for the right moment to enter it.

"We could help," Louise began, the word carrying the full weight of her organisational ambition.

"Or," Laura said, her voice carrying the quiet authority of a girl who spoke rarely and was therefore always listened to, "you could leave them alone."

Charlotte opened her mouth to protest. Louise felt the objection rising in her own chest, the matchmaker's instinct that said surely a well-timed intervention would speed things along.

Charlotte closed her mouth again and looked thoughtful.

Laura's hand moved over Caesar's ears in slow circles. The mastiff sighed.

"They are finding their way," Laura said. "Both of them. And finding your own way matters more than being shown it." She paused. "If you push, you might push them apart. Some things need to come in their own time." She tilted her head. "Like foals."

The analogy landed with the certainty of a horseshoe thrown by an expert. Louise felt her enthusiasm deflate, not entirely, because enthusiasm of her particular strain was not easily extinguished, but enough to recognise the wisdom in it. Charlotte, who understood breeding better than any of them, was nodding.

"She's right," Charlotte said, and the admission must have cost her something, because Charlotte preferred to be the one who was right. She picked up her pencil and turned back to her charts. "We won't interfere."

"We won't interfere *much*," Louise amended.

Something was wrong with Louise and Charlotte, and Eliza could not determine what.

It had begun the day of the breeding, or perhaps the day after. Small things, individually unremarkable, collectively unsettling. Louise had taken to mentioning Lieutenant Llewellyn in conversation with a frequency that bordered on the compulsive. She would begin a sentence about the weather, or the herb garden, or the state of the kitchen stores, and somehow arrive at Llewellyn's name by the end of it, the conversational path as winding and improbable as a river that insisted on flowing uphill. Charlotte, meanwhile, had developed a new habit of looking at Eliza with an expression she could not read, a knowing brightness that sat somewhere between amusement and assessment, as though Eliza were a horse whose conformation Charlotte had only just noticed and found unexpectedly promising.

They whispered. They had always whispered, because they were fourteen and whispering was a constitutional requirement of the age, but these whispers carried a different quality. They stopped when Eliza entered a room. Not gradually, the way ordinary conversation tapered when a new person joined it, but abruptly, with the guilty speed of people caught in an act they knew to be suspicious. Louise would smile. Charlotte would look at her book. The silence that followed was thick enough to spread on bread.

On Wednesday, Louise volunteered to carry a message to the stallion barn informing Llewellyn that dinner would be at six o'clock, which was the time dinner was always at and had been every evening at Belle Haven since before Eliza was born. She ran off before Eliza could point out how silly she was being, returned pink-cheeked and breathless, and reported to Charlotte in a murmur that Eliza caught only the tail of, something about his sleeves being rolled up and his hair being disordered, observations that had no bearing on the question of dinner.

On Thursday, Charlotte asked Eliza, with studied innocence, whether she thought the Lieutenant was settling well at Belle Haven. A perfectly reasonable question, and one Charlotte had never asked before. The way she tilted her head while waiting for the answer suggested the answer mattered more than the question, the way a horse's response to a test mattered more than the test itself.

"He seems content enough," Eliza had said, baffled. Charlotte nodded sagely, as though a theory had been confirmed, and returned to her charts.

On Friday evening, Eliza walked into the study to find Charlotte and Louise bent over a piece of foolscap that was not, for once, a breeding chart. Whatever it was vanished beneath a stud book with the speed of a card cheat palming an ace, and both girls looked up with expressions of innocence so perfectly composed they might as well have been holding signs that read *WE ARE UP TO SOMETHING*.

Enough.

She found Helen in the kitchen, where the late-afternoon light came through the window and caught the gold of Helen's hair as she rolled out pastry. The kitchen smelled of flour and butter and the dried lavender that hung from the beams, and Helen's hands moved with the steady rhythm of a woman who found domestic work not a burden but a meditation.

"Aunt Helen," Eliza said, pulling out a chair and sitting heavily. "Charlotte and Louise are plotting something, and I cannot work out what."

Helen did not look up from the pastry. She turned the dough a quarter, sprinkled a little more flour on it and rolled again. "Are they?" she said, in the tone of someone who already knew the answer and was interested in how Eliza had arrived at the question.

"They whisper. They go silent when I come in. Louise keeps mentioning Lieutenant Llewellyn for no reason. Charlotte keeps looking at me as if I'm a broodmare she's considering for a cross."

The pin paused. Helen's mouth did something complicated, a movement at the corners that was suppressed almost immediately, so quickly that Eliza might have missed it had she not been watching closely.

"I would not worry about it," Helen said. "Girls their age are prone to enthusiasms. It will pass."

"It doesn't feel like it's passing. It feels like it's building."

Helen set down the rolling pin. She wiped her hands on her apron, slowly, the way people did when they were buying time rather than removing flour. She looked at Eliza with the mild, perceptive gaze that had been extracting truths from people for as long as Eliza had known her.

"Leave the girls to me," she said. "I do not think it will be a problem."

This was not satisfactory. Eliza pressed her hands flat on the table and assembled the evidence she had been turning over for weeks, reluctant to deliver it to Louise's mother but now felt she must.

"I think," she said, choosing her words carefully, "that Louise may have developed a tenderness for Lieutenant Llewellyn."

There. It was said. The theory she had constructed from the available facts: Louise's constant mentions of his name, her eagerness to carry messages to the stallion barn, the pink cheeks and breathless reports, the whispered observations about his sleeves and his hair. Charlotte's involvement made sense too, as co-conspirator and confidante. It was the only conclusion that fit the evidence.

Helen's composure broke.

It was not a dramatic rupture. Helen Fallon was too controlled for that. But the laugh that escaped her was genuine and uncontained, a sound Eliza had never heard from her in all their years of acquaintance, and it transformed her face. The composed vicar's wife, the formidable listener, the woman who saw everything and said only what mattered, pressed her floury hand over her mouth and laughed until her shoulders shook.

Eliza stared at her. The laughter was not unkind. There was no mockery in it. But it was unmistakably directed at what she had just said, and Eliza could not for the life of her understand what was funny about it.

"I fail to see what's so amusing," Eliza said stiffly.

Helen lowered her hand. Her eyes were bright, and the smile that remained was warm, the kind of warm that contained knowledge and affection and something that looked very much like recognition, as though Eliza had reminded her of something from her own life that she still found tender.

"Oh, my dear girl," Helen said, and her voice was gentle. "Louise does not have a tendre for the Lieutenant."

"Then what are they plotting?"

Helen picked up the rolling pin and returned to the pastry. The rhythm resumed, steady and sure.

"I have found," Helen said, addressing the dough with the conversational ease of a woman sharing a recipe rather than dispensing wisdom, "that love is very like the weather. It arrives from the direction you are least expecting, and by the time you notice it, everyone around you has already put on their coats."

This was not an answer. It was not even close to an answer. Eliza sat at the kitchen table and turned it over in her mind the way she would turn a stone in a field, looking for what lived beneath it, and found nothing but more questions.

"I don't understand," she said.

"No," Helen agreed pleasantly. "You don't." She laid the pastry into the pie dish, trimmed the edges, and did not elaborate.

Eliza sat a moment longer, understanding gradually that more was not coming. Helen had said what she intended to say, which was one thing, and the one thing was apparently all Eliza was going to get. She stood, pushed her chair in neatly, and walked to the door.

"Aunt Helen."

"Mmm?"

"If Louise does not have a tendre for the Lieutenant, what on earth are those two whispering about?"

Helen crimped the pie crust with her thumb and forefinger, each press neat and even. She did not look up.

"I expect you'll work it out," she said. "You always do."

Eliza left the kitchen more confused than when she had entered it, which was, she reflected, a considerable achievement. She turned toward the broodmare barn, where the horses, at least, made sense. Behind her, through the open kitchen window, she heard Helen laugh again, quiet and fond, and the sound followed her across the cobblestones like a question she could not answer, warm and persistent and impossible to ignore.

Chapter Twelve

THE EVENING ROUTINE WITH Hermes had become a kind of prayer. Not the chapel sort, not the sort his mother would have approved of, but an older kind, the kind that lived in repetition and attention and the laying of hands on something you loved. Llewellyn ran the brush along the stallion's neck in long, even strokes, following the grain of the coat, and Hermes leaned into the pressure the way he always did, his scarred eyes half-closed, his breathing deep and slow. The stallion barn was quiet at this hour. The young colts had been fed and watered and left to the serious business of dozing, and the only sounds were the brush on hide and the occasional shift of weight on straw and, from somewhere beyond the barn door, the voices of two girls who thought they were being discreet.

They were not being discreet.

Llewellyn had been watching Charlotte and Louise for a week, much as a man on picket duty watched the treeline: not staring, but noting the movements, logging the patterns, building a picture from accumulated detail. The picture, once assembled, was remarkably clear.

On Monday, Louise had appeared at the stallion barn door with news that Eliza would be working late in the study and might appreciate a cup of tea brought to her. She delivered this intelligence with the eager brightness of a courier carrying dispatches, and when Llewellyn said he would see to it, Louise beamed as though he had agreed to storm a redoubt rather than boil a kettle.

On Tuesday, Charlotte had asked him, over the stud book, whether he thought Belle Haven was the sort of place a person might stay. She asked it casually, her pencil never pausing on the page, her blue eyes fixed on the chart before her. He answered vaguely, saying that Belle Haven must have been a wonderful place for her to grow up. But the question stayed with him.

On Wednesday, Louise had reorganised the broodmare night watch schedule so that Llewellyn's watches coincided exactly with Eliza's, a feat of logistical engineering that would have done credit to a quartermaster. She presented the revised timetable with an expression of perfect innocence and the faintest flush of pink, and when he queried her she said, "Oh, it just makes more sense this way," in a voice that made it clear sense had nothing to do with it.

On Thursday, both girls had manufactured an excuse to leave them alone in the study, Charlotte announcing she needed a volume from the library and Louise declaring she had promised to help Helen with something unspecified and almost certainly fictitious. They had gone through the door together, and Louise had looked back over her shoulder with the look of a general surveying a battlefield on which the pieces had been arranged to her satisfaction.

He was not a fool. He recognised a campaign when he saw one.

They were matchmaking.

The brush paused on Hermes's shoulder. Llewellyn rested his hand there, feeling the warmth of the horse beneath his palm, and let the thought sit where it had landed. Matchmaking. Between himself and Eliza. Which meant they had seen something, or believed they had, and were working to bring it about.

He was not certain he minded. That was the trouble.

The voice arrived on cue, the one that lived in the back of his skull and spoke with the accent of hard sense and bitter experience. It said: *She is Miss Bell. She is the daughter of a man with the personal favour of the Prince Regent. She runs this estate, and the estate is worth more than your family's farm and every farm in the valley put together. You are a lieutenant on half pay with a leg that will never be right and an arm that aches when the weather turns, and you sleep above a stable because that is where you belong.*

He knew the voice. It had spoken before, in a different register, with a different accent. It had spoken on the day his brother's letter arrived at camp, the letter that said *Rhiannon sends her love* and then, immediately after, the sentence that unwound everything. The voice had said then what it said now: *You were a fool to think this could be yours.*

Hermes shifted, turning his head toward Llewellyn's hand, and the scarred muzzle found his sleeve and lipped at the fabric. The stallion could not see him but knew where he stood, because Hermes had learned to navigate by trust, by the accumulated evidence of hands that were always where they should be.

Llewellyn thought of a night in the broodmare barn, his arms wrapped around a foal that would not breathe. He thought of Eliza's face when the colt gasped. He thought of their hands, joined for a few quiet moments while

Arthur nursed, and the way neither of them had remarked upon it, as if the contact were so natural it required no commentary.

He thought of her standing at the fence after the breeding, her face tilted to the sun, her eyes closed, and the smile that had nothing to do with competence or duty.

The voice said: *She is above you.*

Llewellyn pressed his forehead against Hermes's neck and breathed in the warm, dusty scent of horse. The stallion stood patient, bearing the weight of his silence.

He pushed the voice down. Not away; it would return, as it always did, in the small hours when the candle burned low and the newspapers told him of a war he could no longer fight and a world that sorted people by birth and rank and wealth. It would return, and it would be right about the facts.

But tonight Pompey's head pushed against his knee, the mastiff's brown eyes looking up with the uncomplicated devotion of a creature who did not trouble himself with questions of station, and the yard was quiet, and somewhere in the house a candle burned in the study window where Eliza worked late, and Llewellyn allowed himself the dangerous luxury of not arguing with what he already knew.

He did not name it. Two girls with bright eyes and no subtlety had named it for him, and that was enough.

He picked up the brush and returned to Hermes, and the rhythm of the strokes steadied something inside him that had been unsteady for weeks, and he let it be steady, and he did not listen to the voice.

Serenity had been off her feed since the previous evening, which was unusual for a mare who approached her bucket with the single-minded enthusiasm of a horse who believed every meal might be her last. Eliza found the problem during the morning check: the left rear quarter of the udder was hot to the touch, swollen hard, the skin tight and shiny. When she pressed gently, the mare flinched and swung her head around with a look of reproach that was entirely justified. The foal, a leggy grey colt three weeks old, was already favouring the other teat.

Mastitis. Caught early, the kind that responded well to treatment if you were prompt. Eliza had seen enough cases to know the arithmetic: catch it on the first day and the mare recovered well; wait two days and you were fighting infection; wait three and they might lose the mare, which meant a foal who would have to be bottle-fed because he was too old now for a nurse mare and far too young to wean.

She left Phillip with instructions to keep the foal nursing on the sore teat if the mare would tolerate it, the continued suckling being the best medicine alongside everything else, and crossed the yard to the house. The remedy she wanted was Molly's, written in Molly's cramped hand in the medical journal that lived on the shelf above the kitchen dresser. Molly had developed it over years of trial and refinement, the last version marked with a satisfied tick that was as close to a declaration of triumph as Molly ever committed to paper.

Helen stood at the table, chopping something that smelled of onion and thyme, and looked up when Eliza came in.

"Serenity has mastitis," Eliza said, and pulled the journal from its shelf. She found the page, read the recipe through, and began assembling what she needed. Comfrey leaves from the dried bundles hanging above the hearth. Honey from the stoneware pot. Cider vinegar from the bottle in the pantry. Clean muslin for the poultice. She laid them out on the table, the proportions clear in her mind.

She was measuring vinegar into a cup when Llewellyn appeared in the doorway. His hair looked dusty and his sleeves were rolled past his elbows, and Pompey padded in behind him and went directly to the hearthrug, where Caesar was already installed and disinclined to share. The two mastiffs conducted a brief negotiation involving noses and a single indignant huff before arriving at an arrangement that satisfied neither entirely but gave both enough space to lie down.

Llewellyn looked at the ingredients on the table and then at the open journal. "Mastitis?" he said.

"Serenity. Caught early, I hope." She poured the vinegar and reached for the honey. "This is Molly's recipe. Comfrey poultice with honey and vinegar, applied warm, changed three times a day."

He came to the table. Not to take over, but with the unhurried curiosity of a man who recognised the work and wanted to understand the method. He leaned forward and read the journal entry, his head tilted slightly, the way she had learned meant he was concentrating.

"What proportions?" he asked.

"Two parts comfrey to one part honey, vinegar enough to make a paste. The comfrey draws the swelling, the honey keeps the skin from cracking, the vinegar fights the infection." She was grinding the dried comfrey with the pestle as she spoke, the leaves crumbling into fragments that released a green, earthy smell.

"My Da used something similar on the ewes," Llewellyn said. He spoke in the considered way he always did when offering knowledge rather than opinion. "Same base. But he added salt to the vinegar. Said it drew the heat faster."

Eliza paused. She looked at him. "Salt."

"Only a little. Too much and it dries the skin and makes the cracking worse. But just enough and the inflammation comes down quicker." He met her gaze. "I've seen it work on udders the size of my fist. I'd imagine a mare's would respond the same way."

Eliza considered. The logic was sound. Drawing agents reduced swelling; salt was a drawing agent. The risk was cracking, but if the proportion was controlled and the honey was there to counteract it, the combination might work better than either alone. She picked up the salt cellar.

"How much, do you think?"

He picked up the spoon and measured a small amount into her palm, considered it, and pushed a few grains back into the pot. The pad of his finger was rough and warm against her skin, and the contact lasted no longer than a breath, and neither of them acknowledged it.

At the far counter, Helen said, "I need to fetch more sage from the garden. Louise can help me."

She left through the scullery door. Her footsteps crossed the flagstones, unhurried. Eliza heard her call for Louise, and then the back door opened and closed.

Eliza mixed the poultice. She worked the comfrey and honey and salted vinegar together, and the paste came together thick and green-brown, smelling sharply of vinegar and sweetly of honey and beneath both the clean scent of comfrey. Llewellyn watched, and when the consistency was right he nodded once.

"Write it down," she said. She pushed the journal toward him and handed him the pencil. "Your Da's variation. Beneath Molly's."

He took the pencil in his left hand and wrote in his neat, angular script beneath Molly's cramped lines. *Salt variation. One quarter teaspoon. D. Llewellyn per Thos. Llewellyn.* The letters were smaller than Molly's, more controlled, the handwriting of someone who had written reports and orders and letters home from places where paper was scarce and words were chosen carefully.

Eliza took the pencil back and added beneath his entry: *Applied to Serenity, May 1815. E. Bell.* Her writing was rounder than his, the letters spaced wider, and together on the page the two hands looked like a conversation, each one answering the other, the knowledge of a Welsh hill farm and a Hampshire breeding estate meeting in the margins of a kitchen journal.

The book lay open between them. Their hands rested on the table, his left and her right, and the distance between them was the width of a pencil, and the kitchen was still.

Not the working stillness of two people absorbed in a task. Something different. The poultice cooled in the bowl. The afternoon light fell through the kitchen window and caught the dust motes drifting above the table and turned them gold. From the yard came the faint sound of Phillip sweeping cobblestones, and from the garden, distant enough to be decoration rather than intrusion, Helen's voice saying something to Louise about the sage.

She became conscious of her own breathing. Steady, or nearly so, but the rhythm of it had shifted into something she could hear, the way you could hear your own pulse in a quiet room if you listened for it. Her skin prickled along her forearms, a sensation she associated with the charged air before a summer storm, when the horses grew restless and the sky took on a colour that had no name.

He moved.

Not his hand. His whole body, a small forward shift of weight that brought his shoulder closer and angled his face toward hers. Slow. Deliberate. The movement of a man who was giving her time, every fraction of a second she might need to pull back or turn away or say the word that would stop this before it started.

Eliza did not pull back. She did not turn away.

She was aware of the choice. It sat in her body with absolute clarity, the way a fork in a path sat in the landscape, each direction visible. She could lean away. She could stand, pick up the bowl, carry the poultice to the barn, and the moment would pass, and they would go on as they had been, colleagues and allies and whatever the word was for two people who shared silences and saved foals and wrote their names side by side in kitchen journals. She could do that. It would be safe. It would be sensible. It would be the choice made by the part of her that feared being left, the part that had built its walls from competence and distance and the discipline of never needing anything she could not provide for herself.

She did not move.

The not-moving was the bravest thing she had ever done. Braver than the nights alone in the barn. Braver than facing Thornton's scepticism or the requisition officers' indifference. Braver than running an estate at eighteen while her father was somewhere in Belgium and the letters had stopped coming. She stayed where she was, her hand on the table beside his, and the distance between them closed.

His lips touched hers.

It was not what she had imagined. She had imagined it, she could admit that now, in the private hours before sleep when her mind ran free of the bridle she kept on it during the day. She had imagined something decisive, something that would arrive with the force of certainty and sweep the questions away. What she got instead was this: a quiet pressure, warm and dry, the lightest contact of his lips against hers, lasting no longer than three heartbeats. She felt the roughness of his lower lip and the warmth of his breath and the faint tremor that ran through him, telling her his composure was costing him as much as hers was costing her.

Three heartbeats. She counted them by the pulse in her throat. One. Two. Three.

He drew back. Not far. An inch, perhaps two. Close enough that she could see the variations of grey and blue in his eyes, close enough to feel the warmth of his skin, close enough that if either of them breathed too deeply their mouths would meet again. His eyes searched hers, and what she read in them was a question that had nothing to do with words.

She did not answer. She did not need to. The answer was in the fact that she had not moved, and they both knew it.

Footsteps on flagstone.

The sound came from the scullery, clear and unhurried, the measured pace of a woman who was not rushing and was not creeping but was walking at the speed required to cross a scullery and open a door. Helen's pace. Helen's particular gift for timing.

They stepped apart. The movement was simultaneous and swift. Eliza moved her weight back. Llewellyn leaned away, his hand finding the edge of the journal. They were both looking at the book when Helen came through the door with a basket of herbs on her arm.

Helen set the basket on the counter. She glanced at the table, at the journal, at the two of them with a careful foot of space between them and their faces arranged in expressions of scholarly concentration that would not have convinced a child, let alone a woman who had spent her life getting honest answers before people decided to give them.

She said nothing.

She turned to the herbs and began sorting them, and the ordinary sounds of the kitchen resumed: the rustle of leaves, the creak of the dresser drawer. Normal sounds. Kitchen sounds. The sounds of a world continuing whether you were ready for it or not.

Eliza stood. She picked up the bowl and put the journal back on its shelf. She did not look at Llewellyn. If she looked at him, the composure she was holding together with her fingernails would come apart, and she was not ready for whatever came after that.

"I should see to Serenity," she said. Her voice sounded almost normal.

"Of course," Helen said, from the counter, her back turned, her hands busy with sage.

Eliza walked to the door. She walked through it. She walked across the kitchen garden and through the gate and into the yard, where the late-afternoon sun was warm on her face and the cobblestones solid beneath her boots, and every one of these things was the same as it had been an hour ago and none of them were the same at all.

She carried the poultice to the broodmare barn. She knelt beside Serenity and applied it with steady hands, smoothing the warm paste over the swollen teat, and the mare stood patient and still, and the work was good, and the work was what she knew. Her lips tingled with the memory of a pressure so slight it might have been imagined except that it had changed the shape of everything, as a single degree of warmth changed ice to water, the same substance rearranged into something entirely new.

She finished the poultice and went back to the kitchen and washed her hands and wrote the time of application in the journal beneath their names, and her handwriting was steady, and the feeling that sat beneath her breastbone, warm and terrifying and wholly unfamiliar, did not need words.

Nothing had been said. Everything was different.

Chapter Thirteen

THE HOOVES ON THE lane had a particular sound when they belonged to army horses. Shod for hard roads rather than soft turf, the rhythm carrying the regularity of animals trained to move in formation. Eliza heard them from the yard, where she had been checking the feed store with Thornton, and the sound reached her much as a change in the weather reached the horses: not as information but as a shift in pressure, a tightening of the air.

She set down the ledger. Thornton's eyes met hers, and in them she read the same weary recognition. Another requisition party. They had come three times already this spring, each visit stripping the stables further, taking the fit and the sound and the young, leaving behind what the army did not want: the old, the lame, the pregnant, the blind. Each time Eliza had stood in the yard and negotiated, and each time she had given what she must and kept what she could and told herself the arithmetic still worked.

She straightened her skirts, pushed a loose braid behind her ear, and walked to the front of the yard.

The party was small. Four mounted men, led by an officer whose posture communicated everything his mouth had not yet troubled itself to say. He rode a tall chestnut with a hard mouth and harder eyes, and the man himself was cut from similar cloth: lean, sharp-featured, his uniform immaculate in the way that suggested a batman who ironed with religious fervour. A major's insignia. She noted it the way she noted a horse's conformation, automatically, filing the detail where it would be useful.

He dismounted with the brisk economy of a man who expected someone to take his reins. No one did. His eyes swept the yard, passing over Thornton, passing over Phillip at the water pump, and landing on Eliza.

She watched the assessment happen. It took less than a second and lasted longer than a minute, a single glance that began at her face and ended at her boots and carried the full weight of a conclusion already reached. His gaze touched her skin, her braids, the working dress she wore, and she saw him sort these facts into the order that suited his understanding of the world and arrive at an answer that had nothing to do with her competence and everything to do with the colour God had made her.

He looked past her. His eyes moved to the yard, to the buildings, searching for someone else.

"I require the master of this establishment," he said. He addressed the air above Eliza's left shoulder.

"I am the manager of Belle Haven in Sir Richard Bell's absence," Eliza said. Her voice was level. The levelness cost her something, a coin paid from the reserve she kept for moments when the world insisted she prove what should not need proving. "My name is Miss Bell. How may I help you, Major?"

His mouth thinned. He produced a folded warrant from his coat and held it out, not to her but in her general direction, the gesture of a man handing a document to a servant. She took it, read it, and folded it back along its creases.

"We have no horses fit for army service," she said. "Belle Haven has already provided eighty horses to the requisition this spring. What remains are broodmares in foal or nursing, young stock too immature to ride, and one stallion unfit for service. I can show you the records."

He did not want records. He wanted horses, and his gaze had already found them. Over her shoulder, the near paddock stretched green and lush under the May sun, and in it the dun mare grazed with King Arthur at her side. The colt was five weeks old now, all legs and exuberance, and as they watched he launched himself into a canter that covered the width of the paddock in two dozen ungainly strides before wheeling back to his dam with the triumphant air of a creature who had just invented speed.

"That mare," the major said, and pointed.

Eliza's stomach dropped. She had known this was coming since she heard the hooves on the lane.

"That mare is nursing," she said. "Her colt is five weeks old. He cannot be weaned for months. If you take her, he will die."

The major looked at her. The look said: *And?*

"The army requires horses, Miss Bell." He used her name like a tool he doubted the purpose of. "That mare appears fit. The foal is not my concern."

"The foal should be your concern, Major, because Belle Haven has already given every sound horse we have to give, and we will give more for years to come... in three or four years, that colt will go to Sandhurst and be an officer's mount. But not if you take his dam today." She let that hold for a beat, and then added the final blow. "The army's regulations prohibit the requisition of nursing dams." She was sure of her ground, and anger suffused his face as he realised she knew very well that he did not have the authority to take the mare.

From the stallion barn, seventy yards across the cobblestones, Hermes called.

The sound split the morning. A full-throated stallion's cry, deep-chested and resonant, the call of a mature horse who had caught a scent on the warm air and was answering it with everything his body possessed. It rolled across the yard and rang off the stone buildings and carried the unmistakable declaration of a horse who was neither old nor lame.

The major's head turned. His eyes narrowed, and the calculation behind them was visible.

"What horse is that?"

"The stallion I mentioned. He is not fit for service."

"That does not sound like an unfit horse, Miss Bell." The contempt in his voice had sharpened. He stepped toward her, closing the distance, and his height put his face above hers and his shadow across her, and the positioning was deliberate, a man using the geometry of his body to remind her where the power lay. "It sounds very much like a stallion you would prefer I did not see."

"You are welcome to see him," Eliza said, and her heart was hammering but her voice was steady, steady as the stone beneath her feet. "Follow me, and I will take you to him now."

She turned and walked toward the stallion barn, and did not look back to see if he followed her, because looking back would be a concession, and she would give none to this man who treated her with such contempt.

The stallion barn was cooler than the yard, the thick stone walls holding the night's chill, and the shift from sunshine to shadow made Eliza blink as she passed through the door. Behind her, the major's boots rang on the cobblestones.

Hermes stood in the far stall. He had heard them coming, his head up, his ears forward, his nostrils working the air. The young colts in the nearer stalls shifted and blew, unsettled by the stranger's scent and stride, but Hermes stood still, his scarred head turned toward the footsteps with the careful attention of a horse who mapped the world by sound and smell and memory.

Eliza unlatched the stall door and swung it wide.

"This is the stallion you heard, Major."

The light from the high window fell across Hermes's face. It caught the clouded eyes first, the milky opacity that had replaced the dark intelligence of a warhorse who had once carried a man through smoke and gunfire. Then the scarring. Livid against his silvery coat, the puckered lines radiating from his eye sockets, the rough patches where the skin had healed wrong, the places where the hair grew in different directions or did not grow at all. The cannon blast that had taken his sight had left its signature across his face like a letter even an illiterate could read.

The major stopped walking.

Eliza watched him look. She watched his eyes move from the ruined face to the powerful neck to the deep chest that had produced a call strong enough to carry across the yard. She saw the moment the arithmetic resolved, because his jaw tightened and the tendons in his neck drew taut.

"He is blind," she said. "Both eyes, from a cannon blast he took serving with the 16th Light Dragoons. He cannot see so much as a hand in front of his face." She let the silence do its work. "How useful do you imagine he will be on a battlefield?"

His face changed. The contempt in his eyes did not diminish. It concentrated.

"You have wasted my time," he said. His voice was very quiet, the kind of quiet that sat closer to violence than shouting did. "You have stood in that yard and told me you had nothing, and you have brought me in here to see a broken horse, and I believe you think yourself very clever."

"I think myself accurate, Major!" *He* had no right to be angry. He was the one who had tried to demand a horse he had no right to take, and then all but accused her of lying. Outrage rose, and a note of it must have entered her voice.

His hand came up.

It rose in a sharp, abrupt motion, the movement of a man who was not thinking but acting, his palm open, his arm drawn back, and the trajectory was as clear as a line drawn on a map. Eliza saw it coming the way she saw a horse about to kick, a reading of muscle and intention that happened faster than thought.

She did not flinch. Her body wanted to. Every instinct said *move*, said *duck*, said *make yourself small*, but this was not a horse who could kill with a kick to the head, it was a petty man who would learn the consequences of striking Sir Richard Bell's daughter if he was stupid enough to do such a thing, and so she stood with her chin level and her eyes on his and waited for whatever came next.

What came next was Caesar.

The growl began in a register below hearing, a vibration Eliza felt through the soles of her boots before it rose into audibility. Low, sustained, continuous, the noise of a hundred and sixty pounds of mastiff drawing a line on the ground and daring the world to cross it. Caesar stood in the barn doorway, his massive brindled head lowered to the level of his shoulders, his eyes fixed on the major with unwavering focus. His lips were drawn back from his teeth. The teeth were considerable.

Eliza had not called him. She had not heard him come. He was simply there, his vast body filling the doorway, blocking the light.

The major's hand hung in the air. His eyes moved from Eliza to the dog. The growl did not stop. It held its note, steady and absolute.

Behind the major, the grizzled sergeant cleared his throat.

A small sound. A polite sound. The sound a career soldier made when his officer was about to commit an error that would generate paperwork neither of them wanted to complete. The sergeant stood with his hands behind his back and his face arranged in studied neutrality, but his eyes flicked from the dog to the officer and back, and the message was as clear as Caesar's growl, delivered in a different key.

"Sir," the sergeant said. "I believe we've seen enough."

The major's hand lowered. It descended slowly, his fingers closing into a fist at his side. He looked at Eliza, and the look contained everything his hand had meant to deliver.

She met his gaze. She held it. Her heart was striking against her ribs with a force that surely must be visible, but her face was stone, and she gave him nothing. Not the satisfaction of her fear. Not the flinch he had expected.

He turned on his heel and walked out of the barn. His men followed, the grizzled sergeant casting one quick glance back at Eliza that might almost have been an apology. Caesar did not move from the doorway until the last of them had passed, and then he turned his massive head toward Eliza and regarded her with an expression that, on a creature with less dignity, might have been described as satisfaction.

The hooves receded down the lane, and were gone, leaving the barn in a silence that rang with the memory of what had almost happened.

Eliza stood beside Hermes. Her hands were shaking. She pressed them flat against her thighs and held them there until the tremor retreated to a place where she could carry it without it being seen. The stallion turned his head and breathed against her shoulder, the warm, hay-sweet exhalation of a horse offering what comfort his blindness permitted, and she raised one unsteady hand and laid it against his neck, and stood there with the dog in the doorway and the horse beneath her palm and the fear still running through her like a river under ice.

The yard had the quality of a room after an argument. Nothing displaced, nothing broken, but the air carried a residue of disturbance. Llewellyn noticed it before he noticed anything else, the way he had once noticed the silence that meant a French patrol had recently passed through a village. Thornton stood by the tack room door with his arms folded and his jaw set at an angle that suggested he was restraining himself from extensive commentary through sheer will.

Llewellyn had been in a far paddock, fixing a fence some enthusiastic yearlings had broken through. The work had taken him out of earshot, and he had returned to find the absence of something rather than its presence.

Phillip appeared at his elbow, pale, his freckles standing out like ink spots on paper.

"There was a patrol, sir," Phillip said, the words tumbling. "Requisition. A major, with four men. He wanted the dun mare, the one with King Arthur. Miss Eliza told him no. She told him about the foal and the breeding and all of it, and he didn't care, not a bit. He looked at her like she was..." The boy stopped. His throat worked. "He looked at her *bad*, sir."

"Go on," Llewellyn said. His voice was steady. Beneath it, something had gone very cold.

"Hermes called. The major heard him and said Miss Eliza was hiding horses. She took him to the stallion barn to see." Phillip's eyes were wide. "I was in the hayloft, sir. I could see through the gap in the boards. He raised his hand to her."

"He *struck* her?" Llewellyn said, and did not recognise his own voice.

"No, sir! Because Caesar was there," Phillip said, and the relief in the boy's voice was enormous. "He growled, sir. Properly growled, terrifying! And the sergeant said something, and the major put his hand down, and they left." He swallowed. "They didn't take anything."

Llewellyn nodded. He placed his hand on Phillip's shoulder, briefly, the gesture of acknowledgement he had used with young soldiers who had held their nerve under fire, and the boy straightened beneath it.

"You did well to watch," Llewellyn said. "Where is Miss Eliza now?"

"Stallion barn, sir. She hasn't come out."

He crossed the yard. Pompey fell into step beside him, but when they reached the barn door, Pompey stopped. Caesar lay across the threshold, his enormous body arranged with the deliberate placement of a creature who understood barricades. The dog's eyes were open, his gaze moving between Llewellyn and the yard with the watchful attitude of a sentinel who had not stood down.

Llewellyn stepped over him. Caesar permitted it, which was, in the language of mastiffs, a considerable compliment.

The stallion barn was dim and quiet, the colts out in the pasture. Hermes stood in his stall with his head low, and Eliza stood beside him, her hand moving a brush along his neck in long, steady strokes. The rhythm was unhurried. Her braids were neat. Her dress was clean. Her posture was straight. She looked, to a casual observer, like a woman grooming a horse on an ordinary afternoon.

She was not fooling him. The tightness at the corners of her mouth was there if you knew to look for it.

She looked up when she heard his step, and a shift in her face eased a fraction. She must have seen in his face that he already knew.

"I handled it," she said. Her voice was calm, composed. She returned her attention to Hermes's neck.

"I know," Llewellyn said. He leaned against the stall partition, taking the weight off his leg. "I was only thinking it might be best not to let the mastiffs eat impudent officers. However justified."

The silence held for a beat. Two. He watched the words arrive, watched the corner of her mouth twitch against the tightness that held it, a small struggle between the residue of fear and the thing he had offered in its place.

She laughed.

Not the small, startled sound from the night Arthur was born. A real laugh, full-throated and unguarded, pulled up from somewhere deep in her chest and arriving at her mouth before she could inspect it. Her hand stilled on Hermes's neck. Her shoulders dropped. Her head tipped forward, and the laugh continued, carrying the tension of the past hour and the relief that followed and something else that was simply, purely, joy.

The sound lodged behind his breastbone and stayed. He watched her face as the laughter transformed it, the composure breaking apart, revealing the warmth beneath. Her eyes creased. Her teeth showed white and bright against the darkness of her skin.

He thought: *I would do quite a lot to cause that sound again.*

The distance between them was four feet of straw. He could close it in two steps. He could raise his hand and touch the curl that had escaped her braid at the temple, the same one that always escaped, as though it had ideas about where it wanted to be that had nothing to do with the pins that held it.

Footsteps. Fast ones, lighter than a groom's, quicker than Helen's. The sound of a girl running.

Charlotte entered the barn with a leap over Caesar's hindquarters, a feat she accomplished with the athletic disregard of a fourteen-year-old who had grown up in stable yards. Her fair hair was coming loose, her cheeks flushed, and her eyes held bright alarm.

"Phillip said there was a requisition party," Charlotte said, breathless. "He said there was a major. He said he wanted the dun mare." Her gaze swung between them, reading the scene as swiftly as she read a pedigree. "Did we lose anyone? Tell me we didn't lose anyone."

The moment dissolved. It did not shatter; it changed state, the private warmth dispersing into the wider air of a place that contained other people and other needs. Eliza's composure reassembled itself. She straightened, turned to Charlotte, and her voice was the manager's voice, steady and sure.

"We lost nothing," Eliza said. "Not a single horse. He left empty-handed."

Charlotte's breath came out in a rush. She pressed her hand against her chest, a gesture more dramatic than strictly necessary but entirely genuine. "Thank God."

"Thank your sister," Llewellyn said quietly.

Charlotte looked at Eliza. The look held something older than a fourteen-year-old's relief, something that understood what had been defended and perhaps something of what it had cost, and she crossed the barn and put her arms around Eliza and held on, her blonde head against her sister's dark one. Eliza's hand came up and rested on Charlotte's back.

Llewellyn pushed himself off the partition and left the barn, stepping over Caesar again, giving the sisters the moment. But the laugh was still there, lodged behind his breastbone, warm and persistent. Charlotte's interruption could not take it back. Nothing could. It was his now, and he carried it with him into the afternoon, where the sun was warm and the yard was quiet and the horses were safe for another day.

Chapter Fourteen

THE SOUND REACHED HIM first: a high, percussive squealing that carried none of the conversational quality horses used with each other and all of the raw note that meant pain. Llewellyn dropped what he was carrying and was moving before his mind had finished sorting the information, his body responding to the sound with the same autonomy that had once carried him toward gunfire, the legs obeying while the brain caught up.

He found the yearling at the far corner of the lower paddock, where the hawthorn hedge had grown thick and wild against the boundary fence. The colt had gone through it, or tried to. His hindquarters were still tangled in the briars, the thorned branches wrapped around his hocks and stifles like barbed fingers, and every time the youngster lurched forward the thorns bit deeper and the panic doubled. Blood ran freely down the left haunch, vivid against the colt's golden dun coat, pouring from a gash that began at the hip and curved toward the stifle in a ragged line that glistened in the afternoon light. Horses bled like the dying when they were barely hurt. This one was more than barely hurt, but the volume made it look worse than it was, or so Llewellyn told himself as he approached.

The colt saw him and threw his head up, whites showing, the whole trembling frame cocked to bolt. Llewellyn stopped. He held his hands low and open and spoke, not in English, because the words he reached for in moments of instinct were always Welsh, the ones his father had used in the lambing sheds, the ones that lived in his mouth below language: *there, now, easy, you're all right, you're all right.*

The colt's ears flickered. The trembling did not stop, but the explosive tension in the hindquarters eased a fraction, enough for Llewellyn to close the distance. He placed his left hand on the colt's neck, above the sweat-darkened shoulder, and felt the muscles jumping beneath the hide. He braced his weight against the colt's chest.

Not fighting. He had learned this from his father and from the cavalry and from every frightened creature he had ever held: you did not match your strength against theirs, because you would lose, and the losing would teach them that strength was what mattered. You held. You became the thing that did not move, the solid centre around which the panic swirled and eventually subsided. The colt threw his head. Llewellyn's right arm screamed along the scar line, and he gave it nothing. The colt surged forward and Llewellyn set his feet and leaned into the weight and held, and the holding said the same thing his voice said: *you're all right, I have you, be still.*

He could not free the briars and hold the colt at the same time. He needed another pair of hands, and was calculating how to call for help without releasing his grip when Laura appeared at the fence.

He did not know how she had found them. She carried no stick, had no dog beside her, and the paddock was a hundred yards from the nearest barn. But she came through the rails with the quiet certainty of a girl who knew where every post and beam and stone on this estate sat in relation to her body, and she walked toward the sound of the colt's distress with a headcollar in her hands.

She found the yearling's head. She eased on the headcollar and handed Llewellyn the rope, and then she cupped both hands around the colt's muzzle. The colt flinched. Laura did not remove her hands. She began to hum.

It was not a tune Llewellyn recognised. It had no melody he could have repeated. It was a sound more than a song, low and continuous, vibrating in her chest and her throat, and it moved through her hands into the horse's skull the way warmth moved through stone.

The yearling's head dropped. Not gradually. It descended as though a rope holding it aloft had been cut, the muzzle sinking until it rested in Laura's palms, and the trembling simply stopped. The muscles beneath his hand went slack. The white-rimmed eyes softened and half-closed. The colt stood in the briars, bleeding and tangled and perfectly, impossibly still, as though Laura's hands and her humming had reached into the place where panic lived and turned it off.

Llewellyn stared. He had seen laudanum produce a slower result on men with injuries that required stitching.

Eliza came around the hedge at a run, a leather satchel under her arm. She took in the scene with a single sweep: the tangled briars, the gash, the blood, Laura holding the colt's head, the humming. She went to her knees in the grass and opened the satchel and began pulling out what she needed. She clipped the worst of the briars free with a small pair of shears, clearing the thorned branches from the wound's edges. She sluiced the gash with a sharp-smelling liquid from a bottle in the satchel, and the colt did not flinch. He stood as if carved from marble, Laura's humming the only sound in the still afternoon.

Then the needle. Eliza threaded it with a deftness that spoke of long practice and began to stitch. The stitches were tiny, extraordinary, each one placed with the care of a woman who understood that the distance between a neat scar and none at all was measured in fractions of an inch. Her fingers moved steadily along the length of the gash, drawing the edges together, and the silk thread followed, and the wound closed behind her hands like a seam in a well-tailored garment.

Llewellyn watched her work and held the colt and felt the strange, suspended peace of the moment. The blood had slowed to a seep. Laura hummed. The afternoon sun lay warm across all of them, and the hawthorn that had caused the trouble was in full, obscene bloom above, the scent rising from the white flowers sweet enough to taste.

Eliza tied the last stitch, snipped the thread, and sat back on her heels. She wiped her hands on the linen and looked at her work with the critical eye of a craftsman inspecting a finished piece.

Llewellyn released the halter carefully and moved to examine the wound. The stitches ran in a clean, even line along the curve of the haunch, the edges of the skin meeting so precisely that the gash already looked like something that belonged to the past rather than the present. He had never seen such work, not even in the field hospitals. The army's surgeons would have looked on it with awe.

"There won't even be a scar, I think," he said.

Eliza stood, brushing grass from her knees. "There had better not be. Pa didn't geld him for a reason." She glanced at the yearling, who was now attempting to lip at Laura's sleeve with the serene entitlement of a horse who had entirely forgotten his recent terror. "Pity it isn't his brain."

She was laughing. The sound arrived as it had in the stallion barn, full and unguarded, and his heart felt as though it had grown too large for the space allotted to it, pressing against his ribs, crowding the air from his lungs. He stood there with the blood drying on his sleeves and the laughter filling the paddock and the knowledge that he was in very serious trouble settling over him with a gentle, implacable weight.

Laura lifted her hands from the colt's muzzle and unbuckled the headcollar. The humming stopped. The yearling blinked, shook his head once, and walked away from the hedge with the casual air of an animal who had decided the whole affair was beneath his notice. Laura turned her sightless eyes toward Llewellyn, and on her face was an odd little smile, the smile of a girl who spoke rarely and saw everything despite seeing nothing.

She knew, he thought. *She knew before I did.*

Breakfast at Belle Haven had become a theatre she had not bought tickets to.

Eliza sat in her usual chair with her usual tea and watched the performance unfold with the growing suspicion that she was not in the audience at all. She was on the stage, and everyone else knew the script.

Louise passed the toast to Llewellyn with both hands, as though the rack were made of crystal rather than tin. Charlotte asked him whether Hermes had slept well, a question she had never once directed at any other horse on the estate, and listened to his answer with the attention she usually reserved for the bloodlines of new stock. Laura said nothing, but her silence had a warmth and patience to it, the silence of a girl waiting for someone else to arrive at a conclusion she had reached some time ago.

Helen poured tea. She filled Eliza's cup and then Llewellyn's, and as she set the pot down, her eyes met Eliza's, and the expression on her face was one Eliza decided, firmly and immediately, not to examine. It contained too many things. Warmth, and knowledge, and a tenderness that had nothing to do with tea and everything to do with something Helen had understood long before Eliza had understood it herself.

She drank. The tea was hot and strong and exactly as it always was, and it tasted different, because she was different, because three days ago in the kitchen this man had kissed her and the world had rearranged itself around that fact with the quiet, irreversible certainty of a season turning.

She had not spoken of it. Neither had he. They had continued in their routines, and the work was the same and the words were the same and nothing was the same at all. She was aware of him in a way she could no longer pretend she had not been before. The awareness sat in her body like a low note struck on a string, constant, vibrating just below the threshold of what she could ignore. When his hand brushed the stall door she remembered the feel of that hand in hers. When he spoke she felt the words arrive not in her ears but somewhere lower, behind the ribs, in the place where the kiss still lived.

Three heartbeats. She had counted them by the pulse in her own throat, and the counting had been the act of a woman who needed numbers because numbers were safe, and the kiss was not safe, the kiss was a door she had walked through and could not walk back from because on the other side everything looked different.

She set down her teacup and assembled the evidence.

Louise had been mentioning Llewellyn's name at every opportunity for weeks. Charlotte had been watching Eliza with bright, assessing eyes. Laura had smiled in the paddock yesterday, that knowing little smile directed at nothing visible and everything present. Helen had laughed in the kitchen and said *love arrives from the direction you are least expecting, and by the time you notice it, everyone around you has already been carrying an umbrella for weeks.*

Helen had also said: *Louise does not have a tendre for the Lieutenant.*

Eliza had believed, at the time, that this left the matter unresolved. Louise's behaviour required explanation, and Eliza had looked for it in the wrong place, because looking in the right place would have meant looking at herself.

She pressed her fingers against the bridge of her nose. Across the table, Llewellyn was answering Charlotte's questions about Hermes with the same unhurried steadiness he brought to everything, and his voice moved through her chest like a hand drawn across strings.

She was the one. She was the one with the feelings, the whatever-it-was that had made Louise giggle and Charlotte scheme and Laura smile. And everyone else had apparently noticed before she had troubled herself to look.

The fear rose, as it always did, from the deep, old place where she kept it. The foundling's fear. If you cared for someone, they could leave. She had learned early not to give her whole heart to particular horses at Belle Haven, because the army was rapacious and horses were a business, and they didn't live as long as humans. Anyone who grows up on a farm learns not to give their entire heart to any animal. But Eliza had also learned that people left too. Her birth parents had left her on a church doorstep at six months old. Her father was somewhere in Belgium and had stopped writing; Molly and Clara and Anna had married and gone and were making lives far from Belle Haven. Even Theresa, the only mother she could remember, had gone, because Molly needed her more. Every good thing she had ever held had come with the understanding, pressed into her bones before she was old enough to have words for it, that it might be taken away.

She looked at Llewellyn. He was listening to Charlotte with his head tilted, and his right hand rested on the table, and the scars along his wrist caught the morning light, and she thought of those hands wrapped around a dying foal, squeezing life into it, refusing to stop.

He had not left. He had arrived at Belle Haven with a blind horse and a damaged body and no claim on anything, and he had looked at their need and stayed. He had stayed through the foaling and the losses and the long watches. He had stayed when there was nothing to keep him but the work and the horse and the woman who had not yet understood what everyone else could see.

She rose from the table and went to the broodmare barn, where the horses at least had the decency not to look at her as if they knew a secret she had only just discovered.

Helen watched Eliza cross the yard through the kitchen window and noted, with the skill of a woman who had spent her life reading the weather of other people's hearts, that something had changed. It was not in the walk, which was Eliza's usual brisk stride. It was in the set of her shoulders. They were not squared. They were not braced. They carried their load differently today, as though the load had shifted into a new position that was unfamiliar but not unwelcome.

Helen dried her hands on the cloth and folded it neatly. She poured herself a half cup of tea, drank it standing, and set the cup in the basin.

She had been watching since before the kiss, which she was not supposed to know about and which she knew about with the absolute certainty of a woman who had walked into the kitchen and found two people a careful foot apart with their faces arranged in expressions that would not have fooled a particularly dim sheep. She had said nothing, because nothing needed saying. Eliza was sensible. The lieutenant was honourable. Whatever was growing between them had the quality of good timber: slow, dense, strong. It would bear weight in time. It did not need her hand on it.

But the girls. The girls were another matter.

Helen had allowed the matchmaking to run for two weeks, partly because the impulse was generous and she did not wish to punish generosity, and partly because, in its early stages, the conspiracy had been so transparently inept that it posed no real threat. Louise's rearranged watch schedules and Charlotte's pointed questions and the elaborate excuses had all the subtlety of a brass band performing in a library. Eliza had been too preoccupied to notice. Llewellyn had noticed, Helen was certain, because soldiers noticed things, but he had said nothing, which told her everything she needed to know about his character and his feelings.

The difficulty now was that Eliza had noticed. Not the matchmaking specifically, but herself. Helen had seen it at breakfast, the moment recognition crossed Eliza's face. Eliza had looked at Llewellyn and looked away and pressed her fingers to the bridge of her nose, and Helen had read in that gesture the discomfort of a woman who had just discovered that the whole world could see a thing she had believed was private.

This was the dangerous moment. Dangerous the way frost was dangerous to a seedling: the new growth most vulnerable when it was newest. Eliza's defences were considerable, well-practised, and built to protect against exactly this, the terror of wanting something that could be taken away. If the girls pushed now, Eliza would retreat behind those defences, and the retreat would be swift and total and very difficult to reverse.

Helen could not allow that.

She found them in the corridor outside the study, which was predictable because the corridor outside the study was where all conspiracies at Belle Haven were conducted, being conveniently adjacent to the front hall and the back stairs and offering sight lines in three directions. Louise was talking rapidly in a whisper that could have been heard in the next county. Charlotte leaned against the doorframe with a pencil behind her ear and her arms folded. Laura stood slightly apart, her hand on Caesar's head.

"Girls," Helen said.

Three heads turned. Louise's whisper died mid-syllable. Charlotte straightened. The faintest colour rose in Laura's cheeks, which was as close to a confession as Laura ever came.

"Come with me, please."

She led them to the morning room and closed the door. She did not sit. The girls arranged themselves on the settee, shoulder to shoulder to shoulder, a row of faces that ran the full spectrum from defiance to contrition.

Helen looked at them. She let the silence do its work, the way she had learned from her husband, who was an expert at letting the pause between sentences carry as much meaning as the words themselves. Mr Fallon's sermons were not the kind anyone slept through.

"This is not yours to manage," she said.

Louise opened her mouth. Helen raised one finger, and the mouth closed.

"What is happening between Eliza and the lieutenant is theirs. It is private, and it is fragile, and it is not a project. If something is going to happen, it will happen without your assistance. And if it does not, it will be because that is what they have chosen, and their choice deserves your respect."

Charlotte moved on the settee. Her blue eyes held the brightness of a girl composing her rebuttal with care.

"But we only thought..."

"I know exactly what you thought," Helen said. "That is why we are having this conversation."

Charlotte closed her mouth. Helen could see the objections assembling behind her eyes, the logic that said if two bloodlines complemented each other one ought to facilitate the cross. But Charlotte was also a girl who had spent her life watching horses, and she knew, if she allowed herself to know it, that a mare pushed toward a stallion before she was ready would kick first and think later.

"Eliza is finding her courage," Helen said, and she lowered her voice, because what she said next was not a reprimand but a confidence. "She is doing something very brave, and she will do it in her own time, and the best thing you can do for her is stand back and let her."

Louise's expression was mutinous. Her dark eyes burned with a girl's frustration, one who had identified a problem and been told she was not permitted to solve it. Her lips pressed together. Her hands balled in her lap.

Helen thought, not for the first time, of Louise's real father, because Louise had certainly not inherited her temperament from her mother, nor from her kindly stepfather. No, Louise's innate belief that what she thought, what she wanted, was the only right way to do things had come from the man who had looked at twenty-year-old Helen and decided he was not going to take no for an answer. Helen held her daughter's eyes until Louise finally looked down, submitting with very ill grace.

Laura sat with her head bowed. The flush had deepened. Of the three, Helen thought Laura had the least to answer for, having interfered only minimally, and yet here she was on the settee, drawn into the conspiracy despite her own wisdom, and the sheepishness on her face was the kind that came from knowing you should not have got involved but choosing to anyway because your friends were doing it and it seemed like fun.

Helen let the silence extend. Then: "You may go."

They went. Louise first, her back very straight, her steps crisp with suppressed indignation. Charlotte second, the pencil still behind her ear, her expression thoughtful in the way that meant she was revising a theory rather than abandoning it. Laura last, with Caesar padding beside her, and at the door she paused and turned her head back toward Helen.

"She'll be all right?" Laura said, tentative in a way she rarely was where other people's feelings were concerned. But Laura had not watched any of her sisters fall in love, though three of them were now married; this was a new experience for her and perhaps that was making her uncertain.

Helen smiled, though Laura could not see it. "Yes," she said. "I believe she will."

The door closed. Helen stood alone in the morning room, the sunlight falling across the writing desk in a warm square. She pressed her hand against the back of the chair and thought of Mr. Fallon, who had arrived in her life from a direction she had not been watching. Scared, pregnant, alone, she had come to Belle Haven because she had nowhere else to go, and a quiet, Godly man with kind eyes and red hair had looked at her and seen not a ruined woman but a woman worth loving, and he had loved her with a steadiness that had never once wavered in fifteen years, and extended that love to her daughter, the girl with her father's wilfulness.

Love arrived sideways. It came when you were looking the other way, and by the time you turned to face it, it had already settled in and unpacked its things.

She smoothed the front of her apron and went to see what Cook planned for dinner, because the world continued, and dinner was at six, and some things, unlike love, benefited from management.

Chapter Fifteen

Two chairs stood empty at the breakfast table, and Helen noticed them the way she noticed everything: quietly, and without remarking upon it.

The younger girls were present, subdued in the way of teenagers who had been recently and justly reprimanded. Louise buttered her toast with exaggerated care, her dark eyes fixed on her plate with a studiousness that would have been convincing had it not been so unlike her. Charlotte ate in silence, her charts left in the study for once, the very picture of a girl who had decided to behave but was finding the effort taxing. Laura sat with Caesar's head in her lap and her tea cooling beside her, her expression serene, though the serenity had a slightly chastened quality, like a pond whose surface had been disturbed and was only now settling back to glass.

Helen poured tea and set the pot down. She did not ask where Eliza was. She did not ask where the lieutenant was. She ate a slice of bread with honey, drank her tea, and listened to the sounds of the house and the yard beyond the windows.

"I shall take a walk," she said, to no one in particular.

Louise's eyes lifted from her plate. The speculative brightness Helen had quelled yesterday flickered behind them, a candle not quite extinguished.

"You will stay here," Helen said pleasantly, and Louise's gaze returned to her toast.

The morning was warm and still. Helen crossed the yard unhurriedly. She knew where she was going and was in no hurry to arrive. The broodmare barn stood at the far end, its doors propped open to the mild air, and from within came the sounds of a mare shifting her weight and a foal suckling.

She stopped in the doorway and let her eyes adjust.

The stall nearest the window held a bay mare, standing with her head low, drowsy and content. At her flank, a foal nursed, its small body braced on legs that still looked astonished to be bearing weight. A filly, Helen thought, though her knowledge of horses did not extend much beyond telling the front from the back. The straw was thick with the evidence of the night's labour: soiled towels by the door, a bucket of pink-tinged water, the lantern on its hook burned down to a guttering stub.

Against the wall, beneath the window where the early light fell in a pale rectangle across the straw, two people sat.

They were upright, or nearly so, their backs against the rough stone, their legs stretched out before them. They were both soundly asleep. Eliza's head rested on Llewellyn's shoulder, her face turned slightly toward his neck, her braids coming loose at the temples where the curls always escaped. Her hand lay in the straw beside his, not touching but close enough that the distance could be measured in the width of a stalk of straw. His head was tipped toward hers, his cheek almost resting against her hair.

They looked very young. That was what struck Helen first and hardest. Awake, both of them carried themselves with a competence and authority that obscured their years. But sleep had stripped that away, and what remained were two exhausted young people who had spent the night saving a life and fallen asleep without choosing to, their bodies finding each other the way water found its level.

She stood in the doorway and looked at the two heads inclined toward each other, his fair skin and her dark skin both gilded by the dusty gold filtering through the high window.

She thought of a vicarage kitchen, fifteen years ago. A table, a cup of tea, a man with kind eyes and red hair who had said, simply and without preamble, *I think you are remarkable.* She had been twenty years old and terrified, and the word had landed in her chest like a coal, too hot to hold and too precious to drop.

She coughed.

It was a good cough, decisive and carrying, perfected over fifteen years of managing vicarage teas and parish meetings. It bounced off the stone walls and filled the barn like a sermon.

Two bodies jolted awake. Two pairs of eyes found Helen in the doorway. Eliza's head came off Llewellyn's shoulder as though the shoulder had become a hot stove. Llewellyn straightened so fast the stone must have scraped his back. A foot of space materialised between them like a drawbridge being raised.

Eliza scrambled to her feet and brushed straw from her skirts with hands that were almost steady.

"The bay mare foaled," she said. Her voice was nearly level. "A filly. Straightforward delivery, no complications. We stayed to make sure the foal nursed properly."

"I can see that," Helen said.

Llewellyn had risen to his feet, stiffly, his left leg protesting the night on the stone floor. His face held embarrassment and something that might have been defiance, and beneath both a vulnerability that told Helen everything she needed to know.

She gave him the Look. The one she had refined over years of parish work, deployed on errant choirboys and gossips and the occasional church warden who had helped himself to the collection plate. It had never once failed.

Llewellyn met it for two full seconds, which was impressive, and then inclined his head with rueful acknowledgement.

"I'll see to the morning feed," he said, and left the barn. Not quite running. Moving, however, at a pace that suggested the morning feed was a matter of some urgency.

Helen listened to his uneven footsteps cross the yard. She turned back to Eliza, who stood in the stall with straw in her braids and a warmth along her cheekbones that had nothing to do with the temperature of the barn.

She looked at the foal, who had finished nursing and was nosing at the straw with the bewildered interest of a creature encountering texture for the first time.

"She's a fine filly," Helen said.

"Yes," Eliza said, too quickly. "She is."

Helen reached over and plucked a piece of straw from Eliza's hair, held it up, regarded it, and let it fall.

"Breakfast is on the table," she said, and walked back to the house.

The study door was open when Helen passed it. She paused, looked at the writing desk, and made a decision. She would write to Theresa again today, even though she had written three days ago and not yet received a reply. Not an alarming letter. The kind friends wrote to those away from home and missing it, warm and discursive and threaded through with information for those who knew how to read it.

She would mention the lieutenant. His steadiness, his skill, the way he deferred to Eliza's authority without diminishing it. She would not mention the straw, or the shoulder, or the look on his face when Helen's cough woke him and he found Eliza's head against his neck and Helen's eyes upon him both at once. Theresa would read between the lines, because Theresa always had, and what sat between these particular lines was a young man falling in love with her daughter and doing so honourably, and a daughter falling in love in return with the terrified courage of a girl who had never trusted that anything she loved would stay.

Helen sat down at the desk, drew a sheet of paper toward her, and uncapped the ink.

The weight of her head on his shoulder had left a mark that was not visible and would not fade.

Hermes stood patient beneath the brush while Llewellyn worked dust from his coat, the long strokes mechanical, his mind elsewhere. The moment when his body knew before his brain did that something was different. Warmth against his left side. A weight on his shoulder. The clean scent of her soap cut through with hay and the metallic tang of the night's work. For three or four heartbeats he had been awake and she had not, and he had stayed absolutely still, holding the moment the way he had held the frightened colt in the briar hedge: by not moving, by becoming the thing around which the world could settle.

Then the cough. The scramble. Helen Fallon's face, communicating both amusement and warning in a single glance.

He leaned his forehead against Hermes's flank. At the door, Pompey sighed in his sleep.

The voice had been whispering since the kitchen, since the kiss. It spoke in the accent of home, the flat vowels of the valley, his father's practicality: *What are you doing, boy?*

He knew what he was doing. He was falling in love with a woman who stood above him in every particular the world cared to measure. She was Sir Richard Bell's daughter. She managed an estate that bred horses that could not be bought with money alone, though. When a major had tried to take what was hers, she had stood in the yard and turned him away with facts and courage and a composure that did not bend.

Against this, the voice assembled its inventory. A lieutenant on half pay. A left leg that would never be right. A right arm whose grip failed at the worst moments. A farmer's second son from a valley so narrow you could stand on one ridge and shout to a man on the other, and his worldly possessions amounted to nothing tangible. He had the loyalty of a blind horse, the affection of a dog, and a room above a stable, and every one of those things belonged to Belle Haven.

In the afternoon, he held Serenity while Eliza checked her teats, the mare placid but the colt trying to barge Eliza out of the way, convinced she was stealing his portion of milk.

"Behave, you little devil." Llewellyn put out his free hand to push the colt's quarters away as the small creature turned and tried to line up to kick at Eliza. Laughing, she stepped out of the colt's range, which brought her almost up against Llewellyn. Her foot sank in the deep straw, and she put a hand against the mare's neck to steady herself, right on top of his own hand holding the lead rope.

Her thumb against his knuckle, her palm warm against the back of his.

Neither of them pulled away.

One second. Her eyes on his, and in them a question that mirrored his own: *Do you feel this too?*

He did not move.

Phillip's boots came crashing down the barn aisle, a bucket clanged, and the moment was broken.

Their hands separated. Eliza looked away, moved towards the door. Llewellyn reached to unbuckle the headcollar with hands that were not quite steady.

Evening found him in his room above the stallion barn, the newspaper open on his knee, the candle burning. He was not reading. Below him Hermes shifted, settling for the night, and Pompey lay at his feet.

He was in love with Eliza Bell.

The knowledge was not new. He suspected it had lived in him since the night Arthur was born, since he had looked up from a dying foal and seen her face in the lantern light and felt an unmovable certainty that he had come home.

But naming it changed its weight. The unnamed thing could be carried discreetly, folded small into the private corners of his heart. Named, it filled the room.

The voice said: *She deserves better.*

He thought of a girl in Wales who had said she would wait. Who had not waited. Whose name he no longer spoke, though it sat in him like an old fracture that ached in certain weather. You wanted something, you gave yourself to it, and it was taken.

Below him, Hermes snorted in his sleep. The stallion who should have died on a battlefield, who should have been destroyed when the blast took his sight, who was alive because Llewellyn had refused. Had held on. Had led a blind horse home across a continent because some things were worth fighting for, regardless of what the voice in the back of your head had to say about it.

He closed the newspaper. He blew out the candle. He lay in the dark and listened to the horse below and did not sleep, and the awareness of her, somewhere in the house, would not leave him alone.

The catalogue of moments between them had grown unwieldy.

The kiss. So many moments where she had looked up to find his eyes on her, or he had looked up and she had realised her eyes had been on him for quite some time without her ever really deciding that was where they should be. The night in the straw, waking to Helen's cough with his shoulder beneath her cheek. Her hand on his on the mare's neck, his skin warm and rough, a question in his eyes she didn't know how to answer.

And then, nothing.

She had tried. That was the part that gnawed at her. She had lingered after the evening rounds, standing at the fence where they had stood the day of the breeding, her face turned to a sunset that was merely adequate. He had come to stand beside her, and the distance between their elbows had been the width of a hand, and she had waited, and he had said something about the weather and bid her good evening and walked away, his shadow stretching long across the cobblestones.

She had found a reason to visit the stallion barn after dark, with a question that could have waited until morning and both of them knew it. He had answered thoroughly, standing on his side of the stall door, and she had watched his mouth form the words and remembered what that mouth had felt like against hers, and the memory had risen in her so fiercely she could taste it, and he had looked at her with eyes that held everything she wanted and said, "Good night, Miss Bell."

Miss Bell. She had been Eliza in the kitchen, Eliza in the straw. Now she was Miss Bell again, as if the name could undo what his hands and his mouth already knew.

The evidence contradicted itself. He still looked at her the same way, the grey-blue eyes following her across the yard with what she could now recognise as yearning. An old word, from ballads and the sort of poetry she had never had patience for, but the only one that fit. He looked at her with yearning, and then he stepped back. His eyes said *come here* and his distance said *stay away*, and the contradiction was maddening.

The anger arrived on the third day. Slow and dense, the kind that settled in the bones. She was angry because she had done the hardest thing in her life. She had not pulled back.

And he was retreating.

She had opened a door, and he was stepping backward through it. She had offered something, and he was declining to take it. This was what leaving looked like. Not the slam of a door or hooves on a lane. It was quiet. Careful. A man putting distance where there had been closeness, one *Miss Bell* at a time.

She slept badly.

Morning came grey and overcast, and she rose with a clarity the bad night had produced. The anger had done its work overnight, the way a poultice drew infection, pulling the confusion to the surface and leaving beneath it something hard and useful.

She was going to speak to him.

She sat on the edge of her bed and composed what she would say. She would be direct. The facts were these: he had kissed her, and she had let him, and neither of those things were accidents. He felt what she felt. She had seen it in his face, and she would not allow him to pretend otherwise.

She dressed quickly and pinned her braids and pulled on her boots and went downstairs and across the yard toward the stallion barn.

She was halfway across the cobblestones when she heard the hooves.

Not army horses. She knew that sound too well now, and her body had learned to tighten at the first note of it. These were different. Lighter, quicker, accompanied by the rattle and creak of wheels on an uneven lane.

She stopped.

The sound grew. It came from the east, from the village road, the horses blowing, the wheels protesting.

The carriage appeared around the curve of the lane, drawn by a pair of bays dark with sweat. It turned into the yard without hesitation, as though the driver knew the way, and the wheels ground against the cobblestones, and the horses slowed and stopped, and Eliza recognised the crest on the door.

Chapter Sixteen

THE SOUND REACHED HIM through the open door of the stallion barn: wheels on the lane, the creak of a well-sprung carriage travelling fast, and the quick, blown breathing of horses who had been pushed. Llewellyn set down the body brush and stepped to the doorway, Pompey lifting his head from the straw behind him.

The carriage was already turning into the yard. A pair of bays, dark with sweat, their mouths flecked with foam. The carriage itself was the colour of claret, its lacquered body dimmed by road dust, and on the door a golden crest that Llewellyn did not recognise but which spoke of age and consequence.

Eliza stood in the centre of the yard. She had been walking toward the stallion barn, he noted, her chin set at the angle that meant she had something to say and intended to say it. The carriage had stopped her mid-step.

Charlotte came down the steps of the house at a run, her blonde hair streaming, decorum abandoned in favour of speed. Behind her, Laura descended the same steps with her hand trailing the balustrade and Caesar pacing at her hip.

The carriage door opened. A man stepped down.

He was tall and spare, with grey hair that had once been dark and a face that carried good bones beneath the softening of years. Sixty, perhaps, or near it. He wore a coat of grey wool cut with the understated excellence that only the best tailors achieved, the kind that did not announce itself: the fall of the cloth across the shoulders, the buttons that were not brass but silver, though small and plain.

A very rich man, Llewellyn assessed at a glance, though one who did not care to flaunt it.

The man turned from the carriage and opened his arms, and Charlotte ran into them.

The embrace was not formal. It was a man holding something precious, his grey head bent over Charlotte's blonde one, his hands pressing her shoulders as though confirming her solidity. He drew back and held her at arm's length and looked at her face, and Llewellyn recognised the expression; he had seen it a hundred times if not a thousand as soliders stepped off ships bringing them home from the war and those who loved them looked into their faces.

Laura arrived. The man released Charlotte and turned, and Laura walked into his arms with the certainty of one who did not need eyes to find the people she loved. He held her differently, one hand cradling the back of her head, lips pressed to her brow, and the tenderness was almost unbearable to watch.

Then Eliza, who had crossed the yard and now stood at the edge of the reunion, half a step outside the innermost circle. The man released Laura and turned to Eliza, and his face warmed again, differently. He took both her hands and said something Llewellyn could not hear, and Eliza's shoulders dropped a fraction, and she nodded. The man pulled her into a hug too, which seemed to surprise Eliza, but then tentatively she hugged him back, a smile dawning on her face.

Louise was next, bouncing on her toes and dropping a curtsey that the man waved away before pressing her hand warmly. Helen came last, and she curtsied with composure, but the man took her hand too and said something that made Helen smile in the way she rarely smiled, the way that showed the girl she must once have been before the world gave her reasons to be careful.

The whole tableau played out across the yard like a scene from a painting Llewellyn could not enter. A family, or something that functioned as one, reassembling around a figure whose arrival changed the geometry of the place. The man was not Sir Richard; he had seen Sir Richard Bell once, at Sandhurst. So who this man might be, he couldn't comprehend. He stood in the doorway of the stallion barn and watched in confusion.

Thornton appeared at his shoulder. The old groom stood beside Llewellyn, arms folded, and his weathered face held an expression Llewellyn had not seen on it before. Approval. Simple and direct, the kind Thornton offered to very few things and none of them lightly.

"His Grace," Thornton said, with a nod toward the retreating figure. "The Duke of Allanworth. He comes every summer. Stays two weeks, usually." He paused and added, as if this were the conclusive evidence of character, "He knows his horses."

A *duke*. Llewellyn turned the word over. A duke at Belle Haven, greeted not with ceremony but with embraces, known by the head groom, arriving without warning because the connection was deep enough that warning was unnecessary.

The party disappeared into the house. The yard quieted. The coachman led the sweated bays to the water trough, Phillip scurried out to take them. And then Louise came back across the cobblestones, her quick steps carrying her to the stallion barn.

She stopped in front of Llewellyn and glanced once at Thornton, who took the hint with a grunt and went to oversee the duke's horses.

"You should know," Louise said, pitching her voice low, "who that is, and why he's here."

She told him. Charlotte and Laura were the duke's nieces, his sister's daughters, born out of wedlock and adopted by Sir Richard. The connection was not public. The duke had spent fourteen years ensuring the world did not find out, because the world's judgement fell heaviest on children who had done nothing to deserve it. But privately, in the summers and the letters and the visits, he had loved them fiercely.

And then the rest of it. The duke's son, Matthew, Marquess of Whitmore, had married Clara Bell. Sir Richard's eldest adopted daughter was now Lady Whitmore, and when the duke died, she would be a duchess.

She said it all gently, which was worse than bluntly, because it meant she understood what the information would do to him. She searched his expression for a moment, pressed his arm once, and turned and ran back to the house.

Llewellyn stood still in the doorway. Behind him, Hermes shifted. Pompey leaned against his thigh.

A duke's nieces. A marquess's wife. Sir Richard Bell's estate, where the Prince Regent's favour opened doors and duchesses grew from the same soil as thoroughbreds.

He was a second son from a Welsh hill farm, a soldier on half pay with a leg that ached in the damp and an arm that could not grip a sword. He slept above a stable.

And the woman he loved was the sister of a future duchess.

He turned back to the barn, and Hermes breathed against his hand, and the warmth of the horse's muzzle was the only solid thing in a morning that had moved beneath his feet.

The study still smelled of her father. Not his person, which had been absent too long for that, but the accumulated trace of his presence: leather and ink and the tang of saddle soap he used on his own tack because he said no groom could do it to his satisfaction, though this was not true and everyone knew it.

The Duke of Allanworth sat in the chair by the window. Not behind the desk. He had crossed the study, considered the desk with its towers of ledgers and Charlotte's charts spread all over it, and chosen the window chair instead, settling into it as a man who had sat there before, many times, on summer visits when he and Sir Richard had talked horses late into the evening.

Eliza sat behind the desk. Her feet had carried her there because that was where she sat now, and the chair had moulded itself to her body over the months as a saddle moulded to a rider, and she realised, as she settled, that she had stopped thinking of it as her father's chair some time ago.

Her Uncle William looked older than at Clara's wedding last year, when she had seen him last. The grey had claimed the last of the dark, and the lines at his eyes had deepened, because no doubt the war had added to his burdens as it had added to everyone's.

"You have been busy," he said.

"Charlotte has done most of the bloodline analysis," Eliza said. "I have managed the day-to-day operations. The requisitions took eighty horses this spring. We have been rebuilding from what remained."

He listened. He asked questions, specific ones, the questions of someone who understood horse breeding in terms of commerce. He asked about the broodmares, the foaling season's losses, feed supplies and the price of hay. She answered each one with the facts arranged and ready, because facts were what she trusted and what she offered in return for trust.

He did not interrupt. He sat in the window chair with his long hands folded across his knee and his grey head tilted, and the quality of his listening reminded her of Helen. When she finished, the silence was not empty. It was full.

"Your father," the duke said, and paused. "Your father wrote to me in March, before he went across the Channel. He was afraid he had given you too much responsibility too young." He looked at her steadily. "I think he need not have worried."

The words entered her like a key turning in a lock. This was a verdict, delivered by someone who had known Belle Haven for fifteen years, who had watched it grow from a small breeding operation into an estate whose horses were sought after across England. The Duke of Allanworth managed estates that dwarfed Belle Haven. He knew what competence looked like, and what it cost.

She sat very still. What moved through her was near relief, the deep, structural relief of a beam that had been bearing weight alone and felt another slide into place beside it.

Her father had worried about her. That fact, nested inside the duke's words, glowed. He had worried, which meant he had thought of her, which meant the silence of the last six weeks was not a man forgetting but a man who could not write, and the difference between those two things was the distance between abandonment and circumstance.

"Do you need anything I might provide?" the duke asked. "Resources, connections. If there is anything Belle Haven requires."

She considered the question honestly. She thought of the feed stores, adequate for the summer. The brood-mares, healthy and recovering. The foals growing strong. Charlotte's charts mapping a future built on Eclipse blood and Ballerina's twenty-two years and a blind stallion who had come through fire. Llewellyn's steady hands. Helen's steady presence. Thornton's loyalty and Phillip's eagerness and the accumulated strength of a place that had been stripped of its horses and not of its heart.

"No, Your Grace," she said. "Belle Haven has what it needs."

She watched his face change. A shift at the corners of his eyes, a settling of the mouth. Pride. The real thing, quiet and dense.

Nobody could have done better. The thought arrived without her permission and settled beside the warmth of her father's worry, and she sat behind the desk that had become hers and felt something shift in her spine. Her body straightening before her mind caught up, the verte-brae stacking the way they did when she sat a horse well, when the balance was right.

The duke rose. He crossed the study and laid his hand on her shoulder, briefly, the pressure firm. A paternal ges-ture from a man who was not her father but who had known her father for fifteen years.

"I must be in Portsmouth by nightfall," he said. "But I wanted to see the girls. And to see for myself." He glanced around the study one final time and his mouth curved. "I shall write to your father, when communication permits. He will want to know."

He left. Eliza heard him in the hall, Charlotte's voice rising to meet him, Laura's beneath it.

She sat alone. Everything in its place. Everything as it had been five minutes ago. Everything different, because a man who knew the weight of what she carried had told her she carried it well, and the words had reached into the place where her doubts lived and turned on a light.

The chestnut two-year-old had opinions about being groomed, and he expressed them with the full vocabulary available to a young horse who had not yet learned that humans were not placed on the earth for the sole purpose of supplying carrots. He swung his quarters when the brush passed over his barrel, stomped when the brush found his flanks, and lipped at Llewellyn's sleeve, convinced that pockets existed and contained something worth having.

Llewellyn worked steadily. The handling of young stock was a conversation conducted in pressure and release, and it required patience and attention in equal measure. The colt was well-bred and profoundly convinced of his own importance, which made him simultaneously a pleasure and a trial.

A shadow fell across the stall door.

The Duke of Allanworth stood at the half-door with his arms folded on its top edge, a man's particular leaning, the leaning of one who had spent time in barns and knew how to occupy a stable doorway without alarming the animal inside. His eyes held the assessing warmth of a man who looked at the world the way good horsemen looked at horses: seeing what was there, not what he wished to see.

"A handsome colt," the duke said. He studied the two-year-old, missing nothing. "Douro's get?"

Llewellyn set down the brush. "Yes, Your Grace. Out of a mare called Patience."

"I remember Patience. Richard bred her from a Herod line dam he was very proud of." The duke's mouth curved. "She bit him on the arm the first time he tried to wean her foal. He said it was the most honest criticism he'd ever received."

The anecdote had the ease of long familiarity. Llewellyn said nothing, and the duke did not seem to expect it. His Grace looked around the barn, at the clean stalls and the swept aisle and the tack hung in ordered rows, and his gaze paused on the far stall where Hermes stood with his scarred head turned toward the unfamiliar voice.

"Charlotte tells me she traced the stallion's Eclipse dam line," the duke said. "Seven generations clean, she said, with the satisfaction of a girl who had found buried treasure and was not sure the rest of the world appreciated its worth." He shook his head, but the shake carried pride. "The breeding programme she has designed is remarkable work for a girl of fourteen. For a person of any age."

"Miss Charlotte has a gift," Llewellyn said. It was not flattery.

"She does." The duke was quiet for a moment. Then he looked at Llewellyn directly, the conversational path narrowing from pleasantry to purpose.

"Eliza has been running this estate exceptionally well," the duke said. "Don't you think?"

"Yes, Your Grace. She has."

He did not expand. The truth required no embellishment.

The duke nodded. He was still watching Llewellyn, assembling something, and Llewellyn could not entirely read what.

"I am not sure she could have managed nearly so well without you, however," the duke said. Same even tone, unhurried. "I will be sure to tell Sir Richard my thoughts on that when I see him next."

Llewellyn's hand stilled on the colt's neck.

The duke straightened from the door. He reached over and ran his hand along the chestnut's crest, and the colt, who had been suspicious of every other hand that morning, arched his neck into the pressure with instant trust.

"He'll make a fine horse," the duke said. "Good bone. Good temperament. The breeding is right." He met Llewellyn's eyes once more, and the expression on his face was mild and faintly amused. "Good afternoon, Lieutenant."

He turned and walked from the barn. Through the open door Llewellyn watched him cross the yard to the carriage. Charlotte and Laura stood at the door, and the duke embraced them again, and the grey head bent over the blonde ones.

The carriage door closed. The whip cracked. The bays moved off, and the rattle of wheels receded down the lane, and was gone.

Llewellyn stood in the stall with his hand on the chestnut's neck.

I am not sure she could have managed nearly so well without you.

He turned the sentence over. Professional acknowledgement, certainly: a duke recognising that his contribution had been real. That much was clear.

But then the other thing. The thing that explained why the duke had come to the stallion barn at all, why he had leaned on the door and talked about Charlotte and horses and then spoken Eliza's name.

I will be sure to tell Sir Richard my thoughts on that.

Tell Sir Richard. Eliza's father. A duke, telling a father about a man. Not *useful*. He had said *she could not have managed so well without you*, which placed Llewellyn not beside the estate but beside Eliza, and unless Llewellyn had entirely mistaken that faint amusement at the end, the duke did not object to what he saw.

The voice stirred. It said: *You are reading what you want to read.*

But the voice was uncertain in a way it had not been before. The wall of facts it had built, the irrefutable arithmetic of rank and birth, had not changed. A duke was still a duke. A farmer's son was still a farmer's son.

And yet a duke had come to his stable and spoken to him about Eliza with an expression that suggested the arithmetic was not the only thing that mattered.

The chestnut colt, who had been standing with considerable patience during a conversation that had offered him nothing in the way of carrots, grew tired of waiting. He turned his head and nipped Llewellyn's upper arm with the sharp bite of a young horse who knew exactly how hard to press to make a point without drawing blood.

Llewellyn flinched. The colt looked back with magnificent indifference, the expression of a creature who could not fathom why a perfectly good grooming had been interrupted by a grey-haired man and a conversation about feelings.

"Fair enough," Llewellyn said.

He picked up the brush. The bristles found the colt's shoulder, and the rhythm resumed, and the work was good. But the duke's words would not leave him. They sat alongside the other things he carried: the laugh in the stallion barn, the weight of her head on his shoulder, the three heartbeats of a kiss in the kitchen, and the collection was growing, and he did not know what to do with any of it, and the colt's warm hide beneath his hand was the only certainty he had, and for now it was enough.

Chapter Seventeen

THE BLACK MARE LABOURED slowly, the way old mares sometimes did, as though she had decided the business would proceed at her pace and no one else's. She stood with her head low and her flanks dark with sweat, and every few minutes a contraction moved through her, visible beneath the skin, and she would groan once, low in her throat, and then stand quiet again. The intervals were long. Too long for urgency, too short for sleep. The kind of labour that asked nothing of the people watching except that they stay.

Eliza sat on a straw bale against the wall, her knees drawn up, the lantern hanging from its hook above her left shoulder. The flame was turned low. It threw a circle of amber light that reached the mare's hindquarters and the edge of the stall and no further, and beyond that circle the barn was dark, the shadows deep and warm and close, and the world outside the door had ceased to exist.

Laura had gone to bed a little after midnight. She had sat with them for two hours, her hand resting on Caesar's broad skull, her sightless eyes directed toward the sounds of the mare's labour. When Eliza told her to go, Laura had risen without argument, which was unusual enough to confirm that the girl was genuinely tired. She had touched Eliza's arm in passing, a light pressure that said something she did not put into words, and then her footsteps and the click of Caesar's nails had receded down the barn aisle and into the night.

Which left the two of them.

Llewellyn sat on the straw bale opposite, his back against the partition, his left leg stretched out before him. His right hand rested on his knee. The lantern light found the angles of his face and left the rest to imagination, and Eliza was aware, with the heightened perception that came with exhaustion and proximity, that she had been imagining quite a lot.

She had intended to confront him. That morning, crossing the cobblestones toward the stallion barn, her words had been assembled and ready, sharp as farrier's nails. He had kissed her and retreated. He had looked at her with everything in his eyes and then called her Miss Bell and walked away, and the contradiction was a splinter she could not reach, and she had been going to tell him so.

But a duke's carriage had intervened, and the day had filled with other things, and now it was half past one in the morning and the sharp words had softened in the dark the way hard edges softened in lantern light, and she could not find the anger that had fuelled them. What she found instead was this: a tired man sitting across from her, his face open in the way faces became open when it was very late and the performance of the day had been set aside, and a mare breathing between them, and the barn smelling of clean straw and warm horse and the faint sweetness of the hay stored in the loft above.

She could not start with accusation. Not here. Not at this hour.

"His Grace seemed well," she said, because it was something to say, and the silence had begun to press.

"He did." Llewellyn's voice was quiet, pitched for the barn and the hour. "He came to the stallion barn before he left. Looked at the chestnut two-year-old. Knew his sire and dam both."

"He would. He's known Belle Haven longer than I have."

The mare groaned again. Eliza rose and checked her, running a hand along the flank, feeling the muscles bunch and release. The foal had not yet presented. She returned to the bale and sat, and the sitting felt different now, the way sitting down felt different after you had stood up and moved through a shared space and come back to find the distance between you altered by the going and the returning.

"Do you ever think of leaving?" Llewellyn asked.

The question arrived without preamble, the way his questions always did.

"Leaving Belle Haven?"

"Not leaving. Going somewhere." He turned his hand palm-up on his knee, a gesture that opened the question wider. "London. A season. Clara had one, didn't she? Do you dream of that?"

She almost laughed. The idea of herself in a London ballroom, in silk and satin, making conversation with men whose knowledge of horses extended to the names of the ones they bet on at Ascot, was so thoroughly absurd that it belonged in a novel she would never read.

"Clara's season was a campaign," she said. "She had a plan, and the plan involved a grey horse and the Prince Regent's vanity, and it worked because Clara is Clara. I am not Clara." She paused. "I would be wretched in London. The noise alone would finish me."

He smiled. The smile lived mostly in his eyes, the way it always did, and the lantern caught it.

"Then you're content here."

"I am content here." She heard the word leave her mouth and examined it for truth and found it sound but incomplete. *Content* was a word you might use to talk about a chair you sat in comfortably. What she felt for Belle Haven was larger and less comfortable than that.

"I was found on the doorstep of the church," she said.

She had not planned to say it. The words arrived the way the foal would arrive, when they were ready and not before, pushed forward by a pressure she had been carrying for years without knowing she intended to release it. She kept her eyes on the mare.

"In July. They thought I was about six months old. Nobody knew where I had come from. Black people aren't exactly two a penny in country Hampshire, and not a soul in the parish had ever seen anyone who might have been my mother or father. There was nothing with me. No note, no token, no name." She swallowed. "Sir Richard found me. He was riding past the church and heard me crying and stopped. He picked me up and took me home, because he had two little girls at home already and a nursemaid for them, and Reverend Fallon recorded the finding, and that was that. They decided my birthday should be the sixth of January. Epiphany. Mr Fallon said it was a day of new beginnings."

The straw rustled as Llewellyn shifted, but he did not speak. His silence told her he was listening completely, with his whole body, as you listened to a sound in the dark when the sound mattered.

"Theresa came when I was four. She was meant to be governess to us girls, to Clara and Anna and me, but she married Pa within the year, and after that she was simply our mother. I don't remember a time before her." She paused. The mare breathed. The lantern flame trembled and steadied. "She is with Molly now, because Molly needs her more, and I understand that, and I don't begrudge it, but sometimes the house feels very quiet without her."

She was saying too much. She could feel the words running ahead of her, spilling from a place she normally kept locked, the hidden cellar where the foundling's fear lived alongside the foundling's grief, a place she never opened, and a feeling she had never talked about to another living soul, not even Theresa or Molly, who both knew what it was to be an orphan and unwanted.

"Belle Haven is home," she said. "It is more than enough. It is everything I know and everything I want to know. The thought of being anywhere else is..." She searched for the word and found it waiting. "Unnerving. As though the ground might not hold me."

She had never put that thought into words before this moment. Not even to her father, who would have held her and told her she was safe and meant it with his whole heart, and whose absence was the reason the fear had risen in the first place.

She had said it to a man sitting across from her in a dark barn at half past one in the morning, and the saying of it had cost her something she could feel in her chest, a giving-way, a shifting of stones that had been stacked there since she was old enough to understand what *foundling* meant

Llewellyn was quiet for a long time. When he spoke, his voice was very low.

"Thank you," he said. "For telling me."

The words were exactly right, because he had not tried to fix it or explain it or make it smaller. He had listened, and she had needed him to do that.

The mare groaned again. Eliza rose to check her, and the work steadied her hands, and the dark held them both, and the lantern burned on.

The silence she left behind her words had texture, the way the dark had texture when you sat in it long enough to feel its grain. Llewellyn held it. He held it the way he had held the frightened colt in the briars, by not moving, by letting it settle against him, and what came to rest was the weight of a girl left on a doorstep in July and a woman sitting across from him who had made herself out of what remained.

He was not certain why he began. Later he would look for the reason and find only the hour, the quality of the dark, the way her trust had unlocked something in him that had been bolted shut for two years. He had not told this story to anyone outside his family. His mother knew. His father knew. They did not speak of it, because speaking would require them to choose between their sons, and they loved both, and the choosing would break something that could not be mended.

"There was a girl," he said.

He heard his own voice as if it belonged to someone else, low and careful, the words placed one at a time like stones across a stream. Eliza did not move. Her stillness gave him room.

"Her name was Rhiannon. We grew up in the same valley, below the Black Mountain. Our farms shared a boundary wall and a stream, and I knew her from the time I could walk. The kind of knowing that doesn't need deciding. She was simply there, the way the mountain was there. She's a year younger than me."

The mare shifted. A contraction moved through her, and she groaned, and the sound passed, and the barn settled again.

"When I left for Sandhurst, she said she would wait." He turned the words over as he spoke them, examining them for the last time before he let them go. "I believed her. It never occurred to me not to. She was Rhiannon, and she said she would wait, and the promise was as solid as the mountain."

He had carried the promise through Sandhurst and into Spain and across the hard, bright landscapes of the Peninsula where the dust got into everything and the sun bleached the colour from your uniform and the nights were cold enough to crack stone. He had carried it folded small in the pocket of his mind, the way other men carried miniatures or locks of hair, and on the worst nights it had been enough to hold.

"The letters came for a while. Then they didn't. I told myself the post was unreliable, which was true. I told myself it was lambing season and she would be busy, which was also true. I told myself a great many things that were true enough to believe and not true enough to matter."

He remembered the day his brother's letter came, a beautiful spring day when the birds were singing and it seemed impossible that there was a war raging. The regiment had been in camp, a rare stillness between engagements, and he had been sitting on an ammunition crate mending a bridle when his captain handed him the envelope, creased and crushed and stained. His brother's handwriting was looser than his own, the letters sprawling across the page with the confidence of a man who had never needed to be careful with words.

Rhiannon sends her love. We were married in January.

Nine words. The bridle had gone slack in his hands, and the needle had pricked his thumb, and a single drop of blood had fallen onto the page and sat there, round and red and bright, between *married* and *January*.

"My brother," Llewellyn said. His voice was steady. "She married my brother, seven months after I left for Sandhurst. While I was in Spain. His letter reached me in camp, and the way he wrote it, as though it were news I would welcome, told me he did not know there had been anything between us. She had not told him."

He stopped. The mare groaned again. He listened to her breathing and used it to steady his own.

"Their first child is due this summer." He said it flatly, the way he said things that cost him. "The farm is theirs now. My father still works it, but it's theirs. When I went home on leave, I slept in the room I grew up in and ate at the table I grew up at, and Rhiannon sat across from me with my brother's hand on hers, and the valley that was the only home I'd ever had became a place I could not stay."

The candle in the lantern guttered. The flame dipped and recovered, and the shadows swung and resettled, and Llewellyn sat with the story empty inside him, given to the dark and the woman in it.

He looked at her now. Her face was very still. Her eyes held his, and what he read in them was not pity. Pity would have been unbearable. What he read was understanding.

The silence held a long time. Long enough for the mare to shift and settle again.

"Then we're the same, in a way," Eliza said. Her voice was quiet, the words chosen carefully. "We're both here because here is what there is."

He heard both meanings. The first was literal: two people displaced, washed up at Belle Haven by the receding tide of lives that had not gone as planned. The second lived beneath it, in the word *here*. Here. In this barn. On this night. With each other.

Both meanings were true. He let them rest side by side in his chest the way the two of them sat side by side in the straw, close enough that the distance between them could be measured in what they had not yet said.

He did not say anything. Neither of them moved to disturb the silence.

The silence had changed them. Not visibly, not in any way a person walking into the barn would have noticed, but Eliza felt it in her skin, in the way the air sat against her. They had given each other things they carried alone, and the giving had altered the distance between them, collapsing it in some places and revealing it in others, much as a lamp held closer to a wall showed both the smoothness and the cracks.

She was aware of him with a sharpness that was almost painful. The rise and fall of his breathing. His right hand resting on his knee, the knuckles scarred, the fingers loose. The angle of his jaw in the lantern light.

He had kissed her in the kitchen. Twelve days ago, or thirteen, she had lost count and did not care, because what mattered was the fact: his mouth on hers, three heartbeats, the lightest pressure, and then the pulling back. Since then, nothing. *Miss Bell* and careful distances and a retreat so courteous she could not even call it a retreat without sounding unreasonable.

They had talked. Not like this, not the stripped and honest talk of the last hour, but they had talked, and he had been kind and thoughtful as he always was, and none of it was enough because she wanted him to close the distance again. She wanted the three heartbeats back, and more.

She wanted to know what came after three. She wanted to know what his mouth felt like when it was not being careful.

She did not know how to say this. She was a woman who argued from evidence, and the feeling she carried had no evidence to support it, nothing she could point to and say *here, this proves it*. Only the ache behind her ribs, and the way her body turned toward his the way a plant turned toward light, without decision, without permission.

The mare groaned. Eliza checked her, found no change, sat back down. Closer this time. Not deliberately, or not consciously, but the bale was only so wide, and when she sat, her knee was six inches from his, and neither of them remarked upon it.

The barn breathed around them. The sounds were the sounds of every foal watch she had ever kept: straw shifting, a horse's exhalation, the creak of old timber in the night air. But layered over them was the sound of her own pulse, audible in the quiet the way it had been in the kitchen, and she was certain he could hear it.

He moved. A turning of his head toward her, and his eyes found hers in the lantern light, and the look in them was not the guarded look of the past two weeks. It was open. Raw. The look of a man who had given away his last secret and had nothing left to hide behind.

"Eliza, I..." he said.

Not *Miss Bell*. Two words and a breath. The breath caught, held, and in the held breath she heard the shape of what was coming. Her chest constricted. She sat very still. The sentence hung between them, unfinished, balanced on the edge of his tongue like a horse gathering itself before a jump.

The mare grunted.

Not the slow, weary groan of the contractions that had been coming all night. Shorter. Sharper. A sound Eliza's body recognised before her mind did, the sound that bypassed thought and went straight to the hands and feet, the sound that meant *now*.

She was on her feet. He was on his feet. The half-spoken sentence dissolved into the air, and their bodies were already doing what they knew how to do, moving around each other without speaking, who went where, what was needed.

The mare had gone down. She lay on her side in the deep straw, her neck stretched out, her breathing changed to the hard, rhythmic pushing that was the body's oldest work. Eliza knelt behind her and saw the foal's front hooves emerging, pale against the dark hide, one slightly ahead of the other as they should be, and behind them the nose, pressed against the forelegs, the whole arrangement textbook-perfect, and the relief of a clean presentation after the long, anxious hours was so intense it nearly buckled her.

"Looks good," she said, and her voice was the professional voice, steady and sure, because the work required it and the work was what she gave when everything else was too much to hold.

Llewellyn was at the mare's head, his hand on her neck, keeping her calm, and Eliza watched the foal come. The shoulders cleared. The hips followed. The dark, wet body slid into the straw in a rush of fluid and membrane, and the foal lay still for a moment, wrapped in its caul, and then the head lifted, and the membrane tore, and the first breath came, a wet, gasping inhalation that was the sound of a life beginning.

A filly. Black as her dam, with a small white star between her eyes. She lay in the straw and breathed and blinked, and her mother turned her head to look at her, and the looking was ancient and complete, the recognition of one creature by another that needed no language.

They cleared the membrane and encouraged the mare to stand, lick her foal clean, drink, eat the mash Llewellyn fetched for her. They worked in near-silence, speaking only in the shorthand of the task: *here, ready, good*. The mare nickered, the low vibrating sound that was for the foal and no one else. The filly's ears swivelled toward it.

At half past three, the filly stood.

The first attempt failed. The legs splayed, the hooves skidded on the straw, the small body collapsed in an indignant heap. The second attempt was better. The hind legs found purchase, the forelegs braced, the body rose, trembling, and then the balance came, precarious and miraculous, the weight of a new life held up by four legs that had existed for less than an hour.

Eliza sat back on her heels. Llewellyn stood beside her, and his hand came down to very lightly settle on her shoulder. They watched the filly take her first unsteady step, and then another, and then the muzzle found the mare's flank and began the blind, searching work of finding the teat, and neither of them spoke.

The unfinished sentence hung in the air between them. Two words suspended in the dark. Eliza heard it still, him saying her name in a tone she had never heard from him, low, emphatic. She would hear it for days, turning it over, filling in what might have come next.

But here, now, in the barn at half past three with a foal nursing and the lantern burning low and his arm a breath from her shoulder, she did not chase it. She let it hang. She let the night hold it, along with everything else they had given each other in the dark: the church doorstep and the family who had chosen her, the valley below the Black Mountain and the girl who had not waited, the two meanings of *here*.

Chapter Eighteen

The water was cold. It ran from the pump over her hands in a thin, steady stream, and she watched it carry away the evidence of the night: the dried blood beneath her nails, the fine dust from the straw that clung to the creases of her knuckles. She scrubbed with the hard brush that lived beside the sink, the bristles dragging across her skin, and the sensation was real and present and exactly what she needed, because her body felt as though it belonged to someone who had been awake for a very long time and had given away more than sleep.

The kitchen windows faced east, and the early light came through them thin and grey, the colour of a sky that had not yet decided what kind of day it intended to be. The fire had been banked overnight and the range was barely warm. The room smelled of yesterday's bread and the dried herbs hanging from the beams. Familiar smells. Kitchen smells. The smells of a room that did not know or care that the world had rearranged itself during the night.

She dried her hands on the rough cloth and leaned her hip against the sink and closed her eyes, just for a moment. Behind her lids, the night replayed in fragments: the black mare's slow labour, the lantern, two voices in the dark. Her own voice, saying things she had never said aloud. His, low and careful, each word placed like a stone across a stream. Rhiannon. The valley below the Black Mountain. The letter that arrived on a Tuesday and undid everything.

And then the two words. *Eliza, I.* Spoken in a tone she had never heard from him, low and emphatic, shaped by something that was not caution or restraint but their opposite, and then the mare had grunted and the words had dissolved and the work had swallowed them both.

She could still hear them. They lived in her chest alongside everything else the night had deposited there, stacked and layered and too heavy for the hour.

Footsteps behind her. Helen came into the kitchen already dressed, her blonde hair pinned neatly, her apron tied. She took in Eliza's presence at the sink, the shadows beneath her eyes, the straw caught in her sleeve, and said nothing about any of it.

She filled the kettle and set it on the range. She cut two thick slices of bread and set them on a plate. She fetched the butter and the jam from the pantry, the good jam, the one made from the damson plums that grew against the south wall of the garden, dark and sweet and tart all at once. She placed these things on the table with the quiet authority of a woman who understood that sometimes the most useful thing you could do for another person was feed them.

"Sit," Helen said.

Eliza sat. She ate because the bread was there and her body needed it, though her appetite was buried somewhere beneath the exhaustion. The jam burst against her tongue, and the sweetness of it reached into some tired corner of her and turned on a small, stubborn light. Helen poured tea when the kettle sang and set the cup at Eliza's elbow, and the steam rose in a curl that caught the light from the window.

Helen sat across from her. She held her own cup in both hands and drank, and the silence between them had weight and warmth, the silence of a woman who listened to what had not been said and heard it clearly.

"I was twenty when I came to Belle Haven," Helen said.

Her voice was quiet, conversational, the tone of a woman telling a story she had told before but not often and never carelessly. She was looking at her tea, not at Eliza, and the not-looking was deliberate, a gift of space.

"I was frightened of everything. Of being seen, of being known. I had been a governess, after I was at the Duke Street orphanage with your mother, and the man who employed me took what he wanted and left me to manage what came after, and when I arrived here I was carrying Louise and carrying shame in equal measure, and I could not have told you which was heavier." She paused. The kitchen clock ticked above the dresser. "I had no plan but getting to Theresa, who I knew would help me. And she did; she promised me that I could have my child and find a position, and I knew, with utter certainty, that I would never again trust any man with so much as the time of day."

Eliza's hands stilled around her cup. She had known the broad shape of this story, the way everyone at Belle Haven knew it. But Helen had never told it to her like this, directly, in the first person, with the rawness of a woman offering her own scars as evidence.

"Mr Fallon arrived from a direction I was not watching," Helen said. "He was the vicar. He was kind. He had red hair and a face that was not handsome and a way of listening that made you say things you had not planned to say." The faintest smile touched her mouth. "I did not choose to fall in love with him. I had decided, very firmly, that love was a luxury I could not afford and a risk I would not take. And he simply stood there, being patient and being good, and one morning I looked at him and realised the decision had been made without my permission, and all my careful planning had come to nothing."

She lifted her cup and drank. When she set it down, her eyes found Eliza's.

"The things worth having," Helen said, "are rarely the things you planned for."

The words landed in the place the night had opened, and they did not fix anything or explain anything. They simply sat there, warm and true, the testimony of a woman who had been afraid and had loved anyway.

Helen poured a second cup of tea. She set the pot down and folded her hands in her lap and said nothing else, and the silence held, and Eliza drank her tea and felt the warmth of it move through her chest.

Above them, the ceiling creaked. Then the clatter of feet on the stairs, quick and overlapping, the unmistakable sound of three girls descending at once, Charlotte's voice saying something about mares coming into season and Louise's answering with the eager brightness of a girl who had temporarily forgotten she was meant to be behaving. Caesar's nails clicked on the floorboards. A door banged.

The private hour was over. The household was awake. Helen rose to cut more bread as the voices spilled into the hallway and the kitchen filled with the noise and warmth of the living.

Eliza finished her tea. She set the cup in the basin and caught Helen's eye across the kitchen, and what passed between them required no words, because Helen had already said the only thing that needed saying, and Eliza had heard it.

Her bedroom was beneath the eaves, small and neat, the walls whitewashed and the floor bare boards softened by a single rug Theresa had braided from scraps of worn-out blankets. The bed was narrow, the quilt pulled tight, because disorder in a room felt to Eliza like disorder in a mind, and she could not afford either.

She climbed the stairs with her body making its objections known at every step. Her calves ached from hours of kneeling on stone and straw. Her shoulders carried the weight of the night's labour, both kinds: the physical work of the foaling and the other work, the harder work, the giving away of things she had never given anyone. The landing was quiet. Charlotte and Louise and Laura were downstairs now, their voices distant and muffled.

She unlaced her boots and set them by the door, toes aligned. She pulled the pins from her braids and let the coils loosen, and her scalp ached with the relief of it. She lay down on top of the quilt in her stockinged feet and her working dress, because the effort of changing was beyond her, and the pillow received her head with a coolness that should have been enough to pull her under.

It was not enough. Her mind would not stop.

The ceiling above her was cracked in one corner, a thin line she had traced with her eyes on a hundred sleepless nights, following its branching path the way she might follow a pedigree chart. She traced it now and saw instead the barn, the lantern, the mare's dark flank, and across from her a man telling her about a girl called Rhiannon who had said she would wait and had not waited.

She had heard the wound in his voice. Not self-pity. Something quieter, the ache of a bone that had healed crooked, functional but never quite right, aching when the weather changed. He had carried it across Spain and back to a valley that was no longer his and away to war again, and he had set it down in the dark beside her own.

The church doorstep. She had told him. The words had come out as if they had been waiting for that hour and that listener, and the saying of them had left her not lighter, exactly, but rearranged. Like a room after the furniture has been moved: the same contents, a different shape, and the light falling in places it had not fallen before.

And then he had said her name.

Eliza, I.

Two words and a breath that caught. She turned them over on the narrow bed, examining them from every angle. What came after the *I*? She knew. She had known in the moment, had felt it in the quality of his voice, the rawness of it, the way the two syllables of her name had sounded in his mouth like a door being opened from the inside. He had been about to say something that could not be unsaid, and the mare's grunt had swallowed it, and the work had carried them forward.

She pressed her face into the pillow. The linen smelled of soap and sunlight, the clean domestic scent of a household Helen managed with invisible care.

Helen's voice, from an hour ago: *The things worth having are rarely the things you planned for.*

She had not planned for this. She had planned for the stables, the broodmares, the foaling season and the requisitions and the management of an estate her father had entrusted to her. She had planned for competence, because competence was the thing she could control, the armour she had built from evidence and expertise and the discipline of never needing anything she could not provide for herself.

She had not planned for a man who listened with his whole body and spoke as though he understood that words, once given, could not be retrieved. She had not planned for the way his hand felt against hers, or the three heartbeats of a kiss so careful it might have been a question rather than an answer. She had not planned for the ache in her chest, persistent as a pulse, the ache of wanting something she had spent eighteen years training herself not to want.

The foundling's fear said: *If you reach for this, it will be taken from you.*

She heard it. The voice was old, older than memory. It spoke from the place that knew only the fact of being left, the first and most fundamental lesson her body had ever learned. Reach for nothing. Need nothing. Build your walls high and your competence higher, and when the world comes to take what you love, you will have something left.

She had obeyed that voice for eighteen years. She had obeyed it so well that she had not recognised what was happening in her own heart until three girls with bright eyes named it for her. She had obeyed it through the kiss and the retreat and the nights alone in this bed, tracing the crack in the ceiling and telling herself that what she felt was manageable, a thing she could fold small and carry discreetly.

It was not small. It filled the room.

She turned on her side and faced the wall, and what lay before her was the whitewashed blankness of a surface with nothing written on it.

She was going to speak to him.

The decision arrived not as a thunderclap but as a settling, as a horse settled into its stride after the first unsure strides of a new gait. She was going to find him today, and she was going to say what she could not yet put words to, and the words mattered less than the act of saying them. The evidence was this: he had kissed her and told her his deepest wound and begun a sentence he could not finish, and she had told him hers, and neither of them had flinched, and that was enough.

The fear did not disappear. It sat beside the decision the way shadow sat beside light, inseparable. She would carry both. She would carry the fear of being left and the courage of staying anyway, because Helen had carried both, and Theresa had carried both, and every woman who had ever loved despite good reason not to had carried both, and the carrying was the bravery, not the absence of fear but the refusal to let it be the final word.

Today. When she woke. She would find him, and she would speak.

Sleep came for her at last, the exhaustion pulling her down, and she went under with the decision held close.

She woke to afternoon light, thick and golden, falling across the quilt in a warm band that had crept from the foot of the bed to her waist while she slept. For a moment she did not know the hour or the day, only that her body was stiff and her mouth was dry and the house around her held the hush of a place where everyone had gone elsewhere.

Then the night came back. The barn, the mare, the filly. The dark and the lantern and two voices. *Rhiannon.* The church doorstep. *Eliza, I.*

And beneath all of it, solid as bedrock: the decision.

She sat up. She stood and splashed water on her face, cold from sitting, and the shock drove the last of the sleep from her eyes. She put on a clean dress and rebraided her hair, working quickly, her fingers knowing the pattern. She buttoned her cuffs. She pulled on her boots and laced them tight.

She was still determined. The sleep had not blunted it. If anything, the hours had done what hours did to good steel: the heat of the night had shaped it, and the cooling had set it, and what remained was harder and brighter than what she had carried to bed.

She went downstairs. The hallway was empty, a ribbon of afternoon warmth lying across the flagstones from the open front door. From somewhere in the back of the house came the sound of Helen in the kitchen, and from the garden the rise and fall of Louise's voice explaining something to Charlotte or Laura or both.

She crossed the yard. She went to the stallion barn first, because that was where he was most often found in the afternoons.

Hermes stood in his stall, his scarred head turned toward the door at the sound of her step. He nickered, the low greeting he gave to people he knew. But the aisle was swept clean, the brush hung on its hook. No Llewellyn. No Pompey.

She checked the broodmare barn. Serenity dozing with her colt asleep at her feet, the mastitis healed. The black mare and the new filly, the mare relaxed and comfortable, the filly drinking. No lieutenant.

The tack room. The feed store. The near paddock, where Ballerina watched with tolerant eyes as her twin fillies chased butterflies. No.

She found Phillip at the water pump.

"Have you seen the lieutenant?"

"I haven't seen him this past hour, miss. Weren't he up all night with the black mare? Might be he's sleeping."

His room. She had not thought to look there, because he was never there during the day, but Phillip was right; he must be tired too. She walked back across the yard. Her pace had quickened without her deciding it should. Something was tightening in her chest, a thread being drawn taut.

The staircase to the room above the stallion barn was narrow and steep, built into the thickness of the stone wall, the steps worn smooth by decades of grooms' boots. The only light came from a single small window at the top. She climbed carefully, steadying herself against the wall.

The landing was small. A row of doors, one, standing open.

She stopped.

The room beyond was small. Clean. A narrow bed against the far wall, beneath a window that looked out over the yard. A wooden chair. A shelf with three books and the newspaper. A candle stub in a pewter holder. The room of a man who had learned to live with little and did not pretend he needed more.

On the bed, his travelling bag lay open.

It was leather, worn at the corners, the sort of bag a soldier carried because it was the right size for the things a soldier owned. Inside it, folded with the economical neatness she had come to associate with everything he did, were his few spare clothes. A shirt. A waistcoat. Stockings, rolled tight. The bag was half-packed, as though the work had been interrupted, as though a man had been putting his life into a bag and been called away before he finished.

The floor tilted beneath her. Or it felt that way, a lurch in her body, the sudden drop of a woman standing at the edge of something she had always known was coming.

He was leaving.

The thought arrived with the force of a hand striking water, the surface breaking, and beneath it the cold, the deep, old cold that had lived in her since before memory. The foundling's cold. The cold of a doorstep in July, of arms that had held her and then set her down and walked away. She had been left before. She had been left first, before anything else, and the leaving had written itself into her body much as a brand wrote itself into hide, and everything she had built since, every wall and every moat, had been built against this.

He was packing his bag. The unfinished sentence in the barn had not been a beginning. It had been a farewell. *Eliza, I am leaving. Eliza, I cannot stay. Eliza, I do not want you.*

She could not breathe. She could not stand in this doorway and look at this bag and feel this feeling and continue to be the woman who managed Belle Haven and argued from evidence, because the evidence was a half-packed bag and the conclusion was abandonment and the conclusion was wrong, it had to be wrong, but the fear did not wait for logic, the fear was older than reason and it filled her chest until there was no room for air.

She turned. She went down the stairs too fast, her boot catching the edge of a worn step, her ankle turning, her hand shooting out to catch the wall. The stone scraped her palm. She stumbled, caught herself, kept going, and the fear drove her forward, toward the answer to a question she could not bear not to ask.

She burst from the stairway into the stallion barn and he was there.

He stood just inside the entrance, silhouetted against the bright afternoon, Pompey at his heels. He carried a bucket in his left hand and his sleeves were rolled and there was hay dust on his shoulders, and his face, when he saw her, changed. The mild expression of a man returning from an errand dissolved, replaced by something sharp and immediate, a soldier reading danger.

He set the bucket down. She was coming toward him too fast, her face showing everything she could not hide, and he stepped forward and caught her by the arms.

His hands closed around her upper arms, firm and steady. The grip anchored her. She felt the roughness of his palms through the cotton of her sleeves, the warmth of his fingers, the strength of his left hand and the careful, compensating pressure of his right. Her momentum carried her forward until she was close enough to see the flecks of darker blue in his eyes and the crease of concern between his brows.

"What's wrong?" he said.

She looked up at him. Her breath came in ragged pulls, and her hand stung where the stone had scraped it, and behind her the staircase led up to a half-packed bag that might mean everything she feared or nothing at all, and she did not have the careful argument she had planned, she had only this: his hands on her arms and his eyes on her face.

"Are you leaving?"

The question left her raw and exposed, stripped of every defence she had ever constructed, and she stood in his grip and waited for the answer.

Chapter Nineteen

His face did not break. She watched for it, the way she watched for the first sign of distress in a labouring mare, reading the muscles around his eyes and the set of his mouth. What she saw was worse than breaking. She saw understanding. He understood exactly what she was asking and exactly what it had cost her to ask it, and the understanding moved across his features like wind across water, visible and then gone.

His hands released her arms. Not abruptly, not the withdrawal of a man caught doing something he should not have been doing, but the careful loosening of a grip that had served its purpose. She felt the warmth leave her sleeves where his palms had been.

He reached into his coat.

The paper he produced was folded in thirds, the creases sharp, the kind of fold that came from official hands. The seal was broken but the wax still clung in fragments to the edge, dark red, the colour of something that had once held something shut and now could not. He held it out to her, and this time the gesture was not the major's, that dismissive offering to a servant.

"This came for me two hours ago," he said.

She took it. Her fingers were cold against the paper, though the afternoon was warm, and the coldness was useful because it kept her hands from shaking. She unfolded it and read.

The language was military. Clipped and without sentiment, the prose of an institution that moved men the way Belle Haven moved horses: by record and requirement, with no allowance for what the creature being moved might prefer. Lieutenant D. Llewellyn, 16th Light Dragoons. Medical leave terminated effective the date of receipt. Report to Horse Guards, London, no later than Friday next. The signature was illegible, the rank beneath it was not: Colonel, Adjutant-General's Office.

She read it twice. The second reading did not change the words, but she needed the repetition the way she needed to check a mare's stitches twice, to be certain of what she was seeing before she trusted her own assessment.

Orders. Not a choice. The half-packed bag upstairs was not the work of one who had decided to leave but of a man who had been told to, and the distinction should have eased the constriction in her chest, should have loosened the band of ice that had cinched around her ribs when she stood in his doorway and saw the leather bag with its neatly folded contents. It did not ease. The ice remained, because the result was the same. The paper said go, and he would go, and the reason did not matter to the part of her that had been left before.

She folded the orders along their creases and handed them back. Their fingers did not touch.

She waited.

He would say something now. He would tell her what this meant, whether he wanted it or fought against it, whether the orders were a relief or a sentence. He would say the thing he had almost said in the barn, the two words and the caught breath that the mare's labour had swallowed. He would finish the sentence. *Eliza, I. Eliza, I don't want to go. Eliza, I want to stay.* Something. Anything she could hold, a handhold on a cliff face, a stone in a stream.

He said nothing.

His eyes were on her face, grey-blue in the afternoon light that fell through the barn's wide doorway, and they held everything. She could see it banked behind the stillness of his expression, the way heat banked behind the closed damper of a stove, present and contained and not permitted to escape. He was looking at her the way he had looked at her last night, the look that said *come here* in a language his mouth refused to speak. And she understood, with a clarity that was itself a wound, that he was waiting too. Waiting for her.

The silence stretched between them like a fence neither of them would climb.

She spoke first. She always spoke first. It was what she did, the woman who argued from facts, who met the world with evidence arranged and ready. Her voice came out level, composed, the manager's voice, and she hated the noise of it even as she heard herself producing it, because it was the voice of a woman in control and she was not in control, she was falling, and the voice was the only thing between her and the ground.

"I am sure you will find your feet again," she said. The words were correct. Encouraging. The kind of thing a person said to a soldier being recalled to duty, a sentiment appropriate to the occasion and empty of everything that mattered. She heard how small it was against the size of what she felt, and she could not reach past the composure and the eighteen years of practice to find the real words, the ones that lived in the place where her fear lived, the words that said *don't go, please, don't go.*

She pressed on, because pressing on was what she did when pressing on was the only direction that did not require bravery.

"I am only sorry I have no mount to give you." She looked at him steadily, and this part, at least, was true in a way she could bear to say aloud. "There is not a single horse left at Belle Haven that can carry a rider. Every sound horse has gone to the requisition. What remains are broodmares, foals, and young stock too immature to be ridden." She paused. The inventory was a litany she had recited to the major and to the duke and to herself in the quiet hours when she counted what they had lost, and it served her now the way it had served her then: as a wall built from facts, solid and useless against the thing it was meant to keep out. "You deserve a Belle Haven horse. You have earned one. And I cannot give you what we do not have."

Something moved in his face. A shift at the jaw, a tightening around the eyes, and then a closing, subtle but complete, as if a door she had been looking through had swung shut. She had said something wrong. Or she had failed to say something right. The distinction was the same, and she could not tell which it was, only that the distance between them, the four feet of swept stone and straw dust, had become immense, a canyon opened by courtesy and competence and the inability of two people who carried the same wound to reach across it.

She had given him a horse inventory.

He stood with her words settling over him like dust after a collapse, each one landing in its correct place, factually sound, practically useful, and entirely beside the point. She was *sorry she had no mount to give him*. She was *sure he would find his feet*. The words were those of someone who managed an estate, who dealt in evidence and assets and the clear-eyed accounting of what was available and what was not, and they told him everything he needed to know.

They told him nothing he wanted to hear.

He had shown her the orders and watched her read them, and he had waited. Not for argument. Not for tears. He did not expect either from Eliza Bell, and would not have wanted them. What he had waited for was something smaller and harder to name. A crack in the composure. A word that was not about horses or duty or the practical arrangements of departure. A *stay*, or *I don't want you to go*.

She had given him a horse inventory.

The voice in his head, his father's voice, the valley voice with its flat vowels and its intolerance for self-deception, assembled the evidence with the methodical patience of a man building a dry-stone wall. *She did not ask you to stay. She did not say she wanted you to remain. She spoke of mounts and requisitions, which are the things she knows, the things that matter to her. You are a useful man, boyo. You have been useful here. But useful is not the same as wanted, and the sooner you learn the difference, the less it will hurt.*

He knew the voice was wrong. He knew it the way he knew a horse he was riding was lame before the limp was visible to an observer, a knowledge that lived in the body below thought. He had held her face in his hands in a kitchen and kissed her, and she had kissed him back, and the three heartbeats of that kiss had contained nothing that could be mistaken for gratitude or professional courtesy. He had sat across from her in the dark and listened to her give him the story of her life, the doorstep and the foundling and the fear, and the giving had been an act of trust so enormous it shook him still. He had watched her laugh in the stallion barn and felt the sound lodge behind his breastbone where it remained, warm and stubborn, refusing to be dislodged.

But she had not asked him to stay. And he could not ask himself, because asking would mean placing the weight of his want on a woman who had spent her life learning that the things she loved would be taken from her, and he would not be another weight she had to carry.

So he matched her. He met her composure with composure, her facts with facts, her careful distance with his own, and the matching was a kind of violence done to himself, a blade drawn cleanly across something that bled only on the inside.

"I am sure you will manage perfectly," he said.

The words were true. She would manage. She had been managing before he arrived and she would manage after he left, because competence was her bedrock and the bedrock would hold. He believed this completely. It did not help.

He watched her face for the flinch. Her dark eyes held his, calm and level, her chin at the angle that meant she was bearing weight and would not show it, and the composure was magnificent and it was killing him.

"I shall leave on Friday," he said. The logistics were a mercy. They required no feeling. "I will walk to Basingstoke and catch the post from there. It will have me in London by Saturday evening."

Fourteen miles to Basingstoke. His leg would protest every one of them. He would carry the bag and every mile would be a mile further from Belle Haven and the woman standing before him, and the arithmetic of distance would be the simplest calculation he had ever made and the most painful.

She nodded.

One nod. Small, contained. The nod of a woman receiving information and filing it in its proper place. He was leaving on Friday. Filed and done and requiring no further discussion. She did not speak. She turned.

She walked out of the barn.

Her back was straight. Her stride was even. She crossed the threshold from shadow into the golden afternoon without breaking pace, and the light caught the tight coils of her braids and the squared line of her shoulders. She did not look back.

The yard had never been so wide.

She crossed it the way she had crossed it a thousand times, the cobblestones familiar beneath her boots, the path worn into her body's memory so that her feet could find it without instruction from her mind. Past the water trough. Past the mounting block. Past the rose that climbed the south wall of the house, its buds tight and green, not yet ready to open. Her back was straight. Her stride was even. She was aware, with the part of her mind that operated at a distance from the rest, that anyone watching from the windows would see a woman walking with purpose, and the purpose would be unreadable, which was the same as invisible, which was the same as safe.

She let herself into the house by the side door. The hallway was blessedly empty. Her hand found the study door. The brass handle was cold. She turned it, entered, closed the door behind her, and leaned against it.

The composure held until the door clicked shut. Then it broke.

Not like glass, which broke all at once and made a sound. Like a wall of packed earth in rain, the water finding the cracks and widening them and the whole structure softening and giving way from within, silent and total. Her face crumpled. Her hands came up and pressed against her eyes, the heels of her palms pushing hard enough to see colour behind her lids, and a sound came out of her that she did not recognise, low and wretched, the sound of someone who had held everything for too long and found the weight had finally exceeded her capacity to bear it.

She moved to the chair. Her father's chair. Her chair. She sat and drew her knees up and wrapped her arms around them and made herself small in a way she had not been small since childhood, curled into the leather that smelled of ink and saddle soap and a man's particular ghost, the ghost of one who was on the other side of the Channel and could not help her.

He was going. The fact was a stone in her chest, heavy and cold, with edges. He was going because the army said so, because a colonel at a desk had signed a piece of paper and the paper had more authority over David Llewellyn's life than she did. Friday. Three days. He would pack the leather bag, the one she had seen half-filled on his narrow bed, and he would walk fourteen miles on a leg that ached in the damp, and the post road would carry him to London and London would send him to war.

To war. She pressed her forehead against her knees and felt the fabric of her dress against her skin, coarse cotton, workday cloth. She knew what war did. She had seen it in his body, in the arm that would not grip and the leg that stiffened after standing, in the scars he carried lightly and never mentioned. She had seen it in Hermes's face, the clouded eyes and the livid puckering where a cannon blast had written its name across a living creature. She knew what happened to cavalrymen who went into battle on unfamiliar horses, horses that had not been bred and trained for the chaos of gunfire and smoke and the terrible geometry of a charge.

He would not have a Belle Haven horse. He would have whatever the army gave him, some requisitioned animal, perhaps sound, perhaps brave, but not Hermes, not a horse that had come through fire for him, and she could not fix this. She could not breed a horse in three days or heal his arm with the needle and silk she used on yearlings, and competence, the thing she had built her life upon, the armour she had forged from evidence and expertise, could not protect him from a cannon or a sabre or the sheer, dumb arithmetic of a battlefield where good men died as readily as bad ones.

And she had given him a horse inventory.

The grief twisted sharper. She had stood in the barn with his hands on her arms, his eyes open and raw, and she had retreated. She had spoken about mounts and requisitions, the words of a woman conducting business, and he had heard them and matched them, and the matching was her fault, because she had set the register and he had followed. She had offered him facts when he needed something else. When she needed something else. She had needed to say *I don't want you to go*, and the words had been right there, behind her teeth, pressing to get out, and the foundling's fear had clamped down on them and swallowed them whole.

The fear had won. Eighteen years of practice, eighteen years of building walls and keeping distance, and at the moment that mattered most the practice had held. She had performed composure when composure was the last thing she wanted, and the performance had been flawless, and the cost of it was that he would leave on Friday believing she did not care enough to ask him to stay.

She cried. Not quietly and not prettily and not the way women cried in the novels Charlotte sometimes read aloud in the evenings. She cried the way exhaustion cried, deep and ragged, the sobs pulled up from a place below her stomach, her body shaking with the force of them, her face pressed against her drawn-up knees. She cried for the man in the barn and the foal born at half past three and the sentence he had started and could not finish and the sentence she had needed to start and could not begin. She cried for the girl left on a doorstep who had grown into a woman so afraid of being left again that she could not say the one word that might make someone stay.

The door opened.

She had not heard the knock, if there was one. What she heard was the click of nails on the floorboards, the heavy, deliberate sound of Caesar's claws, and behind it the lighter sound of stockinged feet. The door closed. Footsteps crossed the room, unhurried, certain, moving with the quiet sureness of a girl who had memorised every piece of furniture in this house and could find any of them in perfect darkness because perfect darkness was the only kind she knew.

Laura did not speak. She did not ask what was wrong. She came around the edge of the desk and found the arm of the chair by touch and then found Eliza, and her hand rested on Eliza's shoulder with a pressure that was light and absolute, the same hands that had held a terrified yearling's muzzle and hummed the panic out of him.

Eliza looked up. Laura's face was turned toward her, sightless and calm, and on it was not surprise or alarm or the bright-eyed concern that Charlotte would have worn. It was something older. Something that had been waiting, the look of a girl who had known this was coming the way she knew where the fence posts were and where the stall doors latched, by a sense that had nothing to do with sight and everything to do with the deep, quiet attention she paid to the people she loved.

Eliza had no defences against that look. She reached for Laura and buried her face in her younger sister's shoulder, and the fabric of Laura's dress was soft against her cheek, and Laura's arms came around her, steady and sure, and Eliza cried.

Laura held her. She did not shush her or rock her or say *it will be all right*, because Laura did not say things she could not verify, and the future was not something anyone could promise. She held Eliza the way she held frightened animals, with the whole of her body committed to the act of holding, her thin arms stronger than they looked, her chin resting against the top of Eliza's braids. Caesar came to rest at their feet, his enormous body a warm barricade against the rest of the world.

The sobs subsided slowly. They came in waves, each one smaller than the last, and between them Eliza breathed, and the breathing was ragged and wet and graceless and real. She kept her face pressed against Laura's shoulder because lifting it would mean returning to the composure, and she was not ready. Not yet.

Laura spoke once.

"You haven't told him," she said.

It wasn't a question. It was a statement, quiet and certain, each word chosen with the care of a girl who understood that language was precious and should not be spent carelessly.

Eliza shook her head against Laura's shoulder. The motion was small, defeated, the admission of a failure she could not explain to anyone who had not lived inside her skin and felt the foundling's cold.

Laura's hand moved to the back of Eliza's head. Her fingers found the place where the braids began, the tender skin at the nape, and rested there.

"You will," Laura said.

Two words. Soft and certain. Not a hope but a conviction, spoken by a girl who saw nothing and understood everything, whose gift had always been the knowledge of what was true before the rest of the world caught up. The words settled into Eliza's chest beside the grief and the fear, and they did not dissolve either, but they sat between them, small and warm and stubborn, like a coal that refused to go out.

Eliza closed her eyes. Laura held her. The study was quiet. Outside, the yard went about its business, and the horses called to each other across the paddocks, and Friday was three days away, and the world continued, as it always did, indifferent to the fact that her heart was breaking.

Chapter Twenty

THE CHESTNUT TWO-YEAR-OLD HAD the enthusiasm of
a boy let loose at a fair and the aim of a man trying to thread
a needle in a thunderstorm.

Llewellyn stood at the rail of the breeding yard with
his arms folded and his jaw set against the laugh that was
building in his chest like pressure behind a dam. The colt
had been led in ten minutes ago, bright-eyed and quivering
with purpose, his nostrils flared wide at the scent of the
mare, his whole body vibrating with an energy that said
he understood, broadly, what was expected of him and
intended to give it his absolute all. The mare, a steady grey
called Prudence whose name had never been more apt,
stood at the centre of the yard with the expression of a
woman who had seen everything and was not impressed.
Her ears were forward. Her hind legs were planted. She

chewed a mouthful of hay with the philosophical calm of an animal who had done this before and planned to survive it again.

The colt mounted. Or attempted to. He came at her from a trajectory that would have been more appropriate for clearing a fence, launching himself upward with his forelegs scrabbling at the air somewhere in the vicinity of her hindquarters. He missed. Not by much, but by enough. His hooves slid down her flank, his balance went with them, and he staggered sideways with the affronted dignity of a young horse who could not fathom why the mechanics should prove so complicated.

Prudence did not move. She continued chewing.

Beside him, Eliza made a sound. It was not a laugh. It was the sound of a woman compressing a laugh into the smallest possible space, a tight exhalation through the nose that would have been inaudible if he had not been listening for it with every nerve in his body. Her hand gripped the top rail, and her knuckles were pale, and the corners of her mouth were doing something extraordinary, turning in two directions at once as discipline fought hilarity to a draw.

They could not laugh. The colt was young and easily rattled, and a breeding yard required the same measured calm as a foaling stall. Laughter would undo the whole enterprise. The colt would startle, the mare would lose patience, and the afternoon's careful work would need to begin again.

Discipline held. Just.

The colt circled. He approached again, more cautiously this time, his neck arched and his nostrils working. He placed his chin on the mare's croup and stood there for a long moment, breathing, his flanks heaving with the effort of restraint, and in that moment he looked so precisely like a young man summoning his nerve before asking a girl to dance that Llewellyn had to turn away and press his fist against his mouth.

When he turned back, Eliza was looking at him. Her eyes were bright with the laughter she would not release, and her lips were pressed into a line that trembled at the edges, and the look she gave him was shared conspiracy, two people who understood that the next thirty seconds would determine whether their composure survived.

The colt mounted again. This time the angle was better. The forelegs found their purchase and the quarters drove forward and the mechanics, at last, aligned, the whole performance achieved with the graceless sincerity of a creature who had been born knowing what to do and simply needed his body to catch up with the knowing. Prudence stood. She stopped chewing. Her ears flicked once, backward and then forward, the equine equivalent of a polite acknowledgement that something was occurring.

It was over quickly. The colt dismounted, or rather slid off, one hind leg buckling slightly, and stood beside the mare with his head low and his sides heaving and an air of bewildered triumph. Prudence resumed chewing.

Eliza let out her breath. The sound she made was halfway between a sigh and a laugh, and it escaped her control and filled the yard, warm and unguarded, and Llewellyn felt the sound travel through him and settle in the place behind his ribs where he kept the things he could not afford to lose.

He was storing this. He knew it as it happened, the way a man knew he was memorising a landscape he would not see again: the quality of the afternoon light falling gold across the breeding yard, the dust motes in the warm air, the chestnut colt standing with his head down in the attitude of a creature profoundly satisfied with himself. Eliza at the rail beside him, the tight coils of her braids catching the light, her face open with amusement. The smell of warm horse and dry grass and the faint sweetness of the lime trees beyond the paddock fence.

He had been writing handover notes since dawn. The ledger lay on the desk in the tack room with four pages of his careful script, each entry laid out, the work of a man ensuring that what he left behind would function without him. Thornton's routines. The foaling schedule for the autumn. The feeding regimen for the weanlings. Which mares to watch, which paddocks needed the fence mending he had not got to. The blind stallion's habits: his preference for the left side of the stall, the three-note whistle that brought him, the way he startled at sudden sounds on his right where the blast damage was worst. All of it laid out in the language of handover, the army's word for the moment one man passed his responsibility to another and walked away.

Tomorrow. The word sat in him with the weight of ordnance. He was leaving tomorrow. The post from Basingstoke departed at half past ten, which meant he needed to be on the road by six to make the walk on his leg without rushing.

Nobody knew. Eliza knew, but she was the one person who knew, and neither of them had spoken of it since the barn, since the orders and the horse inventory and the careful, courteous matching of composure that had left them both exactly where they had been, which was nowhere at all. He had not told Charlotte or Laura or Louise. He had not told Helen. He had not told Thornton, though the handover notes were for him, and the old groom would find them on the desk tomorrow morning and read them and understand.

He could not say it. The silence was irrational, superstitious, the magical thinking of a child who believed that closing his eyes made the world disappear. If he did not speak the words, if the shape of leaving did not exist in anyone's mouth but his own, then perhaps the orders would not be real.

But he was a soldier. He knew the difference between hope and delusion, and the border between them was a line he could no longer see.

The colt was being led away, his head high, his step a little unsteady, the swagger of a young horse who had crossed a threshold and emerged changed. Prudence followed at a walk, serene and unruffled. The breeding yard emptied. The afternoon held its warmth.

Eliza leaned on the rail beside him, her forearms resting on the top bar, and her shoulder was close enough that he could feel the heat of her through the cotton of his sleeve. She was looking at the yard where the colt had been, and whatever she saw in the empty space, she did not share it.

He let himself have this. The last uncomplicated good thing. The warmth, the light, the rhythm of her breathing beside him. He held it the way he had learned to hold moments in the field, with open hands, knowing they could not be kept but committing them to the place in the mind where things were stored against the long winters ahead.

The afternoon turned. The light moved. Neither of them spoke, and the silence, for once, was enough.

Charlotte had the stud book open on the flat top of the paddock wall, the pencil working in her small hand, and the expression on her face was the one she wore when the world was behaving according to her specifications. She had watched the chestnut colt's performance with the assessing eye of a girl who evaluated equine encounters as a jeweller evaluated stones: cut, clarity, and the likelihood of producing something valuable.

"Douro's confidence," Charlotte said, not looking up from the page. "And Patience's bone. If the foal inherits even half of what it should, we'll have something worth watching." She paused, the pencil hovering. "Assuming, of course, the colt improves his technique. That first attempt would have been rejected by the Royal Society as physically implausible."

The laughter came easily. It moved through the group the way warmth moved through a stable in winter, and Eliza let it carry her for a moment, the simple pleasure of girls laughing together in the sun. Llewellyn stood a few yards away, leaning on the far rail, and his mouth had curved into the half-smile that she now knew meant he was amused but did not wish to intrude, and the half-smile was like a fishhook in her chest, small and bright and barbed.

Laura sat on the mounting block with Caesar stretched across the cobblestones at her feet, a brush in her hand working through the thick brindled coat in long, slow strokes. The mastiff's eyes were half-closed, his tail giving an occasional thump when the brush found a good spot behind his shoulder. Laura's face was tilted toward the sun, and the light fell across her features, turning her skin to gold and her hair to something close to white. She looked peaceful. She looked as though nothing troubled her, and perhaps nothing did, or perhaps the things that troubled her were held so far below the surface that even the girl who carried them could not always feel their weight.

Eliza watched her sister and wondered. Three days ago Laura had held her in the study while she wept, and Laura had said *you haven't told him* and *you will*, and the words had been spoken with the quiet certainty Laura brought to everything. But they had not spoken of it since. Laura had not asked. She had not pressed, or hinted, or arranged her silence in the pointed way Charlotte might have done.

She had simply continued, brushing the dog and sitting at meals and moving through the house with her hand on Caesar's collar, and if she carried knowledge of Eliza's heart she carried it the way she carried her blindness: privately, without complaint, as a fact of her landscape.

Eliza did not know what Laura believed she had been crying about. The orders, perhaps. Or the feelings themselves. Or the impossibility of both at once, a woman discovering love and losing it in the same breath. Laura might know all of it or none, and the uncertainty was both a comfort and a reproach, because if Eliza could not tell her own sister what was happening, the walls were higher than she thought.

Louise sat on the bench outside the tack room with her hands folded in her lap. Her dark hair was neatly pinned. Her posture was exemplary. She was doing nothing, with a thoroughness that bordered on performance art.

Since Helen's reprimand, Louise had been behaving herself with the visible, self-conscious effort of a girl for whom not interfering was a physical trial. She did not mention the lieutenant's name. She did not arrange the watch schedule. She did not manufacture errands that required both of them in the same room. The absence of these interventions was, if anything, more conspicuous than the interventions themselves. Louise's restraint had the quality of a held breath, and everyone in the yard could hear the not-breathing.

"Charlotte," Louise said now, her voice so carefully neutral it could have been used to calibrate a scale, "shall I fetch you more ink?"

Charlotte looked up from the stud book. "I am writing in pencil."

"Yes," Louise said. "I know. But if you needed ink. For later."

"I do not need ink."

"Right." Louise folded her hands more tightly. Her jaw worked. She looked at the sky as though it might offer her a task she was permitted to undertake, and the sky, blue and placid and unhelpful, offered nothing.

Eliza would have laughed if laughter had not been so dangerous today. The afternoon was warm and ordinary and full of the sounds of a functioning estate. Charlotte was writing the future into her stud book, line by careful line. Laura was brushing Caesar. Louise was suffering nobly. The horses were fed and watered and the foals were growing and the fences stood and the work continued, the great daily work of keeping a place alive, and the place was alive, despite everything the war had taken from it.

This was what she had built. Not alone. With Llewellyn's hands and Thornton's loyalty and Charlotte's mind and Laura's gift and Helen's quiet governance and Louise's ungovernable helpfulness. But the architecture of the days was hers, and the place was standing.

And none of them knew.

Tomorrow morning Llewellyn would walk down the lane with his leather bag and his blind horse would stand in his stall and listen for footsteps that did not come, and Pompey would lie at the barn door waiting, and the space he had filled in their lives would be empty, and they did not know. Charlotte did not know that the man whose horse had given her breeding programme its spine was leaving. Laura did not know that the man she had welcomed with *I'm glad he came* was being taken away. Louise did not know that the matchmaking she had been forbidden to pursue would be rendered moot by a colonel's signature.

Eliza had not told them, because telling them meant making it real, and the superstition was the same as Llewellyn's, the irrational belief that silence could hold back the tide. She also had not told them because she did not know how to say it without her voice breaking, and a breaking voice would require explanation, and the explanation would reveal everything she had spent weeks trying not to reveal, and the walls were crumbling fast enough already.

The afternoon held. Charlotte wrote. Laura brushed. Louise sat. The sun moved across the cobblestones, and dinner was coming, and after dinner the evening rounds, and after the rounds the night, and after the night, Friday.

She pressed her hand against her pocket and felt through the fabric the sharp edge of a folded piece of paper she had taken from the desk in the tack room that morning, on which Llewellyn had written, in his careful script, the handover notes for a man who did not yet know he would need them. She had not meant to take it. She had seen it and picked it up and read the first line and could not put it down, because the first line said *Thornton: the below should serve as a guide in my absence*, and the word *absence* had struck her like a hand across the face, and she had folded the paper and put it in her pocket, and it had sat against her hip all afternoon, the weight of it enormous and invisible.

She leaned on the fence and watched the yard and held the secret and felt its edges press against her.

The candles on the dinner table threw a warm, unsteady light across the dishes, and the roast chicken sat in its own juices on the platter, and the bread was fresh and the butter soft and the room smelled of rosemary and the clean green scent of the herbs Helen had cut that afternoon, and all of it was ordinary, and all of it was unbearable.

Eliza served herself from the dish of potatoes Charlotte passed her. She cut a piece of chicken and placed it in her mouth and chewed and tasted nothing. She reached for her water glass and drank, and the coolness was useful because her throat was tight, the tightness of a woman holding something behind her teeth that wanted desperately to come out.

Charlotte was talking about the breeding. The chestnut colt's first cover, the notes she had taken, the foal she projected from the cross. She spoke with the fluency of a girl whose mind ran on rails of pedigree and probability, and her voice was bright in the candlelight, and Eliza listened and nodded in the right places and contributed a remark about Prudence's previous foals that came from some competent, automatic part of her brain while the rest of her was drowning.

Louise passed the bread with both hands. She complimented Helen on the chicken with the exaggerated sincerity of a girl who had been told to behave and was behaving so hard it had become its own form of theatre. Helen accepted the compliment with a gracious nod and a glance at Louise that said *I see what you are doing and I appreciate the effort*, and Louise beamed, and the exchange was gentle and funny and Eliza felt the prickle behind her eyes sharpen to a sting.

Laura's hand found hers under the table.

The touch came without announcement, Laura's fingers sliding across the linen and closing around Eliza's with a pressure that was light and definite, the way Laura touched everything: knowing exactly where it was, how much force it needed, and what it meant. Eliza's breath caught. She did not look at Laura. She could not, because looking would break something, and the table was small and the candles were bright and Helen's eyes missed nothing.

She held Laura's hand. She held it much as a woman in a current held a rope, not because the holding was comfortable but because the alternative was being swept away.

At the far end of the table, Llewellyn ate. He answered Charlotte's question about the chestnut's dam line with his usual steadiness, his face composed. He spoke about the foal's prospects as if he would be here to see them. He did not say *tomorrow I am leaving* and *the foal will be born without me* and *the colt will cover his second mare and I will not be there to hold the laughter in my chest*. He ate his dinner and he was polite and he was present and he was already gone, retreating behind the composure she had taught him to match, and the courtesy between them was a knife that cut in both directions.

She had seen him with the newspaper that afternoon, standing at the desk in the tack room, his face grim. Not alarmed. Grim in the way of a man reading news he had expected and finding no comfort in the expectation.

She did not know what he had read. She did not want to know.

She had stopped reading the newspapers weeks ago, when the silence from Belgium became the silence that woke her at three in the morning. The papers carried dispatches, troop movements, reports of armies massing on the frontier. They carried lists of the sick and missing from earlier campaigns. She had read the lists once, running her finger down the columns, her heart striking her ribs at every B, and had not found Bell, and the absence should have been a relief but was not, because absence from a list only meant the list was incomplete or the news had not yet arrived. The papers did not tell you your father was safe. They told you only that he had not yet been reported otherwise, and the difference between those two things was a gap wide enough to fall through.

So she had stopped reading. She had let Llewellyn read them instead, without asking him to, without acknowledging the arrangement. He read the dispatches and he said nothing, or he said *the French are massing on the frontier* or *Wellington is still in Brussels*, small pieces of information offered without weight, as though the war were a passing interest and not the thing that might have taken her father and was now reaching back across the Channel to take him too.

When he was gone, she would read them. She knew this with flat certainty. She would pick up the paper each morning and run her finger down the lists, and there would be two names to search for instead of one, and the searching would be a different kind of labour, solitary and unwitnessed.

Laura's thumb moved across her knuckles. A small motion, back and forth, the same motion Laura used on Caesar's ears when thunder rolled across the valley and the great dog pressed against her legs.

Helen was watching. Eliza felt the gaze the way she felt a change in the weather. She kept her eyes on her plate and cut another piece of chicken she did not want and placed it in her mouth and chewed, and the act of chewing required concentration, because if she stopped concentrating on the mechanics of the meal, the tears would come, and she could not cry at the dinner table. She could not cry in front of Charlotte and Louise, who would want to know why. She could not cry in front of Helen, who would already know. She could not cry in front of Llewellyn, who was sitting four feet away and leaving tomorrow and had not finished a sentence that began with her name.

The meal continued. The candles burned. Charlotte talked about bloodlines. Louise offered seconds. Laura held Eliza's hand beneath the table, steady as a heartbeat, the grip of a girl who knew what was coming and could not stop it and would not let go.

Llewellyn set down his fork. He looked at his plate, and then at the table, and then, briefly, at Eliza. The look lasted less than a second. It held everything a look could hold without breaking open. Then he rose, excused himself with a word about the evening rounds, and left the room, and his uneven footsteps crossed the hall and went out through the side door, and the sound of them faded, and he was gone.

Not gone. Not yet. Tomorrow gone. Tonight still here, still in the barn with the blind horse and the dog, still close enough that she could walk across the cobblestones and find him if she had the words and the courage.

Helen began to clear the plates. Charlotte and Louise rose to help. Laura released Eliza's hand, and the absence of the grip was a cold place on her skin. Laura stood, Caesar rising with her, and paused.

"Tomorrow," Laura said, very quietly, so that only Eliza could hear.

One word. Eliza could not tell if it was a question or an instruction or a prophecy. Laura turned and followed the sound of her sisters' voices toward the kitchen, Caesar's nails clicking on the stone.

Eliza sat alone at the table. The candles guttered in the draught from the open door. The newspaper lay folded on the sideboard where Llewellyn had placed it before dinner, and she did not touch it, and the not-touching was its own kind of discipline, the last she had left, and she held it close and waited for the morning.

Chapter Twenty-One

Friday came with birdsong.

Eliza had not slept. She had lain in the narrow bed beneath the eaves and listened to the house settle into its night sounds, the creak of old timber, the distant shift of a horse in its stall, and beyond all of it the silence of a world that did not know or care that a man was leaving in the morning. She had watched the darkness thin at the edges of the curtain, the black becoming grey becoming the pale, uncertain colour of a sky not yet committed to the day, and when the first thrush began its elaborate argument with the dawn she rose and dressed and went downstairs, because waiting in bed for what was coming was worse than going to meet it.

The yard was empty. The cobblestones held the damp of the night, dark and gleaming where the first light touched them. She stood at the pump and washed her face and the cold water ran over her hands and she thought: by ten o'clock he will be on the road.

She had not spoken to him since dinner. She had not gone to the barn. The courage she had summoned in the study, the decision that had settled into her spine like bedrock, had not survived the evening. Or it had survived, but the words had not, dissolving each time she tried to hold them. She had lain awake and composed sentences and discarded them and composed them again, and none of them were right, and the wrongness was not in the words but in the fact that no arrangement of words could bridge the distance between what she felt and what she was able to say.

She filled the kettle. She set it on the range. And then looking out of the kitchen window as she waited for it to boil, she saw something odd.

A boy from the village, fourteen or fifteen, running as though his life depended on it, which was unusual and made her step outside to meet him.

"Bonaparte's beaten! The French are beaten! There's been a great battle, miss, at Waterloo, and Wellington's won!"

He held out the newspaper. It was creased and damp and had been passed through several hands already, the ink smudged where fingers had gripped too hard. Eliza took it. The boy was still talking, the words tumbling over each other, but she had stopped hearing him because her eyes had found the headline and the headline had found the place in her chest where the fear lived and struck it like a bell.

GLORIOUS VICTORY. BONAPARTE DEFEAT-ED.

The dispatch was dated the twenty-first. Three days for the news to cross the Channel, another day for the London papers to travel south to Hampshire by mail coach.

The details were sparse and grandiose in the way of early reports, all triumph and no cost, the language of a nation that wanted to celebrate before it counted its dead.

She read it twice. The print swam. She pressed the heel of her hand against her eye and read it again, and the third reading did not change the words, but the words changed her, the way a key changed a lock: the same mechanism, a different position, and suddenly the door could open.

Her father. Somewhere in Belgium, in the aftermath of whatever Waterloo had been, her father was alive or he was not. The paper did not say. The paper said victory. It did not say at what price, or whose blood had purchased it, or whether a man from Hampshire who bred horses and loved his daughters had survived the day.

Phillip burst from the broodmare barn at a run. The boy from the village had run off there when Eliza took the paper, and behind Phillip came the other young lads, erupting into the yard like corks from bottles, whooping and hollering and clapping each other on the shoulders with the uncomplicated joy of young men for whom the war had been a tax on their horses and their futures and was now, God willing, over. Behind them came Thornton, his face showing pure, unadulterated relief. The old groom looked ten years younger, laughing at the antics of the boys.

Eliza stood with the newspaper in her hands and watched them, and the watching felt like looking through glass, the sounds reaching her muted and distant, as if the news had placed her inside something transparent and separate. She could see the joy. She could not yet reach it.

Through the kitchen doorway she saw Helen. The older woman stood at the table with her hands braced on its surface, her blonde head bowed, her eyes closed. She did not move. The posture was prayer or grief or relief or all three, and Eliza understood, because Helen had known soldiers, had known the cost of wars fought by boys who did not come home, and the victory was real and so were the dead, and Helen was holding both.

Charlotte appeared on the house steps. Laura behind her, Caesar pressed against her leg, and Louise behind Laura. Charlotte stopped in the doorway. Her face was bright and fierce and very young, the face of a girl who understood the news intellectually and was only now feeling it arrive in her body. She turned to Laura, and Laura was already turning to her, and their arms found each other with the practised ease of twins who had been reaching for each other since before memory. Louise's arms came around them both, her dark head between their blonde ones, and the three of them stood in the kitchen doorway and held on, and the holding was the purest thing in the yard.

Eliza stood alone on the cobblestones. The newspaper hung from her right hand, the ink already staining her fingers. Above her the sky had committed itself to blue, the pale, washed blue of an English summer morning, a sky that suggested the world was simple when the world was not.

Bonaparte was beaten. The war might be over. Her father might be coming home.

And the man she loved still had orders in his pocket, and the relief and the grief sat side by side in her chest the way they had always sat, the way they sat in everyone who had ever lived through a war, the joy of survival pressed against the knowledge of what survival cost.

She looked toward the stallion barn. The door was open. Inside, a horse moved, and she heard the low murmur of a voice she knew, speaking to the horse in the careful, steady tone of a man who had fought in the war that was now, perhaps, over, and his voice undid something in her that the headline had not touched.

She folded the newspaper. She crossed the yard.

The cheering reached him through the barn walls the way sound reached a man underwater: present but blunted, the sharp edges softened by stone and timber and the twelve feet of shadow between the doorway and the stall where he stood with his hand on Hermes's neck.

He had heard the boy's shout. He had been at the desk in the tack room, writing the last of the handover notes, the final entry the hardest because it concerned Hermes and the words for how to care for a blind horse who trusted you were not words that fit in a ledger. The shout had come through the open window, high and clear and carrying the vibration of news that could not wait for breath. *Bonaparte's beaten. The war is won.* He had set down the pen. He had stood very still for a long time, his hand flat on the desk, his eyes on nothing.

Then he had gone to the stallion barn, because the stallion barn was where Hermes was.

The dapple-grey stood in his usual position, the left side of the stall, his scarred head turned toward the door. The scars were livid against the pale coat, and the eyes that had once been clear brown were clouded and still, seeing nothing and missing nothing, because Hermes had learned to navigate a world without sight as a man learned to navigate a world without the girl he loved: by feel, by memory, by the stubborn insistence that the ground was still there even when you could not see it.

Llewellyn pressed his forehead against the stallion's neck. The coat was warm, the coarse hair carrying the clean scent of the grooming he had given that morning, the last grooming, the one he had not allowed himself to think of as the last because thinking it would have made his hands unsteady and the horse deserved better than unsteady hands.

Waterloo. A place in Belgium he had never seen. A battle fought three days ago while he stood in a breeding yard in Hampshire and watched a chestnut colt fail to mount a mare, and laughed, and looked at a woman whose face in the afternoon light was the closest thing to peace he had found since coming home from the war.

Home. The word caught. He had used it loosely, the way displaced men did, applying it to wherever the bed was and the roof held. But Belle Haven had taken the word and filled it, the way water filled a vessel, conforming to its shape and becoming inseparable from it, and the thought of leaving was the thought of being poured out onto bare ground.

The men. His mind went to them as it always did, the roll call he carried in his head alongside the living. Sergeant Davies, who had a laugh like a horse's whinny and who had stopped laughing at Salamanca. Corporal Hughes, nineteen years old, who had shown Llewellyn a miniature of his mother every morning as though the showing were a prayer, and who had been shot through the lung at Vitoria and died calling for her. The troop farrier whose name he could not remember, which was the worst thing, worse than the dying, because it meant the forgetting had begun.

They would not come back. However many had fallen at Waterloo, in the mud and smoke of a battle he had not been there for, they would not come back. Their mothers and fathers and wives would receive letters, or would not receive letters, and the absence would be the answer.

Hermes shifted and leaned against Llewellyn's shoulder, the slow, deliberate lean of a horse who trusted the body beside him to take the weight. The pressure was consider-able. Sixteen hands and the muscle of a stallion who had carried men through six years of war, and the lean was not weakness but affection, the horse's way of saying *I am here.*

Llewellyn took the weight. His left leg protested, and he braced against it and held.

Her footsteps crossed the barn aisle. He knew them before they reached the stall, quicker than Thornton's, lighter than Phillip's, with a decisiveness in the fall of the boot that said the woman who wore it knew where she was going and why. The footsteps stopped at the stall door, and the quality of the air changed the way it always changed when she entered a space he occupied.

She did not speak. She leaned on the half-door, her forearms on the top edge, and she waited. He could feel her attention on him, warm and steady, a woman's attention, one who understood that some silences needed company but not interruption.

The barn held them. The sounds of celebration had faded or been absorbed by the stone walls, and what remained was the horse's breathing and the creak of timber and the distant call of the thrush that had been singing since dawn, tireless and oblivious.

"I keep thinking of the men who won't come back," he said.

His voice was quiet. It belonged to the barn and the hour. He did not look at her. He looked at Hermes's scarred face and saw in it every scar the war had left on every creature it had touched.

"I know," she said.

She did not tell him it was over. She did not say they died for something. She said *I know*, which meant she saw what he was carrying and would not try to take it from him or make it lighter, because some things were not meant to be made lighter. They were meant to be carried, and the best a person could do was stand nearby and let the carrier know the ground would hold.

She stayed. The minutes passed. Hermes sighed, the deep, whole-body exhalation of a horse at rest, and his weight eased off Llewellyn's shoulder, and the stallion lowered his head and stood quiet.

Llewellyn straightened. He turned, finally, and looked at her. Her face was composed but not closed. Her dark eyes held his, and in them he saw the same layered thing he felt: grief and relief and the terrible, complicated gratitude of having survived something that was not yet fully understood.

"I still have to go," he said. The words were steady, because they were facts and facts were what she trusted. "Orders are orders." He paused. "But the war is over, if the dispatch is true. And if the war is over, they won't need a cavalry officer with a bad leg and a worse arm. There is a good chance they will release me to half-pay again."

He did not say *I will come back*. He would not make a promise the army had the power to break. But the possibility sat between them in the morning light, and it was the first thing that had sat between them in days that was not a wall.

Her hands tightened on the stall door. He saw the knuckles whiten, the tendons shift beneath the dark skin, and the tightening said more than the composure on her face, and he read it the way he read a horse's body, the small involuntary language that told the truth the mouth would not.

The words had been living behind her teeth for weeks. She had felt them there in the kitchen after the first kiss, in the dark of the foaling barn, in the study with her knees drawn up and Laura's arms around her. They had pressed against the back of her lips like foals pressing against a gate, impatient for the field, and she had held them because holding was what she knew, because the foundling's first lesson was that you did not reach for things that could be taken, and the lesson had been written so deep it operated below thought, below decision, in the place where instinct lived.

She had held them through the horse inventory. Through the dinner where Laura gripped her hand beneath the table. Through the long, sleepless night and the birdsong and the morning that had brought a boy shouting victory. She had held them so long they had become a physical thing, a stone in her throat, a pressure behind her breastbone that made breathing a conscious act.

Half-pay. He had said there was a good chance. The words should have loosened the fist inside her chest, and they did, partially, much as a tourniquet loosened when the bleeding slowed but had not stopped. A good chance was not a certainty. A good chance was the language of one who had been promised things before and learned that promises bent under weight.

She opened her mouth to say something measured. A sensible observation that his injuries alone would be sufficient grounds for discharge. She opened her mouth and the measured words dissolved, and what came out instead was the truth, raw and unvarnished and terrible in its simplicity.

"I don't want you to go."

The sound of her own voice shocked her. It was not the voice of the girl who faced requisition officers and wielded facts like weapons. It was the voice of someone stripped of every defence she had ever built, standing in the rubble.

The silence that followed was immense. She heard her heart in it, and the horse's breathing, and the creak of the barn, and beneath all of it the foundling's voice, the old voice, rising from the cellar where it lived: *You have done the thing you swore you would never do. You have reached. You have needed. You have given someone the power to leave you, and they will, they always do.*

She could not stop. The wall was broken and the water was coming and she could no more hold it back than she could hold back a tide.

"I don't want you to go," she said again, and her voice cracked on the last word, a fracture running through it like the crack in her bedroom ceiling, "and I don't know what to do with that."

She could not look at him. Her eyes found the straw on the barn floor, the worn grain of the stall door, the white crescents of her own knuckles where her fingers gripped the wood. The tears came without permission, welling up from the place the words had opened, warm and relentless, sliding down her cheeks. She did not wipe them. Wiping would require her to move her hands, and her hands were the only things keeping her upright.

His boots shifted in the straw. She heard him move toward the stall door, heard the latch click as he opened it, and then he was in front of her, close enough that she could feel the warmth of him, the warmth she had memorised against her shoulder in the foaling barn and carried with her since.

His fingers found her chin.

The touch was light but certain, the way he touched horses, the way he touched everything: with deliberation, with the understanding that carelessness caused harm. His fingertips rested along the line of her jaw, his thumb beneath her chin, and he lifted her face gently, giving her time to resist if she chose to resist.

She did not resist. She let him raise her face, and the letting was the bravest thing she had ever done, braver than standing before the major, braver than managing an estate stripped of its horses, braver than any act of competence she had ever performed, because competence was armour and this was the opposite of armour, this was standing with nothing between her skin and the world.

She looked at him. His face was very close. His grey-blue eyes held hers, and what she saw was not the careful distance of the past two weeks. What she saw was a man who had been waiting for her to say exactly what she had said, who had been standing on the other side of the same wall, pressing his own palms against the stone, and the wall was gone now and they could see each other clearly for the first time.

He kissed her.

Not the three heartbeats of the kitchen. Not the careful, questioning pressure of a man unsure of his welcome. This was his mouth on hers with intent behind it, weeks of restraint collapsing into the contact, his hand sliding from her chin to the curve of her jaw, his fingers threading into the place where her braids began at her temple. His other hand found her waist, the right hand, the one that could not always grip, and it gripped now, pulling her toward him with a sureness that said the arm remembered what it was for when the reason was sufficient.

She kissed him back. Her hands released the stall door and found his chest, the rough linen of his shirt, the warmth of his body beneath it, the steady percussion of his heart against her palm. She kissed him the way she had wanted to kiss him since the kitchen, since the fence, since the first morning she had looked up and found his eyes on her and felt the ground shift: fully, without caution, without the composure that had kept her safe and kept her alone.

She tasted salt. Her own tears, caught between their mouths, and the salt was the taste of what it had cost her to get here, every sleepless night and every swallowed word, and the cost was enormous and the kissing was worth it, and she knew both things at once with a clarity that was itself a kind of freedom.

The kiss ended the way a wave ended, drawing back with reluctance, the last of it clinging to the shore. His forehead rested against hers. She could feel his breath on her mouth, warm and unsteady, and his hand was still in her hair, his fingers gentle against her scalp, and the distance between them was nothing. A breath. The width of a promise.

"Come home," she said. Her voice was wrecked, low and thick with tears, but the words were clear. "When they've finished with you. Come home. To Belle Haven."

She said Belle Haven because it was the truest name she could give to the thing she meant. Not *to me*, because the words were too large and too new and she was not yet certain her mouth could hold them. But Belle Haven was real. Belle Haven was the stallion barn and the foaling straw and the kitchen where he had first kissed her. Belle Haven was the place where all of it had happened, and if she could not yet say *come back to me* she could say *come back to this*, and the meaning was the same, and they both knew it.

His thumb traced the curve of her cheekbone, following the track of a tear, and the gentleness undid a shift in her that the kiss had not yet reached.

"I will," he said.

Two words. Quiet and certain. The voice of a man who had learned what broken promises sounded like and was choosing to make one anyway, because some things were worth the risk of breaking, and the making was the bravery, and he was brave enough, and she believed him.

He looked around the barn.

The light fell through the wide door in a warm oblong that reached across the swept aisle and touched the edge of Hermes's stall. Dust motes turned in it, slow and gold. The tack hung in its ordered rows, the leather oiled and supple. The water buckets were full. The straw was clean. Every surface bore the evidence of care, the daily, unglamorous care that was the difference between a stable that functioned and one that merely existed, and the care was hers, and he had been part of it, and the being part of it had been the truest work of his life.

He smiled. Not the half-smile he wore to keep from intruding but the real thing, the one that reached his eyes and changed his whole face, and Eliza was looking at him, her cheeks still wet, her eyes dark and bright, and the smile was for her and for the barn and for the cobblestones he could see through the doorway and the paddocks beyond them and the hills beyond those.

"Home," he said.

The word had been hollow for two years. A sound without a room behind it. His valley had been home and then it was not, and the army had been home because it demanded everything and the demand was its own kind of belonging, and Belle Haven had been a place he arrived at with a blind horse and nowhere else to go.

She had given the word back to him. She had said *come home, to Belle Haven*, and the word had filled up again, as a dry stream filled after rain, the water finding the old channel as though it had never been empty.

He kissed her once more. Briefly, because if he did not keep it brief he would not leave. Her lips were salt-sweet, warm, and the softness of them was a thing he would carry until he could come back to her. He drew back. Her hand was on his chest, over his heart, and she pressed once, deliberate, the way she pressed a hand against a horse's shoulder to say *I am here*, and then she let go.

He went upstairs. The bag was packed. He shouldered it. He looked around once at the simple, small room, and then he made his way back down the narrow stairs.

Eliza waited at the bottom, beside Hermes's stall. Llewellyn set the bag down. He stood before the horse.

Hermes's muzzle found his hand, the soft upper lip working across his palm, the blind horse's handshake, his way of reading a person much as a man read a face. The nostrils flared and blew warm air against Llewellyn's wrist. The horse knew him. Had always known him, since the smoke and the whistle and the moment a stallion had come through fire because a man called in the way Belle Haven had taught him must be answered.

He placed his hand on the broad, scarred forehead. The ridged tissue was warm. He stood with the horse and felt the weight of what they had been through settle between them, all the miles and all the fear and the night the cannon spoke and the world went white, and the long walk across a continent with a horse who could not see and a man who refused to leave him.

"Look after her," he said. His voice was low, pitched for the horse alone, though he was well aware Eliza could hear. "She is more stubborn than either of us, and she will not ask for help, and she will need it, and you must give it to her without her asking, which you are better at than I am."

Behind him, Eliza made a sound. Not a sob. A laugh. Wet and broken and real, the laugh of someone who had been crying and found something funny in the wreckage, and the sound went through him like sunlight through a window. He turned and saw her face crumpled and bright at the same time, tears and the ghost of a smile, and the sight was so beautiful and so painful that he had to look away before it undid the last of his resolve.

Hermes nickered. The low, vibrating sound he made for the people he trusted, and Llewellyn pressed his forehead against the stallion's cheek, one breath, two, and stepped back.

He picked up the bag. He eased the strap. Pompey rose and fell into step at his left heel, the dog's place, chosen years ago and never varied.

"Friday next," he said to Eliza. "I will write when I know more."

She nodded. Her arms were crossed over her chest, holding herself together, and her chin was up and her shoulders were square, and the composure was back but different now, not a wall but a bridge, a woman's particular composure, the composure of one who had let someone see what was behind it and was putting it on again not to hide but to stand.

He walked out of the barn. The cobblestones were warm beneath his boots, the morning sun full on the yard, the sky the pale blue that promised heat later. He crossed the yard and passed the mounting block and the water trough and the rose that climbed the south wall, its buds still tight, not yet open, waiting for the warmth that would bring them, and he thought: *I will see those roses bloom. If not this summer, then the next.* He would see them.

The lane began where the cobblestones ended, packed earth and flint, the hedgerows rising on either side thick with hawthorn and dog-rose and the first elderflower. His left leg found its objection early, the shin tightening with each step, and by the third stride the familiar ache had settled in, a companion he neither welcomed nor fought.

He looked back once.

The yard lay behind him, sun-warmed and still. The stable buildings stood in their solid grey, the stone carrying three generations of horse-keeping in its grain. The paddocks stretched beyond, green and rolling, and in one of them Ballerina's twin foals galloped in circles for the pure, delirious joy of having legs.

And at the barn door, Eliza. She stood at Hermes's head, one hand on the stallion's neck, and the horse had lowered his scarred face and placed his chin upon her shoulder, the full weight of it, the blind, absolute trust of a creature who could not see the person holding him and did not need to. Her hand was steady on his neck. She was not waving. She was simply there, the woman and the horse, standing together in the entrance to the place they both belonged to.

He held the image. He pressed it into the place deep in his chest where he kept the things he could not afford to lose, alongside the sound of her laugh and the taste of salt and the two words she had given him that had changed the meaning of everything: *come home*.

He turned back to the lane. The hedgerows rose around him, fragrant and close, and the road stretched ahead, and behind him Eliza stood with Hermes, and neither of them was going anywhere, and he would come back to them.

He would come home.

Chapter Twenty-Two

THE LANE WAS NARROWER than he remembered.

Or he was wider. Not in body, because the rations in Belgium had been poor and the weeks after the battle worse, but in the way a man became wider after seeing certain things, the mind expanding to accommodate horrors it had not been built to hold, and the expansion left you feeling too large for the spaces that had once contained you. The hedgerows pressed close on either side, hawthorn and dog-rose and the heavy, drooping heads of elderflower that brushed his knee as the horse passed, and the scent that rose from them was so thoroughly English, so extravagantly peaceful, that it sat against the smell of powder smoke and turned earth that still lived in his nostrils and the contrast made his throat tight.

The horse beneath him was not his own. A brown gelding requisitioned from somewhere in Flanders, adequate but without distinction, the kind of animal the army produced in quantity and forgot immediately. Sir Richard Bell had ridden better horses before he could walk, and the gelding's short, choppy stride was a constant, minor irritation, like a conversation conducted in a language he spoke but did not think in. His own horses were in Hampshire. The ones that remained. He did not yet know which or how many, and the not-knowing had kept him company across the Channel and up the Dover road and through the long, dusty miles of Kent and Surrey and into Hampshire, where the land softened and greened and the air tasted of chalk and grass and the faintest breath of the sea.

The gate stood open. He passed through it and the cobblestones began beneath the gelding's hooves, the sound changing from the dull thud of packed earth to the sharper ring of iron on stone, and the change was the noise of arrival, and his hands tightened on the reins.

The yard was swept. That was the first thing. The cobblestones were clean, the gutters clear, the water trough full and glinting in the mid-morning light. The stable buildings stood in their solid grey stone, and every door was latched, every hinge oiled, every surface bearing the marks of daily, deliberate attention. The mounting block had been scrubbed. The tack-room window was open to the air. A barrow of fresh straw stood outside the broodmare barn, half-emptied, the work of someone called away in the middle of mucking out.

He rode slowly through the yard, reading it the way he read a horse's body, by the small signs that told the larger truth. The hay store was well-stocked. The muck heap was managed, turned and steaming gently in its proper corner. A row of halters hung on their pegs outside the yearling barn, each one cleaned and repaired, the leather supple. The feed bins were shut against rats. Someone had held this place together with both hands, and the holding had been thorough.

But the riding horses were gone. He noticed their absence the way you noticed a missing tooth, by the space where the thing should have been. The lower paddocks, which in summer would have held a dozen hunters and hacks, were empty. The schooling ring stood unused, its surface baked hard. The cross-country fences along the ridge, which he had built himself over three summers, cast their shadows on undisturbed grass. The war had reached into his yard and taken what it needed, and what it had left behind was the breeding stock, the future, the animals too young or too old or too pregnant to carry a soldier.

He passed the stallion barn. Through the open door he caught the movement of a grey shape in the dimness, a horse he did not recognise, and he marked it for later and rode on.

Ballerina's paddock lay beyond the kitchen garden, sheltered on three sides by the old stone wall and the line of lime trees his grandfather had planted in the year of the American war. He saw the mare first. She stood in the shade of the largest lime, her bay coat darkened by the shadow, her head low. She was carrying her age openly now, the sway in her back deeper than before he left. But she was plump, her coat glossy, and she was alive, and when his eyes found the two small shapes beside her the tightness in his throat became something else entirely.

The foals. Twin fillies, almost four months old, leggy and bold, chasing each other in tight circles through the long grass with the pure, extravagant joy of creatures who had never known anything but safety. One broke away and galloped the length of the fence line, her tiny hooves drumming, her tail a dark flag behind her. The other followed, and they met at the corner and reared and struck at the air with their forelegs in a miniature battle that was all play and no consequence, and Ballerina watched them with the tolerant, sleepy expression of a mother who was content to let the young be young.

Eliza was at the fence.

She leaned on the top rail with her forearms crossed, her face turned toward the foals. She wore a working dress, the sleeves rolled to her forearms, the fabric faded from washing. She was sturdy and still and entirely herself, the girl he had left standing in the yard four months ago with the weight of an estate on her shoulders, and the weight had not broken her. He could see that from thirty yards. The set of her spine said it. The calm of her hands on the rail said it. The way she watched the foals said it. He dismounted, eyes on her, but did not cross the space between them. Not yet. He was savouring being home, the solid feel of Belle Haven beneath his boots, this land where he had been born and bred, had loved his wife and raised six remarkable daughters even though truly, none of them were his.

The dogs found him first. Caesar's deep bark broke the stillness, the massive sound rolling across the yard, and behind it Pompey's answering bay, and then they were coming, both of them, the two great brindled shapes covering the distance with the flat, driving run of mastiffs who had identified something that required their immediate attention. Caesar reached him first, his huge head driving into Richard's thigh hard enough to stagger him, the tail swinging with a force that could have cleared a table. Pompey arrived a half-second later and reared up, enormous paws on Richard's chest, and the weight nearly took him off his feet, and the gelding shied sideways, affronted, and Richard laughed.

The sound of his own laughter surprised him. He had not been certain he still knew how.

She turned because the dogs told her to.

Caesar's bark was unmistakable, the deep boom that came from a dog the size of a small pony, and it was not the bark he used for strangers. Strangers received a sound like masonry collapsing, low and terrible and designed to make a man reconsider his choices. This was different. The bark of recognition, urgent and joyful, and beside it Pompey's answering cry, higher and wilder, the two dogs calling to each other and to the thing they had found with an excitement that could not be contained.

She turned.

A man stood in the sun just a few yards distant. Tall. Dark-haired. The gelding behind him was unfamiliar, but the man was not. The man was the shape she had been searching for in every approaching figure on every road for four months, the shape her eyes had manufactured from shadow and distance a dozen times only to dissolve upon inspection, and this time the shape did not dissolve.

Her father.

The composure she had built and rebuilt and carried through every requisition and every foaling and every sleepless night and every morning she had opened the newspaper and searched the lists and not found his name broke. It did not crack or crumble. It fell. The whole structure, all of it, the competence and the steadiness and the manager's voice and the eighteen years of practice at not needing anything she could not provide for herself, went down at once, and what stood in its place was a girl whose father had come home.

Her hands left the fence. Her knees were uncertain. She took a step and then another and her boots found the grass and the grass held her and she was walking and then she was running, the working dress catching at her legs.

He met her. His face was thinner than she remembered and there were lines around his eyes that had not been there in March and he was wearing a coat she did not recognise, and none of it mattered because it was him.

His arm came around her shoulders.

Not both arms. One. The gesture was not an embrace but a settling, as you settled a hand on a horse's withers to say *I am here*. His arm was heavy across her shoulders, carrying the smell of road dust and sweat and the faint, foreign scent of wherever he had been, and beneath it all the smell that was simply him, leather and horse and the soap he had used for as long as she could remember.

"Well done, my girl," he said. His voice was quiet, pitched low, meant for the creature beside him and no one else. "Well done."

That was all. He did not ask what she had done or how she had done it. He did not request an inventory or a report. He looked at the yard, at the swept cobblestones and the mended fences and the full water trough and the foals galloping in Ballerina's paddock, and he said *well done*, and the two words held everything: the trust he had placed in her when he left, the knowledge that the trust had been met, the recognition that what she had held together had cost her.

It was enough. It was so far beyond enough that the word itself seemed small and foolish, a cup held up to an ocean.

She leaned into his arm. She pressed her face against the rough cloth of his coat and breathed, and the breathing was ragged, and she did not care, because her father was here and the ground was holding and the foundling's fear, the old, cold certainty that the people she loved would leave and not come back, had been wrong. It had been wrong this time. The leaving had an ending, and the ending was his arm around her shoulders and his voice in her ear and the dogs circling their legs with tails that struck like cudgels.

At the fence, Ballerina raised her head. The old mare's ears came forward, and she walked to the rail with the careful stride of a horse who was moving more slowly each year but had not yet forgotten what urgency felt like. She stretched her neck over the top bar and her nostrils worked, and the soft sound she made was not a whinny but something lower and older, the sound a mare made when the person who had lifted her from the straw as a newborn foal came back into range of her senses.

Richard's hand found the bay muzzle. He stood with his arm around his daughter and his palm against the horse he had given to his wife because he trusted this mare with something infinitely precious, and they stood.

Then they went inside. The hallway received them, cool and dim after the bright yard, and the sound of their entry travelled through the house, finding every corner.

Charlotte came first. She appeared at the top of the stairs with a stud book in her hand and her blonde hair escaping its pins, and the word she had been forming dissolved when she saw him. She was down the stairs in a rush, the stud book dropped on the stairs, her arms around his waist before he had crossed the threshold, and the sound she made was not words but the bright, uncontrolled cry of a girl who had been brave for months and did not need to be brave for one more second.

Laura came behind her. Slower, her hand on the wall. She did not rush. She descended the stairs with the careful sureness of a girl who knew every surface by touch, finding the dropped stud book with her toe and stepping over it. She reached the bottom and stood, her face tilted slightly upward, her sightless eyes directed toward the rise of Charlotte's crying.

"Laura," Richard said. Just her name.

She walked to him. Her hand found his arm and travelled up it to his shoulder and then to his face, her fingertips light against his jaw, reading him the way she read everything. Whatever she found there satisfied her, because she nodded once and leaned in and let him hold her.

Helen appeared from the kitchen with flour on her hands and her apron dusted white. She stopped in the doorway and looked at the man surrounded by his daughters and his dogs, and her expression was complex and private, the look of a woman who had kept watch over another woman's family and could now, at last, hand the watch back. She wiped her hands on her apron, and she smiled, and the smile was warm and full and faintly trembling at the edges.

"Welcome home, Sir Richard," she said.

Louise stood behind Helen, vibrating with the effort of not throwing herself across the hallway. Her dark eyes were bright. Her hands were clasped so tightly the knuckles showed white. She bounced once on her toes, caught Helen's glance, and composed herself with visible, heroic restraint.

"We are so very glad you are home, sir," Louise said, and the words came out in a rush, and the formality was betrayed entirely by the crack in her voice, and Richard looked at her over Charlotte's head and his mouth curved.

"I cannot tell you how good it is to be home, Louise. Thank you, both of you, for helping to take care of my girls."

Eliza took him to the stallion barn after they ate a hasty meal of bread and soup Helen and Louise pulled together, when Helen had satisfied herself that he had eaten enough and Charlotte had been gently prised from his arm and Laura had returned to her chair by the window with Caesar at her feet and the household had collected around his presence like sediment after a disturbance, finding its new level.

The walk across the yard was short, but she began talking before they reached the door, because the words had been waiting for him the way the yard had been waiting, maintained and orderly and ready to be handed back. She started with the requisitions. The facts came first, because facts were what she trusted, and the facts were these: thirty-seven horses taken in the first round, the unbroken three-year-olds in the second, the major with his papers and his indifference and his insistence that the army's need superseded the estate's. She told him the plan they had made with the three-year-old colts, destroyed in that second requisition, and that they had then looked to the younger colts, and of course to Hermes.

Richard listened. He walked beside her with his hands in his pockets, reading the yard as she had seen him read it a thousand times. He did not interrupt. He asked no questions. His silence had the quality of a vessel being filled, and she poured into it.

They entered the barn. The light was cooler, filtered through the high windows. The smell was the smell of her life: clean straw, warm horse, oiled leather, and beneath it the sweetness of a stone building that had housed horses for three generations and absorbed them into its walls.

Hermes stood in his stall, left side, as always. His scarred head turned toward the door. The ears came forward. The nostrils widened, working, reading the air. He found Eliza first, and the low nicker came. Then the nostrils widened further, and the head lifted, and the stallion stood very still, assessing the second set of footsteps with the careful attention of a horse who had learned that not every stranger was safe.

"This is Hermes," Eliza said.

Her father had stopped. She watched his horseman's eye do what it did, the swift assessment that took in conformation and condition and scars and clouded eyes in a single sweep. She saw him register the dapple-grey coat, the powerful shoulder, the clean legs. She saw him register the blindness. His face did not change, but something behind it did, a shift in his attention, the way light turned when it passed through water.

"He was sent from Belle Haven as an unfinished three-year-old, seven years ago," she said. "Charlotte identified him. His mother was Celestine, the granddaughter of Eclipse."

She watched the word land. Eclipse. The greatest sire of the century, the foundation stone of every Thoroughbred worth the name, and her father knew what it meant.

"I remember Celestine," her father said. "And her grey colt. Unpromising, I thought him, but I didn't geld him because of that bloodline. I never thought he'd come back to us, not after all this time. What happened to him?"

"A lieutenant brought him back," she said. "David Llewellyn. Sixteenth Light Dragoons. He was at Sandhurst when Molly demonstrated the whistle."

Richard's head turned. She saw the connection made instantly, because her father had invented that three-note call and Molly had taken it to Sandhurst and the rest was history, the kind that lived in a horse's memory rather than in books.

"His first engagement," she said. "The horse he was riding, Osiris, was shot from under him. He was surrounded, certain of capture. He remembered the whistle. He gave the call, and this horse came to him through cannon smoke and musket fire and carried him to safety. He rode Hermes for two more years. When a cannon blast blinded him, the lieutenant refused to have him destroyed. He walked him home."

She had not planned to tell the story with this much detail. But the story demanded its own telling, because the man who had lived it mattered and the horse who stood before them was the living proof.

"We didn't call him Hermes," Richard said. "The lietenant named him that?"

"Yes."

"We'll have to give him another name for the stud books. We had a stallion called Hermes when you were a little girl, a great chestnut, do you remember?"

Eliza shook her head. "Charlotte knew about it, though. We've been calling him Hermes the Blind, for the records."

"That'll do well enough, then."

Richard stepped forward. He raised his hand slowly, giving the horse time, and offered the back of his knuckles to the scarred muzzle. Hermes investigated. The nostrils flared, the soft lip worked across Richard's skin, the blind horse's ritual of introduction. Then the head dropped, and the stallion stepped forward and pressed his forehead against Richard's chest with the slow, deliberate pressure of a horse who had made a decision.

Her father's hand came up to rest on the broad neck. He stood with the stallion leaning against him, and his face held an expression she had seen only rarely, the expression of a man who understood something about a horse that went beyond breeding and conformation, into the territory of what an animal had survived and what it had chosen to become.

"We've put him to thirty mares for next year," Eliza said. "Charlotte has the breeding charts. The Eclipse dam line is irreplaceable. His sire line runs through Mercury, so we cannot cross him with Mercury-line mares, but the possibilities beyond that are extraordinary. Charlotte can show you. Charlotte will insist on showing you. We put him to Ballerina too. I know you weren't going to breed her again but her foal died and she took on those twins and she's so healthy, and she liked Hermes, she was a dreadful flirt with him..."

She heard herself talking faster. She told him about the two-year-old colts, the chestnut's first cover. She told him about the bay mare who had carried twins and died, and the twin fillies who would have starved if not for Ballerina. She told him about the black mare's long labour and the filly born at half past three, black as her dam with a white star between her eyes.

She told him about the work the lieutenant had done. The words came differently when she spoke of him, though she could not have said how. She said he had mended fences and cleaned stalls and carried feed and done every task without complaint and without pulling rank. She said he had deferred to her authority and had never tried to overrule her. She said there were five foals alive who would have been lost without his skill, his hands steady in the small hours, his patience with a frightened mare. The way he had seized King Arthur, the colt who hadn't known he had been born, and squeezed and squeezed him until the colt seemed to wake up and scrambled to his feet. She said Charlotte's breeding programme existed because he had brought Hermes back to them, and the thirty foals they would produce next year would carry bloodlines nearly lost to a cannon blast and the army's standing orders on the disposal of blinded animals. She said he had received orders recalling him to London and had left on foot because there was not a single rideable horse left on the property to carry him.

She said all of this. She did not say the rest.

She did not say that he had kissed her in the kitchen and she had kissed him back. She did not say that he had told her about Rhiannon in the dark, or that she had told him about the church doorstep, or that the telling had changed the shape of her in ways she was still discovering. She did not say that his unfinished sentence lived in her chest like a second heartbeat. She did not say that she had wept in the study while Laura held her. She did not say that she had told him *come home, to Belle Haven*, or the way his thumb had traced the track of a tear down her cheek, or that she had watched him walk down the lane until the hedgerows swallowed him and had stood at the barn door with Hermes until she could no longer pretend she might still see him if she looked hard enough.

She did not say she loved him. She had not yet said those words to anyone, including herself, in any arrangement she trusted to be accurate and complete.

But she heard herself. She heard the way his name surfaced in her account like a stone in a stream, unavoidable, the current parting around it and reforming and parting again. She heard the quality of her voice when she described his hands in the foaling stall, and the care in the breeding yard, and the patience with the blind horse who trusted him. She heard what the words were doing beneath their factual surface, the way a river's noise told you about the depth beneath even when you could not see the bottom.

And she suspected her father heard it too.

Richard stood with his hand on Hermes's neck. He had not interrupted. He had not asked a single question, which was itself remarkable, because her father was a man who asked questions the way other men breathed, reflexively and without ceasing. His silence said he was letting her speak, and his silence also said he was listening to more than the words, hearing the spaces between them with the attention of a man who had raised six daughters and loved a woman who had once been a governess with no prospects and had learned, in the process, that the most important things people said were the things they could not quite bring themselves to say.

His blue eyes found hers. Clear and steady and very kind. The kindness was the worst part, because it told her he knew. Not the details. Not the kiss or the sentence or the specific geography of a heart that had opened itself against its own better judgement. But the shape of it, as a horseman knew a mare was in foal before the belly showed, by the change in her eye and the way she carried herself and the subtle alteration in the quality of her attention.

He knew. And he did not ask. He simply stood with his hand on the blind stallion's neck and looked at his daughter, and what passed between them was the oldest form of love, the love that saw clearly and held its tongue and waited for the person it loved to be ready.

"He sounds," Richard said, "like a man worth knowing."

The words were simple. They could have meant anything. They could have been the polite acknowledgement of a competent employee, the assessment of a useful officer, the observation of a gentleman about another gentleman. But they were none of those things, and they were all of them, and the way he said them, quietly, with the faintest curve at the corner of his mouth, told her he was saying something larger and trusting her to hear it when she was ready.

She nodded. Her throat was tight. The stallion breathed between them, the slow, even rhythm of a horse at rest, and the barn held them in its cool, quiet stone, and the afternoon light moved across the floor in its warm arc.

Her father's hand rested on Hermes's neck. Outside, the yard was clean and the foals were growing and the roses on the south wall had opened while she was not watching, the tight green buds unfurling into white. The summer was here. The war was over. And somewhere on a road between London and Hampshire, a man with a leather bag and a limp might already be walking home.

Chapter Twenty-Three

THE LETTER ARRIVED ON a Tuesday, carried by the regular post from London, and Theresa held it at breakfast with a delighted smile, though she decried the creased and crumpled state of the paper. It had taken a long time to come from Vienna, across a continent reeling in the aftermath of war.

"March the fifteenth," Theresa read aloud. "A girl. Seven pounds and healthy, and Clara recovering well, though the doctor insists she must rest at least two months before attempting the journey." She looked up from the page, her brown eyes bright. "She says Anna has been impossible. Anna has reorganised the entire household in Vienna and has begun calculating the most efficient route home, and Lord Ashburton has given up arguing with her because, and I quote, 'one might as reasonably argue with the tides.'"

Charlotte laughed. The sound filled the parlour with a warmth that had nothing to do with the July sun pouring through the open windows and pooling on the faded carpet. She sat on the floor beside Laura's chair, her legs folded beneath her, a stud book balanced on one knee because Charlotte was never more than arm's length from a stud book. Laura smiled, her face turned toward the sound of their mother's voice, her fingers resting on Caesar's skull.

The curtains stirred in the breeze. Beyond the window, the yard lay in its mid-afternoon quiet, the cobblestones pale with dust, and beyond the yard the paddocks stretched green and rolling.

"They would have waited longer than eight weeks to leave, with the turmoil," Theresa said, folding the letter along its original creases. "But I think they must be on their way by now. They could be home any day. All of them. Clara and Matthew, Anna and Ashburton. Home."

Home. The whole family, gathered beneath one roof for the first time since the war scattered them. Clara, who had gone to Vienna before Eliza could memorise the new shape of her sister's face as a married woman. Anna, whose mathematical mind and fierce practicality Eliza had missed with a specificity that surprised her, the way you missed a particular tool from a workshop rather than tools in general, and her husband, whom Eliza had met so briefly at Matthew and Clara's wedding she could not quite bring to mind what he looked like.

Eliza smiled. She said the guest rooms would need airing and the linens checked, and Theresa nodded and said she would see to it, and the conversation turned to preparations. Laura volunteered to arrange flowers, recruiting Louise. Charlotte said she would have the breeding records ready for Anna's inspection, because Anna would want to see the accounts within the first hour, and this was not a criticism but an acknowledgement of a sister's nature offered with affection and the faintest competitive edge.

The talk flowed around Eliza like water around a stone. She sat in her chair and ate her toast and listened and nodded, and beneath her composure something pressed against her ribs with a steady, patient ache.

The family would be reunited, since Molly and Tim would surely come too with baby Alexander. All of them. Every Bell, every husband, every child, gathered in the house where the walls knew their voices. It was right and good and she wanted it with an earnestness that embarrassed her, the earnestness of a woman who had spent four months holding the place together and was ready to share the weight.

But in her heart the family was larger than the letter described. In her heart it included a tall man with a Welsh accent and a careful way of handling horses and a sentence he had begun and could not finish, and that man had walked down the lane seven weeks ago with a leather bag on his shoulder, and he had said he would write, and he had not written.

Seven weeks. She had counted them the way she counted days to foaling, marking each one off, and the post arrived each morning and each morning it carried nothing with his handwriting on it. She had stood at the hall table and sorted the letters with hands that did not shake, because shaking hands would have been noticed, and she had filed the absence quietly, without comment.

There were reasons. The army was a mechanism of staggering inefficiency, capable of moving a hundred thousand men across a continent but incapable of releasing one lieutenant in a timely fashion. The post was unreliable. He might have been sent somewhere before being discharged. He might be on his way. The reasons were sound.

The foundling's fear did not care about reasons.

The fear said: *He is not coming. He said he would write and he has not written, and a man who does not write is a man who has decided.* The fear said: *You reached. You said come home, and the hope is dying, because this is what happens. The people you love walk away.*

She pressed her thumbnail into the pad of her finger, a small, sharp point of pain. Theresa was talking about the nursery. Two babies in the house. Molly's Alexander and Clara's girl, seven pounds and healthy, and the joy of it was real and Eliza felt it, a warmth in her chest that sat directly beside the cold, because she had never known a happiness that was not accompanied by the awareness of how easily it could be taken away.

"Eliza?" Theresa's voice, gentle. "Are you quite well?"

"Perfectly," Eliza said. She stood. "I should check on the weanlings before the evening feed."

She left the parlour. She crossed the hallway with her shoulders squared and the ache as constant as a pulse, and behind her the family talked about homecoming, and she carried the silence of the one person who had not come home, and the carrying was familiar, and the familiarity was the cruellest part, because it meant she had been right all along. The walls had failed anyway, and the sky beyond them was enormous and empty, and she walked into it alone.

Theresa found her eldest daughter in the stallion barn, as she had known she would. Ever since she came home, Eliza had been spending a great deal of time there, more than she ever had before.

Theresa paused at the entrance and let her eyes adjust. The barn's interior held a cooler register, the stone walls banking the day's warmth. The smell was one she had loved since before she had language for loving: straw and leather and warm horse and the faint mineral scent of old stone. She had come to Belle Haven as a governess fifteen years ago, a thin, uncertain girl from an orphanage who knew little about horses except that she loved them, and the barn had been the first place she felt safe, because horses did not judge you for being plain or poor or unsure of your place in the world. They judged you only for how you handled them, and Theresa had learned to handle them well.

Eliza stood in the stallion's stall with a body brush, working in long, firm strokes along the horse's barrel. The brush moved with the grain of the coat, each pass releasing a shimmer of dust that caught the light from the high window. The stallion stood with his head low and his scarred eyes half-closed, leaning into the brush with the boneless contentment of a creature who trusted the hands upon him completely.

Theresa watched. She had been watching Eliza with the patient attention of someone who understood that subtle differences told the truest stories. The yard was immaculate. The horses were healthy. Charlotte's breeding charts were remarkable. Eliza had done everything asked of her and more.

But something had shifted. There was a weight in her daughter's silence that had not been there before. The composure was intact, but it had the quality of something being held rather than something that simply was, and Theresa knew the difference, because she had held her own composure for years before Richard had gently, patiently, shown her that putting it down would not mean falling apart.

She stepped into the barn. Eliza's brush paused for the briefest moment, the hesitation of a woman deciding what face to wear.

"Don't stop on my account," Theresa said. She leaned on the stall door. The stallion's scarred head turned toward her, the clouded eyes unseeing but the ears attentive.

Eliza resumed brushing. Her face was composed. Of course it was. Eliza's face was always composed, even at four years old, and the composure had worried Theresa then and worried her now, for different reasons.

"I had letters from Helen while I was away," Theresa said.

She kept her voice mild. She did not look directly at Eliza. She looked at the stallion, because she had learned from Helen that the most effective way to get an honest answer from a guarded person was to give them a direction other than your eyes to face.

"Helen is a thorough correspondent," Theresa continued. "She wrote about the requisitions, and the foaling, and Charlotte's breeding programme, and how hard you were working. She wrote about the household accounts, which were in such good order that Anna will be disappointed to find nothing to correct." She paused, letting the silence do its work. "She also wrote about Lieutenant Llewellyn. Rather more, I should say, than your letters contained on the subject."

The brush stilled. The stillness lasted two heartbeats, and in those two heartbeats Theresa read the whole story, or enough of it, because a mother knew what a stillness like that concealed.

"Is there anything you would like to tell me?" Theresa asked. The question was an open door. She would not push through it. She would stand beside it and wait, the way she waited for shy foals who needed time before they would come to her hand.

Eliza's back was to her, and her shoulders were square, and for a moment Theresa thought the composure would hold, that Eliza would turn with a measured account of a useful officer who had contributed to the estate and departed in good order, the facts arranged like cutlery on a table, neat and gleaming and telling you nothing about the meal.

Eliza turned.

Her face was breaking. Not the controlled fracture of a woman permitting herself a moment. The whole surface going at once, the way ice broke on a pond in spring, cracks appearing everywhere simultaneously, too many and too fast to stop. Her mouth opened and no words came. Her eyes, those dark, steady eyes that had faced down requisition officers and managed an estate stripped bare, filled with tears that spilled before she could catch them.

The brush dropped from her hand. It struck the straw with a soft sound that was somehow louder than any sound Theresa had heard in months. And Eliza, her most self-possessed daughter, the girl who had never cried in front of her, not when she scraped her knees and not when the village children said cruel things about her skin and not when Theresa had explained, carefully and kindly, the story of the church doorstep, stood in the stallion's stall and wept.

Theresa's heart seized. She had expected deflection, or a careful admission in the manager's voice. She had not expected the walls to come down all at once, as if the lieutenant's name had been the last brick and the removal of it had brought the structure crashing inward.

She opened the stall door and crossed the straw, and Hermes shifted to make room, his blind head turning toward Eliza's weeping with an alertness that was not alarm but attention, the focused concern of a creature who understood distress and did not shy from it. Theresa's hand found Eliza's shoulder, and beneath her palm she felt the tremor, the shaking of a body that had carried too much for too long and was finally setting it down.

"Oh, my darling," Theresa said, and her voice caught, because the sight of her strongest daughter in pieces was a thing she had not prepared for, and the not-preparing was its own kind of grief, the grief of a mother who had been away when her child needed her and could not make up the distance now, could only stand in the wreckage and hold on.

She had not meant for this to happen.

She had not meant to cry. She had not meant for Theresa to see her like this, cracked open in a stall, the walls lying in rubble. She had planned to carry it the way she carried everything: privately, without complaint, invisible from the outside.

But Helen had written letters. And the question had been so gentle, the door held open with such patience, that the composure had not cracked so much as dissolved, the way salt dissolved in warm water, the structure simply ceasing to exist.

She could not stop. She pressed her hands against her face and the tears ran between her fingers and her breath came in ragged, graceless pulls. The shame was enormous. The shame said: *You are Eliza Bell, you manage this estate, you argue from facts, you do not fall apart in a horse's stall because a man you kissed twice has not written to you.* The shame said: *Get up. Wipe your face. Give your mother a measured account and move on.*

She could not get up.

Hermes moved. His scarred head came around, slow and deliberate, the careful motion of a horse navigating by touch and sound and the geometry of trust he had built within the walls of his stall. His muzzle found her shoulder. The soft lip worked across the fabric of her dress, reading her, and then his head dropped lower and pressed against her arm. He was leaning into her. The way he had leaned into Llewellyn in the barn, the full weight of his trust offered without reservation.

She turned into him. She buried her face in the thick grey mane, the coarse hair rough against her cheek, and the mane smelled of grooming dust and clean horse, and beneath it the warm, alive smell of a creature who was here, who was solid, who would not walk down a lane and disappear. She gripped the mane with both hands and held on.

Theresa's hand was on her shoulder. Her mother was speaking, the words arriving through the roar of Eliza's own breathing, shapes rather than sounds.

She tried to speak. Her mouth opened against the horse's mane and the words came out broken, each one a shard of something that had once been whole.

"He said he would write," she managed. The sentence was wretched. It was the complaint of a girl, not a woman, and she heard how small it sounded against the scale of what she meant. "He hasn't. Seven weeks. And I told him to come home, I said it, I said the words, and he said he would, and he hasn't written, and I don't know."

She did not finish. The not-knowing was the worst, worse than grief, worse than the foundling's certainty that she had been left again. The not-knowing was a door that could open onto anything, and she could not see through it, and the not-seeing was driving her mad.

Theresa's hand tightened on her shoulder. The grip said *I am here*, and it was not enough but it was something, the way Helen's hand had been something on the morning after the foaling.

Outside the barn, a mastiff barked.

The sound was enormous, the deep, rolling boom that shook the air, felt in the chest before the ears could parse it. Eliza knew that bark. She had lived with it for years, and this was not the bark for strangers. The stranger bark was low and terrible, designed to rearrange a man's priorities. This was the recognition bark. The bark that said a known person, a loved person, had come within range.

A hand settled on her back.

Not Theresa's. Theresa's hand was still on her shoulder, small and warm and maternal. This hand was larger. It covered the space between her shoulder blades with a breadth and weight that was entirely different, and the warmth came through the cotton of her dress and reached her skin, and the touch was careful, deliberate, the touch of a man who understood that carelessness caused harm and chose, always, to be gentle.

"Don't cry, cariad," said a voice behind her. Low, steady, with the slight lilting vowels of a man from a Welsh valley. "I'm home."

The world stopped. It did not slow or shift. It stopped, much as a heart stopped between beats, the absolute stillness of a mechanism suspended at the top of its arc before gravity took hold.

She turned.

He stood right there in the stall. The red coat was travel-stained, the facings faded, the buttons dull. He was thinner than she remembered, the bones of his face more prominent, the jaw sharper. His dark hair needed cutting and there was road dust on his boots and his right arm hung at his side with the careful stillness she knew meant it was aching, and his grey-blue eyes were on her face, and in them was everything, everything he had carried across seven weeks and whatever miles lay between wherever he had been and this barn, written in a look so clear and so unguarded that the reading of it required no effort at all.

He was here. He was real. He was standing in the barn where she had kissed him and told him *come home*, and he had come home, and the foundling's fear, the old, cold voice that had said *he will not come back, he will not come back*, was wrong. It had been wrong. And the wrongness was the most beautiful thing she had ever felt, a warmth that started in her chest and spread outward until it reached her fingers and her toes and the roots of her hair.

Eliza let go of Hermes's mane. She stepped toward him, and the step was the bravest thing she had ever done, braver than the first time, braver than the words in the barn, because this time she was stepping toward something real and present and not a decision made in exhaustion or a sentence spoken in desperation but a man, whole and here, who had kept his promise.

The young man said "Pardon me, ma'am" with the automatic courtesy of a soldier raised to mind his manners, and then he moved past her as though she were a gate rather than a person, one hand already reaching for her daughter, and Theresa found the space she had occupied taken by a man in a faded red coat who filled it completely.

She stepped back. She did not mind the stepping back. Motherhood had taught her that there were moments when a parent's role was to be present and moments when it was to be elsewhere, and Eliza's body language was speaking a dialect Theresa had not heard from her before.

Eliza's arms went around his neck.

The motion was not graceful. It was not the restrained embrace of a young woman raised to composure. It was the lunge of a creature reaching for the solid thing in a flood, both arms flung up, her hands finding the back of his neck, his collar, the rough wool of his coat, gripping fiercely. She held on. Her face pressed against his shoulder, her whole body drawn up against his, and the sound she made was not a word but a breath, the shuddering exhalation of a woman who had been holding her breath for seven weeks and had finally been given permission to let it out.

Theresa watched from the aisle, and felt no surprise.

She had known. Not the details, because Helen's letters had maintained a discretion that spoke of a woman who understood the difference between informing and interfering. Helen had written about the lieutenant's competence, his respect for Eliza's authority. She had written about his horse, the blind grey stallion who stood looking as unsurprised by the proceedings as Theresa felt. She had written that his departure had been particularly felt by Eliza.

And Theresa, who had known Helen Fallon since they were girls in the Duke Street orphanage trading crusts of bread and whispering in the dark, had read those words and understood everything they contained.

The lieutenant's chin rested against the top of Eliza's braids. His eyes were closed. His face held an expression Theresa recognised, because she had seen it in her own mirror, years ago, on a governess who had come to Belle Haven expecting nothing and found everything. The expression a person wore when they arrived at the place they were meant to be and felt the rightness settle into their bones.

Eliza was crying still, but differently now. The sobs had softened. The ragged sound of breaking apart had become the quieter sound of putting herself back together, the tears falling gently, the storm passing. Her hands had moved from his collar to his shoulders, her fingers curled into the wool, and the grip was no longer desperation but certainty, a woman holding something she intended to keep.

His mouth was against her hair. When he spoke, the words came rough and low, pitched for her alone, the Welsh lilt thick with the effort of holding himself together. "I tried," he said. "I started it a dozen times and burned each one because I didn't yet know what I could offer you." His arms tightened. "I couldn't bear to send you anything less than a promise, and until I stood in front of your father I had no promise to make."

She did not lift her face from his shoulder. She only pressed closer, and the small shake of her head against the wool of his coat said *nothing to forgive* as clearly as if she had spoken the words aloud.

Hermes stretched his neck forward and placed his scarred muzzle against the lieutenant's arm. The blind horse breathed against the red sleeve, nostrils working, and then sighed, the deep, whole-body exhalation of a creature satisfied that the world was, for the moment, arranged correctly.

Footsteps behind her. The measured stride of a man who had walked this barn a thousand times.

"That's Lieutenant Llewellyn, I presume?" Richard's voice was low, pitched for her ears alone, amused and moved in equal measure.

Theresa's hand found her husband's. His fingers closed around hers, warm and familiar, the hand that had held hers when he asked her to marry him and she had been too astonished to speak, and then too happy, and then too frightened that the happiness would be taken from her, and none of those fears had come true. Almost fifteen years, and his hand still fit hers as though the bones had been shaped for the purpose.

"I certainly hope so," she said. Her voice was steady, but the corners of her mouth were doing something she could not control, the tremble of a woman caught between laughter and tears. "Otherwise, Helen left a lot more out of her letters than I would have expected her to do."

Richard's breath left him in a sound that might have been a laugh, quiet and warm, and his thumb moved across her knuckles in the slow, deliberate stroke that was his way of saying *I love you* without words, the language of years compressed into a gesture so small it was invisible to anyone who did not know what to look for.

They stood together in the aisle and watched their daughter be held by a man who had walked home to her, the blind stallion patiently waiting his moment of greeting when the humans were done with their emotions. The afternoon light fell through the high windows and caught the dust motes and turned them gold. Beyond the barn the yard lay in its quiet order, the paddocks green under the July sun. The roses on the south wall had opened at last. White, abundant, climbing toward the eaves with the extravagant persistence of living things that would not be kept down, their petals catching the light and holding it the way this place held everything: gently, stubbornly, with the deep, patient faith that what was planted here would bloom.

Chapter Twenty-Four

THE PLUMP WOMAN WITH the kind eyes said something to Eliza that he did not catch, the words pitched low and maternal, and her hand settled on Eliza's arm with the gentle authority of a woman who had been guiding children through difficult moments a very long time. Eliza's fingers loosened on his coat. She stepped back. Her face was swollen with crying, her dark eyes red-rimmed and bright, and she looked at him with an expression that was not yet joy but was no longer grief, the face of a woman standing in the wreckage of a wall and discovering that the landscape beyond it was not the wasteland she had feared.

She went with her mother. Her footsteps crossed the barn aisle and passed through the door, and the afternoon light caught her braids and the squared line of her shoulders, and then she was gone, and the space she had occupied filled with the warm, heavy quiet of a stable in July.

The quiet had a shape. It was the shape of Sir Richard Bell, who stood in the centre of the aisle with his hands in his pockets and his clear blue eyes on Llewellyn's face, a man's eyes, one who had just watched a stranger hold his daughter while she wept, and who was now taking the stranger's measure with the unhurried attention of a horseman assessing an animal he had not yet decided to trust.

Llewellyn had rehearsed this meeting. He had rehearsed it on the road from London, and in the coach from Basingstoke, and during the walk up the lane with his leg protesting every stride. He had composed an introduction: his name, his rank, his regiment, his connection to Belle Haven through Molly's demonstration at Sandhurst.

Every word of it was pointless in the face of what Sir Richard had just seen, which was not a competent officer conducting legitimate business but a man with his arms full of someone else's daughter, his eyes closed, his whole body curved around hers as if she were the only solid thing left in the world.

There was no recovering from that, but the words were all had, so he said them anyway.

"Sir," he said. His voice came out rougher than he intended, scraped raw by the road and the weeks and the last five minutes. "Lieutenant David Llewellyn. Sixteenth Light Dragoons. I served in the Peninsula and in Belgium, and I was at Sandhurst when your daughter Molly spent a summer there working with cadets in eighteen-twelve."

Sir Richard nodded. The nod was neither encouragement nor dismissal.

"I have come to ask your permission to marry your daughter."

The words left his mouth stripped of every preamble he had planned. He had meant to build toward them, to establish his character, his record, his prospects. Instead the sentence had escaped like a horse through an unlatched gate, and it stood between them now, impossible to recall.

Sir Richard's expression did not change. Llewellyn pressed on.

"I should tell you what I have to offer, and the answer is very little. My family's farm in Wales belongs to my brother. I have no estate and no income beyond my half-pay, which is forty-two pounds a year. I am attempting to sell my commission, but so is every other lieutenant being discharged, and the price has dropped to nearly nothing. My right arm was injured at Vitoria, and my left leg in Belgium, and neither is fully healed."

He was listing his deficiencies the way Eliza listed horse inventories, methodically, by category. The comparison struck him as he made it, and it would have been funny in a different moment, the two of them so alike in their retreat to facts when uncertain of their ground.

"I have not compromised your daughter." The words felt wrong. They reduced the kitchen and the foaling barn and the kiss on that last morning to the language of propriety, a ledger entry where there should have been a poem. "I have kissed her. Twice. Nothing more. I would not, I have not, I would never take advantage of your trust or hers, and I know that my circumstances are not what a man should bring to a woman of Eliza's worth, and I know the distance between what she deserves and what I can provide."

He was losing the thread. The composure he had maintained by sheer effort of will was crumbling.

He drew a breath. He found the last thing.

"If you refuse me, I will go. I will walk back down that lane and I will not return. I will not contact her. I will not place the weight of my want on your family or your household. You have my word, sir, as an officer and as a man."

He said it. He meant it. And as the words left his mouth his right hand found the edge of Hermes's stall door and gripped it, the knuckles going white, the tendons standing out, the arm that could not always grip gripping now with a force that said the body knew what the promise would cost even if the mouth was willing to make it. The wood bit into his palm. Behind the door, Hermes moved and pressed his scarred muzzle against Llewellyn's wrist, the blind horse's handshake, and the warmth of the horse's breath was the only thing keeping him upright.

The silence stretched. Sir Richard stood with his hands in his pockets, his dark hair touched with grey at the temples. His face held the blankness of a man thinking deeply and refusing to be rushed, a man who understood that the most important decisions were made slowly and that the pressure to decide quickly was almost always wrong.

Llewellyn waited. The dust motes turned in the warm light and somewhere outside a thrush sang, tireless and oblivious, and his hand gripped the stall door as though it were the edge of a cliff.

Sir Richard asked one question

"Do you love her?"

Four words. No preamble. No reference to the inventory of deficiencies Llewellyn had laid out, the empty pockets and the bad arm and the worse prospects. The question bypassed all of it, and the answer came up before thought could intervene.

"Yes."

The word left him with a force that surprised him. It came from the place where he had stored the sound of her laugh and the taste of salt and the weight of her head against his shoulder.

"Yes," he said again, because once was not enough. "With my whole heart. Since before I had any right to. Since the morning I arrived and she stood in this yard and managed me with more authority than any colonel I have served under, and I knew, before I could name it, that she was the steadiest thing I had ever seen, and the bravest. I have been to war and seen acts of extraordinary courage, and I have still never met anyone braver than your daughter."

Sir Richard's face changed, the blue eyes warming by a degree that would have been invisible to anyone not watching with the desperate scrutiny of a man whose future depended on the reading. The corner of his mouth moved. It wasn't quite a smile, but it might be the beginning of one, held in reserve.

Richard turned his gaze to Hermes. The stallion stood in his stall, his scarred head low, the patient, attentive stillness of a horse who understood that something important was happening and was content to wait.

"I don't know why you think you have nothing to offer," Richard said. His voice was conversational, almost mild. He nodded toward the stallion. "You brought us a great-grandson of Eclipse; a stallion when we had none left, who has thirty foals coming next spring who would otherwise not exist. His legacy is beyond price."

The words landed strangely. Llewellyn's mind was still braced for refusal, the muscles of his thought clenched against a blow that was not coming.

"But he was already Belle Haven's," Llewellyn said. The horse had been bred here, born here, sent away as an unfinished three-year-old from this very stable. "I only brought back what was yours." Belle Haven-bred stallions didn't belong to the army; they were only loaned, and must be returned if they survived their service. He had learned that from Molly at Sandhurst, when she saved the chestnut stallion Apollo from being destroyed after a vindictive colonel tried to declare him dangerous, and he had used the knowledge to save Hermes when he could not bear to lose the horse who had saved him.

"And without you, he'd be dead."

Richard spoke with the quiet certainty of a man who knew perfectly well what the army did with blind horses. The standing order was destruction. A horse that could not see could not serve, and the army dealt with liabilities without sentiment. Every other officer would have followed the order.

Llewellyn had refused. He had looked at the horse who had come through cannon smoke because a three-note whistle said *come*, and he had refused. Not because the horse was valuable; he had not known about the Eclipse line. He had refused because Hermes had saved his life, and that meant there was a debt to pay, and he had the words to do it: *he belongs to Belle Haven and he must go home.*

Llewellyn's hand loosened on the stall door. The grip released, finger by finger, the white knuckles filling with colour. His palm ached where the wood had pressed its grain into his skin. He felt the ache recede and something else take its place, warm and spreading, rising from his chest, the feeling of one who had been carrying a weight so long he had forgotten it was there and had just been told he could set it down.

Sir Richard extended his hand.

The handshake was firm. The grip of a horseman who had held his family together through a war, meeting the grip of a man who had done what he could with what he had and brought home what mattered. Their hands met, and nothing more needed to be said about it.

Richard turned back to Hermes, reaching to pat the strong grey neck, and Hermes huffed out a warm, oat-scented breath. The two men the stallion loved best: the one who had helped him into the world and taught him to carry a rider and to be fearless, and the one who had called him through fire and fought with him and brought him home when he could no longer see. Both were with him, and Hermes was content.

"Thirty foals," Richard said. He was smiling now, the full smile. "A whole new line. Charlotte is going to be insufferable."

"She already is," Llewellyn said. And the sound that came out of him was laughter, real and unguarded, and Sir Richard laughed with him, and the barn echoed with the sound, and Hermes stood between them, blind and patient, carrying a future neither of them could see and both of them believed in.

The damp cloth was cool against her sore eyes.

She sat on the edge of her bed and let Theresa press the folded linen to her swollen lids, as you let a farrier lift a horse's hoof, with the passive cooperation of a creature who understood the tending was necessary. The cloth smelled of lavender. Theresa wrung it and refolded it and pressed it again, her hands gentle, the hands of someone who had spent fifteen years turning care into a language more reliable than words.

Eliza's own hands lay in her lap. They were a woman's particular hands, the hands of one who had just gripped a man's coat as though the fabric were the only thing between her and a fall, and the memory was still in her fingers, the roughness of the wool, the warmth beneath it.

She did not know what was happening in the barn.

The not-knowing had a familiar shape. It was the shape of every morning she had sorted the post and not found his handwriting, every night she had counted the days. The foundling's voice was speaking again: *He will be refused. Your father will send him away. You reached, and now you will pay.*

But there was another voice. Quieter, steadier. Laura's voice, saying *you will*. And beneath it, the voice of the man who had called her *cariad*, a word she did not know but understood the way you understood music, by what it did to the body rather than what it said to the mind.

Theresa lifted the cloth. She studied Eliza's face and nodded, as if to say, *not too bad*.

"The blue dress, I think," Theresa said. She moved to the narrow wardrobe. "It suits you."

The ordinariness of the instruction was a kindness. It said: *we are not going to discuss what happened in the barn. We are going to put on a clean dress and go downstairs and deal with what comes next.*

Eliza let herself be dressed. She stood while Theresa fastened the buttons at her back. The blue muslin was soft against her skin, finer than her working dress, and the change of fabric felt like a change of register, the shift from the woman who managed horses to the woman who was about to learn her fate.

"I was terrified of your father," Theresa said. Her voice was conversational, almost light. She smoothed the fabric across Eliza's shoulders. "When I came to Belle Haven. I thought he would see through me in an instant. A barely trained governess who knew nothing about anything. I expected him to send me away within a week."

Eliza turned. Theresa's face was soft with memory, her mousy brown hair escaping its pins, brown eyes warm.

"He didn't, of course," Theresa said. "He saw through me in a day. But what he saw was not what I was afraid he would see." She paused. "Your father has a gift for seeing what people are, rather than what they lack."

The words came to rest. Eliza held them and breathed.

Footsteps below. Voices in the hallway, low, indistinct.

Theresa's hand found her elbow. They descended together. The stairs were narrow and the banister smooth beneath Eliza's hand, and each step brought the voices closer, and her heart was in her throat the whole way down.

The study door was open.

Her father stood by his desk, the desk where she had sat and wept with her knees drawn up and Laura's arms around her. The room was the same. The leather chairs, the smell of books and saddle soap. Everything the same, and everything changed by the man who stood beside the window.

He was smiling. Not the half-smile. The whole of it, the one she had seen only that day when the chestnut colt failed to mount the mare and their shared laughter pressed against the walls of their discipline. The smile reached his eyes and warmed them, and in the warmth she read the answer before her father spoke, because some things did not require words, only the willingness to look and the courage to believe what you saw.

She went to him. The three steps across the study were the simplest she had ever taken, because they carried her toward a certainty, and certainty was the thing she had wanted all her life without knowing she was allowed to want it. He took her hands. Both of them.

"You have my blessing," her father said. His voice was quiet, steady, carrying the calm he used with horses when the important thing was the tone before the words. "In case it wasn't already clear."

Eliza looked at him. His blue eyes held hers, and in them she saw the man who had lifted her from a church doorstep and given her a name and a home and a family and had never, not once, made her feel that the giving was conditional.

"Of all my daughters," Richard said, "Eliza is the one I always suspected would end up staying at Belle Haven. It is in her heart and soul, and she has proved herself more than capable of managing it during even a severe crisis."

The words struck home with the weight of recognition. She had managed his estate. She had held his horses and his breeding programme and his household together, and he had come home and said *well done*, and now he was saying this, the larger thing, placing her at the centre of Belle Haven not as a temporary steward but as its future.

"I could not have done it without him." Her voice was thick. She looked at Llewellyn, whose hands tightened on hers. "Without David. None of it."

Her parents smiled. The two of them, side by side, her father tall and slightly greying and her mother plump and plain and beautiful in the way kindness was beautiful, and the smiles they wore were the same smile, the smile of two people who had loved each other for fifteen years and learned that love did not require grand gestures but only the willingness to show up, day after day, and do the work.

"I don't think that's quite true," her father said. "But I am very glad you will have such a capable assistant as your husband."

Husband. The word arrived in the study and stood among them like a new foal, unsteady on its legs, blinking at the light. She felt Llewellyn's hands shift around hers, the grip finding a new position, and the adjustment was the physical equivalent of the word: a rearrangement, a settling, two things that had been separate discovering they fit.

She looked up at him. His eyes were on her face, and the smile had softened, becoming quieter and more private, the look of a man who had been given permission to want what he wanted. His thumb moved across her knuckles, a single pass, the same gesture her father used with her mother, and the echo was so precise and so unconscious that it told her everything about the kind of man he was and the kind of life they would build.

Outside the study window, the paddocks stretched green beyond the barns, and in them the horses stood in their patient, beautiful arrangements, the mares with their foals, the yearlings and the two-year-olds, and in the stallion barn a blind grey horse was standing in his stall, his scarred head turned toward the door, listening for the footsteps he knew, the footsteps that had walked away and come back, as they always would, as long as there was a home to come back to.

She held his hands. He held hers. And the future, which had been a door she could not see through, swung open at last, and beyond it was Belle Haven, and she let herself believe.

Epilogue

Belle Haven had never been so noisy.

From the kitchen came the clatter of plates being laid for a table that had required two additional leaves and still could not comfortably seat everyone who needed seating. From the parlour came the thin, determined wail of a baby who objected to something, possibly everything, and from the paddock beyond the lime trees came the answering whinny of a mare who felt the same.

The baby was Alexander Richard Blair-Fortescue, which was a lot of name for a little boy, but he was doing his best to live up to it already. He was five months old and had the lungs of a town crier and the disposition of a small, furious emperor, and his mother was carrying him across the cobblestones toward where Caesar lay in a patch of sun with the air of a dog who could not be troubled by anything short of the Second Coming.

Molly stopped three feet from the mastiff. She held Alexander against her hip, her thick black hair escaping its bonnet, her face wearing the expression of a woman who loved all large animals but was experiencing a moment of rational doubt about introducing her infant son to a creature that outweighed him by roughly a hundred and seventy pounds. Caesar opened one eye. It regarded Alexander. Alexander regarded it. The wailing stopped. A fat hand extended, fingers grasping, and the baby's grip found Caesar's ear, immediate and total, the grip of a creature who had discovered something magnificent and intended to keep it. Caesar's tail thumped once against the cobblestones, the sound like a mallet on a drum. Pompey appeared from the stallion barn, assessed the situation, and lay down on the other side of the baby. Alexander released the ear and grabbed a handful of Pompey's jowl instead, and the dog bore it with the stoic patience of a soldier enduring inspection.

Molly laughed. The sound was bright and uncomplicated, the laugh of a woman who had walked from London to Hampshire at fourteen because she loved horses and had never once regretted the walk, and Eliza felt the sound settle into the yard and become part of its texture.

They had all come home.

Clara had arrived four days ago with her husband and their baby daughter, two months older than Alexander but somehow infinitely more delicate. They had named her Sophie, for Matthew's grandmother. Clara carried her with the careful, slightly terrified competence of a first-time mother who had read extensively on the subject and discovered that reading and doing bore almost no resemblance to each other. She was thinner than Eliza remembered, and her fair hair was pinned with less than her usual care, and the sight of her imperfection was somehow more reassuring than perfection would have been, because it meant Clara was real and present and not the polished memory Eliza had been carrying.

Anna had arrived with her. Anna and Lord Ashburton, who had driven them all from Dover in a hired coach with the efficiency of a man accustomed to moving across continents at speed. Anna had walked into the house, surveyed the accounts Charlotte had prepared, and found them in such good order that she stood in the study for a full minute, the ledger open before her, her face unreadable, before she closed it and said, "Well. I shall have to find something else to correct." The faintest smile. "Give me an hour."

The wedding was twelve days away. Eliza had insisted on waiting. She had looked at Llewellyn across the breakfast table, their first breakfast as an acknowledged, publicly visible pair, and said, "I want them all here." She did not say *I want witnesses*. She did not say *I want every person I love in the same room so I can look at them and believe it*. But he had heard it, the way he heard everything she could not quite say, and he had nodded, and Mr Fallon had called the first banns the following Sunday, his kind face beaming from the pulpit.

The horses had come back too. Not all of them, not nearly as many as they would have wished. Some were buried in Belgian fields, or sold, or scattered through the army's vast, indifferent machinery. But twenty-seven of the original requisitioned horses had been returned, arriving in groups of three and four, led by soldiers who seemed as relieved to be rid of them as the horses were to be home. Sir Richard had been offered his pick of army surplus to replace those that would not return, and he had chosen carefully, the horseman's eye finding quality beneath poor condition, potential beneath neglect.

The yard was filling. the clatter of hooves on cobblestones, which had become a memory during the worst of it, was once again a daily, ordinary music, and the ordinariness was the miracle, because ordinary meant the place was alive.

And then there was Ashburton.

Lord Ashburton had discovered Hermes on his first morning at Belle Haven, and the discovery had produced in him a state of excitement so intense and so sustained that even Anna had begun to look at her husband askance. Three days in, and Ashburton was still talking, his cheerful face alight with the fervour of a man who had spent a decade at racetracks across Europe and knew what he was looking at.

"Crossed with Thoroughbred mares, the foals could be extraordinary," he had said at dinner, for the fourth time, gesturing with his fork in a manner that endangered the gravy boat. "Charlotte, you've put him to Prudence, yes? And the bay with the white socks? The conformation on those mares alone, combined with that bloodline, you could produce horses that would win at Newmarket."

Charlotte, seated beside him, had produced a breeding chart from beneath her napkin with the speed of a conjurer producing a rabbit. "I have projections," she said, and the word *projections* carried the weight of a girl who had been waiting for precisely this audience for months.

They had not stopped talking since. Eliza found them daily in the tack room or the study, bent over Charlotte's charts, their voices weaving together in a duet of pedigree and probability that could go on for hours. Charlotte carried the stud books to meals. She carried them to bed. Laura reported that Charlotte had been muttering about dam lines in her sleep, and the report was delivered with the flat, fond tolerance of a twin who had spent fourteen years accommodating her sister's obsessions.

Sir Richard listened. Eliza had watched him listening, the quiet attention of a man weighing the future. The army would not need as many horses now. The war was over, the demand for cavalry mounts reduced, and the estate that had bred warhorses for two generations must find a new purpose or wither. Racehorses. Thoroughbreds. Ashburton's enthusiasm and Charlotte's genius gave the idea shape, and Eliza could see her father turning it over, fitting it into Belle Haven the way a new fence was fitted into old ground.

The place was evolving. She felt it the way she felt a change in the weather, the shift that preceded a new season. Belle Haven would be different. Not diminished. Different. And she would be at its centre, where her father had placed her and where she had always, without knowing it, belonged.

She leaned against the doorframe and watched Alexander pull Pompey's ear with the fearless grip of a boy who did not yet know the world contained things to be afraid of. Molly was laughing, her hand on Caesar's back. The sun fell warm across the cobblestones. From the tack room came Charlotte's voice, rising with excitement, and Ashburton's answering exclamation, and the rustle of pages being turned at speed.

Eliza breathed. The breath went in carrying the scent of warm stone and horse and rosemary and the sweetness of the lime trees, and it came out carrying something she could not name but recognised, the feeling of a vessel filled, a channel no longer dry.

The foundling's voice was still there. It would always be there, she suspected, the small cold whisper that said *this can be taken from you*. But it was quieter now. It spoke from a greater distance, and the distance was not emptiness but the space made by the people who had stayed and those who had come back.

The grass was at its thickest in the lower paddock, a deep, vibrant green that reached halfway to Hermes's knees.

Eliza leaned on the fence and watched him graze. The long line ran from his halter to Llewellyn's hand, slack and swaying with each movement of the stallion's head. He worked the ground with methodical contentment, his blind head low, his scarred muzzle buried in the clover. Each pull of grass came with a soft, tearing sound, then the slow grinding of his jaw, and the rhythm of it was the oldest music she knew, the sound of a horse at peace.

The sun sat low above the ridge. Its light came across the valley at a slant, turning the fields from green to gold and back, the shadows of the lime trees stretching long. Beyond the fence the land rose toward the hills, and in the middle distance three mares stood nose to tail beneath an oak, their foals lying in the grass at their feet, small dark shapes who had never known a world at war.

Llewellyn stood beside her at the rail. His forearms rested on the top bar, the right arm bearing weight it had not been able to bear three months ago, and the ease of the posture was its own kind of recovery, the body finding new competencies as a blind horse found new paddocks, by patient, repeated effort. He smelled of soap and leather and the faint tang of the liniment he used on his leg after long days, and the smell was so familiar now that its absence would have been a wrongness, a missing note in a chord she had learned to hear as complete.

The distance between them at the rail was the width of a hand. Close enough to feel the warmth. Close enough that his sleeve brushed her arm when either of them shifted.

The distance had its own grammar now, different from the careful space of the early weeks, different from the compressed closeness of the barn. This was the distance of people who had passed through the difficult part and arrived at the place where proximity was not a negotiation but a fact, as unremarkable and as necessary as breathing.

She put her fingers to her lips.

The whistle came out clear and bright, two short notes and one that rose sharply, the sound travelling across the paddocks with a carrying power that had nothing to do with volume and everything to do with pitch, the frequency that generations of Belle Haven horses had been trained to answer. Her father had invented it. Molly had taken it to Sandhurst. A lieutenant had used it on a battlefield when his horse was dead and his life was ending, and a grey stallion had come through cannon smoke because the call said *come*.

Every head came up.

Hermes stopped chewing. His scarred face lifted, ears forward, nostrils wide. The three mares raised their heads in unison, necks arched and ears pricked toward the sound. The foals woke and scrambled upright, alerted by their mothers that here was something that attention should be paid to. In the yearling field, thirty young horses turned as one. In a far paddock, the chestnut two-year-old who had failed so spectacularly at his first cover and improved so dramatically at his second stood with his head high and his chest broad and his whole body oriented toward the whistle like a compass needle finding north.

The yard stilled. For a held breath, every horse on the property was looking the same way, toward the woman at the fence who had blown the call.

Then Eliza blew another note, the note that said *not you, the call is not for you*. The mares lowered their heads. The yearlings returned to their grazing. The foals, finding nothing alarming, began a game of who-can-run-fastest. The world resumed.

Hermes nudged her. His muzzle found her hip with the unerring accuracy of a horse who had memorised the exact location of pockets on every person he trusted, and the nudge was not subtle. It was the insistent, velvet-lipped demand of a stallion who knew that a whistle was frequently followed by a reward and saw no reason why today should be an exception.

She laughed. She reached into her pocket and drew out a slice of apple, and Hermes took it from her palm with a delicacy that contradicted his size, his lips working the fruit from her skin with the gentle care of a creature who understood that the hand that fed him was worth being careful with.

"Still works," Llewellyn said.

His voice was quiet. His eyes were on her, and the half-smile was there, the one she had learned to read, though there was nothing reserved about what lay beneath it.

She looked up at him. The afternoon light fell across his face, catching the line of his jaw and the place where his dark hair curled against his collar and the grey-blue of his eyes, which were the colour of the sky before rain, or after it.

"It brought you here, didn't it?" she said.

The words came easily. They were simple and true, the simplest true thing she had said to him, because Molly had given him the whistle, and the whistle had brought Hermes through fire, and Hermes had brought Llewellyn to Belle Haven and to her.

He looked down at her. The half-smile opened into the whole one, the rare one, the one that changed his entire face and made something behind her ribs turn over slowly, much as a foal turned in the womb before it was ready to be born.

"Yes," he said. "It did."

He put his arm around her shoulders. The weight of it settled against her the way a saddle settled on a horse's back, finding its place. His hand rested on her upper arm, warm through the cotton of her sleeve. She leaned into him. The leaning was easy now. She had spent eighteen years learning not to lean on anything that could be taken away, and the unlearning had been the hardest work of her life, harder than foaling, harder than requisitions, harder than standing in a barn and saying *I don't want you to go*. But she had done it. She was doing it now, her weight against his side, her shoulder beneath his arm, and the ground held, and he held, and the holding was not a promise that nothing would ever go wrong but a promise that when it did, they would be standing together.

In the far paddock, three foals tore through the long grass, their small hooves drumming, their manes flying, running for no reason except that running was what they were made for and the evening was warm and the field was wide.

Eliza watched them. She stood at the fence with the man she loved and the blind horse who had brought him to her, and the paddocks stretched green and gold beyond the rails, and the air carried the scent of fresh grass and warm horse and the faint sweetness of the roses on the south wall.

The foals ran. And Belle Haven was solid ground beneath their feet.

I hope you've enjoyed reading *Miss Eliza Takes The Reins!*

I knew, from the moment I conceived the storyline for this book, that it would be both the emotional heart of the series and the closing of a chapter. The war is over, and Belle Haven must adapt... and Charlotte saw before any of them the direction it must go. That girl has Plans. Unfortunately, she's going to have to wait a few years, because a foal must gestate for nearly a year, and then grow for another three before it's old enough to race... but once Hermes' first offspring are ready, England's racecourses won't know what hit them.

You can read about Charlotte's plans – and how they don't turn out quite as she expects – in *Miss Charlotte Makes A Mess*, coming soon!

Also By Catherine Bilson

The Blushing Brides Series

An Earl For Ellen
A Marquis For Marianne
A Duke For Diana
A Captain For Clarissa

The Bookshop Belles series (co-written with Ebony Oaten)

Estelle's Ardent Admirer
Marie's Merry Gentleman
Louise's Christmas Champion
Bernadette's Dashing Doctor
Matthew's Willing Widow(exclusive gift for newsletter
subscribers)

The Brides of Belle Haven series

A Bride For Belle Haven (prequel novella)
Good Golly, Miss Molly
Miss Clara and the Marquess
Miss Anna's Mistake
Miss Eliza Takes The Reins
Miss Charlotte Makes A Mess
Miss Laura In Love
Miss Louise Meddles

Regency Novels

His Darling Duchess

Phoebe And The Pea
Kidnapping Lord Blaymire
The Captain's Runaway Bride
The Wassail Wager
The Bride Said No
St. George and the River Horse (exclusive for newsletter
subscribers)

Christmas Courting (collection of novellas)

American Pioneer Romance

Coming From California
Returning From Rhode Island

Pride & Prejudice Variations

The Best Of Relations
Infamous Relations
Mr Bingley's Bride
A Christmas Miracle At Longbourn
Grief and Grievances
The Second Mrs. Bennet
A Loss At Longbourn
The Meddling Matlocks
Possession and Prejudice
Lydia and the Colonel
The Ghosts of Pemberley
The Secret Diary of Anne de Bourgh (forthcoming)

The Crime & Consequences Trilogy

Malice and Misfortune
Rivalry and Ruination
Intrigue and Inheritance

Follow us on Facebook or Instagram, or

sign up to the Shenanigans Press newsletter to find out about our latest new releases!